Book I

# The Hero

of

# No Last Name

THE Templum Three
Saga

# C.A. Zitzelberger

Beware of Attack Ducks Publishing

Sacramento, California.

First Printing, 2014

ISBN-10: 0985785403

ISBN-13: 978-0-9857854-0-6

LCN: 2014901880

Printed in the United States of America

*Book design by C.A. Zitzelberger*

Dedicated to:

My husband, John,
for telling me I should write.

*In Memory of:*

Evelyn Tanaka
February 21, 1913 – December 2, 1998

&

Frances Zitzelberger
May 12, 1922 - May 20, 2011

# CONTENTS

"We're fools whether we dance or not,
so we might as well dance."

# INTRODUCTION

*In many ways, it was beautiful. It was how it was meant to be. Her fingers ran through her tangled hair, pulling hard upon the knots, yet there was no pain or discomfort. She turned to her reflection in the mahogany mirror atop the heavy dresser. It was too difficult to tell which parts belonged to her and which did not, though there was something that she wanted to find on the other side. Looking down, she saw an expensive watch lying beside a folded pair of glasses. She turned to the other side and saw a set of earrings next to a woman's hairbrush. She sighed as she leaned against the tabletop and tried her hardest to ignore the growing circle of blood.*

*She stared down at his body, knowing there was nothing to wake him. He was dead, and there was no doubt in her mind about that. He had been cold for over an hour now.*

*Against her will, tears began their steady flow. They rose up, and then floated away. Her knees were weak, and the plush carpet greeted her with such swiftness that she was almost sick upon it. Bright flashes of obscure figures greeted her with aggression, but she somehow knew they were nothing but falsities. Fingers, that almost seemed alien, dug into the soft cushion of his final resting place. It was so soft and so inviting that part of her wanted to die there as well. After all, there was no turning back now.*

*Knees, bleeding freely from her marks of survival, also sunk into the clouds of woven fabric below as her head began to fog. Her sliced palms finally finished absorbing the impact of her fall, and an inviting rush of air filled her lungs. An icy burn radiated in her bones and, yet, she was unnervingly sure of its hollowness. Her vision scattered as her eyeballs* swung toward their farthest periphery. Needle-thin beams of light pierced the window sheers, casting the dust in shadows and intensifying her heart's aching. She rolled onto her back and allowed gravity to siphon her body toward earth. The ceiling seemed strangely distant until she noticed the speckled darkness that had stained the new coat of paint.

It was his blood, wet and bright red.

Her vision panned back, and she saw the entirety of the crimson art spattered across the ceiling. The shadows played off the textured finish, and she was momentarily mesmerized. They flittered like demons, dancing to the dawn of a new day.

The walls changed color and softened. She tried to lift her head, but the invisible weight upon her was so crushing that it quickly became futile. Her blood pumped as she became aware of its flow and noted the new hole in her skull. She debated panic but decided that it wouldn't do much good. Her arms clutched her chest once more before falling heavily to her sides. Muscles, tight and overworked, melted downward as she closed her eyes. The carpet was still inviting as a final, easier resting place. Then she smelled the smoke and remembered why she was there.

Black clouds of life-stealing vapor charred her lungs as she felt the heat from the flames that were now looking to devour the fragile walls. They swayed before her with flickering tongues of orange and yellow. His body had been closer to the fire and was already ablaze. It would soon be time to sleep and to finally rest. She knew death was near and understood that she could do nothing to save herself.

Her eyeballs flitted around the room with the curiosity of a newly-admitted hospital patient, and she knew it was hopeless. The heat sashayed toward her as her body finally failed completely. She watched the brilliant streaks of fiery color leap closer and closer until they were racing up to the sleeves of her shirt. The story of her life had begun in flame so it seemed appropriate. Her body tensed. Panic filled her in preparation for the pain that would arrive and remain within her for eternity.

It never did, though she had waited for it, and then the lie was apparent.

"It's time to wake up."

●

Camilla woke with a start. Her lungs burned for air as her arms flailed desperately against her tattered blanket. She took a deep, cooling breath as her heart thundered with the echoes of rushing water. Her stomach ached but not out of hunger.

Cam had grown quite accustomed to night terrors but the intensity at which her mind had simulated her own death was frightening. No dream had ever felt so debilitating. She propped herself up on the edge of the bed as her body slowly recovered.

Her eyes scanned the bedroom, trying to confirm its validity. Familiar paper-thin walls surrounded her, bleak like the constantly gray horizon. She shivered as a cold wind threatened to bring the brittle building to ruins. The old world structures the slaves inhabited were a danger from their age alone.

The moon winked in through the cutout in her wall that functioned as a window. She stared at its pearlescent glow as she curled up on her cot and forced herself to rest in anticipation of the long day of work that awaited her.

Cam's dreams had been slowly growing intense and strange, having begun several years ago when her parents had died. Despite their peculiarity, she enjoyed them more often than not. The worlds she dreamt of were always different and always a better alternative to reality.

A cold draft rose and fell into the bedroom. She shivered but smiled to herself at the thought that there could be another world worse than this.

CHAPTER 1
# CRIPPLING THE INNOCENT

The pain throbbed as Cam clung to her chest with both hands and gasped. Her heart shook like a violin strum as she steadied herself against the stony, cavern wall. The sharp pangs continued to rattle in her chest like an adding machine as an eerie cacophony of voices rose. She spun around at the new sound but knew that it was useless. After all, she was the only one who could hear their bellowed moans.

The fingers of her free hand ran twitchily across her temple as she silently struggled to regain control. She knew that if a guard witnessed her moment of weakness, it would mean death. Gritting her teeth, she forced herself to concentrate on anything else.

She stared at her hands. Bones jutted from beneath the skin due to a lifetime of malnutrition but she was still able-bodied enough to work long hours in the Raquineste Mines.

A whip cracked. She and the other slaves of the Gi Force Regime cowered instinctively. Sweat poured down her back as she felt the critical eyes of the nearest soldier. Her hands burned as she clenched them. Both were severely calloused from years of hard manual labor. She pushed sweat-coated locks of golden brown hair back before turning to check on her little brother Kevin, whose slave abbreviation was Ke, to see that he was hard at work just as she had expected. He was only ten years old, nearly eight years her junior, and stood barely taller than his pick.

Slaves always abbreviated their names to the shortest possible form in the following of an old tradition. At the reinstatement of slavery, slaves began referring to each other by short nicknames to conserve what little energy they had. After a while, full names were only spoken at funerals as a sign of final respect.

The days were long and painfully tedious. She was exhausted but managed to fixate on the drive of her pick. She watched its peak rise and fall as it hit the dense earth.

*Up and down.*

*OVER AND UNDER.*

She inhaled sharply at the sound of the voices, halting her impending panic. It wasn't necessary for her to turn around to observe her surroundings as she knew precisely what was occurring behind her. As with every day, all the other slaves were droning on just as she was. Their picks rang with a continuous rhythm, a melody of misery.

Out of the corner of her eye, she saw the guards pass by as they performed their hourly inspections. Their weapons slapped against their legs as they marched a death knell of thundering footsteps. She had learned to read the time in the sunless mines by their hourly presence. It was the guards' fifteenth and final inspection of the day.

"It's almost over, Cam," Ke whispered in an excited rush. "Can we go to Tom's house again?"

"Maybe, I'll ask if we see him."

"Oh, we'll see him," Ke said with a wink. "He *always* looks for you."

Cam rolled her eyes at him before turning back to her work. She and Tom had been friends since his family had appeared in the Slums two years previous. New slaves of all ages and races were added to the ranks every day, but he had been different from the others.

"Shift's over!" shouted the nearest guard as the work horn blared. "Shift's over!"

The slaves swarmed into a crowd and began to move slowly out of the mine. Guards stood at the mine's periphery, tripping the slaves at random with the butts of their guns, laughing derisively as they watched them struggle to stand on worn and trembling legs. Cam and Ke walked up the steep slope that led to the entrance, avoiding the guards as much as possible by staying in the center of the throng. Once out in the evening air, she chanced a look around to locate Tom but was unable to find him in the masses.

"Let's just go to his place," Ke suggested as his stomach growled. "He's got to be on his way there anyway."

Cam tussled his wavy, brown hair in agreement as they began to walk down the main road, Hangyaku. The road was severely deteriorated. Loose chunks of old world cement sat at the edges of the curving road, its banks of gravel kicking up dust with the slightest movement. She sighed as they trudged down the bleakest of rivers, the one that always led them to desolation.

One of the central living quarters in the Slums was located at the end of the road on the western side of town. It was a sixteen story building settled along a falcated road. The building was darker and even more decrepit than its surroundings. The stairs creaked ominously with every step and the walls were shedding their graying paint.

Tom lived in unit thirty-four with his parents. Cam paused before the door and rapped her knuckles sharply against it. Dust burst from the brittle door jamb as if to portend the crumbling of the entire building. They waited, but no one answered.

"Well, that's several layers of odd," Cam said. "Someone's always here after shift."

She knocked again as Ke stepped beneath her to knock as well. There was no answer.

"Where is everyone?" Cam asked Ke. "Usually they come right home to take care of Wes."

"Yeah," Ke said, his youthful face falling slightly at this. "I miss Wes."

She forced a smile.

"Me, too."

Wes was Tom's father, an ordinary man in appearance who had worn tattered, wire rim glasses under a mop of thick hair. While most in the Slums were apathetic to the very concept of living, Wes somehow managed to maintain a relentless drive for happiness. He was like Cam and Ke's parents had been in that respect.

Then he contracted the sickness that Vinestra, the rare and deadly mineral the slaves mined for, inflicts upon touch. It had only been one month after she had first met him. Now, he lay in a deep slumber that would eventually lead to death.

"So, Tom's really not here?" Ke asked as he pressed his ear against the thin door, listening for movement. Cam shoved him back, protesting to his rudeness though no one cared about manners in the Slums.

"I guess not." Cam sighed as she thought of the strange and delicious foods they usually enjoyed at Tom's house. Steamed vegetables were their typical choice of dish though, sometimes, they even had butter. "I think we'd better go home. Mel won't have any food for us if we don't hurry."

Together they walked off toward the shambles they called home. Ke began regaling stories of the dreams he'd had the night before in great excitement. He always enjoyed being the storyteller.

"—and then there was a huge fire!" he exclaimed, throwing his little arms into the air for emphasis. "BOOM! I was knocked over and this big dragon-beast-thing came down. Whoosh! He took me up into the sky, away from these stupid gray clouds. It was awesome!"

"Sounds pretty awesome," Cam said, smiling. His storytelling was always a favorite pastime of hers.

Ke then began retelling his favorite parts of the story in greater detail as they entered the house. They were immediately welcomed by the ripe scent of Kaibe, the most common food in the Slums as it was provided for free. It was a thick paste the color of ashes and its taste was something akin to aging rubber.

"Hi, Mel," they chorused. Mel was their godfather. He was the only one who had attempted to help them after their parents' death when Cam was thirteen.

"Oh, I thought you two might be at Tom's," Mel said as Ke gave him a hug. "It's lucky for you I still made enough for three."

Mel was growing older in years, but his commanding air was still clear. He was tall with an imposing posture and steely eyes that could effortlessly turn from comforting to stern. A few wrinkles had set in around his mouth and forehead, bearing his age, and Cam had been noticing how tired he appeared lately.

Mel smiled warily at them. Ke immediately began telling him about his day while Cam trudged over to their sofa, a dirty blue cushion less than an inch thick. She sat down and stared at her surroundings.

By the front door, was a low dining table that they had made out of mismatched bits of particle board. Behind the dining area, sat a small sink and a wooden crate that they used as a countertop. In the same room, by the farthest corner, was a large hole covered by a cardboard lid that served poorly as a toilet. Apart from the main living area they had one small, dank bedroom. Mel slept in the main room on the sofa while Cam and Ke shared the bedroom, separating their room by a moth-eaten sheet.

Ke sat down next to Cam and reached under the mat to pull away the floorboard beneath. If one were to look in this secret compartment, they would have seen a rather extensive collection of varying tomes. It was their family secret, a treasure of stolen literature that they hid desperately under the sofa. Ke pulled out a thin book made from rich paper and settled down to read.

"You're reading that again?" Cam asked as she reached under the floor for her own book. "You're getting too old for pointless fantasy books, little brother."

"They are not pointless!" Ke protested as he opened the book with renewed enthusiasm. "You think the history books are the only ones that have the truth, but these do too."

"Oh, really? Your point there was not exceptionally clear. Fantasy books are fictional and, thus, not true."

"Maybe they're written fictionally to entertain by using larger than life characters and plots to parallel their morals," Ke said smartly. "The evil in my books may not be 'real,' but they represent real things. At least *my* books tell me how to defeat them."

Cam stared, a bit stunned.

"Come and eat, you two," Mel said as he placed plates of foul Kaibe on the table.

Cam and Ke went to join him. They sat around the table, telling stories and jokes to avoid discussing reality. Ke broke into the story of his dream again. His little arms waved dramatically through the air while Mel laughed.

They spent the remainder of the night shoveling down Kaibe, pretending it were anything else. They continued to talk and share stories until the moon had passed high above them. Their laughter echoed off the paper thin walls, reverberating through the dilapidated dwelling with the rich warmth of the living. For Cam, this was her family and the only happiness she had managed to find in her nineteen years as a Raquineste slave.

●

The morning sunrays were just striking the other side of the continent as the first work horn blared, alerting the slaves to wake up. Cam shot upward, the bed creaking in her wake, and put on her clothes.

She only had a few items that she could truly call her own. Two graying, threadbare shirts and a pair of torn, black pants created half of her possessions. She had one pair of old boots that were too big and speckled with holes, ensuring she could feel every jagged rock through the soles.

She had just finished tying up her frizzy hair when a shuddering force, all too familiar, rattled in her limbs. Sharp pangs struck her heart as the first whispers trickled into her ears.

*Ocean's rising.*

Her body shook as it fought for oxygen, and she feared that today would finally be the day her mind and body disintegrated.

*RUN WHILE YOU STILL CAN.*

The attacks had begun nearly a decade ago during puberty but, even so, the sudden pain and fear was something she could not become accustomed to. Each time the precipitous ache erupted, she had the dreadful feeling that she was falling with no hope of a safe landing. After which, it was only a matter of time before she would begin to hear the screams.

"Cam, hurry up!" Mel shouted, his voice booming into the room. "You know what they do to those who are late!"

Cam managed to take two deep breaths which steadied her just enough to reply.

"I'm almost ready!" she shouted back as the smallest tendril of a whisper etched itself in her ears. She took a deep breath and forced the pain down as trembling fingers fumbled under her flat mattress, searching for her most prized possession.

She quickly pulled out a silver necklace with a small, circular ornament. In the center of the circle was a gray-silver stone, the same color as her eyes. It was smooth to the touch but had the appearance of rich velvet. She toyed with the clasp but dared not put it on for, if anyone saw it, they would undoubtedly try to steal it. Instead, she stared at it as her fingers played lightly against the stone. It was the only thing she had inherited from her parents and it always helped her to cope.

"Cam. We are not going to be the Colonel's next skinning victims!" Mel shouted, his voice deadly serious.

She quickly put the necklace back in its hiding place as the curtain to her half of the room flew open.  Mel stood, livid, along with Ke who appeared worried.

"Damn it, Cam, I won't wait for you."

"Sorry, Mel.  I'm ready."

"Geez, Cam," Ke said. "What took you so long?"

"It was nothing," she muttered then, seeing the look on her little brother's face, patted him firmly on the head and smiled.

They walked quickly through the desolate streets, disturbing the road's constant dust in their wake.  Most of the inhabitants had already left to avoid punishment.  They ran at a hard sprint to reach the mines, barely arriving on time.

The workers were already being led into the dark maze of the mine by assigned groups.  Blank faces by the masses flowed forward, their picks slung over the shoulder or held at the side.  Every day Cam's heart sank amid such hopelessness as she was forced to join their melancholy ranks.

Mel stopped before the second cavern to work, but Cam and Ke, always the adventurous ones, continued down with the thinning crowd until they reached the end.

"End of the line, Ke," Cam said.

"You say that every day," Ke groaned. "Every day the end of the line just moves further and further in."

Cam and Ke stopped at the deepest section of the wall.  She drew her pick high over her shoulder and dug it into the side of the cave.  She struck over and over, picking away at the hardened earth.  With each throw, she waited for a resplendent light to emerge from the crevice she had made in the hope it would reveal Vinestra.

Vinestra was effulgent when found.  It glowed brightly as if to visually announce its value.  Its discovery meant two hours off the next work day, making the reward unworthy of the risk for most.  Cam still pursued it even though she had personally seen the lethalness of raw Vinestra on several occasions.

An old and familiar knot began to form in her shoulder muscle as she listened to the crescendo of picks.  Every day was another concert of unnecessary death.  Screams echoed from those who were struck with a whip as grunts of overexertion and vomiting bellowed from those who had reached the brink of their energy levels.  But the worst sound for Cam was the crying from those who were losing a loved one to Vinestra's sickness while they were forced to work.

Most days, they droned on for hours with nothing eventful happening, but today was different and somehow she had already known. Cam felt a small hand on her elbow and she turned to look at Ke.

"Cam! Cam! Look at this!" Ke whispered excitedly. Cam peered over his shoulder and gasped at the warm glow emanating from the stone. The Vinestra he had unearthed was larger than her fist.

"That has to be one of the biggest pieces of Vinestra ever mined," she said.

"I know," he said as his innocent gaze grew into hardened determination. "Cam, maybe we could keep it. We could take Mel and run. We could live in Tengoku, the capitol! We'd have a better house and real food! We could sell it somehow..."

"Ke, don't say that," she said harshly. "We can't steal from the Gi. They'll know, they *always* know. We should just signal someone."

She spun, searching for a guard. Then, for a moment, her mind flitted away as she fantasized about being among the citizens in their illustrious buildings. What would it be like to truly be free? An excited trembling rolled down her spine as her inklings of wealth were cut short.

She turned back to Ke and saw his eyes fixated on the Vinestra. He straightened his little shoulders determinedly then smiled at her as she felt the trembling of an internal earthquake in her chest again. Their eyes locked and her body screamed for action.

"Ke—"

"Sorry, Cam, but we need it more than they do."

A look of inexplicable resolve came over him as he reached for the stone, his little fingers curling around the gem. She saw the hole in his glove a moment too late.

Ke smiled, triumphant, but it was short lived. A large hand struck his face with a force powerful enough to knock out a full grown man. His minute form flew through the air and thudded against the stone wall.

"Thief! We have a thief!"

A crowd began to surround them, both slaves and the Gi Force alike. They all stared at the unconscious boy on the ground as blood quickly encircled his head. Murmurs rose into the air until a man, round-bellied and red-faced, appeared. It was Colonel Holkstoin of the division that overlooked the mines, the Army of Eden. His fat face twisted into a small smirk at the sight of Ke.

"No! Leave him alone!" Cam shouted.

Armored hands forced her still. She tried to call out to Ke but another hand silenced her. She struggled hard against their bonds, wanting only to break free and save her innocent little brother.

"Idiotic little boy," Holkstoin muttered as he extended a short leg and kicked Ke in the side. Cam tried again to scream. "Do the workers of the Raquineste Mines not know better? Our good graces are what keep you fed and sheltered. You should be grateful. Instead, dim-witted boys like this feel that thievery is the best way to show respect."

His metal-toed boot hit Ke's side again.

"What a waste," Holkstoin remarked. "Now, get back to work. You know full and well what will become of this boy."

The workers quickly returned to their labor as the sound of dull picks against hard stone began to reverberate once more. Cam could do nothing but stare at her brother as he lay on the ground. She barely noticed the guard's dirty looks in her direction as he squeezed her more tightly.

"Colonel, what do you make of her? She's his sister it seems," the guard said, a cold hand drifting to places no man should touch without permission. "We haven't had a plaything for a while now."

Some of the other guards looked at the Colonel, just as hungry for his approval. Cam struggled against them, fingers searching for her pick that had fallen earlier.

"Do what you want," Holkstoin said, waving a lazy hand in the air. "Just clean up when you're done."

"Thank you, sir," he said. They began to drag her away just as her fingers managed to find the rough handle of her pick.

She ducked her head and swung the pick backward as hard as she could with one hand. The rusted tip punctured his eye with a nauseating squish before breaching his skull. He dropped her, moaning in pain. Guards sprinted toward her from every direction, encircling her. She quickly noticed one without his helmet and ran at him. Her bony but powerful fist struck his undefended face, sending him to the ground and creating an escape route. She had never been more grateful for the self-defense lessons she had been receiving from Tom.

Ke was so close now. She ran toward him as his eyes fluttered open. They were glowing intensely with silver instead of their usual brown. He raised his hand up to her and she felt warmth spread from her head down to her shoulders. He smiled, eyes bright.

"Ke?"

Then, before she could utter another word, the world went black.

# CHAPTER 2
# SURVIVAL

Images flashed behind Cam's eyes like horrific fireworks. She could see Ke and hear his body thumping over the mine's rocky ground. A sharp pain radiated at the base of her skull as her eyes began to flutter. She murmured, tasting salt over her cracked lips. She was thirsty.

"Ke!" she shouted, sitting up.

Iron bonds bit into her flesh as she struggled against them. Her eyes opened amid bits of dust. She immediately knew where she was and the realization caused a sweeping cold to settle in her core. She was in the Prison of the Gi.

Then a voice broke the silence. "I couldn't wait for you to wake up."

There was little time to take in her surroundings as she saw a guard staring at her with malice through the bars. Her eyes widened and she retreated further into her cell as she realized the man standing before her was none other than the one she had defeated in the mines. A thick bandage was wound over his eye to cover the damage she had inflicted but his smile was sick and triumphant.

"Really? You were waiting around for little, old me? Sounds like you have way too much free time," Cam said, spitting at his feet as she hid her trembling hands.

"I wouldn't talk to me in that tone if I were you," he said, unraveling the bandage. "Don't think yourself so high and mighty. Defeating a Gi Force soldier is not so simple."

Her mouth fell open. His injury was gone. Not a scratch remained on his eye. It was as if she had never pierced him with the pick.

"You look so shocked," he said, his grin widening. "The Gi are all powerful and you are nothing but a piece of meat about to be whipped raw."

"No," she muttered, realizing her fate.

He was speaking of the Whipping Post that sat in the center of the western hills. The location was ideal as it enabled the citizens of Tengoku to watch the destruction of the Slums.

"The Whipping Post," she breathed.

"Oh, yes, in about five minutes time."

Her head fell. Her body shook as it usually did but, this time, fear had not just permeated her senses but also overwhelmed them. The marks she had seen on the others were caused by the cat-o-nine-tails the Colonel carried. The Colonel was always a coward and his weapon proved it, to hit from a distance without the enemy being near was his brand of warrior.

She cried, tears falling salty and true into her hands. She thought of Mel, Tom and Ke. Half of the people who endured the Colonel's whipping never returned home. They were lost bodies, graves that no one visited as no one knew where they were. She cried even harder.

Several more guards joined him. "That's right. They're about to drag you away and make you pay for your indiscretions."

She said nothing. Her head was bowed low and her thoughts were racing. They were going to cart her off like an animal to the slaughter. She would soon be just another slave massacred at the Whipping Post. She would soon be dead.

"Oh, don't cry," one of the other guards said mockingly as they chained her. "Bitches as worthless as you can't cry when they're getting what they deserve."

"Don't worry," the first guard said, stroking her check as she felt the urge to vomit rise up. "We'll make good use of the empty body once Colonel Holkstoin is finished!"

They slung her, hands and ankles bound, onto a flat cart. Jagged metal caught her skin and her wrists bled against the chains. They pushed her out of the prison into the daylight. She stared up at the sun in wonder, having never seen it before with the constant fog of the Slums. It was so bright.

Pain returned to her heart as the familiar voices rose in her head, chanting inaudible riddles. Soon the decrepit cart, covered in blood of which only a fraction was hers, stopped before the Whipping Post.

"And now, you see the criminal for who she is!" Colonel Holkstoin shouted as he joined her at the post. He held a shiny, gold microphone in his hand as he spoke to the crowd that had gathered. "She's the ungrateful bitch who attacked one of our hardworking guardsmen yesterday!"

The crowd booed. She noticed that half of them were close to her age. They were so energetic, so excited for the carnage they were about to witness.

"Tie her to the post!"

Her lungs filled to shout out a plea, but no words came. The soldiers tied her to the cold pole. Holkstoin took casual steps toward her as her heart thundered painfully.

"Shall we begin?" Holkstoin asked. He unrolled his whip and turned to her. "Ready? You will certainly feel this first strike!"

The whip snapped, cracking against her skin. Her muscles locked in brutal agony. She cried out, tears falling quickly.

"Again? Again?" Holkstoin asked the crowd. They cheered as he cracked the whip again and, this time, she felt her skin part sharply from its equal. Warm blood began to fall, rolling down her raw back. She had hoped for another brief respite, but the next strike came almost immediately. They continued ceaselessly on as the crowd's cheering heightened.

She lost count after twenty.

*Mercy. That's all you have to say. Just give in. They want to hear you beg. If they want my humiliation, then they can have it...*

She raised her head to cry out a plea but, before she could open her mouth, something caught her eye. She blinked several times before she was able to focus on a figure in the distance. He was so far away but she knew, unmistakably, that it was Tom. He stood over the farthest hill, by the fence that encased the Slums. His face held no expression as he leaned against a blackened tree, watching. A breeze flew by as the whip cracked again. He stared at her, eyes boring into her, cutting holes deeper than the whip as a newfound sense of strength erupted in her. She raised her head.

*They underestimate me.*

The whip struck again, leaving nine more marks against her flesh.

*I am going to survive this. I have to.*

Her blood flowed down to her ankles, but she no longer cared.

*Ke needs me!*

She remained still for the rest of the whipping. The harder Holkstoin hit, the greater her resolve became. She did not cry out again, her tears no longer feeding the earth. His strikes grew fiercer and fiercer in response to her sudden resilience. Her body fell limp, but her head was still held high.

Holkstoin could not continue at that pace for long. Eventually, he dropped his whip to his side and took several deep breaths. His hands were blistered and she took comfort in this as her back bled a river of red. Hot blood trickled down her legs, splitting between her toes. She watched it roll over the ground, cutting between the soft dirt in the same way water carves the earth.

"Enough," Holkstoin shouted, his exhaustion plain. "Has she had enough? Has she bled her crime's worth?"

The crowd cheered.

"Then she shall return to her work," he said. "She shall be the Gi's slave until she dies!"

A guard stepped forward and cut her free of the post while managing to keep her hands secured tightly. She fell, not realizing how close to death she was. Then, through the blur of her vision, she saw Tom. He smiled a smile that screamed survival, and she knew she would live. She could not feel the soldier's rough grips or the wounds freshly bleeding upon her back. The only feeling that was with her was survival.

CHAPTER 3
# COLLAPSE

Cam awoke in her own bed that night. A dark curtain had already fallen over the decaying town as images of Ke and Tom clung to her mind. Ke laying on the ground, in a crumpled heap, was at the forefront. She screamed out loud as some of the wounds on her back broke open to bleed with her cries.

"Cam, stop it," Mel said, pushing into the room with a small bundle of torn cloth. "The whole west district will hear you. The guards will come and I'm not thinking you want to see them again."

"Mel," Cam said, weakness coming over her. She glanced at the sheet dividing the room and heard ragged breathing. "Ke?"

Mel turned, following her gaze.

"He's sleeping, Cam."

"No." Fresh tears spilled down her cheeks.

"I'm sorry."

"No," Cam protested as she tried to rise. More of her lashes split and fresh blood stained the mattress as tears of pain joined tears of loss. "He-he's fine. He's fine!"

"Cam, don't you remember the whipping?" Mel asked, face white. "Ke was sinking into Vinestra's poison before you even made it to him. He's already asleep."

Cam fell back onto the flat mattress, barely conscious of turning over to let Mel tend her wounds. A vital piece of her had been stolen and was breaking apart. Ke had fallen into the bad slumber. She had not saved him, and she fell asleep with that thought invading her dreams.

•

Cam woke with a start the following morning and felt the itching of the mattress against her wounds. She moaned and rolled from the bed, eager to part from anything so uncomfortable. She reached for her locket as a deep pang struck her chest that she knew could only be Ke.

The memories of the previous day's whipping had already begun to slip but then, with a horrid flash, they burst through her mind with ferocity. She bit her lip, feeling bile rise and fall into her mouth with the sudden searing pain of her raw wounds. Then the wind blew in through the pane-less window, bringing the sound of ragged breathing to her ears. She looked up through pained vision toward the dark blue sheet that separated her from Ke.

The sheet was thin, old and smelled of mold but it was the only barrier they had had available. Then she heard another raspy breath and stood instinctively. Her body was numb as she moved closer to the sheet, her clammy palm outstretched. The harsh breathing continued as she pulled the divider away and saw Ke.

He was lying on his back in his thin, little cot. A gray blanket lay over his body and his little arms were at his sides. His usually cheerful face was still and his skin was overly pink. If she had not known better, she would have thought he was merely sleeping.

"Cam," Mel said, coming into the room. He stopped at the sight of Cam kneeling over Ke. "It's time to go to work."

"Right…" she muttered as she stared blankly at Ke. "Time to go."

•

Cam arrived on time and began her duties with an angry voracity. Her emotions were tumultuous and she could barely feel the weight of her pick as it slammed into the earth. The other slaves avoided her, but she was apathetic. She could only feel Ke and the stinging of the whips. The day passed without incident and she swept through it dazed.

The night had fallen with an especially heavy cover of fog. The gray clouds had darkened gloomily but, as it was the end of spring, the weather struck her as unusual. She stopped and glanced up at the sky with the unnerving feeling that the earth could also feel her pain. Perhaps it was preparing to cry with her.

The streets were emptying quickly as everyone hurried home but Cam stood, still staring at the sky. She blinked and looked down at the jagged gravel cutting her toes. Her feet were bars of weighted steel as she continued to trudge down Hangyaku, the road that always led to nowhere. She walked for several minutes, leaving drops of blood along with her footsteps. The sun had fully set, and the darkness was consuming, but at that moment Cam wanted nothing more than to be consumed.

She put one foot on the first stair of the staircase then stopped. The breeze blew her hair around as her blank eyes stared unfocused on the next step. She looked up at the sky again and turned around as the familiar pounding in her chest returned. The idea of going to her unit was not appealing.

Instead, she walked around the building and found herself in front of a gnarled old oak. She let out a heavy sigh and leaned against it. The clouds were furling together as a delicate breeze blew by. She sat down beneath the tree and stared for several minutes at the sky, hoping that a meteor would crash into the Slums or that a flood would wipe them clean.

"Cam."

"What are you doing here, Tom?" Cam asked, recognizing the voice. She turned to him. He was tall, though starved in appearance like all slaves, with a mess of dark brown hair.

"Thought you might want to train a bit," he said, leaning against the dying tree.

She thought of a snide remark before deciding that training would probably keep her mind away from the things that were slowly destroying her. She stood.

He grinned and charged forward, keeping his body angled as he swung. Cam jumped back, twisting her skinny torso away from each blow, but he was exceptionally swift. He jabbed, aiming for her throat, and she was too slow to react. She fell back in frustration and awe, as always, at his lightning speed.

"You think you're being slow, but you're just being lazy," he said, helping her up. "Might want to work on that. It'll help with the, you know, not getting hit."

She rolled her eyes, brushing the dirt from her already dirty pants and repositioning herself.

"Go," he said. She stepped back against his advance, using her forearms to knock him away. "Faster."

His foot work was eloquent and quick like a rapid beat. Cam felt her mind meld with her body's movements as she continued to block. Her confidence grew until she looked back and realized that she was rapidly losing ground. In her haste to keep up with his pace, she tripped over a rock.

"Be aware of your surroundings, Cam," he said. "Peripheral vision is your friend."

She grunted and stood, readying herself again.

"You know a lot of techniques now, but you need to work on your instinct," Tom instructed. "Let everything else go."

She slid her foot backward and let her weight fall upon it. She tried to concentrate on the training exercise, but her mind kept wandering up to the room where Ke was.

"Come on, Cam," Tom said, returning her focus to their sparring. "Let's do it already."

"In your wildest dreams," she taunted, raising her fists.

Tom smirked as he rushed forward. His fist swung an inch from her nose. She dodged successfully, but the action caused her to lose balance and she stumbled again.

"That was just terrible," he said.

"I'm doing the best I can," she replied as she repositioned.

"No, you're body's here but your mind's elsewhere," he said, striking several mock blows. "There's nothing you can do for Ke right now."

His words felt intrusive and it angered her. He flew toward her and she knocked him away with more force than she had intended. Tom frowned.

"Don't talk about him," she said firmly. "I'm fine."

"Oh, really?" he asked as he, almost lazily, blocked her. "I'd beg to differ. You appear to be at the beginning stages of implosion."

He switched back to an offense stance and attacked.

"I'm fine, Tom!" she shouted. "Back off!"

Her hands struck his, never nearing their intended target. Her body picked up speed with her newly found fury as she blocked each new blow with utter effectiveness.

"Cam, you're like a dying star," he said. "It's only a matter of time before you collapse. You can't run from this forever."

Something in his words struck her harder than his fists ever could. Her mind had already been a perplexing jumble of interwoven complexities, but now it was masked by the one thing she had been trying to suppress.

Tom jumped forward and swung his leg in a move intended to trip her. Under normal circumstances, when she sparred with him, it would escalate to a point where she was barely able to track his movements. The wind picked up as time slowed and she felt her arm move up. Her hand wrapped around his foot, stopping him dead. His eyes snapped to hers as she threw him back.

"You want to know the truth?" she asked, her body moving in a symphonic rhythm to his parries. She grabbed his shirt and threw him to the ground. "You really want me to say it?"

He jumped to his feet and jabbed, but she grabbed his incoming arm and shoved him back. He lurched into the old oak tree, and it trembled from the impact as their eyes met, blue against gray.

"It's my fault," she said.

"Wait, what is?"

"It's my fault Ke's dying."

"How do you figure?" Tom asked.

She slumped down under the blackened tree.

"I knew what he was going to do," Cam confessed. "He's my baby brother. We think alike, and when I saw that chunk of Vinestra, I wanted it too. I wanted to help my family. I wanted to help myself. I was selfish. If I hadn't been wasting time thinking like that, then I could have stopped him. I could have saved him."

Tom sat down next to her.

"Honestly, you couldn't have saved him," Tom said. "He was going to do what he wanted, when he wanted. Like you said, you two are a lot alike. You're both impulsive. You often act without thinking."

"Really? Those weren't even close to being words of comfort."

"But you two are both good and so are your intentions," Tom continued. "Ke made a mistake, but it was not without good purpose. You made a mistake for the same reason. Mistakes happen but, in the end, Ke was just trying to do what was right and that's what really matters. At least, that's what I think."

They sat in silence as the desolate clouds overhead unleashed a torrent of glossy waves. The rain fell, drenching them in their solace. She watched the rain cascade to the ground, leaving craters in the gray earth. Water ran through her hair, tumbling over her face and dampening it to a much darker brown as her body began to shake. Cam's mind had been temporarily freed of its invisible captors upon her confession but, in its place, a more sinister exploit came to fruition and it was rooted in revenge.

Tom placed a warm hand on her shoulder. She turned to him and saw a small hint of worry flit over his face.

"What?" she asked.

"Nothing," he replied quietly. He gently squeezed her shoulder then stood up to leave. "It's getting late. Mel will be worrying about you. You should go home."

A sad smirk crossed her face. "Right, I should go home."

CHAPTER 4
# CONFESSIONS AT DEATH'S DOOR

The next day was the worst Cam had ever experienced. Her exhausted body no longer had the fuel of anger or the numbness of shock to sustain it. Relentless, burning waves rolled over her, but the physical pain was infinitesimal in comparison to the agony of her loss. After her shift ended, she went searching for Tom.

The darkest of nights flowed into the Slums as a bitter cold mercilessly battered the already fragile buildings. Cam, legs still sore from that day's work, walked quickly toward Number 34. The candlelight from the nearby homes was duller than usual as a generous fog had rolled in. She quickened her pace, but no lights were on at Number 34 when she arrived. Only a shadowy figure was visible, huddled by the wall.

A dark home was always a bad sign in the Slums. She moved closer, afraid of what she may find.

"Tom?" she asked cautiously.

He was crouched low to the ground, his head resting uneasily in his hands. He was shaking horribly and his skin was ghost white. She waited, but no response came. His hands were clenched into fists, knuckles whiter than the moon.

"Tom? What's wrong?" she asked again.

"It's my...dad," Tom said as his shaking grew worse. He turned his head to face her and his eyes were frightening. "He died."

The words came out like an echoing of death's sentiments.

"What? When?"

"Not sure. He was dead when we came home."

"Oh, Tom," she said, kneeling down. Her hand came to rest awkwardly on his shoulder. It was odd for her as she was not well versed in the art of comforting. He withdrew roughly, throwing her comfort aside. "I'm sorry."

"Don't be sorry."

"I know that's not what you want to hear," Cam said sheepishly. "But I'm here for you, you know, if you need me."

"That's great, Cam, but you don't understand. No one was there for *him*," Tom said. "If I..."

"You couldn't have done—"

He flinched at her words, and his stare became cutting. "No one was there, Cam. *No one* was there for him!"

He stood abruptly, fists clenched. His expression, filled with such sorrow and fury, brought tears to her eyes. Then, with a sudden out of characteristic loss of control, he kicked the old iron railing and sent it flying down to the street. He turned back then fell against the wall and slid down to sit on the crumbling porch again.

"Are you going to be okay?" she winced as soon as the words left her. She knew the answer before Tom could respond. This was the first time she had experienced someone else's loss and she was ignorant of how to act. When she had lost her parents at age nine, she had known then that the concept of "being okay" no longer applied. The question she had asked would have angered her as well. "Never mind, that was a stupid thing to say."

He looked up.

"Don't worry about it," he said, forcing softness into his tone. His fists uncurled and fell to his sides.

They walked into the house in silence. The room was dark and they could hear his mother, Shun, crying. Cam sat down at the dining table in her usual spot. She glanced across at the empty chair, Wes' chair.

Memories of Wes, prior to the sickness, ran through her mind. She remembered dinner with Wes, Shun and Tom. They had been such a happy and complete family. Wes was always the one making everyone laugh. He would tell the most absurd but hilarious stories that kept everyone's spirits up.

Cam turned, realizing Tom had not sat down with her. He was still standing by the front door, jaw rigid as he stared at nothing.

"It's not right," he muttered to himself. "None of this is."

"Of course it isn't," Cam said, but he did not seem to hear her.

"I mean, *this* was supposed to be simple. Now, I don't even know what my actual mission is anymore," he said.

"Your mission?"

His brow furrowed, and he avoided her eyes as he became increasingly interested in a bent fork that was sitting on the table.

"Okay, Cam. I've got to tell you something..."

"That's ominous."

"I wanted to tell you sooner. Actually, truth is I had no idea how I would tell you without it resulting in you punching me in the stomach or something," Tom said as her stare became acerbic. "You know how we sometimes hear about rebel groups causing the Gi some well-deserved trouble?"

"Yes," she said cautiously.

"Well, Cam, I'm one of them."

He cringed, waiting for her reaction, as her eyes narrowed.

"Okay," she said, after a moment.

"Wow. Really? That's not the response—"

She stood and punched him in the stomach, cutting him off. He grunted and fell into one of the chairs.

"Good, I'm glad we got that out of the way," he said with a grimace. "By the way, Mom's one, too. Obviously, we're not really slaves. We're members of a rebellion group known as the Equintas. My Mom's actually one of the leaders, of sorts. That's also why we always had such good food because it was grown at our home in the mountains."

"Of course it was," she mocked, crossing her arms. "By the way, I always knew something was up. For one, you were way too good at hand-to-hand combat and—"

"Cam, that's not the important part," he interrupted. "You need to know that you've been lied to your entire life. The Gi Force are not just your slave masters. Their deception goes much deeper."

"Deception," she pondered. "That sounds a lot like what you've been doing this whole time."

"There is definitely truth to that," he said, his shoulders falling. "But it's the Gi who hurt Ke and they are the ones who have been lying about what Vinestra really is."

"What do you mean?"

"Vinestra doesn't cause the sickness. The Gi Force does."

She took a step backward.

"That's not true," she said.

It was impossible and she refused to believe it. Of all the things she had been told, no matter how wrong or horrible, she had always taken comfort in the fact that they were true.

"Actually, Vinestra is something really spectacular," he continued.

"How can you say that? How can you say that after Ke? After your father?"

Tom reached for her apologetically, but she backed away further.

"Listen to me, Cam. Vinestra is a *good* thing," he said. "It boosts the natural aptitudes one has, whether that's physically, mentally, or something else. Basically, it elevates you to the best that you possibly can be. Its power is immense, and for that reason the Gi made this elaborate cover up for it. We, slaves, mine it for them and we're told it kills upon contact. Thus no one here will touch it and accidently discover their secret."

"No," she said, voice beginning to waver.

"I swear, it's the Gi Force," Tom continued. "They did all of this. Didn't you ever wonder how they could refine something so 'dangerous' without dying? It's because everything they say is a lie. Vinestra *is* more powerful in its raw form but, even refined to almost nothing, it can still prolong life and subtly enhance one's natural talents."

"Wait, then how have they been making people sick?" Cam asked. "How did they make Ke sick?"

"Poison," he said, "with a synthesized version of cyanide that contains an inhibitor to block the creation of methemoglobin. They administer it to anyone who touches Vinestra. By doing this, they're able to keep up this charade, keep up the fear."

"But *when* could they do this?"

"They do it when they carry them away after exposure. We learned that when Wes got sick and Mom followed the guards. What? You don't believe me, do you?"

She let out a long sigh.

"I wish I didn't, but I actually do," she said. "I just really feel like I should hit you again for having been such a stinking liar. You could have told me, you know."

"I was just following orders. I would have told you, but my instructions were very clear. I was told both on paper and in-person that I had to keep our identities secret above all else," Tom said testily. "But, after Wes died today, I realized that I could do so much more for the rebellion if I *didn't* follow orders, so I saw no reason to continue keeping the secret from you. See, my Mom and I were sent here to search for this thing. We haven't found it, so we're just wasting our time while people like Wes and Ke suffer. We could be spending our time helping them directly instead."

"How?"

"For me, before I came here, death in the Slums was just death," he said. "People die here so often that you grow accustomed to it, but now I think I really understand what we're fighting for."

"Well, that's very epically dark and all but I still don't understand your point," Cam said.

"Like I said," he whispered. "What's happening in this world is not right. The Gi think they're invincible, but they bleed just like we do and they can die just like we can. I won't let Ke suffer the way my father did. Ke won't be alone. I'm going to save him and the whole damn Gi Force army won't be able to stop me."

Her mind was frozen and she felt tears coming at the thought of Ke. At that moment he was asleep in his bed, in the bad slumber.

"Cam," Tom said. "We need to escape then break into the capitol."

"Break into Tengoku?" Cam asked. "I think you're bordering on delusional now. Also, the escaping bit seems kind of out there, too."

"We broke in, didn't we?"

"Okay, that is factual," Cam conceded.

"We need Aeraden. It's somewhere in the Ether and we're going to find it," Tom said. He stared at her pointedly as though she would know exactly what he meant.

"Can you not tell from my blank expression that I have no idea what you're talking about?"

"Okay, you heard the stories of the Ether, right?"

"Yes, but aren't they just stories?" she asked. "I mean, an underground government facility...actually, make that a top secret, underground government facility where they manufacture genetically altered foods and perform mad science experiments."

"It's all true, Cam," Tom said, brushing her rant aside.

"Of course it is," she sighed. "So, what does that have to do with the Air-de-been?"

"Aeraden," Tom corrected. "It's locked away in the last chamber of the Ether, in their main Vault. Aeraden is the healing stone. No one knows where the Gi found it, but it can heal just about any disease or wound that is nonfatal which, luckily for us, includes the Gi's supposedly incurable poison. Granted, if it's administered before the last stage of the sickness...though that's technically also a theory, I guess. Actually, it's all really just a theory except for the part about the stone being real."

"So, you're saying that if we have the stone than there's a chance to save Ke?"

"Exactly."

She sighed.

"Okay, I need you to confirm this for me because a lot of weird just occurred in very quick succession, and I'm, well, somewhat addled," she said. "You want to escape the Slums then illegally enter Tengoku and steal a magical stone from the Gi Force, all in the hopes of saving my kid brother?"

"Indubitably," Tom said. "Preferably without getting caught."

"Logically."

"So, are you in?" he asked, extending his hand to her.

Cam stared at him with disbelieving eyes, but she knew her decision was already made. If there was any chance to save Ke, then she had to take it.

"Of course I am," she said as she shook his outstretched hand.

CHAPTER 5
# THE ETHER

Cam left Tom's house, emerging into the damp, hazy night. Consequences and dangerous notions allowed her mind to stray toward revolutionary conclusions. She was a slave and had been since infancy. All of her life, successful rebellion against the Gi was unheard of. Any show of displeasure while working was considered to be criminal sedition constituting a painful, sometimes deadly, punishment. Cam had only ever heard of one attempt of premeditated murder against a Gi officer, and it had resulted in horrific failure. The man was captured, burned, whipped, and then died from blood loss as the result of a gruesome sodomy. Cam remembered how the Gi had left his skinned and disemboweled body hanging by the mine's entrance as a reminder to obey.

Cam recalled the memories of other such atrocities she had witnessed over the years and felt nauseated as she recalled each one in detail. She was disgusted but, at the same time, every injustice only helped to fuel her drive to save Ke. She wasn't going to let Ke be another statistic or let Wes' or her parents' deaths be in vain.

Cam stepped onto the platform of her floor and saw the faint glow of a candle through the only window. Mel was sitting at the kitchen table as she walked in. He wore a worried look as he toyed with a plate of the Slums' version of bread, grot.

"Mel?" Cam asked. "What are you still doing up?"

"I was worried about you," he said. "I heard about Wes..."

"Oh."

"I'm sorry. He seemed like a nice fellow," Mel said, struggling to find the words. "I have some food here, if you're hungry."

Cam sat down.

"I don't really feel like talking," she said as she tore off a piece of grot.

"That's fine," Mel said. "I can just keep you company for a bit."

"Alright, thanks," Cam said, forcing a smile for her godfather.

They sat for a while in awkward, growing silence. Cam stared at her food, chewing it slowly as time ticked away at an inexorably sluggish pace. Irritation wracked her nerves as this was time that she could be spending to further map out their infiltration plans or to study the Gi's military structures. Any time not spent on their plan, on saving Ke, felt like a waste to her, and it was with this thought that a radical idea came to her.

"Mel," Cam said, looking up. "Remember the stories about the Ether that you told me when I was little? Could you tell them again?"

"What?" Mel asked, caught off guard by the sudden introduction of voice. She felt her internal clock continue its undeviating journey as the seconds of silence escalated her panic.

"Please," Cam said, her voice involuntarily revealing an edge of desperation.

Mel's eyes narrowed and, for one nerve-racking moment, Cam thought he might say "no." But then his smile turned warm, breaking the tense rigidity of fear that had enveloped the small space between them.

"Well, the legend goes that the Ether is a place within Tengoku," Mel said. "It was supposedly a sanctuary for the rulers of the land. A long time ago, strange creatures played there and the ground was so fertile that the land for hundreds of miles around produced the finest wines known to man. The people who were allowed to live there lived for hundreds of years and were blissfully content until their dying day. The land described in the old stories, with its rolling hills and lonely oaks, sounds remarkably similar to where we live now. So I guess that would make the Gi, as they are the rulers of this land, the ones to occupy the Ether today. That is if the Ether were real. The rumor associated with this old myth is that it explains the extensive food resources the Gi have despite the dead land and—"

Mel had noticed Cam's prompt attention and curiosity at the subject.

"But you know that's just a story, right?" Mel asked. "There is no *real* Ether."

Cam fiddled with her food.

"Well, I heard it's true," Cam said, probing further. "I heard that they have food there and medicine—"

"That's a bunch of rubbish," Mel interrupted with a laugh. He clapped Cam's hand, a bit too entertained by the notion, but Cam pressed on.

"I don't know. I heard that they even have real beef, not just that synthesized stuff they advertise on the big boards," Cam said, her hands playing with the graying napkin.

Mel raised his eyebrows. Meat was difficult to come by as the animals died when they grazed on the poisoned earth. It had been hundreds of years since any animal had been seen roaming the rolling hills surrounding Tengoku.

"Cam, you're a smart girl," Mel said, squeezing her hand. "What would make you believe this nonsense? Oh wait, I know, it was probably Tom telling you old wives tales again."

"No," Cam said defiantly, "but if they can grow those bio-altered vegetables there then animals are not a far reach!"

Mel froze; his hand hovered over his rusty plate. His expression conveyed irritation but Cam could see something else voicing its turn in her godfather's mind, something that she could not discern. Then his expression warmed again as he threw a piece of grot into his mouth. She stared at him, perplexed, and he smiled wide.

"Cam, why do you want to know?" he asked, clearly exasperated. "The Ether's contents aren't released to anyone but the highest ranking officials. I mean, the only ones who are even allowed to enter the Ether to begin with are those with at least a B class security clearance—"

Mel paused, lips parted as the expression on Cam's face confirmed the amount of knowledge he had revealed. Cam felt her heartbeat quicken as she stared, disbelieving, at her godfather.

"That was a lot of detailed information for a simple wives tale, specifically that last part."

"Well..." Mel stammered.

"Mel, what do you know?" Cam asked. "I mean, how do you know?"

"Never mind how I know," Mel said as he took a large sip of his greenish water, grimacing at the bitter aftertaste. "Oh, but I do know they have pork..."

"Mel?"

"What do you want, Cam?"

"I'm just curious," Cam said, heart beating with the excitement of new knowledge. It seemed impossible, but her own godfather knew the inner workings of the Ether. Maybe he also knew of Aeraden. "If it's real, I want to see it. I understand they have other things in there besides altered meat and vegetables..."

"You mean Aeraden."

Cam's heart stopped. The word and the knowledgeable ease at which Mel used it left her frozen.

"Do you know—"

"I know some things, but I'm not about to tell you," Mel admitted. "It's for your own safety, sweetheart."

Cam frowned.

"But, Mellech..."

Mel's head snapped up at the mention of his full name as he had not heard it uttered in a very long time.

"Is this so important to you that you would speak my entire name?" Mel asked as he wrenched his hands. Cam saw an opening for manipulation and seized it immediately.

"I have to save Ke," Cam said, pleading. "Mellech, don't you want to save him, too? He's suffering at this very moment. He'll never wake up if I don't do something and you're the only one who can help me. Don't you love him, too?"

"Cam, how can you even say that?" Mel asked, his brown eyes softening with sadness. "I love Ke as if he were my own child."

"Do you?" Cam asked, her voice purposefully cold. "If you love Ke and you love me, then help. All I want is Ke back and I probably won't be able to do it, but I have to try. I can't stay idle on the sidelines to his death march. Besides, it's not fair what they force us to do or what they do to us with their poisons—"

Cam stopped. She had not intended to divulge so much information, but her mind had rambled against her will. Mel was staring at her with a contemplative expression.

"What?" Mel asked. "What was that about the Gi's poisons?"

"Uh," she said. She needed to change the subject as she knew some things must be kept secret. Her mind reeled and she couldn't piece together a sentence to save her life. "Um, well, I was being metaphorical."

"Okay," Mel said, confused by Cam's odd response. "What was that a metaphor for?"

"Well, it doesn't matter now," Cam said quickly, trying to drop the subject. "What's important is that I need to save my little brother and you can help me, but you're refusing."

"Ke's been strong just to make it this far," Mel said, a faraway look in his eyes.

"Mel," Cam said, her hands clenching into fists. "I'm not going to ask how you know everything you do, but I need your help. I have to save Ke. I can't lose anyone else to this."

Mel stood, setting his napkin on the table. The gray desolation of their lives seemed to grow even more palpable in the awkward silence of the room. The walls were closing and swelling with Mel's every breath as Cam waited. She looked at her godfather, pleading with him the way Ke pleaded with Cam in her dreams. After several tense moments of desperate thoughts, Mel's hands resettled upon the table.

"Firstly," he said. "There are many obstacles. The guardians of the Ether are fierce and far more powerful than you."

"I'm stronger than you think, Mel," Cam boasted. "I can fight anyone if it came down to it."

"Well, the guardians aren't all human," Mel said. "Some are creatures that are far more deadly than any mere man."

"Creatures?"

"Here," Mel said, moving to the fireplace and removing a worn brick from the wall. Cam had never known about this hiding place before. She stepped closer. Mel's hands swiftly searched the crevice before removing a brown leather-bound book. "Read this. It may help."

Mel handed Cam the book. The leather cover was embossed with a picture of a red-skinned creature with sharp teeth and horns. A stream of curving fire fell from its mouth and formed a circle around its body. She stared at the drawing before the title drew her eye.

"It's the *Book of Trappings*!" Cam exclaimed, holding the worn book tightly. "How did you get this? It's the forbidden stories and historical accounts of the Trappings Era. You told me that the Gi had them all burned and that only two copies remained. One's in the Gi's Museum of Eden and the other is in the Lord General's personal library."

"Just read it, Cam. Read it and maybe you will fully understand the foolishness of what you plan to do. Maybe you'll think better of it. What happened to Ke is not right, I agree wholeheartedly with you there, but if you do this then I'll" —he shuddered— "I'll never see you again. I know you don't want to lose Ke, but I don't want to lose you, too."

Mel was staring at the floor as he spoke. Cam grinned then threw the book down on the sofa and hugged her godfather. As a family, they had never been especially open about their emotions thus the action was awkward for both of them at first. Cam felt a tear roll down her face as she had never been so grateful for assistance in her life. In the other room, Ke's rattling breaths turned into a coughing fit. They were already becoming more frequent. Mel quietly released Cam.

"Remember, I'm not trying to help you do anything," Mel said, "but I'm also not trying to hold you back. You and your brother have always been...what's the word?"

"Impulsive?" Cam suggested, a smile at the edge of her lips.

"Right," Mel said. "So, if you're going to do something stupid then you should at least be well-informed. Now, go to bed."

Cam patted him on the shoulder as she walked into her bedroom, lit a candle and opened the book. She sat for what felt like an eternity, running her fingers over the brittle cover. It had been the longest week of her life, and the impossibility of the book before her only added to the surrealism. The hours passed slowly as she sat with the book in her hands. Ke's breathing was the only sound that could be heard. The moon was large and creeping in through the window before she turned to the first page:

*The Book of Trappings, Edition Two*

*By the Gi Force and its honor, the previous records of this text were manufactured incorrectly to represent falsehoods. The forthwith is a true and accurate account of the Trappings Era. Please enjoy this record in its entirety.*
*The Almighty Gi Will Never Die.*

Cam rolled her eyes at the Gi's motto but pressed on, reading quickly through the first few chapters.

*Chapter Seven: Oni-Orochi*

*14 December, Year of the Serpent*

*The Armistdan Order had mostly fallen by the night of the twelfth of December. Their forces were finally diminished by the Markstre Force. Our spy infiltrated their camps as a lost traveler and managed to kill the majority by poison to their water supply. Only the leader, Edan, and his two closest warriors, Mylioth and Cardenash, still live.*

*The entrance is almost free to those who have searched endlessly for it. Its powers are reflected in the opulent earth. We are close to what we seek.*

*Tomorrow, at the break of dawn, we will force through the entrance and finally find eternal life.*

"The Armistdan Order," Cam whispered.

Cam had been taught that their story was just a myth. The Armistdan Order had been a small force that had inhabited the nearby area three hundred years previous. During the Final War, the last war known to man, their small army was responsible for the Slaughter of the Serpent. The Armistdan Order was only a few hundred strong, but they decimated over one thousand of the Gi's platoons during their occupation of the Tengoku area. That was the story Cam overheard the soldiers telling each other in the Raquineste Mines. It was meant to be a motivational story for the soldiers to show them how the Gi triumphed through adversity. She had thought them to only be myth.

She turned back to the book. Her eyes were dropping from her exhaustion, but the next section compelled her to continue.

*15 December, Year of the Serpent*

*I cannot even begin to describe the horror of today's events. I do not know how to explain everything I have seen but, even as I write, the blood of my comrades pours onto these pages.*

*The entrance was at the end of a large cave. We could feel it drawing us in and I knew we were close.*

*We encountered nothing for the first few hours in the cave. The cave's paths were level and easy to traverse. Our crew was jovial, excited beyond description, that was until we met the beast.*

*A monster is the best description I can provide. It stood like a man, but it had scales the color of blood and enormous pincer-like claws. The Captain ordered the men to charge and, at this, the beast changed. Its body grew and morphed until it stood nearly fifteen feet in height. The men fought valiantly to fend off the beast, but there was no way to defend ourselves as the beast's breath was not like ours.*

*It was fire.*

*It scorched the front lines and gave serious injury to the Captain and myself. I was knocked to the ground and suffered a blow to the head. All I can remember now were its ruby red eyes staring at me through a veil of red and black scales. I thought I was going to die in that cave, but the Captain stood his ground. Despite his injuries, he managed to pierce the eyes of the great beast. It soon fell and whimpered to the Captain's side, beaten and tamed.*

*For this creature, so great and powerful, could not be slain. The Captain kept the creature naming it Oni-Orochi. I later discovered the creature may have been a demon of some sort. I, being a man of pure science and absolute rationality, had not been familiar with the old legends or myths. I did not know of these creatures' existence. I believed that they were mythical, fictional, story tales for the young but, here at the entrance, they were real.*

"Demons. Okay, that's troublesome," she muttered to herself as she continued to read.

She learned that the Armistdan Order had been real. According to the *Book of Trappings*, the Armistdan Order was a group of thugs who sought to stop the Markstre from spreading their messages to the people. In the end, they were dwindled down to their core leaders: Edan, Mylioth and Cardenash. According to the book, they were the fiercest and most horrible of the Armistdan. She turned the page and found herself staring at an artist's rendition of the three.

Edan was broad shouldered and draped in chains. In his hand was a sword as long as one of the Gi's pickup trucks. Cam squinted at his likeness and noticed his face was distorted as if it had been done in a different medium than the rest of the picture. His expression was angry, almost bestial.

Cardenash was a very large, muscular man with legs like tree trunks. He held a flail in one of his meaty fists and his expression was like that of a wolf's. His teeth were bared and saliva ran thickly between his teeth. Then she turned her attention to Mylioth and was struck dumb by the image.

He very subtly resembled someone she knew, but she could not put her finger on it. He was tall with pointed features and a slender build. In one hand was a tanto and, in the other, a bow though, just like Edan, his face seemed almost inhumane.

She turned to the next page and found herself at a new chapter. Her eyes widened as she held the book closer to her face.

*The Discovery of a Sanctuary: The Ether*

●

Cam stayed up through the night, skimming the final chapters as quickly as she could before her shift started. She decided not to sleep as there was little point. Instead, she dressed early, fed Ke and gave him fresh blankets.

"Cam," Mel said, yawning. "You're up early."

"I had a good night's sleep," she said with a small smile.

Mel eyed her before stepping forward.

"Oh, did you take care of Ke already?" Mel asked, peering behind the curtain.

"Yup."

"Well, then I guess we'll head off to the mines a little early," he said.

They walked slowly down Hangyaku and out of the Western District. Mel was staring up at the barren trees and the gray smog that was a permanent fixture in the Slums. He was smiling and it was making her nervous.

"You know, Cam," Mel said, crossing his hands over his chest. "I gave you that book in the hope that you would see the dangers. I hoped it would dissuade you from going."

"Oh, trust me, it did," Cam lied.

"It did?" Mel asked disbelievingly.

Cam forced the most sincere smile possible.

"Yes, I promise," she said as they came to the entrance of the Raquineste Mines.

Many of the workers were already gathering, forming lines. Soon the bell rang, and the first group moved in. Mel parted from Cam at his usual point while she continued to hers. She was set to put her pick into the ground when Tom came up next to her.

"Tom," she said, halting her pick in midair.

"Cam, this conversation couldn't wait—"

"That's what I was thinking, too. You'll never guess what I found out," she whispered, interrupting him. "The Ether *is* real and I know what guards it! I read a book last night. Oh, and you won't believe this, Mel knew about Aeraden!"

"You were speaking so fast that I only understood Ether and Aeraden out of that," he said. She took a deep breath. "Now, what were you saying about Aeraden?"

"Mel knew about it," she repeated slowly. "He gave me the *Book of Trappings,* and I read it, all night. Every word."

"How did Mel get one of those?" Tom asked, his expression becoming severe.

"I have no idea," Cam said, "and I wasn't about to pry when he was giving me information about the Ether."

"Sure, sure," Tom said distractedly. "But this means we're leaving."

"What?"

"We need to leave as soon as possible," Tom repeated.

"Are you sure we'll be ready?" she asked.

"No, but we'll have to be."

●

*Everything was dark, and she was unable to feel. She thought she was running though she could no longer be sure. The surrounding black was utterly suffocating. She tried to adjust her vision in the hope that the world would return, but instead she found she was incapable of using sight at all. Her brain instructed her legs to move, to run, but there was no certainty the message had been received and executed. There was just an unending void. She was drowning and could neither save herself nor experience her body's final flicker of life. She needed the safety of land and liberty from the crushing darkness, but all was still within her purgatory.*

*What was happening? Was this death?*

*Normally, that thought would have been like a shot to the heart, a bullet of psychotic panic, but there was nothing. She knew her body was heaving with tears yet, again, there was no sensation. She was broken, and this was the punishment for the failures of her dreams. This everlasting pit of null was the hell she deserved.*

*Then she heard it.*

*A faint thump, rhythmically even, had begun to pulse. It rose slowly in volume and at a torturous rate. The tiny noise caused excitement to boil as she attempted to locate the sound. Her body was still numb, nonexistent, but she could finally hear as they engraved themselves into her eardrums, the rising story of a rebirth. The beats were repetitive, already bordering on maddening, yet they were glorious as they were the confirming echoes of her own heartbeat. She smiled and ran on.*

*The welcome beat had soon been joined by other melodies. Her ragged breathing rose with her pulse as a delicate melody began to form. She listened and realized that her body was still obeying her as her only restored sensation continued to swell. Pattering against her awakening eardrums came the clomping of her boots against pavement, each step leaving a scar of aural permanence behind. She pushed forward with renewed resolve just as the burn of winded lungs and the ache of cramped muscles began to trickle toward her brain. A fine layer of cool sweat began coating her skin, falling where her tears had been and replacing them. She grinned outright as she tasted the saltiness and smelled her unwashed clothing. She stared ahead, her sight gradually returning. Then she saw that the outline of a door had broken deep within the darkness.*

*The aria of her exertion was rapidly joined by the whistle of the wind picking up. Her feet were suddenly light as her pace effortlessly doubled. She ran on and, with the assistance of the new gust, flew forward at an inhuman rate. The darkness melted, running bright with effulgent gold. The glass towers she had seen jutting from the capitol were now, already, trapping her in their avaricious clutches. The golden sidewalk was her guiding beacon. She was nearing the door and could not help but immediately note the tiny figure before it instead.*

*It was a boy. He was standing before the door, facing away from her. He turned, face frail. Cam opened her mouth to shout his name as she threw her body into a hard sprint. The scar from his recent tragedy was still too fresh. The wind bellowed and moved with increasing speed until her velocity was nearly uncontrollable. She stumbled quickly to a halt before him, knowing that she had little time to spare.*

*"Ke," she rasped, gripping his shoulder. "Ke, are you alright?"*

*He smiled, his skin rosy and his face fuller.*

*"Hi," Ke said. "Camilla of No Last Name."*

*The words etched themselves deep, invoking lost memories.*

*"What?" she asked, palms sweaty and cold. "What do you mean?"*

*"Don't fight who you are."*

*Cam looked away, focusing on the door as if the act by itself would eliminate the need for her to answer if she simply stared with enough concentration. Somehow, Ke always knew the truth.*

*"I guess I don't really know who I am," she admitted, uncertainty deep. They were silent for a moment as Ke continued to stare. She looked up, forcing eye contact and a confident smile, "but I do know that I'm the one who will save you."*

*Ke shook his head.*

*"That doesn't really matter anymore," he said, his brow furrowing in a way that aged him to adulthood. "After all, you aren't just my hero."*

*"What do you mean?"*

*"That was always your problem. You could never see, but you will soon," Ke said. "There's always a truth that your blindness is hiding."*

*"No, saving you is all I have left!" she shouted, civility gone. "There's nothing else to see."*

*The way the poison had robbed him of his warmth, had begun to siphon his light was criminal and was her only mission.*

*"You must see it, Cam. When the time comes, you'll need to be more than you are now," Ke said. "My life doesn't matter in this fight. You must remember the bigger picture."*

*"No, you're wrong," Cam pleaded as they stared, both lost in their own arguments. "You need to live, you must! I need you..."*

*"No, you don't. It'll be okay," Ke said. "Just remember, I'm alive in you."*

*Ke's little arms were suddenly wrapped tightly around her. Comfort had been her job to carry out before, not his. She shut her eyes, trapping her hot tears in a dam of delicate flesh. He was too young, too innocent, to waste away trapped inside his own shriveling, poisoned body. He released her. She reached out to seize him, eyes still closed as she formulated the words needed to convince him it was better to stay. Her jaw twitched open to speak, but a new voice was interrupting her.*

*"You failed. He's already been gone for some time now."*

*Cam's eyes flew open. Where Ke had stood was, instead, the swirling shadow of an unknown woman. She grasped Cam's hand forcefully, her dark hair draping her face into obscurity. Cam spun, searching for Ke as he had only just been present. But she could not find him anywhere.*

*The unidentified woman began to cackle, her voice rumbling at a hauntingly low volume. Anger, unwarranted and unexpected, bubbled beneath Cam's skin as she increased her grip on the mysterious stranger's palm, purposefully causing harm, as nails bit her sharply in return. The woman sneered, and Cam felt movement in the corner of her own mouth. Her lack of responsibility was the basis for her defeat. She stared as the stranger's hair fell back, and the streetlights illuminated her face.*

*It was the eyes. Thick lashes framed a wash of silver. Cam shifted to run but was frozen.*

*They had no mirrors in the Slums. Cam had only gleaned blurred peeks in puddles, and yet, she was certain this woman was another version of herself.*

*"We couldn't protect him, but that's okay," the other Cam said. "Now, just remember..."*

*Their left hands flew up, holding each other's jaws in vice-like grips. Cam was dazed from her failures with Ke, from losing him. Their right hands closed into fists that were then thrust powerfully into the other's chests. Blood erupted outward like a geyser. Cam heard ribs shattering followed by two synchronous squelches as she gasped. She moved her gray eyes upward and met an identical pair as the bitterest cold settled in her empty core. The other Cam smirked as they wrenched their bloody fists away. A still-beating heart was clutched tightly by each.*

*"...I'm alive in you, too."*

•

Cam awoke, tired and panicked from the vivid dream, before she remembered that it was the morning of the slaves' monthly day off. She readied herself quickly and left the unit to find Tom waiting for her.

They walked down Hangyaku together in silence, each beating over their foolish mission. They eventually settled themselves under a dead tree. The twisted branches, gnarled by time and death, littered them in spotty shade. She sat down and caught a falling leaf as she watched the others of its kind fly away. Tom pulled a book from the sack he had brought and opened it with a flourish.

"I can't believe we're going to do this," Cam said in a rush. "So, what do we need to do? How do we escape?"

"In the underworks."

Cam looked up in disgust and shock.

"You mean the sewers? The place where the poop goes to live out the rest of its days?"

"Yes," he said. "It's the only way. The fences are all patrolled so there's no way to climb over without being seen. Trust me, we've tried other means before and it results in being killed by the Gi Force."

"Okay. How do we get into the sewers?"

"Right there," Tom said, pointing toward the back of the church. "There's a drainage grate big enough for us to slide through and it's the only one that's completely hidden from view of the towers. Once we're in, then we just have to remain on a northwestern route."

Cam reclined back with a look of wonderment.

"Wow," Cam said. "That sort of sounds like an actual plan."

"I'm very smart," Tom said with a grin.

They planned most of the logistics, deciding to leave at midnight when the spotlight was the only pertinent threat. The journey would take at least two days. Gathering enough food for the journey would be difficult but they could eat rats, if necessary. Water was their only real obstacle while in the underworks, though they were willing to weaken themselves if it meant a successful escape.

"Now, what did you find in the *Book of Trappings*?" Tom asked after they had completed their plan. She handed him the book which he took in amazement.

"There's a chapter that talks about the Ether and the Ether only," Cam said. "It also talks about these demons. Specifically, this one called Oni-Orochi."

"Oni-Orochi?" Tom asked, looking up.

"Yeah, funny name, I know," Cam said. "Anyway, after reading it, I don't know how we are going to get passed the Gi's security. The Ether supposedly has its own protection and I'm not even sure what that means but it sounds like it's probably bad, potentially fatal."

"The fact that we have this book is really crazy," he remarked as he skimmed the pages. "When we get into Tengoku, we'll be much more prepared for breaking into the Ether. You ready for this?"

"Not even a little bit," Cam said. "But I'm still willing to go."

"Good," Tom said. "Then we'll leave tomorrow as planned."

•

That night, Cam lay upon the rough burlap of her mattress. It was the last time she would sleep on it, and she knew she would not miss it. She had already taken the divider sheet down and packed everything she owned in it, which wasn't much.

She glanced over at Ke from her position on the tattered bed. His little body had been slowly shrinking.

"I can do this, Ke. I can save you."

# Chapter 6
# WHICH WAY THE WIND BLOWS

It was the day. A day to be blended with any other one, but today she was awake well before the first work horn. Her only possessions were packed into the bag she had made from the old bed sheet.

She went to work as she normally would and the day inched by at a torturous rate. Each throw of her pick seemed to last an eternity. Her nerves were fried and the voices came to call on her twice. It was the first time she had had an attack since Ke fell ill.

When the shift finally ended, she made it a point to walk home with Mel. They chatted as they traversed Hangyaku, at which time Cam realized that she would probably never walk the road again. Something in that thought made her smile.

"—and lately I've been getting these strange pains in my back. I think I hurt myself more than I thought last week," Mel said. He turned to look at Cam who was not listening. "Cam?"

Cam started.

"What?"

"You've been distracted this whole time," Mel said.

"I'm sorry. I'm just tired," she lied.

"Well, that makes two of us."

Once home, they ate a peaceful dinner, but Mel's back and leg pain forced him to go to bed early. Cam had to restrain the urge to hug the man who raised her good-bye as any act out of the ordinary would have given away their plan.

Cam thought about taking a nap but knew that her anxiety was going to prevent her from sleeping. Instead, she decided to sit with Ke whose little figure had grown so gaunt. She was rereading the *Book of Trappings* when she heard a soft knock on her bedroom wall.

"Cam," Tom whispered through the walls. "You ready?"

"I'll be out in one second," she whispered back.

She kissed Ke on the forehead and grabbed her bag. She was almost out the door when she remembered that her most prized possession was still coiled inside the mattress. Her heart jumped in her throat at the mere thought of leaving her necklace behind. She grabbed the delicate chain, threw it around her neck and crept out the door.

Tom and Cam left the West District together via the Back Alley. It was midnight and, in the crushing darkness, it was feeding time for the Lost. Chills ran up Cam's spine at the ravenous looks on their faces. Rodent intestines and bloodied feathers dripped from their mouths as their razor sharp teeth chewed the bones with an animalistic voracity. She shuddered.

They emerged on a rarely used back road that led to the sewer grate. They glanced down the street through the din to find no one awake, let alone near. Most in the Slums greatly valued every moment of sleep.

Every night was a never-ending nightmare in the Slums and the mornings were the wakes for the dead, testaments to the terror of never truly waking up. Tear-sodden men and women joined the ranks going into the mines each day, confirming to her that someone else had died. They worked as hard as they could, blistering their hands and crying into the mine's deep earth.

Tom was right.

What was happening in the Slums was wrong. They shouldn't be dying by the droves night after night. Cam shook as she and Tom opened the grate.

"Don't puke," he said.

He said it like a joke, but she braced herself as the most horrid smell blew into her face. She gasped. Tom lowered himself into the sewers and extended a hand to her. She gagged again as the breeze blew the acrid smell upward, but she determinedly reached for him and lowered herself down.

She fell hard onto old, damp concrete as her feet slipped against layers of slimy residue. The smell was so potent that Cam leaned against the closest wall and was painfully sick. She felt her body about to lurch again when Tom's hand began to gently rub her back. Her muscles relaxed slowly as she spit the taste from her mouth.

"Wow, you did exactly what I told you not to do," he joked as he helped her up. "Seriously though, it'll only get worse from here. Right now we're close enough to home, to where we started, that we can go back."

Cam wiped her mouth and turned to him. Her determination was evident in the burning light that emanated from her eyes. It only took one look for him to know to press on.

They began to trek down fetid passageways on slippery floors that were stained brown and green. Cam slowly grew accustomed to the smell after being sick until her stomach was empty. Together, they walked for an entire day in tired silence.

Passageways turned into narrow crevices that rose and fell as they progressed. The flow of sewage had become their putrid guiding star. They attempted to eat several times but found that it was better to remain hungry in their current environment. Soon, the sewer had taken them so far down that it became impossible to discern whether it was day or night. They walked beyond the point where their bones ached and their muscles burned. After several more hours, they had grown exhausted enough to determine that rest was required for sake of risking injury.

"Where do we sleep?" Cam asked as she collapsed from the throbbing pain in her legs.

"I think you just answered your own question," he noted, looking down at her. "We can set up camp here."

Cam began building a small campfire. Tom pulled out the dried fruits and vegetables he had packed along with a couple of bottles filled with dirty, smoke colored water gathered from the Slums' wells. Pungent drafts spiraled constantly through the passageways as the fire grew strong enough to warm them both.

They managed to eat small portions of their meals as the fire seared the air, lowering the rancidity. Afterwards, Tom laid the blankets out over the layer of slime glowing dully atop the mottled concrete.

"Well, we should get some sleep," Tom said.

Cam nodded, sitting down on the frayed blanket. It's lonely, tattered threads scratched her bare legs, but she ignored it as she settled down.

"Good night, Tom," Cam said.

"Yeah, you too," he replied and, within seconds, they were both fast asleep.

•

A few hours later they awoke and continued on, following the markers left by the Equintas years previous. They marched forward, barely speaking due to their exhaustion, as the slick path beckoned them further on their arduous journey.

It was nearly a full day of monotony later that the landscape began to change. An eerie chill supplemented itself in their environment as the walls grew dark. Upon closer examination, Cam found that the color had not changed at all. The walls had simply gained a thick coat of blood.

They pushed on, despite the ominous tension, until they found themselves in a large circular room. Cam gagged as the air smelled even worse there than in the rest of the sewers.

"Um," Cam whispered as she stared at the bones strewn ahead of them. "Are those bones human?"

"Looks like it," Tom said grimly.

"I don't like this," she said as a rib cage cracked under her feet.

"Just stay close," Tom said. "We'll be fine—"

*Splash.*

"Tom, what was that?"

They turned as a large ripple spread over the water's surface.

"I don't know," he stammered.

*Splash.*

"Tom?"

Then the sewage erupted upward. Brown sludge rose, expanding like a flower bud opening as it cascaded across the circular room in a dirty rain. Tom and Cam stared transfixed as a colossal tail rose out of the water.

It was the size of a telephone pole and covered in slimy scales. It swung toward Cam with mighty force, knocking her backward. Her body struck the slimy stone wall with a cacophonous crunch and she crumpled to the ground, unconscious.

The water grew still again as Tom turned to Cam lying unconscious on the filthy, stone floor. He ran to her and checked for her pulse while his own pounded loudly in his ears. He found it immediately and breathed a sigh of relief. A breeze swirled through the chamber as he leaned forward to pick her up. He had barely raised his feet to move when a soft feminine voice began to echo enchantingly throughout the chamber.

Tom stopped and took a defensive step back. The water began to ripple again, joining the melody of chilling whispers. The water parted ways and Tom felt his jaw drop as he saw what appeared to be a woman emerging from the sludge.

She floated above the murkiness just enough to reveal her eyes. They were like gasoline in water, dark with shifting cascades of metallic rainbows, but it was the size of the creature itself that put Tom on guard. If he was guessing correctly, based on the estimated mass of its head, the creature was around fifteen feet tall. Meanwhile, the song continued its tranquil lullaby as the two, man and beast, stared at each other. Tom felt his adrenaline peak as the beast blinked with translucent eyelids then let out a terrifying roar. Sewage cascaded over the stone walls as it lunged out of the water.

Tom jumped out of the way with almost inhuman speed, but the monster was just as fast, and it followed his every move. It had the torso of a woman with an unnaturally small waist. Long masses of clumped hair covered its naked chest and fell down its scaly legs. Its long tail whipped through the air menacingly as it chased Tom with fury, slamming hard into the chamber wall. He saw Cam stir at the sudden noise.

"Cam!" he shouted. "Wake up! We need to move, now!"

She rolled over as her eyes slowly focused on him. Then they widened in fear as the large beast loomed, its immense body casting a formidable shadow. Saliva and blood fell from its mouth as its tongue lashed forward. Its scales matched the color of the sewage, sick green, and its eyes burned bright. Cam opened her mouth to scream, but was stifled as Tom picked her up and began to run.

"Put me down, Tom. I can run myself!" she exclaimed.

He smirked.

"Trust me, you can't run as fast as I can."

He raced out of the chamber, choosing one of the narrower passages as it appeared too small for the beast to swim through. The small breeze seemed to follow them as his speed grew. The temperature surrounding them plummeted. Her skin grew cold as her hair whipped her face with such force that the skin broke. Soon, the winds billowing around them were so great that Cam was forced to bury her face in his shoulder. The air beat at her as they covered nearly a quarter of a mile in under thirty seconds. Tom turned back and saw that the water behind them was still before he slowed his pace. He set Cam down in as small alcove as he leaned against the wall to catch his breath. She backed away from him, staring at him with fear.

"What the hell just happened? Who are you?" she exclaimed. "Wait, make that *what* are you? Actually, I don't care. Yes, I do. No, I don't. You're probably an alien, an alien who saved me so he could take me back to the mother ship and dissect me slowly—"

"Not an alien," he interrupted.

He took a step toward her and she threw her fists up defensively.

"I will try my very hardest to defend myself," she warned. Cold sweat beaded her forehead, negating any power in her statement.

"Cam, let me explain."

He reached his hand into his pocket and withdrew a small switchblade.

"That's a weapon," she said, pointing at him fearfully. "That could be used to do something bad and it is not putting me at ease even a tiny little bit!"

"I'm not going to use it, weirdo," he said. "*Look* at it."

He tossed the blade at her feet. It was only a few inches long and it was inlaid with a silvery stone. Cam recognized the material immediately. She picked up the knife, examining it with fervor. It precisely matched the jewel dangling around her necklace.

"You're probably wondering why they're identical," Tom said. "It's because they're both Vinestra."

She turned to him with widening eyes.

"How's that now?"

"Remember how I told you Vinestra enhances certain aptitudes in a person?" he asked.

She nodded, unable to respond vocally.

"Some people find that they are amazing dancers or that they are born mathematicians. Others find that they are very proficient with a certain weapon or that they can negate gravity," Tom said. "Mine is that I can harness the air and manipulate it. I can also muffle my footsteps, so that they're undetectably silent."

"So, back there, you were using the wind to essentially fly at high speeds," Cam said slowly.

"Yes," Tom said. "See, I got this knife from my Mom when I was little. Before the Gi took over, when the truth about Vinestra's powers was still widely known, parents would allow their children to touch it around age five to discover their power so they could learn how to use it. At that same time, they would also give them an object with a highly refined version of Vinestra in it."

Cam raised her hand.

"Not to sidestep the point, but you're telling me your Mom gave you a knife when you were five?" Cam asked with a raised eyebrow. "She always struck me as much more sensible."

"It belonged to my dad. It's usually jewelry or a pen or something like that," Tom said. "But, anyway, this version keeps the powers or aptitudes of the child from degrading as well as protecting them from negative thoughts. However, it's not concentrated enough to actually cause your ability to manifest. But that's why you never gave in to the despairs of the Slums and—"

He stopped. Cam opened her mouth to speak, but he threw a hand up to shush her. He turned and she followed his gaze ahead of them.

The passage ahead was dark as it appeared to split left and right. Then the sound of water slushing against stone met their ears. Tom grabbed his knife and Cam recoiled as the archway to the next passage exploded and the beast appeared.

Stones flew through the air in a rain of destruction. Tom, using his talent of remarkable speed, was able to dodge each piece. Cam, on the other hand, managed to evade the largest stone in her trajectory but was then struck by one slightly smaller. It landed squarely below her ribcage causing her to lose balance and tumble into the waterway of the sewer.

Tom quickly raised both hands. The wind followed his command and funneled, creating a thick tornado-like barrier around the monster who was slithering its way into their passageway. Sewage rose into the twisting cyclone as the beast roared with anger. Debris viciously encircled the creature, leaving thin gashes over its scales. It tried desperately to escape but was beaten back by the brutal winds. It opened its mouth to bite through the barrier only to lose half of its forked tongue in the force of the tornado. Tom grinned at the small triumph as he felt his knees begin to buckle. He knew he could not maintain such a powerful spectacle for long. Already, the strength was ebbing from him.

Meanwhile, Cam had managed to extricate herself from the revolting water. Tom noticed just as the beast turned its attention to her. He grunted, pushing the winds with increasing force as he ran to her. He wrapped his body over her as he tried to sustain the wind barrier. He had grown pale, and Cam could feel him shaking. The monster charged toward them repeatedly but was unable to break through. Cam's mind spun as she tried to regain her equilibrium.

"We'll get out of this, Cam," he grunted. "I promise! I'll—"

Then his body went limp and he collapsed, pinning her to the ground. The tornado dissipated as the monster reared its head and prepared to lunge again.

Cam threw the hand that was not trapped under Tom toward the beast. Adrenaline coupled with desperation came over Cam as it flew forward, free of any barriers or hindrances.

"Stop!" Cam screamed as she watched its orb-like eyes dart toward her. "Please, stop!"

She shut her eyes and clutched Tom, preparing for death. Her breath quickened in anticipation, but second after second passed and nothing happened.

The air was still and the sounds of the raging beast had ceased. Cam cautiously opened one eye and peered up. The beast had retreated slightly though it growled low and maintained its fixed gaze through its oily, black orbs. Cam stared back, unable to move. It tilted its head to the side and eyed her quizzically.

"Uh, Tom?" she whispered, tapping him with her weak and numb fingers. "Tom, wake up. We're not dead."

His eyes opened as she poked him in the armpit. He slowly pushed himself up, freeing her. He turned and saw the beast, watching them with softened posture. It was silent as Tom stared in shock.

"How the hell?"

"I don't know. I just said 'stop' and it did," Cam said. "Although, I'm thinking the 'how' is not as important as the fact that it's not attacking us at the present. Maybe we should take this moment to run?"

The beast tilted its head as an odd feeling began to tickle Cam's senses. She shook her head in confusion when she suddenly realized that the curiosity she was feeling not her own. The creature's dark eyes bored into hers. She crawled forward as a strange, low rumble began to reverberate through the air. Cam stared at Tom, but he did not seem to notice the noise.

It grew in volume and began to override her other senses. She could see Tom's mouth moving but was unable to hear what he was saying. Her body was numb as the air grew oddly still. She looked around as a sense of emptiness settled upon her. It crept into her mind like an icy tendril before assuming her sense of sight. Then a string of intricate coding filled her field of vision.

Cam froze as an array of strange symbols ran past her, reaching faster and faster speeds until her eyeballs were twitching uncontrollably. Her chest was tightening, and she could not breathe. Then they were suddenly gone as quickly as they had begun.

She inhaled. The sounds of the sewer and Tom's voice came crushing over her in a tumult. She blinked, trying to steady the ringing in her ears.

"Hey, are you listening? Look at how obedient it's being," Tom said as she shook her head. "It's like a pet, a gigantic man-eating pet, but still obedient like a pet."

The beast growled and Cam felt anger rise in it. She laughed as indignation erupted in her as well.

"What?" Tom asked, having taken a few steps back.

"I think you pissed it off," she said, a realization coming over her. "You insulted it by calling it a pet. Independent creatures like this don't tend to take orders."

Tom's face paled like ice as he turned to Cam.

"What? You don't believe me?" Cam asked. "In fact, I just communicated with it and kept it from dismembering us."

"Wait, you what?" Tom asked. "Are you saying it communicated back?"

"In a fashion, I suppose," Cam replied with a shrug of her shoulders.

Tom was slack-jawed and seemed to be at a loss for words. Meanwhile, the beast still appeared to be quite upset. It growled again and moved a few feet closer to Tom.

"If I were you," Cam said, putting a hand under his chin to close his mouth, "I would apologize to it, now being preferable if you value your limbs."

"Oh," Tom said, staring upward. "Sorry?"

Cam felt the beast's fury subside. Its anger had been like a sweltering heat that had culminated to a point of such intensity it had no more room to grow, leaving the only option of implosion.

"We don't mean any harm, granted, we couldn't really harm you much to begin with as you are quite a bit more powerful than us," Cam rambled to the monster. "Anyway, we just need to pass through."

It blinked in what appeared to be agreement then turned and dove quickly into the murky sewer water. She watched it swim away as its long dorsal fin cut a razor-sharp path through the muck. Once Tom was sure that the beast was gone, he rounded on Cam.

"Okay, Cam," Tom said. "What the hell was that? It listened to you! How did you do that?"

"I don't know," she said, shrugging her shoulders casually as if this were a normal, everyday occurrence. His lack of coolness was causing her to be nervous. "I just understood it."

"Oh, of course," Tom said disbelievingly. "Now, what did you mean when you say you 'understood it?'"

"I told you. I don't know," Cam said, irritation growing. "I didn't initiate the communication. It just happened."

Tom's face contorted into an odd mix of excitement and fear.

"Come on," she said, grabbing him by the elbow and pressing onward. "We should keep moving."

Tom went without protest. He was quiet as they doubled back to collect their belongings and he remained silent as they began to further their journey along the dank sewer passages. Cam was nervously attempting conversation as they silently tread down the slippery paths.

"It's crazy, huh?" Cam said. "You know, that monsters actually exist."

Tom grunted in agreement, still deep in thought.

"You know," Cam said, eyeing him questioningly. "You never really seemed like the type to believe in weird, potentially paranormal stuff."

"If I fight it and it nearly kills me then I really have no problem accepting its existence," Tom said.

"Okay, valid response."

She left him to his thoughts as he seemed very distracted. They traveled for roughly an hour after the strange events before they saw a faint glint of sunlight from above. They both stopped and looked up at the surface. A grate was visible and they could clearly see open sky. Tom climbed the nearest access ladder.

"I'll check," he said.

"Okay," Cam said. She watched him ascend as she allowed her mind to wonder back to the beast again.

It had communicated with her. It had spoken to her, presenting its voice in some kind of code. She knew that, hidden within the layers of complexity, the beast had shared its emotions along with a single word. She focused on the word and began to decipher it with trepidation, somehow already knowing the key. With fluid focus, the letters melded together and reformed until a single word became apparent.

"Leviathan," Cam said.

Somehow she knew that "Leviathan" was the beast's name. The creature had been attempting to introduce itself. She sighed in confusion as the weight of something unknown crushed her mind like a vice.

"Hey, Cam!"

She blinked, refocusing up the ladder at Tom who was sliding down to her with a wide grin.

"Cam," he said. "We're here."

# Chapter 7
## Among the Citizens of Babylon

They emerged from the sewers into an alley behind the largest grocery store Cam had ever seen. It was nearing noon as the sun was set high above them. She stared up at the sky and basked in the sunlight that she had never enjoyed before.

Nearly every building in Tengoku was golden. The store they stood behind was part of a long strip mall. The building was white with gold trim and hundreds of cars dazzled from the surrounding parking lot.

"Wow, it's so big," Cam remarked, "and clean."

"Turn around," Tom said.

Cam nearly fainted at the sight of the hundred-story towers that densely filled the skyline. Gold and glass twinkled down at her. She stared for several minutes before Tom quietly grabbed her hand and guided her down the alleyway toward the front of the building.

"Are we going to one of those big buildings?" Cam asked as he pulled her along.

A loud commotion ahead interrupted his answer. Cans clanked as a woman screamed. They looked at each other then ran toward the sound.

"Stop!" the same woman shouted. "Please, leave me alone!"

A man's disjointed voice erupted. "You little bitch!"

"Someone, help!"

Cam and Tom turned the corner to see a small woman with chin-length, straw-colored hair. She was very petite at only five feet tall. The man had her cornered against the wall and appeared to be intoxicated. She moved to kick him and missed. Anger fell over the man as he grabbed her fiercely by the shoulders and slammed her hard against the wall.

"Stop!" Cam shouted.

She ran forward and punched the man hard in the kidney. He dropped the woman, doubling over.

"Are you okay?" Cam asked, rushing forward. In her haste, she did not notice the man rise with his fists ready to strike.

"Cam, duck!" Tom shouted.

Cam grabbed the girl and they tumbled to the ground. The wind picked up as Tom stepped forward. He grabbed the man's wrist and brought it down swiftly over his knee. The sound of bones shattering filled the air as Tom threw him against the wall. The man turned to face him, clutching his broken arm.

"Get the hell out of here," Tom said. The man nodded and lurched out of the alley with as much speed as he could muster in his drunken state. The woman looked up at Cam as she tried to straighten her skirt.

"Are you okay?" Cam asked the woman.

"I'm fine, you damn moron," the woman sneered. "I can take care of myself."

"What? You looked sort of cornered," Cam said as she tried to suppress her irritation.

"I could have handled it," the woman said angrily. "You both are absolute idiots."

The woman pushed Cam away as she stood. She picked up her purse then began to walk out of the alley. Cam turned to Tom in disbelief as the woman glanced back, catching their expressions. She sighed loudly and returned to them.

"You really thought you were helping me, didn't you?" she asked, her green eyes filled with annoyance.

"Well, yes," Cam said, eyebrows furrowed.

"Goddamned tourists," said the woman as she opened her purse. She opened a luxurious leather wallet and emptied it of bills. "Here, take this."

The woman pushed the money into Cam's hands.

"Sorry, it's only about five thousand GV. I don't carry much anymore now that debit is on your ID," the woman said.

"But *why* are you giving this to us?" Cam asked.

"No one ever genuinely tries to help others in this city," the woman shrugged. "It's kind of annoying but in a refreshing sort of way. By the way, you two smell really awful."

She clamped her purse shut then gave them a short wave. Her kitten heels clicked as she turned and strutted out of the alley. Cam faced Tom as the money crinkled in her palms.

"Was that weird? I've never met a citizen before so I have no frame of reference," Cam said. "She was upset with us for helping, but she actually wasn't? In fact, she was grateful enough to give us reward money for the assistance that aggravated her..."

"No, that was very weird," Tom said. "The few citizens I've encountered before were all pretty much drunk, pretentious douchebags. She, at least, seemed sober."

"I guess that's a plus," Cam said as she looked down at her clothing with a grimace. "Though she was correct in stating that we smell."

They each changed into the only other items they had with them. Then they discarded the soiled clothes as well as their rations.

"So, what's next?" Cam asked.

"We need to find my Mom's black market connection here," Tom said. "We can get IDs and supplies from them."

"We need to *find* them?" Cam asked. "As in, you don't know where they are located?"

"Actually, I'm really not even sure who they are," he clarified. "But don't worry, I have a vague notion."

•

"A mall?" Cam asked Tom as they entered Tengoku's Grand Furta Plaza, the location of the world's largest mall.

"Actually, we're looking for a store inside the mall that sells mattresses," Tom said. "Now, come on."

Cam followed Tom out of her the periphery of her vision as she took in the plaza which spanned over sixteen city blocks. The surrounding buildings towered high, blocking out the direct rays of the sun. They cut through the garden with its long hedges and brightly-colored flowers then followed the path to the mall's entrance.

The air swirled around them as they were hit with industrial air conditioning. A collage of golden escalators ran upward around the building's interior.  An atrium rose from the first floor up to the sixty-seventh before arching into a glass ceiling.  A thin, manufactured waterfall ran from the center of the roof and fell into a fountain on the first floor.  The fountain had a white stone base and glass walls that rose nearly twenty-five feet tall.  In the center stood a large, abstract statue that looked like an enormous drop of orange dye.  Everywhere she turned she saw brightly lit storefronts and eager customers.

"Over here," Tom said.

Cam turned and followed him to a large screen displaying the directory.  Tom clicked on the home goods category then began to browse through them.  Bustling bodies pressed against them, pushing them out of the way.  She had never been in such a crowded environment before.

"There's only one mattress store," Tom said. "It's number 347 on the fifth floor.  It looks like it's just across the catwalk when we get off the elevator."

They made their way forward.  Cam coughed at the introduction of so many new smells.  Perfumes, industrial cleaners, and mediocre food flooded her senses.  Her head began to ache as they entered the elevator.  They ascended slowly as Cam drummed her nails on the rail with increasing speed.

When they reached the landing, they were pushed out onto a walkway by the crowd surrounding them.  Cam stumbled and, in that misstep, she lost Tom in the maddening swarm.  She stood, disoriented, as the crowd pressed upon her.  She felt her body begin to shake as an invisible knife stabbed her heart.  Panic rose as she realized her sense of direction was impossible to recover in the overwhelming, alien environment.

She stumbled forward with the crowd, searching for Tom.  Several times, she caught the sight of someone with the same hair color or a similar coat, but none of them were him.  Her panic grew as the smells, the bright sun, and the buzzing chatter clouded her mind.

The crowd edged her on until she saw a shiny, gold bench.  She shoved her way toward it as her body trembled in pain.  The bench was her only chance to get away, to save herself.  It loomed closer and closer as a pretty beacon of salvation.  Her breath caught sharply in her chest as she approached.  Her reflection in the polished railing appeared beaten and haggard.

*What's it going to be?*

JUMP OR FALL?

Cam reached the railing and grasped it with white knuckles. She looked down and saw the large fountain. Its ornate branches of reds and oranges burned brightly against its glass walls. The water below reflected the colors in swirling masses of blood and flesh. Her head began to spin as she turned to the bench.

It was now occupied by a woman and her three children. Cam's panic doubled instantly as she felt herself being siphoned back into the crowd. Her nerves ran over mental needles and fictional razorblades as she felt a warm hand grip her arm. She gasped as her body was spun.

"Geez, you're pathetic," Tom joked. "You can't even stick with me in a crowd?"

She ignored him, looking away as she caught her breath, before trekking across the catwalk. Tom followed closely behind as she determinedly wound a deft path through the slow-moving people. Her eyes darted over the stores, taking in the wares. She stared in at the soft rugs and rich furniture with amazement as she had only ever known threadbare blankets and cardboard box tables.

"There it is," Tom said.

They approached the mattress store then passed under its large neon sign. The store was overflowing with customers. California king mattresses with plush pillow tops called to her, though the air smelled of plastic and dirty shoes. Tom indicated for her to follow. He led her toward the back of the store as a man approached.

"Hello!" the man said with a grin. "Looking for a new mattress today?"

"No, I'm just looking for sheep," Tom said, emphasizing the word "sheep."

The salesman laughed nervously at Tom, avoiding direct eye contact.

"He's just being weird," Cam said nervously. "In fact, he's drunk. Yes, that makes the most sense, this man is saying these things because he is drunk."

The salesman grew even more disconcerted by her statement as he swiftly moved on to another customer. Cam rounded on Tom.

"Really? Sheep?"

"Yes," Tom said, his eyes fixated on a bearded man unlocking the back door. "Never mind, that's the person we need to talk to."

"How do you know?"

"I'll fill you in later," Tom said as they casually followed the man.

They approached the back door. Tom glanced behind them then pushed on the door handle. They both stepped into a dark storage room. The air smelled strongly of cigarettes and whiskey. Tom handed her his pocket knife as they moved.

"Just in case," he whispered.

"Of?"

"Why do you always need clarification?" he asked.

"Maybe because you're vague as shit," Cam retorted.

Then they heard an ominous click.

"Need more clarification than this, honey?" came a brusque voice. Cam turned and saw the bearded man. He was holding a Smith and Wesson 686 revolver mere inches from her face.

"No, I think I'm good," Cam said with a forced smile.

"Here," the man said as he threw a pair of handcuffs to Cam. "Put those on the boy there and move slow. The room's soundproof so I ain't afraid to scatter your gray matter to other side of this room."

Cam took the handcuffs and clasped them slowly around Tom's wrists. They clicked over several times as she tightened the bond. Then she took a couple of deliberate steps away from him before returning her gaze to the bearded man.

"Good, now come here so I can do the same to you," the man said. He pulled another pair of handcuffs from his pocket with his free hand. "Put your hands out in front of you."

She walked forward, hands held out as she had been instructed. Her heart was beating rapidly again, not out of panic but out of adrenaline. She knew she had to do something to untangle the situation, but she was unsure as to what. She only knew that it would be something impulsive and necessary.

"Good girl," the man said.

"I like to think so," Cam said with a grin as she grabbed the man's arm. His hand had been extended over her arms, giving her the perfect opportunity to strike. She pulled him down and cut her elbow into his face. He grimaced and fell backward with his newly inverted noise. Cam did not hesitate. She was upon him in seconds as she wrenched the revolver from him. One of his calloused hands came down and struck her hard. Blood fell from her as she retreated with the gun in her hand. She pointed it at him threateningly as she kicked him in the ribs. "Don't move. Like you said, this room is soundproof."

"True, but I doubt you'll pull that trigger," the man said.

"What makes you think that?" Cam asked as she tossed Tom the keys.

"Oh, please. You're *actually* a good girl," the man said. Cam felt the gun waver in her hands. "I can see that in your eyes."

"Doesn't mean I won't pull the trigger, aimed right between your eyes, if I have to."

Her eyes had darkened. She readjusted her grip on the pistol with the intent to kill. She did not like how cavalier he was when he was the one being threatened.

"Cam," Tom said. "Remember what we're here for."

Cam nodded, pushing aside her anger as she slowly lowered the gun. Tom turned to the man.

"So, listen up as you have no weapon and cannot defend yourself against us," Tom said, grabbing the man by the collar and pulling him to his feet. "I'm looking for sheep."

"Really? Now's a terrible time for humor," Cam scoffed.

But the man was staring up at Tom with quizzical interest.

"Whose flock you seekin?'" he asked.

"Isaac," Tom replied.

The man cocked his head and grinned.

"Then ya'll lucked out," he said. "They're in the office today."

"So, you'll take us then?" Tom asked.

"Sure thing," the man said as Tom released him. "Name's Gregory, by the way. Let me show to our humble storefront."

•

Cam followed Tom as he followed Gregory through the storage room down to a subbasement. Rows of heavy shelving and stacks of mattresses decorated both sides of their path.

"So, why did you ask for sheep?" Cam asked curiously.

"It's the only thing my Mom really told me about her contacts," Tom said. "It's their code phrase plus the ram's head tattoo on his forearm is their symbol."

"Us 'specialty' traders like to symbolize ourselves with a sheep or a ram," Gregory said. "Allegorical, you know?"

"Um, no," Cam said.

"Our network is the biggest, most complicated one in the whole world," Gregory continued. "Our group is known as 'Isaac.' Birmings, next town over, has 'Constantine,' and they're almost as big. But, even with so many members, we still have to do business underground or we'd get caught by the Gi. The code phrase helps us distinguish real customers from undercover agents."

"It also helps that you all seem to hang out in the back of mattress stores," Tom added.

"—and why is that?" Cam asked.

"Dunno, actually," Gregory said. "It's just always been that way. Guess it's because mattress stores have big warehouses. More room for the illegal doings, you know?"

"Yeah, I guess," Cam said.

"Speakin' of which, I forget to ask what you two want," Gregory said. "Got to get you to the right person, you know?"

"Just take us to the person who usually deals with Shun of the Equintas," Tom said.

Gregory stopped. He turned to Tom and looked him up and down.

"You're her kid then?" he asked. "You're Krytos' shining star? The hope of the rebellion?"

Gregory stared at Tom's lanky, malnourished frame with amusement.

"I guess so," Tom replied. "Now, who is the person we need to see?"

"If you're who you say you are, then you get to talk to Wenda."

"Wenda?"

"She's our unofficial leader of sorts. You know, everything's got be 'unofficial' in an organization like ours," Gregory said. "Mainly, she's the one who starts removing thumbs when things get out of line."

"Sounds like a classy lady," Cam muttered as Tom elbowed her.

"Here we are," Gregory said as they stopped before a large, red door. "Wenda, customers!"

There was a short pause before a raspy voice answered. "Bring 'em in."

Gregory nodded to them and opened the door. Tom and Cam stepped into a drab office, overfilled with storage furniture and unfiled paperwork. The walls, floors and ceilings were made of gray cement. Heavy shelving and a variety of sizable safes lined the walls. A shoddy oak desk sat in the center and, in that desk, sat Wenda. She was an older woman with wild, white hair and narrow eyes. A cigarette sat in her mouth as she counted stacks of GV.

Gregory pushed them into the cheap, plastic chairs that sat before the desk. Cam's chair scraped loudly against the floor as she moved it forward.

Wenda looked up and her sharp, hazel eyes widened. Cam stared back resolutely, thinking it was some form of initiation. Wenda eyed them both quizzically for several more moments before reclining in her chair. She took a long, rough drag from her cigarette.

"So, this is how this works," Wenda said, flicking her ashes onto the floor. "You tell me what you want then I'll tell you what I want in return. Then we'll discuss terms. If we don't agree, then I'll start slicing off pieces of your tongue until we do...or until you are unable to speak. Whichever comes first. Remember, I don't need the Equintas so much as they need *me* for supplies and trading route. I have no issue with killing you both."

Wenda smiled widely.

"We just need First Tier IDs and fifty thousand," Tom said. "It can be fake GV, we don't care so long as they pass."

Smoke furled out of Wenda's nostrils as she snuffed out her cigarette.

"That's doable," she said as she lit another. "Though, the IDs are a strange request from the Equintas. You know that'll be twenty crates each, right? Plus four more for the cash."

Tom gulped, showing a flash of hesitation, before recovering. "Ten each."

"Ten? Come on, kid. Are you high?" Wenda asked, lip raised incredulously.

"I think we can make do without the IDs for now then," Tom said to Cam. "We'll go to Constantine, since we aren't in a rush."

He stared at Cam pointedly and she knew to play along.

"We'll probably get better service there, too," Cam said.

They both stood and walked toward the door. They had only made it a few steps before they heard Wenda grumble loudly followed by the lighting of another cigarette.

"Fine," Wenda said, throwing a hand up. "Seventeen."

"Fifteen," Tom said.

Wenda stared hard at Tom, but it was already too obvious that she needed whatever was in the crates.

"Okay, fifteen," she said through gritted teeth. "Write down the names you want."

Wenda shoved a piece of paper at Tom along with a pen. Tom quickly wrote two names on the paper. She took it, rose from her chair and moved to the other door in the room. Her hand was on the knob when Tom spoke.

"Hey, while you're at it, could you also recommend a place for us to stay?"

●

Wenda begrudgingly returned an hour later with two, small cards and a stack of GV. She tossed them on the desk without making eye contact. Tom took them and looked them over.

"Up to par?" Wenda sneered.

Tom let a smile escape him as he turned up to Wenda, flipping the cards between his fingers.

"They'll do," he said.

"Good," Wenda replied. "Now, Gregory here will show you out. Remember, I expect 34 crates to be at the outpost by the end of the month."

Tom nodded then stood with Cam behind him. She could feel Wenda's eyes piercing the backs of their skulls as Gregory held the red door open for them and they exited.

●

Gregory led them back to the mattress store. The fluorescent light burned Cam's eyes as she heard the door shut followed by the clicking of multiple locks.

"So, where to now?" Cam asked as Tom handed her one of the IDs. "Hotel?"

"I think that's our only option," Tom said.

They quickly maneuvered out of the store and into the massive golden mall. They located another directory then navigated to the first floor tourist kiosk. The machine was tall with a large display. Pictures of smiling tourists were plastered across the screen and down the sides of the machine itself. They dispensed a guidebook and another city map. Tom flipped it open to the index then to the section on lodging.

"Looks like this is the cheapest one," Tom said. "The Grandier Hotel."

"That name makes it sound like the most expensive one," Cam said with a raised eyebrow.

"Well, let's go and see what it's like," Tom said. "We probably won't need to stay for long after we get a plan together. Plus, we can always go back to Wenda for more GV."

Cam agreed. They walked at a brisk pace through the city. They followed the directions on their map, navigating through congested intersections and sidewalks, until they arrived at the world famous Paradise District.

The Paradise District contained the world's largest concentration of business and culture pertaining purely to entertainment. Rows upon rows of casinos, theaters and theme parks lined the streets. The collective clamor from the intoxicated citizens perusing the establishments was a blanketed roar of gluttony.

Cam stared up at the varying skyscrapers twinkling down in gold and glass. The buildings were decorated elaborately in their own themes. One was in the shape of an enormous hot-air balloon while another had a waterfall rushing down its hexagonal face. Each of the magnificent structures was overwhelming but the most impressive, by far, was the Metraline.

The Metraline was the Lord General's tower. The city of Tengoku was built abutting the face of the Western Tutamen Mountains, surrounding the Metraline which was itself built partially into the rocky mountainside. It was the only building in the city that was not golden. It was a muted slate during the day and lit silver at night. A wall, over five stories tall, surrounded the grand structure. Guards marched continuously along the top and by the single entrance while snipers held watch from the many surrounding guard towers. It was within the walls of this safeguarded fortification that Aeraden resided.

The crowds thickened the further in they went. The early evening had arrived and, with it, the dinner rush. They kept checking their path on the map until they were finally upon their destination.

It was small in comparison to the surrounding glass behemoths. The entrance doors were made of multi-paned glass with a complex gold pattern interlaced between the layers. The words, Grandier Hotel, were written over the entrance in lighted, silver script. The double doors were opened for them by two uniformed men who eyed their disheveled appearances with suspicion.

Their shoes squeaked against the white marble floors as they entered the brightly lit lobby. A plush, circular sofa sat in the center wrapped around an oversized arrangement of brightly colored flowers in a polished vase.

"*This* is the cheapest hotel in town?" Cam asked under her breath as they passed a room that appeared to be both a bar and a spa. "That's marginally hedonistic."

"Just a bit," Tom said. "I don't think a single one of them would last a day in the Slums."

Cam laughed hollowly as they made their way to the front desk. A tall brunette with a sharply pointed nose looked up at them. The shiny nametag clipped to her breast declared her name to be Yvonne.

"Good afternoon. Welcome to the Grandier," Yvonne said with a wide smile that pulled her face taut. "How may I help you?"

"Do you have any rooms available?" Tom asked.

Yvonne looked down at the glass screen on the counter, the smile never leaving her face. The reflection of her whitened teeth against the luminous lights was blinding Cam.

"Well, look at that, you're in luck. We do have one room open," she said, looking up. "You know how it is in summer. We're usually booked completely full."

"Right, lucky us," Tom said. "So, what's the rate for this room we are so fortuitous to have acquired?"

Yvonne's smile twitched.

"Eight thousand, sir," she said. "Our regular rooms are all booked. This is for our lowest-end suite."

"Of course it is," he replied, counting their counterfeit GV. "For two nights."

He shoved the money on the counter and Yvonne took it, her face frozen in the smile again.

"Wonderful, sir," she said. "May I get your name?"

Cam looked up in slight panic. She had not thought to examine her ID to see what name Tom had picked for her.

"Thomas Graystone," he replied.

"Thank you," Yvonne said, as she typed into the glass screen. "May I also see IDs for both of you?"

Tom was already sliding the card across the counter as Cam fumbled in her pocket to locate hers. She found it and accidently threw it at Yvonne in her haste and apprehension to produce it. It struck Yvonne square between the eyes, leaving a small red mark as she yelped.

"I am so sorry," Cam said after a moment as Tom turned away to laugh.

"It's quite alright, ma'am," Yvonne said through gritted teeth as she retrieved the fallen card and resumed inputting their information.

"Way to not draw attention to us, by the way," Tom whispered, a small grin still on his face.

Several patrons had turned to search for the source of the noise. Their judgmental eyes bored holes into their already holey clothing. Cam shrugged lamely as they turned back to Yvonne, who pulled out a small card reader and swiped their cards through. Cam watched apprehensively, but a green light flashed on the machine, and Yvonne continued her work.

"Looks like we're all set. Here are your cards back, along with your room keys," she said.

"Thanks," Tom said as Cam picked up her ID.

A citizen number was typed across the top. Her fingerprint was on the left and her personal information was on the right. Apparently, she lived in the city of Birmings that lay fifty miles to the west and her name was Camilla Leona Stofnam. She frowned as a man in the same blue uniform as the doormen approached.

"This is Baertel," Yvonne said. "He's our grounds guide and he will show you to your room. Have a very pleasant stay."

Baertel was a wiry-haired man with kind eyes and jovial smile that emanated an empathy that the other citizens seemed to lack. He shook both of their hands with enthusiasm.

"Let's get your bags and we'll head to the elevator," he looked around, realizing that they only had one very small bag. "Or, we'll just head to the elevator."

Baertel turned on the heels of his glossy loafers as Tom turned to Cam.

"...and our conspicuousness continues," Tom whispered.

They followed Baertel behind the front desk to a hall with multiple elevator doors. One of them was already open, preparing to go up, and Baertel ushered them in. Two figures were cuddled in the corner while the scent of sweet, heavy cigar smoke curled up toward the ceiling. A dark-haired man in his mid-forties, wearing a Gi Force armed services uniform, had his arm wrapped around a tall, svelte woman, clad in a pink evening gown. They were laughing loudly and falling against each other.

"So, I've been invited to the Lord General's annual gala," the dark-haired man boasted loudly to the woman. "Perks of being a commissioned officer."

He winked at her and she kissed him sloppily.

"I can't wait, baby," she giggled.

They fell further into the corner together, oblivious to the strangers sharing their elevator car. Cam stared at the ads flashing on the walls then at her shoes then back at the ads, trying to ignore them. The ding for their floor soon rang and Baertel held the doors open for them.

"This is our floor," he said. "It's just up here, to the left."

They exited into a wide, high-ceilinged hallway decorated with glass sconces.

"So, what brings you to our fair city?" Baertel asked.

"Vacation," Tom replied flatly.

"That's nice," Baertel said. "Where you guys from?"

"Birmings," Cam said then added under her breath, "...apparently."

"Always liked that town," Baertel remarked brightly. "Nice places to live there. My cousin's got a flat in the Dupree Building. Imagine that! Can't wait 'till it's my turn to try for First Tier. I could move into the Southerland Villas over by Karmen's."

"First Tier, what—" Cam began, but Tom shook his head for her to be silent, "—what could be better?"

Tom nodded, approving of her self-correction.

"Not much, ma'am. Not much," Baertel said, avoiding her eyes. They stopped before a large set of white double doors. "Anyways, this is your room."

Tom slid in his key and the locks clicked open as Baertel opened the doors. Cam felt her jaw fall slack.

It was a gorgeous room. A large sectional made of luxurious, ivory leather sat in the center, facing a television screen that encompassed the entire northern wall. Beautiful abstracts hung at regular intervals, and a plush area rug sat atop the hardwood floors. A full kitchen and bar ran along the western wall before opening into the hallway that led to the bathroom and bedrooms. The eastern wall was composed of floor-to-ceiling window panels and a glass door that led out to the patio and the breathtaking view of Tengoku's Paradise District, brilliant with the light of the nightly attractions.

"Everythin' look good here?" Baertel asked, noting the silence.

"Looks fine to me," Tom said, handing Baertel a tip. "Right, Cam?"

"Uh," she said. Her brain was overwhelmed by the new environment. "Yes, it's all very large."

Tom, now standing behind Baertel, threw his arms up in annoyance.

"That's good, I guess," Baertel said, turning to shake Tom's hand again. "Well, I can be reached at the blue button on your phone. The hotel directory is in this binder. It was nice to meet you guys. Ya'll enjoy your stay."

He tipped his hat, leaving their room with a smile. The door closed and Cam let out a low whistle.

"This is insanity!" she exclaimed. "I mean, is this really what it's like to be a citizen? This sofa cushion is almost as big as my bedroom back in the Slums."

She sat on it and sank into the pillowed top.

"Remember, this is the 'cheap' hotel," Tom said, shaking his head. "Imagine what it's like in the big hotels. This suite could probably fit in the bedroom of one of those."

"That seems highly posh and unnecessary," Cam noted. She felt the handle on the side and tentatively pulled on it. Her body flew backward as the end seat she sat upon reclined abruptly. She looked up at Tom who was now upside down to her. "What in the fiery hell just happened to me?"

"That's a recliner," Tom laughed. "It's so you can appear to be sitting when, in fact, you are actually lying down."

"So, it's a bed?" she asked slowly.

"I guess you could use it that way," he said. "I think it's really just for sitting though."

"That doesn't make sense," she said. "This place is weird."

She tried the handle again, hoping to gently return to her previous position. The back slammed upward and she flew out of her seat, landing on the soft rug.

"Okay, I don't like the furniture here," she said as Tom helped her up. He was laughing uncontrollably.

"Why don't you just sit on the barstool?" he suggested as she took her new seat. "I'll make us some food and then we can try to figure out what to do from here."

Cam agreed as Tom rummaged in the fridge. A few minutes later they had turkey sandwiches and orange juice. She had always dreamed about the amazing food the citizens must enjoy. She had seen the massive billboards at the edge of the city, displaying happy citizens as they devoured bottle-grown steaks. It never occurred to her that the food may actually be bland.

"Disappointing, isn't it?" Tom asked, holding up his sandwich.

"To say the least," Cam muttered, mid-bite. Then she looked around and smiled. "On the other hand, I think we should revel in the fact that we're in a Tengoku hotel and that we haven't been arrested, tortured, or maimed by anyone in the Gi Force. Our plan is playing out mostly in the way that we wanted sans sewer monster, of course."

"It is astonishing that we've made it this far," he replied. "Although, now comes the hard part."

"Harder than the nearly fatal encounter back there with the poo monster?"

"Well, now we have to break into the Ether and then into the vault that has Aeraden. There will be a large quantity of very well-armed soldiers as well as other deadly security measures," Tom said. "Oh, and did I mention that I don't actually know the vault's specific location? I just know that it's in the Ether and the Ether is under the Metraline."

"Okay, so we just need more information," Cam said.

"*Classified* information," Tom corrected. "The word 'classified' connotes something much more difficult to attain. We need access to high security data and I don't know how we would do that, short of kidnapping a high-ranking officer."

Cam turned to him with wide eyes.

"Tom, I have an idea."

"It involves the insanity that was my sarcastic comment, doesn't it?" he asked hesitantly.

"Maybe," Cam conceded. "But I think we could actually make that work. Do you remember that couple we just saw in the elevator?"

"The Smelly-Get-A-Goddamn-Room-Repugnantons? I recall them vividly," Tom said.

"You said we need a high-ranking officer, so—"

"Rotten-Tooth-Cigar-Breath was not a high-ranking officer. He was a first lieutenant," Tom interjected. "He wouldn't have access to what we need."

"This is where letting me finish my sentence would be helpful," Cam said. "Do you remember what he was bragging about? He said he was going to be at a place where *all* the officers will be? The—"

"—Lord General's gala," Tom finished.

"Correct," Cam said. "If we could party crash, it would be like a concentrated pool of applicable targets. It would be a start, at least."

"That's a really good idea," Tom said disbelievingly. "I wasn't aware you were capable of having those."

"You're just jealous that you didn't think of it first," she replied as she put their used dishes in the sink. "Now, what's the plan?"

"I say we follow the guy, incapacitate him and his date then take their place," Tom said. "He's the lowest rank of commissioned officer, so there are hundreds of others just like him who will be there. If we're careful, no one will notice we switched places."

"Stands to reason," she said. "Plus, you two do look a little alike."

"Thanks," Tom said sardonically. "That's a fantastic ego boost."

"Hey, I was just stating something factual," she said then she yawned loudly, remembering that neither of them had slept much in the last few days.

"I think we both need sleep," Tom said. "We have a long road ahead of us and we'll need the energy."

"I concur," she replied. "I've never had the chance to go to sleep before the sun fully sets. It sounds nice. Good night."

"Night."

She walked down the short hallway and chose a room. The ornate bed before her was easily the most lavish piece of furniture she had ever seen. Thickly woven sheets lay tucked under a down comforter. The notion that it was hers to sleep in was almost unbelievable.

The white, glass wall opposite the bed was another screen similar to the one in the living area. Two wooden nightstands, painted gold, sat on either side of the bed. The surfaces of both of them were miniature versions of the television screen and were emblazoned with the hotel's logo. She fished through the closet and found an oversized nightshirt that also displayed the logo. She undressed, threw it on, and settled herself into bed.

The mattress was soft and her body was tired. She sank into the comforts of the bed and closed her eyes. She tried to relax, but she was sitting on the edge of a brewing wave of panic. Adrenaline was still pumping through her veins and her body was frayed from the stress. Her restive sleep of late had brought her little respite and the anxiety of such had proven to complicate the simple matter of just falling asleep. She rarely dreamt anymore and, when she did, they were exceptionally vivid. She pulled the bedspread up to her chin, snuggling within the foreign comforts of an alien city of glutton, and drifted into an uneasy sleep.

# CHAPTER 8
## UNDER THE GUISE OF VANITY

*The room was empty. Golden floors opened to golden walls. The ceiling was lost in the shadows of its own height. A healthy breeze was tunneling around the space. She turned to Tom, his back was to her as he stood before a stone door.*

*She called out his name. He ignored her as he reached for the handles. The ornate door was dark and heavy, no kin to the regal room. It slid open just enough for Tom to sidle through. He disappeared into the darkness and was gone.*

*Her feet fell with increased speed. She reached the door just after it had fully shut. Her hand encased the handle, pushing tentatively, only to find it locked. She turned to face the room in the hope of seeing it filled with something, anything at all. But it was empty. A sudden pain jolted in her leg, and she looked down.*

*A white crab was beside her, watching her intently. It clicked its claws and gestured toward the door. She shook her head, trying the handle again to demonstrate her continued denial of entry. The crab sagged a little, seemingly frustrated. It pointed to itself, then toward her, then toward the door. She was dubious as she leaned forward and scooped up the creature. It jumped delightedly in her hands then scrambled onto her shoulder. She raised a skeptical eyebrow but obeyed as she knew she was meant to open this particular door above all else. She stepped forward, grasped the handle, and swung it unhesitatingly downward.*

*An audible click resounded in her ears as the door slid open. She turned to the crab and smiled before entering.*

Brilliant light met her as the door closed with a clangorous thud. Gold permeated her field of vision as she blinked several times in an attempt to prevent the gilded light from hindering her further. She took a clumsy step, colliding with something anomalous. Her eyes adjusted, focusing on the still and porcellaneous face of an ostentatious woman.

She knew of such women, having already seen their decadence on display in the city streets. She looked about the room and saw hundreds of other avaricious citizens adorned in their own gaudy vestments, their cavalier postures tragedies to their inconsequentiality. They did not turn to stare at the sudden intruder. They were stiller than statues.

The crab nipped at her. She looked up and saw the same heavy stone door from the previous room with Tom, again, standing before it.

She rushed forward, maneuvering between the frozen figures of jubilant citizens. Some held wine goblets while others were petrified mid-laugh, unaware of what was occurring. Tom had his hand on the handle and was already vanishing through the door when she careened to a halt at its threshold. She pulled the handle and flew into the next room.

She stopped. Again, she was blinded and, again, she found herself in the same golden room. However, this time, the room's occupants were no longer in the suspended thralls of delectation. The little crab was clutching her tightly as she drew herself up and took a cautious step.

One hundred sets of eyes were upon her. She ignored their solemn stares, searching for the door she was always meant to find. She located it just as it was being hurriedly closed. His name tumbled from her lips as a gust of wind was suddenly extinguished ahead of her, and she was impelled to move. The room was silent, save for the slapping of the soles of her boots as the unwavering eyes of the citizens bored into her. She took a few more steps, hurrying to save herself from the fear that was rising icily within. She shuddered as the disquieting spectators spun to track her slow progression, but she pressed on, knowing it was still imperative that she follow him.

They revolved soundlessly in her direction as though on a mechanical dais like a ballerina in a music box. Their shallow breaths were silent, only made noticeable by the slight warmth they produced. She tripped, falling amid a rainbow of ballroom gowns and jewels. Her shoulder struck the hard ground as the crab was catapulted from her sight, and she was, again, alone. She wondered if she should have run instead of carelessly continuing on. She pushed herself up as dozens of shadows began to encircle.

The doll-like men and women moved to surround her. She was trapped and did not have the means to protect herself. Their faces remained stolid and their eyes unblinking as they leaned downward. Painted lips and darkened eyes encroached further upon her. The last store of bravery she had saved depleted itself as she could now see why they had frightened her so. Their pupils were inhumanly dark like chasms to something unknown and treacherous. Tom would not wait for her to find him. Panic began to take its wretched hold when she heard a fainting tapping.

She fell back, searching for the sound. She pursued the rhythm until she saw the crab waving madly at her. Now, against her fleshy prison of well-dressed citizens, she understood that they would not actively prevent her escape. They were fearsome only because they were what she had once feared.

She sat up, ignoring all their penetrating stares as she broke free of the shadowy wreath and knocked the living mannequins away. They did not break their falls. Their bodies collapsed like toppled chess pieces, like the pawns that they were. She scooped up the crab and ran for the door. It opened dutifully at her touch as she and the crab proceeded on.

A dense darkness met her, eradicating what light remained in her eyes. She bumbled blindly through until she felt her shoe sink then stick to something that had pooled upon the flat marble. Then the blinding light returned with ferocity. Her head was swimming as the floor tiles churned. She focused on the pattern, trying to steady herself, when she realized that there had previously been no pattern to the tiles. The new swirls were simply a part of the elegant splatter of fresh blood.

The room was littered with bodies, stained crimson. The same door stood at the opposite end, but this time Tom was facing her with a cold smile. He waved his hand, beckoning her forward. She turned to the little crab. It nodded purposefully then pointed at the door. She sighed then forcefully lifted her stuck foot, ignoring the eviscerated body that lay beside her, and waded further into the gory mess.

Blood sloshed high over her ankle, soaking her socks. Empty faces screamed silently upward, their eyes as hollow as they had been in the previous room. She kicked aside the entrails and severed limbs that blocked her path. At times, she was forced to physically climb over the piles of human remains. There would be no autopsy for any of these bodies as their cause of death was as apparent as their innards.

*Tom watched, waiting patiently, as she trudged through the blood. She emerged by his side, her clothes and hair clinging uncomfortably. Then he opened the door, and they crossed the threshold into the black of the next room.*

•

Cam shot upright as the sun broke through the sheers into the hotel room. The clinking of dishes in the other room told her that Tom had already awoken. She stared out at the sunlit city, regaining her bearings from the unrest of her nightmare. Then she dressed and joined Tom for another tasteless meal. As it was still early, even by the average soldier's schedule, they decided to plant themselves in the lobby and wait for the man to exit.

The only activity came from the bistro where a few hotel patrons stood, sipping foamy drinks. They settled themselves in two cushioned armchairs that offered an unobstructed view of the lobby.

"We should order something," Tom said, standing. "They'll probably kick us out if we don't. Want anything in particular?"

"I don't even know what coffee tastes like, so surprise me?" Cam suggested with a shrug.

Tom nodded and left to join the line. Cam turned to the table set between their chairs and began to examine the literature. Most were magazines or pamphlets for establishments in the Paradise District. She picked through fashion magazines and television guides until she came across a thin book. It was black with a golden sun cross in the center, the symbol of the Gi Force.

She picked it up, curious as she had seen the very same book in each room of their hotel suite and in various kiosks at the mall. The binding cracked with the innocence of new information and the pages smelled potently of ink. She turned to the first page.

*The Edicts of Gi Citizenship*

*Section I: Societal Tiers and Placement*

*For the safety of all citizens, the first edict decreed by the Lord General is the predetermined division of the assets of all citizens with the creation of societal tiers and mandated placement. Three societal tiers exist with placement assigned as follows.*

*Placement into the* Second Tier *is governed by parentage or by ruling of the Magistrate. All* Seconds *will be granted employment within any Gi city limits and are required to work five shifts per week. Compensation will be made via the Bank of the Gi in the form of electronic Gi Avari [GV] credits (see Section II-A for more information on currency) and living quarters in the appropriate district will be assigned by the Housing Department (see Section VI-A for more information on housing).*

*Placement into the* First Tier *is governed by parentage or by completion of the Tier Transitional Placement Probation Program (see Section IV-C for more details on the TTPP program or on the Sanctions Department). Compensation, in accordance with the System of Livelihood, is dispensed regardless of employment. Living quarters in the appropriate district will be assigned by the Housing Department.*

*Placement into the* Golden Circle *is governed by the Lord General and his immediate council.*

*Establishments within city limits that are designated by Tier and promoted as such may only be patronized by declared Tier(s). Inter-Tier socialization must remain limited to professional or necessary interactions as deemed acceptable by the Sanctions Department. Breach of interaction laws is punishable by law and will result in disciplinary action (please see Section IV-A for more information on the Sanctions Department and the interaction laws).*

"Having fun?" Tom asked.

Cam looked up and saw a cup of coffee being held out to her.

"I'm having, um, confusion," she said, taking the cup as she turned back to the book. "This is what that Baertel guy was talking about before, isn't it? About wanting to be First Tier, but being stuck in Second?"

"Yup," Tom said, sitting down.

"Social tiers, mandated by law?" she asked perplexed.

"They're slaves here too, Cam," he replied. "They just get to live in fancier houses and booze away the fact that there really is no such thing as freedom, at least not under Gi rule."

Cam frowned. She took a sip of her coffee, sputtered then spit it out. The barista looked over, offended.

"What the hell is this?" Cam asked Tom quietly.

"Um, coffee," he said.

"It tastes horrible," she said, sniffing it tentatively.

"It does taste better when the beans are actually grown instead of manufactured," he said. "Still, damn, stay somewhat cool."

Cam set her cup down as the officer they were looking for walked out of the elevator. She tapped Tom on the shoulder and he followed her gaze. They waited for him to reach the exit before standing and following him.

They shadowed him as he walked several blocks to one of the Gi's training facilities for the military. Security was heavy and they knew they could not follow any further. Instead, they visited several shops in the area that had a view of the building as they waited nearly nine hours for him to reappear. Afterward, he returned to the hotel and went up to his room which they learned was number 1123.

They continued to track his every movement for the next two days, during which time he did not deviate from his routine with the exception of the visits from his girlfriend. In that time, they had gleaned very little about the man himself aside from the fact that he was a new transfer from another division and that his stay at the Grandier Hotel was temporary as he waited for permanent First Tier housing in the Serrano District. He also drank immoderately and often smelled strongly of alcohol. They knew they could manipulate his constant inebriation to their advantage the following night, the evening of the Lord General's gala.

●

They opted not to follow the man that day, instead electing to flush out their plans then wait for him to return from work in the hotel's bistro. Promptly at six fifteen, he came through the double doors with a freshly lit cigar between his teeth.

Cam and Tom stood as the man took long strides to the bank of elevators. They joined the group of people waiting and were sure to enter the same car he did. The elevator moved swiftly upward and Cam felt her heart begin to race as the crowd thinned at each stop. When they reached the eleventh floor, they exited first and mingled by the directory while the man proceeded in the opposite direction to his room. He was stumbling slightly, already a bit drunk.

They waited another minute then continued on their way to room 1123. When they arrived, Tom pressed his ear quietly to the door.

"Is he making his own bourbon in there or something?" Cam asked as the sharp scent of alcohol struck their faces.

"Television's on," Tom whispered back. "So, he's drunk and distracted. That's good."

They both listened through the door, facing each other so they could monitor activity at both ends of the hallway. The man's voice soon pushed higher than the volume of the television, begging to be overheard.

"Sure, I know that, honey, but I've been having this strange feeling lately," the man said as he took a long drink. "I'm not happy...

"I know. I know this sounds weird, but I don't feel like I'm doing what's right. Life doesn't seem right...

"Yes, I know this is my only choice."

There was a long pause followed by another deep swig.

"No, baby, it isn't you," the man continued. "I love you so much and that's the point I'm trying to make. I want us to be happy together but I need, I don't know, a purpose...

"No, I guess I don't know what I meant by that...

"No, I would never do anything that stupid...

"I'm sorry. Please, don't be upset."

He took another long drink then set the bottle down and clicked his lighter on.

"Sure, I understand," he said. "You have a good time with your friends...

"No, don't worry about me. I don't really like crowds and I wasn't looking forward to this gala anyway...

"Yes, I am grateful for what I have. I'll talk to you later."

They heard the click of the phone as he hung up. The mattress deflated and the volume on the television rose.

"Ready, Cam?"

She turned to the door. The eavesdropped phone call they had just overheard had shone them the first bits of personal information about the man. She felt sick with new guilt as she nodded for Tom to proceed.

He pulled a pilfered keycard from his pocket and unlocked the door. The soft beep of the lock was drowned by the evening news. They pushed the door open just enough to slide sideways into the room. A closet door stood partially ajar and they slipped inside, hiding in the shadows of his jackets.

"What now?" Cam whispered.

"We wait," he whispered back.

The television continued to roar as they watched him through the slats. They stayed huddled on the floor of the closet for another ten minutes as he drank himself into a grand stupor.

He stood and walked to the sliding door that led to the patio. An overused ashtray sat on the little glass table. He reached for his cigar, relit it then leaned against the railing.

"I'm going for it," Tom whispered.

"What? What are you going for? I thought we could just wait until he passed out."

"The gala started thirty minutes ago. We can't wait any longer," he reasoned as he signaled for her to remain hidden.

He pushed the closet door open then crept up behind the man. His footfalls were perfectly silent as he edged closer. A large, decorative vase sat in a niche in the wall. She watched as he raised his hand in its direction.

A small wind, concentrated solely around the vase, formed quickly. The vase rose off of its perch, hovering a few inches in the air. Tom manipulated it further forward until it was just above the man's head. Then he clenched his fist and the air surrounding the vase dissipated instantly. It fell with a dull thud upon the man's skull and he slumped to the floor, unconscious.

"Quick, Cam," Tom said. "Help me get him to the bed."

Cam stared at the blood that was encircling the man's head, unable to move.

"Cam!" Tom said with more urgency.

She ran forward and grabbed the man's legs. Together, they heaved him onto the rich bedding. She watched as his blood continued to seep from him, staining the pillowcase. The saliva evaporated from her mouth as nausea rose upward.

"Cam, we have stuff to do," Tom said, his tone more gentle. "Come on."

They tore through the room, searching for the items they needed. Tom opened the closet they had hid in and found formal clothing for them both. Cam searched through the nightstands and the dresser, looking for the invitation. Then she opened the television cabinet and saw a regal envelope propped inside.

*To: First Lieutenant Eric Von Clousen and Guest*

She picked it up as her eyes wandered back to the bed, to the man whose name she now knew. The nausea returned and she tried to concentrate on Ke. It would all be worth it, in the end.

"Good, you found it," Tom said, coming up behind her. "We need to go."

She nodded and followed him out of the room, watching as Eric Von Clousen's blood dried on his fingertips.

●

They dressed quickly in their stolen clothing and managed to catch a cab heading toward the hall where the gala was being held. They rode in silence, Cam playing twitchily with her necklace as the heavy tulle of her dress constricted her breathing. The lights of the brilliant buildings flew by them in a multi-colored blur as they turned into the Financial District. Their cab came to a sharp halt before the bustling convention center.

The broad building was white with a wide patio that tumbled into an elaborate garden. The white brick fence was covered in vines and was lined by perfectly square boxwoods. Dozens of guests were milling around the entrance, dressed in the finest attire the city's tailors had to offer. A heavyset man in a white tuxedo stood by the door, greeting guests and validating their presence on the list he held in his hands. Tom handed him their invitation, and they were ushered in with no difficulties.

Once inside, Cam stared up in wonder at the magnificent domed ceiling of the foyer and the detailed mural of gold and silver fireworks painted against it. They maneuvered through the grand archway that led to the ballroom, eyeing the uniforms as they tried to select the best target.

The ballroom rose to a staggering one hundred feet, and its grandeur gave Cam vertigo. White pillars stood around the room, and the walls were covered in a finely embossed wallpaper. The warm, wooden floors were shined and reflected the abundant light. Long tables draped in fine tablecloths lined the space, each topped with different platters of food. Cam stared curiously as she watched people dipping sweets into a large, chocolate fountain. They stopped before one of the champagne tables as a large woman with auburn curls approached them excitedly.

"You look so familiar," she said, tapping Tom on the shoulder. "Are you the gentleman my husband and I met last week? At the Overton's party? Eric, wasn't it?"

"No, I'm sorry, I think you have me mistaken with someone else," Tom said as he began to pull Cam away, but the woman followed.

"Really? He carried a very similar little trinket with him," she indicated a small, silver locket that hung from one of the buttons on his wrist. "Plus, you two look awfully alike."

Tom gave Cam the shortest of bewildered expressions before addressing the woman. "Sorry, still not him."

"Oh, well, my mistake then," the woman laughed, extending her hand. "I'm Meredith Draper, by the way."

"Thomas Graystone," Tom replied, reciprocating the handshake. "This is Camilla."

Cam smiled and shook the woman's hand as well.

"Lovely to meet you both," Meredith said. "So, are you new to the military, Thomas? My Harold's been in for several years, but he was posted out of the GFAF headquarters in Curro City for most of it. He just got transferred back here and I can't tell you how happy I am to be in the capitol again. Oh, look, there he is talking to the General! He's the one wearing glasses."

They turned in the direction Meredith was pointing. Several guests were mingling on the large balconies that overlooked the dance floor. Three men were standing against the railing, deep in conversation. The lowest ranked man wore glasses and was unmistakably Meredith's husband. He stood beside a middle-aged man with prominent cheekbones and cold eyes who bore the insignia of a Brigadier General. Beside him stood a man who Cam knew by name and reputation. His name was Bacchus Murphy and he was the General of the Gi Force Armed Forces, second in command only to the Lord General himself.

"My Harold looks so nice in his full uniform," Meredith mused. "Wouldn't you agree?"

"Uh huh," murmured Cam, though she had not heard a word of Meredith's last statement. She and Tom were staring in open shock as two young women entered the balcony.

The tallest was very striking with long curls of strawberry blond hair. She wore a risqué, red dress and her face was painted with heavy makeup, but she was not nearly as interesting to them as the other woman. The other woman was tiny, short and thin. She wore a simple black dress and appeared to be bored. Cam remembered the bright green eyes vividly from when they rescued her in the alley mere days before.

"Meredith, who's the shorter girl there?" Tom asked as Cam leaned in with interest.

"Oh, that's Rhea Murphy," Meredith said. "Her sister, Aurelia, is the girl in the red dress. They're General Bacchus Murphy's granddaughters. Their father is the Brigadier General there."

"Interesting," Tom muttered.

"I know, isn't it?" Meredith asked. "You almost never see her at these things."

"Really?" Cam asked. "Why's that?"

"Well, I don't want to gossip or anything," Meredith said, smiling as she leaned in. "But I heard she's a bit of a troublemaker. Apparently, she likes to start fist fights with grown men twice her size. She has some complex about something. I heard she broke a man's arm in seven places once. Could you imagine that tiny thing doing that?"

"No, not really," Cam said as she turned toward Rhea again, wondering if she even topped one hundred pounds. "She's really small."

"Exactly," Meredith said, polishing off her glass of champagne. "I said the same thing, but the rumors came from such a variety of very reliable sources that I think I would be a fool to discount them! Oh, look there, my sister and her husband just arrived. Would you both excuse me?"

They nodded as Meredith picked up a new glass of champagne and hurried toward the entrance where another redheaded woman stood waving. Cam turned to Tom.

"I think that was the information we were looking for," Cam said.

"Agreed," Tom said. He glimpsed up at Rhea. "Target acquired."

•

Cam and Tom made a prompt exit shortly after their encounter with Meredith, returning to the hotel just before midnight. The nightly entertainment scene was reaching its peak and the lobby was overflowing with citizens. Baertel tipped his hat as they passed by his station on their way to the elevator. They continued up to their floor, discussing the new angle of the mission in low whispers.

"Well, we can't just waltz into the Serrano District," Tom said. "That's where the Golden Tier citizens live, and they guard that place almost as well as they do the Metraline."

"We could head back to the shopping center where we first met her," Cam said. "Maybe she'll show up there."

"I guess, seems like a long shot though," Tom said as he pulled out their hotel key.

"It's kind of our only shot right now," she said. "Unless you've got something better."

"I'm working on it," Tom said pointedly. He opened the hotel door and they both stopped.

The lights were on and the television was blaring. An empty beer bottle sat on the counter and a heavy, leather jacket was strewn atop one of the barstools. They heard the toilet flush, and Tom pulled out his switchblade. He signaled for Cam to stay back as they saw the light from the bathroom spill into the hallway and the shadow of a man emerge.

The breeze blowing in from the open window grew to a sudden roar and the man turned just as the gust struck. He flew backward, striking the wall with enough force to knock the paintings from their hangings. Tom was upon him in a second, wrenching the man's head upward as he held the blade to his neck.

"Who are you and what the hell are you doing here?" Tom demanded.

"Whoa! Calm your shit, man!" the stranger said. "It's me!"

Tom pulled the man to his feet and spun him around. Cam crept closer, also curious to see the face of the intruder. He was marginally shorter than Tom. His skin was deeply tanned, causing the starkness of his short, white hair to be even more pronounced.

"Gun?" Tom asked. "Holy crap! Cam, it's Gun!"

"Cam?" Gun asked, peering around Tom to look at her. "Who the hell is she?"

"Excuse me? Who the hell am *I*?" Cam asked angrily. "I think you should be telling me who the hell *you* are first!"

She rolled up her sleeves, fists clenched.

"Whoa, let's all take this down, well, a lot of notches," Tom said, his voice purposefully low and calm. "None of us wants the neighbors calling the guards. So, I'll make introductions. Gun, this is Camilla. She was a Raquineste slave before she decided to join our side."

Gun looked Cam over as she stared menacingly back.

"Cam, this is Gunnar Harko," Tom said. "He's one of the Equintas."

"Like one of your rebel guys?" Cam asked.

"I happen to be *the* Bladesman of the Equintas but whatever," Gun muttered. "And, dude, you can put me down any day now."

Tom released him with an apologetic shrug.

"What are you doing here?" Tom asked him.

"What do you think? I'm looking for you, obviously," Gun said incredulously as he meandered to the refrigerator and opened a new beer. "You only abandoned your post, abandoned your Mom, broke into the capitol city, promised Wenda a gazillion crates that we don't have, and apparently stole a slave."

"Neither one of us believes in slavery so, technically, I didn't 'steal' her," Tom corrected.

Gun rolled his eyes.

"It's time to go home, bro," Gun said. "Things have changed up there and we need you on point."

"Wait," Cam interrupted. "He's not going anywhere. I need him here 'on point' helping me get Aeraden."

Gun raised an eyebrow at Tom.

"What the hell, Tom? Why didn't you just promise her the moon while you were at it?" Gun asked as he turned to Cam. "You're savior here is an idiotic asshole. You two have about as much of a chance of stealing Aeraden as I do growing a pair of wings out of my butt. Sorry to be harsh, but it's true."

Cam opened her mouth to retort, but she couldn't formulate a good one.

"The visualization of you growing wings out of your butt has sort of spearheaded this conversation," Cam said, shaking her head.

"I'm not going with you," Tom said to Gun.

"Dude, don't be stupid. You're coming home," Gun said. "If you don't, I'll knock your ass out and leave this Cam chick here to fend for herself."

"You'd leave the innocent, recently-freed slave in Tengoku alone among the most highly concentrated population of Gi?" Tom asked, eyebrow raised. "Your threat lacks substance."

Gun's eyes narrowed.

"Fine, it does," Gun conceded. "Just please go home so that I can go home. I miss real food and my own bed."

"Sorry, Gun, but it's not happening," Tom said. "She and I have a better chance of stealing Aeraden together than we do with the best of our squad."

"Really?" Cam and Gun said together. They looked at each other then back at Tom. Gun had stopped smiling.

"For one thing, I'm one of the squad best so I call bullshit," Gun said. "Sure, you're you and I guess that counts for something. But she's just some girl—"

"You don't know what I know," Tom interrupted, voice rising with his irritation.

"You could easily fix that by telling me what you know, you know?" Gun gave him a sideways look.

Tom's eyes passed from Gun to Cam then back to Gun.

"Fine," Tom said. "She's 'of No Last Name' and she probably has more power in one of her nose hairs than you do in your whole goddamn body. There you satisfied, now?"

Gun's mouth fell open as he collapsed into one of the barstools.

"Wow," Gun breathed as he finished his drink with a flourish. "I mean...wow."

"I know," Tom said.

"You *need* to tell Krytos."

"I know, but right now?"

"Uh, yes, right now! He'd make another run at Aeraden with that kind of information," Gun said.

"Wait, really? You think so?"

"Yeah."

"Then we could bring you in and the other elites..."

"It'd be the most badass strike against the Gi ever. Better even than the Comuneros taking down that ship," Gun said excitedly.

Cam stared between them as they continued to talk as if she were not there.

"It would be stupendous if one of you could explain what the hell is going on," Cam remarked loudly.

They both stopped and turned to her.

"Yes, that's right, I am still here," Cam said annoyed. "Still here and still confused."

Tom turned to Cam with a grin.

"I think we should go with Gun," Tom said.

"You mean we should abandon our plans and let my little brother die," Cam said hotly. "I can tell you right now, I won't agree to that."

"No, we'll be coming back soon and with more firepower," Tom said, grin widening. "A lot more, mostly because of you."

"Right, now you need to explain the weirdness that was your aforementioned statement in regards to my 'power' and my lacking of a last name," Cam said. "Of which, you do know that the latter can be said about *all* Gi slaves the world over?"

Tom looked away. He opened his mouth to speak then promptly closed it again.

"What is it?" Cam asked skeptically.

"I'm trying to figure out a way to say this that won't result in you hitting me again," Tom said.

"Then stop saying things that warrant you getting hit," Cam said through gritted teeth.

"Let's just say then that you deserve an explanation and it will be given to you at the appropriate time," Tom said vaguely.

"Now not being that appropriate time?" she asked.

"Correct, now not being that time," Tom nodded. "Though if you would accompany us to—"

Tom doubled over as Cam punched him in the stomach. Gun laughed outright.

"Shut up, Gun," Tom sputtered as he leaned against the counter. "Cam, you are unnecessarily violent."

"Well, you unnecessarily resemble an ass," Cam retorted.

"What? That didn't even make sense," Tom said.

"Oh man, this story is going to be retold a lot," Gun said happily from behind them.

Tom stopped and took several pained breaths.

"As I was saying," Tom continued. "If you would accompany us up to Rebel's Glade, our home, then not only will we come back for Aeraden with an army, but you'll have everything explained to you and more."

Cam looked from Tom to Gun then back to Tom.

"Give me your word that we'll come back and save Ke," Cam said.

"I absolutely give you my word on that," he said, extending his hand symbolically.

She looked at his outstretched hand then up at him. She thought of Ke and of the poison circulating in his veins.

"I guess I'll go then," she said, shaking his hand.

"Good," Gun said, piping in. "Then we need to go, now."

•

Cam could hear Tom running through their suite as he gathered the supplies they required for the journey. She was in her room, filling her new backpack. They had purchased a case of water and had split it evenly between them. She decided to take every free amenity the hotel had to offer. Miniature toiletries and packs of cotton swabs were settled haphazardly in the front pocket of the backpack. The clock on the glass wall read just after eleven o'clock as the late night news blared on.

"Thank you, Chantelle," the male anchor, Victor Thelm, said. "In other news, last night in the Paradise District, the body of First Lieutenant Eric Von Clousen was discovered by a maid at the Grandier Hotel."

Cam dropped the sewing kit she had been holding and looked up.

"Tom!" she shouted as Eric's picture flashed on the screen. "Tom!"

"What?" he said, alarmed as he burst into the room.

She pointed as footage of the crime scene played. He sat on the edge of the bed, mouth open.

"Police say his murder was exceptionally violent," Victor continued. "A full homicide investigation has begun and—"

Tom grabbed the remote and turned it off. Cam felt sick.

"I didn't..." Tom began. "He was alive when we left. I checked."

"That doesn't matter," Cam said. "He's still dead."

"No, the injury I caused couldn't have killed him," Tom gulped. "I didn't use that much force..."

Cam reheard the sickening thud of the vase against Von Clousen's skull and shivered. There had been so much blood.

The phone rang and Tom answered it. He spoke quickly and quietly. Cam stared at his hands and she could see the blood again. Tom hung up and turned to her.

"That was Gun," he said. "He's wants us to hurry."

"Right," she replied, quietly as she mechanically resumed packing. "Yeah, we've got to go."

CHAPTER 9
THE RESISTANCE

Cam and Tom met Gun in the lobby, both choosing to remain silent about what they had just learned. Together, they left the Grandier Hotel and made their way to the Golden Fire Casino where the Equintas had built a secret route leading to their town of Rebel's Glade.

Cam had seen the Golden Fire Casino earlier as it was one of the city's landmark casinos. It was shaped like a hot-air balloon, themed whimsically with depictions of blue skies and golden trees. Blue and gold lights flashed across its spherical front as advertisements for the latest shows took their turn across the boards. Its boggy interior was crammed with slot machines and gaming tables. The heavy smell of smoke suffocated the air, choking Cam, as they navigated the dizzying casino floor.

"It's just over here," Gun said to Cam, pointing to the circular entrance of a club.

A large neon sign flashed "Garden of Sin" as a monstrous beat reverberated from within. The doorman looked up from his post and nodded them entry as he recognized both Tom and Gun. Cam followed them down a dark hallway, through thick curtains, and onto the crowded floor.

They maneuvered around the sweaty patrons and empty glasses toward a door that read "Employees Only." Gun produced a keycard and swiped it through. The lock beeped as he swung the heavy door open to reveal the kitchen. There were only a few on staff, and none of them acknowledged their presence. Gun stopped before one of the large, industrial refrigerators.

"This way," Gun said as he opened the refrigerator door.

"You want me to go in the fridge?" Cam asked.

"Just get in," Tom said, shoving her forward.

Tom and Gun followed her then shut the door. Gun lifted a faux-can off of the shelf to her left, revealing a switch. He flicked it and the wall behind them began to vibrate. Cam turned as the wall slid to the side, opening into a dark staircase.

"Watch your step," Tom warned. "We really sucked at building stairs when we first made this."

Cam frowned as they descended the steepest steps she had ever seen. To worsen matters, they appeared to be nearing a cave system and the accumulated moisture left the walkways dangerously slick. Eventually, they emerged onto a narrow cavern path. Tom picked one of the torches off the wall and lit it.

"This path goes under the Paradise District and out of the city," Tom said. "From there, we have faster means of transportation."

They continued down the dark passageway for quite some time. What began as the distinctly musty smell of a basement morphed into the clean earthiness of stone and condensation. The air was crisp in a way that was completely foreign to her.

"So, what can I expect when we get there? How pissed off is Krytos exactly?" Tom asked Gun tentatively. "I imagine a lengthy lecture's coming my way."

"Yeah, Krytos was pretty steaming mad at you when I left," Gun said.

"Wait, I've heard that name before," Cam interjected. "Back in the city."

"Krytos is the leader of the Equintas," Tom said.

"Oh, that's right," Gun said, pointing his finger at Tom. "You promised Wenda like a hundred crates. How in the name of the devil's fuzzy sphincter are we going to make that happen?"

"Actually, it was 34 crates," Tom corrected incredulously. "Though I may have promised her they'd be delivered by the end of the month."

Gun stopped and turned slowly to face Tom.

"That's not going to happen," Gun said.

"I know that it's not, but I needed her help," Tom argued.

Gun shook his head at Tom as they continued down the path.

"Excuse me, but what are in the crates?" Cam asked. "I gathered it's something valuable."

"You gathered correctly," Gun said as he poked Tom in the shoulder. "Why don't you tell her what's in those crates?"

"Fruits and vegetables—" Tom began.

"Right, but fruits and vegetables that are not...?"

"...not grown in a lab—"

"—because they're grown in...?"

"...the ground," Tom finished.

"What?" Cam asked in amazement.

"That's right," Gun said. "The earth back home is not poisoned like the Gi's is. We can grow *real* food there, food that actually has a taste and a smell. Food that is more than worth its weight in gold."

"I take it then that 34 crates is a lot," Cam said.

"Here's some perspective for you. We produce about one hundred and fifty per year. Right now, so late in the season, we have twelve," Gun said. "So, yup, we're gonna be a bit short on that order. Thanks, Tom!"

Gun shook his head again as Tom tensed. Cam stared between them uncomfortably as they continued on.

"So, this town of yours, this Rebel's Glade," Cam began hesitantly, attempting to break the silence, "what's it like?"

"It's small," Tom replied as Gun continued to huff. "At least it was last time I was there. Remember, I've been in the Slums for the past two years."

"It's still pretty small," Gun said, smiling. "It's nice that way though."

"Where is it exactly?" Cam asked.

"Well, you know how Tengoku was built into the western face of the Western Tutamen Mountains? Well, there's another bigger mountain range east of it," Tom said. "Rebel's Glade is nestled in the valley between them."

"Oh, and be warned," Gun added. "Everyone there's been exposed, so we have a pretty eclectic group."

"Exposed?" Cam asked.

"To Vinestra," Gun said.

"So, everyone there has powers like Tom's thing with air?"

"Been showing off again?" Gun asked disapprovingly.

"Please, I don't do that," Tom said.

"Of course you don't," Gun said sarcastically as he turned to Cam. "But, yes, everyone there has something of a special talent."

"Interesting," Cam said as she pondered the thought. "What's your power then?"

A smug smile crossed Gun's face.

"Mine's awesome. As in it will blow your freaking mind," Gun said. "See, I can pick up any weapon and instantly master the ability to use it."

"That's why he's our Bladesman, or the second-in-command of the offensive squads," Tom said.

"Whoa," Cam said as she tried to imagine what it would be like to absorb knowledge so quickly. "So, what's Krytos' ability then? It must be something crazy powerful if he's the leader."

"It is," Tom said. "Mainly, because he has two."

"You mean he has two powers?" Cam asked.

"He can freeze things, make projectiles out of ice," Gun said.

"He can also make these portals," Tom added. "We use them often for quick escapes, though he claims the power isn't fully developed yet."

"Probably making you wonder what yours is, huh?" Gun asked.

"I have a power?" Cam asked, disbelieving.

"Duh," Gun said. "Everyone's good at something."

"We'll find out when you're exposed to Vinestra," Tom said. "I mean, if you want to do that."

Cam grinned as a shiver of excitement shot up her spine.

"You just offered me the opportunity to discover my super power," she said slowly. "I'm really not going to turn you down."

Soon, they found themselves at the entrance to a much larger cavern. The vast ceiling domed high over their head and the walls showed signs of being manually widened. Tom aimed the torch down the tunnel. A set of train tracks ran north while a parallel path had been marked for future installation.

"Whoa, you guys finished laying this side already?" Tom asked, staring around. "This is the Equintas' own little railroad, Cam. The finished side is for the fast car and the unfinished side will eventually be for supply freight from Tengoku. Before Mom and I left, they were only halfway done."

"Krytos broke two more cells since you left," Gun said. "We've got more talented folk to help now."

"They broke cells without us?" Tom asked skeptically.

"Our intel's better now," Gun shrugged.

"Cells?" Cam asked as she followed them along the tracks.

"It's the Gi's secret prison in the Ether under the Metraline," Tom said. "It's where they take the people that they either really want to examine or that they really want to punish."

"What do you mean?" Cam asked.

"The Ether is a labyrinth of laboratories," Tom explained. "The people in the cells are their test subjects for various human experimentations. It's essentially unending torture, if you're lucky enough to even survive."

"It's where most of the population of Rebel's Glade came from," Gun said as he stared resolutely ahead. "It's where I came from."

"Oh," Cam said.

"Come on," Gun said, picking up the pace. "The truck should be up here."

"The truck?" Cam asked as she stared at the railroad tracks dubiously.

Cam followed them up the path where an old pickup truck was parked. The tires had been removed and replaced with drive wheels that were locked to the track.

"Everything's been enhanced and tweaked quite a bit," Gun said. "I think she's tops out around one hundred and fifty, now."

"I don't really have any reference for what that means, but it sounds cool," Cam said.

Gun jumped in the driver's seat while Cam and Tom sat on makeshift seats in the covered bed.

"Hang on!" Gun shouted as the engine roared.

Cam felt a pull in her abdomen as the truck lurched forward, picking up speed with every second. The wind whistled loudly in her ears and she laughed in exhilaration as the truck found its top speed. Within an hour, they were able to see the tunnel's end.

•

They exited the truck and approached the circle of light ahead of them, frosted in green and white. Cam stepped to the edge and gasped aloud at the picturesque landscape before her. She was too overwhelmed to speak. She had never, in her wildest dreams, imagined such places existed.

Before her was the most stunning landscape. The mountain peaks were drizzled with a fine layer of melting snow. Far below, ran deep valleys peppered with vast evergreens that stood tall like arrows jutting from the rocky earth. She could hear the sound of rushing water nearby. Mountains, even higher than the one she stood upon, surrounded them. They were glowing an illustrious silver in the bright sunlight with faces like brightened elephant hide, flat and marred by wrinkles. She turned to the southeast and found most of her vision obscured by blue. A vast lake stretched out before her in vivid azure.

"Come on!" Gun shouted from farther along the path. "We can still get there before dark!"

They followed him, arriving at a wide riverbank. The river rushed as Cam saw a small boat nearby, tied to a tree.

"We're just outside Rebel's Glade now," Gun said. "We can get you some real food soon. Hell, we can get *me* some real food soon."

They set the boat out into the river and took turns rowing. Cam leaned over the side and saw little fish swimming with the current. Their scales reflected the sunlight like diamonds. She reached a trepid finger below the water's surface and watched in amazement as they scattered. Then a foreign cry, loud and purposeful, shattered the air as she looked up and saw an eagle. Cam, who only knew barren earth and gray skies, was paralyzed by the display of natural beauty.

Their boat traversed the flowing river, cutting angular lines in the glossy water. The river widened as the boat worked its way through the forest. The mountains loomed, snow-peaked and expansive. Melted snow ran along the craggy mountainside, joining the river by way of miniature waterfalls. The mountains were even more majestic from her perspective at their base. She stared upward but could not see the top.

Their boat drifted around the river bend as the mountainsides began to shrink. Spread before them was a valley, long and entrenched between the mountain ranges. Trees blanketed much of the valley like a thick, woolen blanket. She had never seen so much greenery.

"Uh, hang on to something," Tom said. Cam looked at him confused. "Now would be a fine time to start listening to me, Cam."

Then she realized what he was referring to. She had been too preoccupied with the view to notice that the river was quickly becoming a waterfall. Before she could fully comprehend what was happening, the boat lurched and they began to fall.

"Falling! We're falling relatively fast here, wait, make that dangerously fast!" Cam screamed in panic.

"I think you took a wrong turn back there," Tom said calmly to Gun.

"Nah," Gun said.

"Are you two crazy?" Cam shouted. "The ground is approaching more than just a little bit swiftly!"

She gave up and screamed as Tom and Gun sat quietly in the plummeting boat. The trees drew closer and closer. The wind rushed around her as her heart beat wildly in her chest. Cam shut her eyes, waiting for a squelchy impact.

It never came. Strong gusts blew in and she opened her eyes to find the boat hovering at an angle, a few feet above the ground. Mist surrounded them, adding a soft sheen to the air. She looked over at Tom only to see his eyes closed in concentration. He slowly exhaled and raised his hand. The boat leveled, hovering parallel to the river as they began to descend gently like a feather. Cam grinned in amazement until she saw Tom begin to struggle.

Sweat dotted his forehead as his expression turned rapidly into a grimace of exertion. Then they fell into the water. They were only a few feet from the bottom, but the impact was enough to cause them all to fall on their backs as water rushed over the boat.

"Ouch," Cam said. "Do you guys really travel that way every time?"

"No," Gun said, standing up. "It was Tom's idea. He thought you'd like the view, I mean we usually take the mountain pass...whoa, Tom, you okay?"

"Yeah," Tom muttered, leaning his head on his arms. "Sorry about the landing. I didn't know it would be that hard to control. My Mom does it for all the newcomers."

"No, it was fine. Scary as hell and somewhat harsh to the upchuck reflex, but fun," Cam insisted, "so, thank you."

"You're welcome," he replied as they continued down the river.

●

The river in the valley was broad and crystal clear. It followed nearly parallel with the mountain ranges as it weaved through the trees and smaller vales. The sun was setting, casting warm hues of orange and pink over the water. Cam's spine tingled with anticipation as they traveled farther in, nearing their destination.

"Hey, look! We're almost there," Gun said.

"See that mountain, Cam," Tom said, pointing to a mountain that was shorter than the rest. It was rounded at the top and its sides were like flattened platinum. "We're at its base."

Gun maneuvered the boat closer to the dock as Tom tied it up. Cam could see the lake, dark and tranquil, further down the river. The dock led to a path that cut between the thick trees. Night had fallen as Cam peered into the forest.

"Jeez, how much farther is it?" Cam asked. "By the way, good job on hiding your town."

"We try," Tom replied sarcastically.

"Then it should be noted that you've found success," Cam said.

They exited the boat and trudged down the road. The trees began to part quickly as they entered the forest. Cam saw smoke wafting upward as a wide, open plain became visible. Dozens of structures stood clustered together though none were large or lavish. Most were humble cottages constructed from local timber, though each was distinctly unique from the other. There was something in the atmosphere different from anything Cam had ever experienced before. The town itself seemed to breathe with life.

"Look at that," came a voice as they approached. "Gun actually accomplished his mission."

A young man walked over and gave them an awkward wave. He was lanky with a boyish face and dark hair. His kind brown eyes were slightly angled, magnified behind his rimless glasses. Cam saw that he wore strange white bands around his forearms. She stared, trying to discern what they were. He noticed her gawking and shyly put his arms behind his back.

"Please, you're talking to the pro here," Gun gloated.

"Hey, Sammy," Tom said, giving him a brotherly hug. "This is Camilla."

"It's just Cam really," she corrected, holding out a hand.

"Samson Casey," he replied, shaking her hand. "Good to meet you."

Then a rustling wind blew between them. Cam turned and saw Shun walking toward them. There was no visible anger on her face as she turned to Cam, ignoring Tom.

"Hi Camilla," she said with a smile. "Are you okay? I know all of this must be terribly overwhelming. Thomas was far beyond reckless in his actions and I am sorry for that. I thought I had raised a more responsible son."

She turned to Tom, scathingly, at the last part.

"It's okay, really," Cam said.

She smiled again as she faced Gun.

"As always, excellent job," she said to Gun. "Thank you."

"No problem, Shun," Gun said. "Would it be alright if I turn in for the evening? It was exhausting bringing them all the way back here."

"I'll bet," Shun said, eyeing Tom.

"Me too, I'm on shift at the clinic," Sam said. "I just wanted to say hello before I started."

"Sure," Shun said as both Gun and Sam left. "Thomas, take Camilla home. She'll be staying with us while we figure out the housing situation. I'm sure she's tired and would like to rest."

"It's good to see you, too, Mother," Tom said sharply as he grabbed Cam's wrist. "Come on, let's go. The house is this way."

They left Shun and walked along a path that led to the center of town. Tom began rattling off names and facts but Cam was unable to properly absorb the new information. Her attention was captured by a house, smaller than the others, that rested near the center of town. A wooden wind chime echoed soft notes in the evening breeze and a rocking chair swayed as if it had just been occupied moments before.

"Whose house is that?" Cam asked.

Tom smirked. "That's Krytos' house."

As they walked by, Cam couldn't shake the strange feeling that she was being watched. Then a whiff of cigar smoke met her nose and she turned to find its origins. A pair of powerful onyx eyes met hers from the darkness of the open doorway. Someone *had* just been in the rocking chair.

"Here we are," Tom said, gesturing to his left at a small house. It was green with white trim and was the only one other than Krytos' house that was built in the craftsman style.

"It's great," Cam replied, grinning. They walked up the stairs to the porch. Tom held the door open for her as she stumbled through on tired legs.

From the tiled foyer, she could see a living room to her left and a small kitchen to her right. The house was very neat. Wooden floors, polished brightly, gleamed beneath her feet and there was not a speck of dust to be seen. Their furnishings were simple with subtle modern lines, and the smell of fresh lemons and clean, mountain air filled the space.

"My room's this way. You can sleep there," Tom said. She followed him down a short hallway to a bedroom.

"This is really nice, cozier than I'd expected," Cam said, sitting on the bed.

She put her hand on the soft quilt. It was beautiful and held all the charm of being handmade. She felt Tom's eyes move to rest upon her as she looked up. They stared at each other, beyond the point of awkwardness, with relief and pride at their arrival.

"Well, get comfortable," Tom said, finally. "You should probably relax. I'll be in the living room if you need anything, okay?"

"Okay," Cam replied. Tom grabbed the door handle, about to leave. "Tom?"

"What?" he asked. She jumped to her feet and hugged him as tightly as she could. He looked oddly taken aback.

"Thanks, you know, for everything," she muttered, releasing him.

"You're welcome," he said. Then he grabbed the handle again and left.

She lifted the blankets and climbed underneath. Her body relaxed as she curled herself under the sheets. The warmth of the blankets enveloped her as their heaviness helped her to fall into yet another dreamless asleep.

●

Cam woke in the darkness of midnight. She heard a door slam in the hall and arose to investigate. She heard shuffled footsteps as she pressed her ear to the keyhole.

"Thomas, get your coat," she heard Shun say. "We're telling Krytos now."

"I don't think I need to wake him for this," Tom said.

"You said you were sure," Shun said in a grave tone.

"I am," Tom said. "She spoke to that *demon*. Only the true descendant could do that."

"Then you need to tell him," Shun said exasperated. "Tell him that you finally found her, Camilla of No Last Name."

There was a short but punctuated silence.

"Let's go," Shun insisted.

Cam heard the scuffle of footfalls followed by a door closing. She curled up under the warm blanket but knew that she wouldn't be able to fall back asleep. Instead, she threw the covers off and turned on the light, causing the already overworked generator to rumble even more.

The room was small. It was clean like the rest of the house, albeit a bit barren. The heavy scent of cedar rose from each drawer she opened though most were nearly empty. Dust danced through the air and she sneezed as she made her way to the closet.

To her surprise, the closet was rather chaotic. A few shirts and pants hung on wooden hangers. Beneath them sat a bow, two short swords and an exquisite rifle. On a shelf, sat a box of ammunition and, on the floor below it, a quiver of arrows.

She continued her inspection and found that the rest of the space was filled with books. She scanned the titles. Most of them were history books she had never heard of. Her eyes flirted with each title until she had several of interest picked out. She took the books back to the bed and began to read. After an hour, she heard the door to her room open.

"Can't sleep?" Tom asked.

"Not when you two are slamming doors," she said, sitting back on the bed. "So, mind telling me what that was all about?"

"Damn, I was hoping you hadn't heard any of that," Tom said, half-smiling. "Part of the terms of me *not* being demoted for my disobedience is that I have to keep my mouth shut until he can tell you himself, tomorrow. Sorry."

He seemed almost embarrassed. She grabbed his hand and squeezed.

"It's really not a big deal," Cam said.

He squeezed her hand back and leaned into her, his presence permeating her circumference of personal space.

"Well," he said. "Tomorrow is going to be a *very* good day and you will have all of your questions answered."

He stood to leave.

"Good night," he said.

"So far," she said and he smiled as he shut the door.

## CHAPTER 10
## WHEN IT RAINS

The morning dew had just settled upon the trees as Cam walked out onto the porch and took in the serenity. A bench stood on the patio under a wind chime that was singing the softest of songs. Cam inhaled. She could smell the trees and the river water mixed with the sweetness of the fresh rain. She glanced around. No one seemed to be awake yet. She slipped on her shoes and began to wander around the site.

Houses of varying shapes and architectural designs were circled inside the large opening between the trees. A large fire pit, surrounded by log benches, sat at the town's center. The ashes from the previous night's fire had barely been disturbed by the nightly winds. The ground was soft and damp below her feet as she found herself concentrating on her footfalls.

"Hey, Cam."

She started and looked up to see Tom.

"Want a tour?" he asked.

"Yes, I do," Cam said, staring around. "It's really pretty here."

"Oh, come on, don't downplay it," he said with a crooked smile. "It's gorgeous."

They walked along a path that led them to a vast open field. The stark mountains were covered in glimmering ice and the trees wept cold tears of dew. The land was rich and barely affected by man.

"Let's go to the training fields first," Tom said. "I think everyone's already there."

He led her through the buildings to a vast field at the mountain's base. She squinted in the bright morning light and saw that a large group of people were congregated. Tom waved, greeting everyone and making introductions. As they approached the edge of the field, Cam spotted the man she knew must be Krytos.

He was tall and muscular. His skin was a deep, velvety molasses and his authoritative eyes were bold like obsidian. He wore a navy happi coat over his clothes and was standing at the opposite edge of the field, crossing his powerful arms as he watched everyone gather. His presence was silent but impossible to miss.

Shun was standing beside him, talking quickly. He laughed, showing moon white teeth. His smile accentuated a long scar that ran down his left cheek. Then, as he relaxed his stance to gesture toward the field, she saw something even more striking. Spiraling, silver scars of various widths ran from between his fingers to his elbows in an elegant pattern of permanent pain.

"What are his scars from?" Cam asked.

"I'm not sure about the ones on his arms," Tom said. "He never told me, but the one on his face is from the beast that guards Aeraden in the Ether."

She turned quickly to him.

"You mean the beast we would've faced had our plan continued?"

"Maybe," Tom said sheepishly.

She furrowed her brow, giving Tom a skeptical look. When she turned back to the field, she found herself staring into the critical eyes of Krytos. He gave her a short nod before stepping out onto the field.

"Scrimmage!" Krytos shouted toward the crowd. "Positions! Two teams today. Let's keep it simple."

Excited chatter erupted as the players broke off into two groups. A competitive edge could be seen gleaming in each of their eyes like a freshly sharpened blade as a thin boy came onto the field. She watched him paint a perfectly straight line for the line of scrimmage. Tom instinctively took a step forward, but Krytos put his hand up.

"Don't be such an asinine host, Thomas. Sit this one out," Krytos said to the disappointment of others on the field as well as Tom's. "Stay with Cam. Teach her the game."

Tom nodded. He looked disappointed for a moment but then turned to her and smiled.

"So, what is the game?" Cam asked.

Tom was about to answer when a woman of about thirty came bounding toward them. She was a fair blonde and her smile made her nose crinkle. She was easily the most cheerful, upbeat person that Cam had ever seen.

"I'll sit with them, too," the woman said to Krytos who nodded his approval. "Hi, I'm Alexandria Perrins. Alex for respectable short, not slave."

"I'm Cam."

"Of course, but what's your true name?" Alex asked.

"Oh, it's Camilla."

"But, dear, that's only your first name," Alex said. "What if I meet another Camilla? I won't have any way of distinguishing you two verbally. I suppose I could refer to you as the one with the gray eyes, but what if this other Camilla I meet later also has gray eyes? Then I'd really be in a pickle."

Cam stared and when she didn't answer promptly, Alex added. "Thomas, what's her name?"

"Like she said, it's Camilla," Tom said.

Alex smiled and playfully smacked him on the shoulder.

"You're just being difficult, now. If her name was just Camilla then she'd...well, she'd have no last name at all..." Alex said, trailing off.

She looked at Tom with wide eyes as he nodded.

"Is she—"

"Yup, at least *I* think so," Tom said.

Her mouth fell open and she took Cam's hand with glee. "It's great, no, wonderful to meet you!"

"Uh, thanks. It's nice to meet you, too," Cam said awkwardly, shaking her hand as a portly man wearing silver glasses came to stand beside Alex. She smiled and took his hand in loving embrace.

"This is my husband, Max," Alex said to Cam. "Max, this is Camilla...of No Last Name."

Max's eye widened as he shook Cam's hand.

"Really?" Max exclaimed.

"It would be really quite awesome if you didn't tell everyone about this yet," Tom said to Alex. "At least wait until we find out for sure."

"Oh, fine," Alex pouted. "It's just exciting news!"

"Not as exciting as you two getting married. Congratulations!" Tom said, quickly changing the subject as he clapped Max's shoulder. "I'm sorry I missed it."

"Please, you were on mission!" Alex said with a grin. "It was a quiet ceremony anyway. Krytos officiated and we had it on the west shore of the lake."

"That sounds like it was amazing," Tom said.

"I'd better get back, sweetheart. It was nice to meet you," Max said. He kissed his wife on the cheek before heading toward the edge of the field.

"Oh, I'm sorry," Tom said, turning back to Cam. "I forgot to tell you about the game."

Cam listened to him as he explained the rules of the day's game which was a simple scrimmage. It was a basic free-for-all with each person being allowed to use their powers how they wish to hit a member of the other team. Once tagged, you were out for the round.

"Does anyone get hurt playing this game?" Cam asked, knowing that Tom's or Gun's could easily hurt someone.

"Oh, no," Alex assured her. "See my Max standing there. Watch him."

She followed Alex's gesture and watched Max with interest. He closed his eyes, a look of contentment washing over his face, as a burst of neon light fell over each player. The light encased each person like a cocoon.

"I don't quite understand," Cam said.

"He's a protector," Alex explained. "His power is to shield others."

Cam nodded, amazed.

"Wow, that's awesome and probably rather handy," Cam remarked.

"Shut up, you guys," Tom said, shushing them both. "The game's about to begin."

Krytos walked to the edge of the field. He placed his hands on his hips and surveyed them.

"Alright, now let's show our newcomer what power really is," he said with a smirk. "Begin."

The action began the moment after Krytos had spoken. Several points were scored in the first few seconds as bolts of lightning and high-powered jets of water flew. Several people quickly showed their powers were in physical combat. Gun flew forward and pulled a wooden sword from his side. He swung it with fantastic grace, striking three shields in an instant.

"So, I gather you've done this before?" Cam asked Tom.

"Our boy here was the reigning champ before he left on assignment," Alex said proudly. "Have you seen him fight yet? He's fantastic."

Cam smiled and turned back to the field. She saw a small boy on the field that she had missed earlier due to his size. He could not have been older than Ke. He jumped out of the way of a bolt of lightning and slammed his tiny fist into the earth with unbelievable strength. The ground divided away from him, creating a grand rift. It rode forward with such force that six people on the opposing team were knocked onto their backs.

"Shun likes to say that he makes the earth speak," Alex said. "We call him Bobby. He doesn't know his real name. He came to us as a baby from the Ether, born and orphaned in that wretched place."

Out on the field, a very thin man, identified by Tom as Matty, melted into the ground only to reappear behind one his opponents who he hit with a surprisingly powerful fist. The match continued in this manner through five rounds. The score was dead even until the very end of the game.

Krytos threw his hand into the air at the close of twenty in-game minutes. The players stopped and turned to face him. Gun's team had won by three with one hundred and two points.

"Good game, everyone," Krytos said. The players rushed up to him as he began throwing compliments. "Tia that was an excellent display...Matty, yes, you have improved your strength...Yes, Bobby, I saw that hit and it was incredible..."

Cam felt a rush of warmth from Krytos that she had not expected. She had thought he would have been an emotionless, authoritative leader like the ones she was accustomed to as a slave. But he wasn't. The Equintas were not his warriors to command, they were the family members he had managed to save. All of these people, who had been orphaned by life and terrible circumstance, had a home here. Cam turned to Tom, who was engaged in the game, and felt more alone than she had in a long time.

•

The scrimmage continued behind Tom and Cam as they left. Tom had suggested they take a walk to the river so she could see the town's periphery. The grass was still laden with moisture as they walked the perimeter of the Equintas Camp. Stray droplets of water struck them as they walked silently down to the river's edge.

They stopped at a clearing where the trees had grown together to create a small alcove. The river trickled along as Cam dug her foot into the soft sand of the bank. She looked at Tom. He had taken a seat and was staring through the breaks between the boughs. She sat with him.

"So, this is what an actual forest looks like," Cam noted as she thought of the Slums and the lifeless decay of the land.

"Yup, good and green," Tom replied. "This is what the world, the whole world, should be like. Natural biomes. Naturally dispersed energy. Just natural life in general, you know?"

Cam nodded as she pushed her hands into the sand. She felt the grainy texture sift between her fingers as she pulled them upward. It was heavy and fell quickly.

"You know," she said as she watched a blue bird settle itself across from them. "I never even knew such places still existed. To be honest, I never thought the stories about the rebels were true either."

"Well, that's because we're always hiding and we're really good at it," Tom said, his tone tensing. "You know, most people know what's right. It's only because they're given limited choices that they choose the wrong one. To pick between what is right and will kill you versus what is wrong and represents your salvation, I don't know."

He trailed off as he tossed a flat pebble into the river.

"I guess," Cam said. "But then what is truly wrong? What makes anything moral?"

"Wrong is what is wrong to you," Tom said.

Cam stared at him, awash with confusion.

"I'm beginning to gather that this is not some haphazardly chosen topic," Cam said. "What's going on?"

"It's nothing," Tom said. Cam gave him a knowing look and he frowned. "It's just that I've been thinking about Wes a lot since we got here."

"Your father?"

Tom laughed.

"Yeah, my *father*," he said. "I've been thinking about his death a lot lately. I could have done something. I knew about Aeraden. I had limited resources, but I could have at least tried. It was wrong not to even attempt it."

"But you did attempt it when you took me to Tengoku to save Ke," Cam said. "In fact, you're still doing it by gathering your forces here to help."

"I should've done it for Wes," Tom said, voice rising as he stood. "He saved me once and I couldn't return the favor because I guess I'm just that worthless, just that fucking weak."

"No, you aren't," Cam said firmly.

"You don't understand. That man was my hero," Tom said. He began to pace. "Now, he's dead and I'm alive. Me! The scared little bastard who couldn't just break the rules to save the man who was everything my real father should have been!"

He stopped and turned to Cam. She had her mouth parted, the words trying to form on her tongue.

"What was that again?" she asked.

Tom took a deep breath and slowly sat down.

"Well, I guess there really is no reason to hide it anymore," Tom said. "Wes wasn't my real father."

"Right, that's what I thought you said. Care to explain that one further?"

"Wes was not my father though I do credit him for making me who I am today," Tom said and then, seeing Cam's expression, added. "Let me explain. We came to the Slums like I'd told you, but we met Wes along the way. My Mom and I had been attacked by an off-duty soldier. I killed him but not after he had stabbed my Mom. It was my first big, undercover mission. I didn't know what to do when I saw her bleeding out. We were undercover and had no supplies. I just remember apologizing to her over and over because I knew that I couldn't save her."

Cam thought of Ke and the moment when she had seen the hole in his glove.

"She was dying and I was just falling apart when Wes came along. He was just out walking and heard the commotion. He came to our aide," Tom said, reflecting on the memory of his hero with deep admiration. "Together, we carried her up to unit 34. He bartered for medical supplies and gave us shelter for months while she recovered. They fell in love. She told him everything about who we were and what we were doing in the Slums. She planned on bringing him here when were done with the mission. But then he got sick."

He stopped and took a deep breath.

"You have to understand, Cam, I never met my blood father, but Wes was everything I imagined him to be. He truly cared about others. He loved life, in all situations, and he fought the sickness like hell to continue loving it," he said. "I should have fought for him in that same way."

Cam did not know what words, if any, would bring him comfort. Instead, she remained silent.

"But I didn't," Tom said. "Because I was too scared."

"What do you mean? Scared of disobeying Krytos?"

"Please, give me some credit," Tom scoffed. "If it was that simple, I would have went off mission the moment I learned he was sick."

"Then what was it?"

"You know the scar on Krytos' face, right?" Tom asked and she nodded. "When I was a kid, he made a doorway that led almost directly to Aeraden. He took a team of the Equintas' best, my mom included. But something was there when they arrived, blocking the entrance. Krytos tried to fight it..."

Tom sighed.

"In the end, the lives of the Equintas outweigh the dangers of getting Aeraden," Tom said. "But I do know Krytos is devising a plan as we speak. He always believed the cure for the sick would be the first step in freeing the slaves and educating the Tengoku citizens. It would open the door to truly freeing us all. I trust him and I always have. I never thought to defy him for anyone before."

Tom looked up as it began to rain, soft and nearly silent.

"After Wes died," he said, through clenched teeth. Cam felt the wind blow quick and harsh as Tom clenched his fists in anger. "After Ke got sick, I knew that the plans didn't matter anymore. Death was death, but Wes' death was the first death of someone I actually loved."

He turned to her and she expected to see anger or maybe tears, but he was smiling.

"Cam," he began. "You're the best and weirdest friend I have ever had—"

"Really? Weirdest? That's quite the achievement considering you live in a town full of superheroes," she interrupted.

"Hey, come on, I'm trying to say something nice here," Tom said. "Wes' death showed me what love and loss truly are, and you gave me the motivation to be brave. Because of you, I'm pretty sure I did the right thing this time."

They stared at each other. The rain was falling with the gentlest touch, becoming a mere whisper as it sliced the air, and the rain was amplifying the natural colors that surrounded them, making them shine glossy and fresh. They were so close that only a few raindrops managed to fall between them. Then Cam heard a rustle as a loud voice spoke.

"Why are you guys sitting in the rain?"

They turned to see a dark shadow emerge by one of the trees.

"Volpi?" Tom asked.

"What's a Volpi?" Cam inquired as a tall woman stepped into the light. "Oh, I see now. It's a person."

Volpi had warm, sun-bronzed, russet brown skin and striking, angular features. She was wearing a black tank top over loose-fitting jeans that were held up by a studded belt. Her hair was shaved and shaped into a spiky, indigo mohawk.

"Good to see you too, Tom," Volpi said. "It's been a while."

"Sure has," Tom said. There was a strange pause where the conversation halted and Cam was no longer there. Tom coughed. "Uh, this is Camilla. Cam, this is Volpi."

"I don't really give two shits who she is," Volpi said, stepping closer. "This is *our* place, Tom. You don't bring outsiders here."

"When did you become such a haughty bitch? The color green does not suit you at all," Tom said harshly.

"Don't flatter yourself," Volpi scoffed.

"Sure, whatever you say. Cam, let's go," Tom said as Volpi's face became a look of indignation. Tom turned and glanced sideways at Volpi. "I did always prefer your natural hair color, by the way."

Cam followed beside him as they left, her eyes diverted to her shoes as she tried to ignore the feeling of Volpi's eyes boring into the back of her skull.

●

The light was ticking over the horizon and the last needles of sunlight were detangling themselves from the sky. The open field was empty. A grand fire had been lit in the center of the village and torches were alight at every building.

"You guys coming to dinner?" came a cheery female voice from behind them. They turned to see Alex smiling at them. "Max is already inside. We should hurry before everything's gone."

They walked toward the community center, the largest building in town. Alex carried the conversation effectively by herself. She informed Tom and Cam of everything that had transpired over the last two years. Cam, having no frame of reference for the information, let her mind wander. The building they approached had three curved platform steps that led to double doors. The thick wooden doors were propped open as the most tantalizing and delectable scents wafted out into the town.

"Wow, these carvings are so intricate," Cam remarked as she gazed at the building's exterior. They told stories of demons, battles, and warriors. They covered the entire exterior from every pillar to every wall. "They're beautiful."

"Milo did them," Alex said.

"Who's Milo?" Cam asked.

"I think you probably saw him drawing the lines of the field earlier," Alex said. "Krytos freed him two years ago, right before Tom left. This is his power."

"Visual arts," Cam said as she followed one particular storyline that wrapped diagonally around the nearest pillar.

"Poor boy said he was stuck in the labs since he was seven," Alex said. "He spent six years in there."

"How did he last for so long?" Cam asked.

"I'm not sure exactly," Alex said, placing bitten fingernails against her chin in thought. "He never talks about what happened down there. He'll only talk to Krytos about that. Krytos has become something of a father figure to poor Milo, which is good because I always thought Krytos would be a great dad."

Alex stopped then turned to face Cam.

"You know, now that I think about it," she said. "Krytos mentioned something about Milo's old cell mates. One of them told him stories to keep him from being afraid. She told Milo that he would be saved someday and that he just had to survive until that time came."

"At least he wasn't alone in there," Cam said.

They both fell quiet as Tom nodded toward the community center's doors.

"Well, I think we've stood out here in the cold night for long enough, especially when hot food is on our table," Tom said.

Tom and Alex pushed forward with Cam at their heels. As she passed the threshold, the magnitude of the room's understated brilliance overtook her.

"Wow," Cam said.

"Take off your shoes, please," Alex requested as she removed her own. Cam followed suit, setting her boots on the large shoe rack. "I'm going to find Max. See you guys later!"

The room was warm and the walls were the same color as the forest outside. The walls were lined with enormous bookshelves, occupied by an array of tomes. Stunning old world weapons hung beside them, shined to glossy perfection. Dozens of circular tables filled the room, each surrounded by mismatched chairs.

As she ventured farther in, her gaze was drawn upward. The ceiling was high and lined with exposed beams. Large skylights filled the space between the beams, flooding the room with refreshing, natural light. She could see the moon, faint and white, fighting with the sun for domination of the sky. Her bare feet were tingling, and it was then that she noticed the floor. It was composed of silver tiles that seemed to emanate a subtle glow. She stared at them for a moment until she realized that they closely resembled the little bauble of Vinestra she wore around her neck.

"Hey," Sam said from a table just ahead of them. "Sit down, we made sure to save you two a seat."

They took seats across from Sam, Gun and Volpi. Tom fell into their conversations while Cam's attention was stolen by the platters of food congested in the center of the table. There were trays filled with cheeses, flatbreads, and crackers. Next to them was a cloth-lined basket filled with thick squares of soft focaccia. Two half-empty bottles of wine and a carafe of water stood in the center. Two large bowls were crammed between the plates, one held a simple salad while the other held minestrone. The main courses were creamy alfredo, lasagna, and meatball marinara.

Cam filled her plate with a bit of everything, wondering if her eyes were too big for her stomach. She grinned down at the freshly-cooked noodles and the crisp, green salad before her. She could tell simply from the rich, appetizing smell that the food before her was going to be the best she had eaten in her life thus far.

"Are you getting enough to eat there, Cam?" Gun asked, chortling as he bit a chunk out of his bread.

"Probably not," she replied, throwing a very large piece of lettuce into her mouth. "I would've gotten more, but the plate's too small."

"Pig," she heard Volpi mutter beside her.

Cam chewed and swallowed quickly in embarrassment. She turned to Volpi, readying to riposte, when Tom spoke first. "Yeah, this is the first time she's eaten real food in, well, in ever. So, she can eat until she throws up if she really wants to."

Sam groaned and slammed his fork on the table as he turned to Tom. It was apparent that he was Tom's closest friend in Rebel's Glade.

"Not this, again. How about you leave Volpi alone, Tom?" Sam asked. "You're being rude."

"What? *I'm* being rude? But she—" Tom sputtered indignantly. Sam gave him a reproachful look. "Fine, whatever, I'll just let it go then."

"Thank you," Sam said, his tone indicating his recurring role as mediator. He smiled at Volpi, but Volpi was too engaged in glaring at Cam to notice. He then clasped his hands together and spoke briefly under his breath. Cam cocked her head and turned to Tom.

"What's he doing?" she asked quietly.

Tom finished chewing. "He's praying. Sammy's one of the last living Christians in the world since the Lord General outlawed every other religion but his own."

Cam frowned, reclining in thought. The conversation moved to Tom as everyone was anxious to hear of the events that led to his momentary defection. The room around them was alive with the energy of dozens of discussions and hearty laughter. Cam was unaccustomed to large social gatherings and she felt rather out of place among their close-knit family.

Each time the conversation moved to Cam, every occupant of the table moved to stare, and her heart rate doubled. She fiddled with her fork or her napkin as she replied, trying to delay her first reaction of running. The voices whispered in her ears, incomprehensible but just as audible as the dialogues that were occurring around her. She concentrated on her food and ate three full plates followed by two slices of cake. Everyone, including herself, was quite surprised by how much she had ingested.

"Most people do that at least once when they get here for the first time, though not quite to the same impressive extent," Tom said as they put their dishes away. "Was it good?"

"No, I've had better," Cam said jokingly. "You know, back in the Slums, where I ate food that resembled chunks of half-dried vomit."

"I appreciate the imagery, but I'm still sort of trying to digest here," Tom said.

She followed him toward the front door where they put their shoes back on and stepped into the night.

"So, you ready to officially meet Krytos and get your questions answered?" Tom asked.

"I think so," she said.

"You better be sure," Tom said with a wink. "Because your whole life is about to change."

# Chapter 11
## Descendants

Night had fallen and the stars were radiating glimpses of the past. Tom held the door open as she walked into Krytos' small house. The space was illuminated by a variety of candles. It smelled of tobacco and old paper. A small hand-woven rug sat in the dining room with a wooden table at its center. Milo was sitting at it, drawing on a sketch pad with speed as Krytos closed his book.

"Hi, Krytos, I'm Cam," she said, throwing her hand out. "Camilla, actually."

Krytos stood, appraising her as he shook her hand.

"Nice to meet you. Please have a seat," he said, gesturing to the dining table. "Your mother should be here shortly, Thomas."

Krytos exhaled and a cloud of smoke encircled the little room. Tom sat by Milo, while Cam took the chair next to Krytos. She could see him more clearly and, again, refrained from staring at the silver scars.

"Nervous?" Krytos asked Cam.

"What? No, I'm not nervous," Cam said quickly. "Not nervous at all about the vague mysteriousness regarding the seemingly significant information you're about to disclose."

Billowing smoke rose around Krytos in thin, intertwining tendrils. "It's okay to be nervous."

He smiled. She tried to smile back as the door opened abruptly. Shun rushed in, carrying a bag overflowing with papers.

"I'm here," Shun said, shedding her coat. "I think I have everything."

"Thank you," Krytos said.

There was a long pause where no one spoke. Then Krytos exhaled, blowing a smoke ring over the flame of the nearest candle, and sighed.

"Camilla, we have been waiting for this for so long," Krytos said. "I don't know quite where to begin."

Cam furrowed her eyebrows.

"How much do you know about the Armistdan Order?" Krytos asked.

"Only what I read in the *Book of Trappings*," Cam said.

"How did you manage to get a copy of that?" Krytos asked, his tone suddenly heavy as he and Shun exchanged glances.

"My godfather, Mel," Cam said slowly. "Only it was a funny copy. The book's pages were deteriorating, but the binding was almost new."

"Ah, a delusory book or 'lying books' as the kids here call them," Krytos said. "They are any book that has been rewritten by the Gi to represent them in a more favorable light. I assume it tells an auspicious tale of the Markstre? It probably shows the Armistdan Order as savages trying to halt the Markstre's spread of equality. Did you know that the Markstre and the Gi Force are actually one in the same? Halfway through the Final War, the Markstre changed their name to the Gi Force so they wouldn't be as easily associated with the destruction they had caused."

"It *was* something like that," Cam said surprised.

"Well, despite the Gi's attempts to extinguish the truth, you still have basic knowledge of the Armistdan," Krytos said. "They were led by the Templum Three: Edan, Mylioth and Cardenash. These men were not the brutes the Gi portrayed them to be. They were simply the guardians that stood in their way."

"Stood in the way of what?" Cam asked.

"The entrance to the Templum Ortus and the many treasures it purportedly yields," Krytos said. "Three hundred and fifty years ago, the Markstre were flooding the lands in search of the Templum Ortus. Lady Halderin saw their approach and knew that the entrance was vulnerable. She turned to the Armistdan Order, a small untrained band of villagers who only wanted to protect their home at the base of the mountains, and granted their three bravest the ability to stop them through the power within Vinestra. Thus the Templum Three were created."

"Lady Halderin?" Cam asked.

"The story goes that she's from the other world, the Templum Ortus. She gave them a collective power, a power that would give them an enormous advantage," Krytos said. "Together, the Templum Three could summon any or all of the Seven Demons of Ortus Canitia."

Krytos paused. Cam's eyes flitted over the room's occupants. They all stared at her in anticipation.

"I don't, um, know what that means," Cam admitted.

"Well, from what Thomas has told me, you've already encountered one," Krytos said, "...in the sewers?"

"Leviathan?" Cam asked. "That was a demon?"

"You didn't think that a gigantic, fanged mermaid was normal, did you?" Tom asked, eyebrow raised.

"Well, maybe," Cam conceded. "But, hello, ex-slave here! Scavenging birds and sickly rats were about the height of my zoological experiences."

"The Seven Demons of Ortus Canitia guard the *other* side of the entrance to the Templum Ortus. When needed, the Templum Three could bring them to our realm and ask them to fight with us," Krytos said. "The demons are still out there, as you know from your run-in with Leviathan, though they have not been seen in hundreds of years. If we could bring the new guardians together then they could summon the demons to aide us and we could end the Gi's reign forever."

"The *new* guardians?" Cam asked.

"The responsibility of guardianship has been passed down by each of the Templum Three to the firstborn of the new generation," Krytos said. "Together, the three descendants form the new Templum Three. Shun, the document, please."

Shun handed Cam a folded piece of parchment.

"See, we've been looking for you for a long time," Krytos said.

Cam took the document and began unfolding. It was far larger than its compacted state made it appear as she continued unfolding until the paper lay flat. Tiny squares and circles filled the space along with severely cramped handwriting. She squinted at the circle nearest the document's bottom edge and read:

*Camilla of No Last Name*

"What is this?" Cam asked, looking up.

"It's a genogram of your family," Krytos said. "Go ahead, give it a thorough read through."

Her eyes darted to the right of her name where Ke's was then upward along the vertical line connecting her to her parents. She squinted at the paper, noticing the color of the line running between her and her father was silver.

"Why is the line different between my dad and I?" Cam asked, her fingers tracing the shallow embossing.

"Just follow it," Shun encouraged.

Cam looked down again and followed the silver as Shun instructed. It traced up through several generations of people she did not know. She noticed some did not even have first names by their lines, although each of them was designated by "of No Last Name." She scanned faster, her hand roving up the document until she reached the top. Then the ambient noise in the room died away as her senses became fixated on the name. She looked up, her wide gray eyes locking with the deep brown of Krytos'.

"Edan?" Cam asked.

"Yes," Krytos said. "Camilla, you are his descendant and one of the Templum Three."

Cam fell back in her chair, dizzy from the overabundance of thought swimming in her head. Her first thought was that it was all a joke, but Tom's somber expression conveyed otherwise. She looked at the genogram then back up at Krytos.

"Okay, highly metamorphic information aside, how do you figure it's me?" Cam asked. "You've only identified half of my ancestors here. How can you be sure?"

Krytos and Shun turned to Tom.

"They're sure because I'm sure," Tom said, "and I'm sure because of what I saw back in the sewers with Leviathan."

"What do you mean?" Cam asked.

"You were able to communicate with it, Cam," Tom said. "You *made* it stop attacking us."

"I didn't make it stop, so much as I just asked it to," Cam said, her voice quieting under the weight of their gazes.

"The powers bestowed by Lady Halderin were powerful but, while the Templum Three could summon the demons, only Edan was granted to ability to communicate with them," Krytos said. "Did Thomas explain how Vinestra works?"

"He said that touching it hypes up your natural gifts to insane levels," Cam said.

"That's right," Krytos said. "I'm assuming he also told you that the jewel around your neck is Vinestra."

"He did," Cam said as her fingers automatically clutched the necklace.

"It appears to be too refined to have enhanced your abilities to the desired levels," Krytos said. "But I'm guessing it was just enough to bring out a bit of Edan's communicative power while leaving the other dormant."

"Whoa!" Cam exclaimed, holding up a hand. "Leaving dormant the other what now?"

"About one in every one hundred million people has two powers that develop with the introduction of Vinestra," Krytos said. "Myself included."

"That's right. Tom told me you can do crazy stuff with ice *and* make portals," Cam said.

Krytos let a grin slide across his face as he puffed his pipe.

"So, what was Edan's other power?" Cam asked eagerly.

"First, I think it's more important that you learn about the other two descendants," Krytos said. "Even if we find that you are Edan's with certainty, we still need all three of you together to summon."

"Oh, right," Cam said. "So, Mylioth and Cardenash, right?"

"Yes," Krytos said. "For Cardenash, we have very little information. We're not even sure what his power was precisely though we believe it was something physical."

"Well, what about Mylioth?" she asked. "What do you know about him? About his power?"

There was silence that was punctuated only by the scratches of Milo's pen as he drew with fervor. Cam looked around, waiting for someone to continue.

"I did just ask that question out loud, right?" Cam asked.

She turned to Tom who looked at her with apprehension.

"Mylioth's power was with the air," Tom said. "He could manipulate it and move with it at its pace."

Cam stared at him for several moments before allowing a hollow laugh to escape her.

"Of course," Cam said a bit angrily. "You're Mylioth's descendant then?"

"So they tell me," Tom replied.

Cam shook her head.

"So help me, Tom, if Krytos and your Mom weren't here, I'd punch you so hard right now for being such a huge ass," she said. She paused, took a deep breath, and turned to Krytos. "Okay, but he and I make two descendants. Two, not three."

"Applause for your remedial math skills," Tom muttered.

"So, you're wondering who the third is?" Krytos asked.

Cam nodded.

"To be honest, we don't know who it is," Krytos admitted. "The genealogy for Cardenash's line has an abrupt break in it that leaves no trail behind. In fact, we're missing the most recent five generations of him."

"Five?" Cam asked in shock. "Five generations? How can you not be able to find five generations?"

"Oh, quite easily," Krytos mused.

"We've had leads," Shun said, speaking up for the first time. "None of them panned out though."

"But we'll find him," Tom added.

"Or her," Cam corrected.

"But that doesn't concern *you*, Camilla," Krytos said, snuffing his pipe. "At least, not yet."

"What does concern me?"

"Well, firstly, we want to give you an opportunity to touch raw Vinestra, to see with certainty that you are Edan's descendant. For, if you are, his second ability should manifest almost immediately," Krytos said. "Secondly, we'd like to extend an invitation to you to join the Equintas. Regardless of whether or not you are Edan's descendant, we want to help you and we want you to find a home here. Thomas told me about your little brother and I think we may be able to do something for him as well."

Cam pondered his proposal, knowing that if it meant help for Ke then she would agree to anything.

"Okay," she said. "Count me in."

●

Krytos, Shun, and Tom led Cam out into the darkening night toward the training fields. Tom turned to her.

"You're sure you want to do this right now?" Tom asked. "You know you can wait, if you want."

"Nope," Cam said. "We're not waiting. I want to know if I'm Edan's descendant tonight."

Tom shrugged as they stopped in the center of the field farthest from town. Max, the shield generator, was already there waiting. Shun ran about, lighting the several lanterns that surrounded them. Cam could soon see deep cracks and craters scattered across the earth where they stood.

"Okay, Camilla," Krytos said. "Remember, the effects of exposure grow greater with age. This may be rather intense."

"I know, you already read me the disclaimer," Cam said with a nervous smile.

Shun and Tom moved to stand behind Max as his neon shields burst down upon them. Krytos stepped toward Cam and pulled a small box from his pocket. He opened the lid, revealing a glowing shard of pure Vinestra.

"Whenever you're ready," Krytos said.

He placed the box in her hands as another shield appeared, encasing him as well. Cam looked down at the sliver of Vinestra and thought of Ke. She had failed to save him before, but this opalescent mineral before her was her second chance. She moved her hand, hovering just about the milky glow.

"For Ke," she whispered.

She brought her hand down over the Vinestra. Light exploded over the field, illuminating everything around her for a mile, then she screamed and was catapulted backward through the air.

CHAPTER 12

FIRE AND ICE

Thundering sparks of heat detonated like percussion waves in her ears, culminating to a nearly painful point before they ceased. She could not move or speak. She was not even sure if she was breathing. Her mind was a broken film reel, spinning images of new truths too quickly for her to comprehend. Her blood burned, boiling with the surge of new power, as she stared up at the starry sky.

She screamed again.

Her voice tore through the air with crushing fury. Her muscles tightened as tears of agony rolled down her face. She flipped onto her stomach, trying to lift herself up. Another scream ripped itself from her throat as her attention became fixated on the escalating rate of her heart. She reached up to her chest, fingers clinging her shirt, as the repetitive thumps ran closer and closer together. Then her body burst into bold, yellow-orange flames.

"Cam!" she heard Tom shout.

She turned to him as another wave of devastating pain crushed her, followed by another and then another. The fire grew, building upon itself, until the entirety of Rebel's Glade was lit from her flame as if by the morning sun. Then came the heaviest blow, and she felt her body collapse onto the now grassless field.

"Cam," Tom said again as he reached her. "Cam, are you okay?"

She looked up at him, weakly.

"Did I do it?" she asked, her voice a hoarse whisper. Krytos, Shun, and Max approached. She turned feebly to them. "Am I Edan's descendant?"

Krytos laughed as he kneeled down beside her.

"Edan's second power was with fire," Krytos said. "So, yes, you are his descendant."

She smiled.

"Right on," she murmured. "So, what's next?"

"Now, you start training," Krytos said. "Tomorrow morning, we'll meet right here."

"Okay, sounds good," she said, voice trailing as her eyes drooped shut and she fell unconscious.

●

*The forest sped by Cam in an ever-increasing blur of deep greens and shadowy blacks. The wind was cutting. Her boots smacked against the compacted earth and scattered pine needles as she chased the elusive figure racing ahead of her.*

*"Camilla, where are you going?"*

*She stopped. The wind rushed on, carrying the implausible voice farther into the forest. It rang in her ears, leaving behind the smear of something so familiar but so foreign.*

*"Dad?"*

*She turned and saw her father smiling warmly at her, gray eyes twinkling.*

*"Hi, sweetheart. It's been a long time."*

*His smile broadened, reminding her of the times when he had told her she had made him proud. She clenched her jaw to keep it from shaking as she ran to him, embracing him tightly as she ignored the blood that had begun to pour down his white shirt.*

*She wanted the dream to end, to cease before it became a nightmare, but that very thought only hastened the transition. The creeping shadows on the trees retreated as the forest brightened, allowing her to see more clearly. Hot blood splashed against her scalp, seeping between her and her father. It rolled down her face, pooling inside of the ear that was pressed against him. She squeezed him tighter, holding on as her tears joined the trail of blood.*

"Camilla—"

"No," she pleaded. "Not yet..."

The soft ground began to shift into pavement as the trees faded, morphing into streetlamps.

"Stop running from this, Camilla."

She felt his hands move to her shoulders. The swift dance of the forest winds fell stagnant with the thick air of the city.

"You must face this."

He gently pushed her back, his comforting hands abandoning her. The sun burned her eyelids as she forced them to remain shut.

"Open your eyes."

She watched the deep reds on the inside of her eyelids flitter in a complex mosaic as she ignored his request.

"OPEN YOUR EYES!"

His voice cut her eardrums as she heard the busy streets and local shops fall into silence. Her eyes flew open against her will like a window shade abruptly being drawn. An audible gasp escaped her as she stared into the increasing horrors of the bloody store.

"See why it's so important that you pay attention," he said. "I never had the chance."

Cam felt something cold and heavy drop within her as she doubled over and was suddenly sick. The trembling in her body increased as the blood cascaded down her father's face from the empty sockets where his eyes had just been.

He touched the dark, sticky webbing, and she knew bad news was imminent. "I never had the chance to see. None of us did."

Cam frowned at his words. She spun about and saw that the street was amassed with dozens of people she had never met. Each of them was missing their eyes, each streaked with bloody tear stains just like her father. They faced her as their varied voices rose together in chorus.

"We never..." they said through motionless mouths.

Their bodies condensed as they encroached upon the small circle of space occupied by Cam and her father.

"...never had the chance..."

Their rising voices reverberated in Cam's chest, and it froze her. Their gouged eye sockets, still fresh and wet, stared in her direction.

"...the chance to see."

They stopped, stopped speaking and stopped moving. They stood, facing her with impassive expressions. She was becoming panicked when she turned to her father and asked. "Dad, who are these people?"

"We never had the chance to see, Camilla," he said, disregarding her question. "But you do."

Silence fell just as a flash of light filled the street, blinding Cam as she threw her hands up to shield herself. The winds iced and were still. Then an explosive crackle broke the air, and a panorama of raging flames met her eyes.

"Dad!" she screamed.

The sun began to set, washing the sky in vibrant vermilion like the fire that fell in great blankets. The intense heat was mugging, and the assaulted oxygen had diminished. The people surrounding her ran alight with the ferocious flames, screaming silently toward the sky as they burned. Cam turned. The flames engulfed her father as well, but he stood unwavering as the flames melted the skin from his bones.

"Dad," she breathed. "No."

"Cam, what are you doing?"

Cool air blew over as a hand fell on her shoulder and she turned up to see Tom.

"Stop doing this," he said.

"Tom?"

"You should just face what you've done."

"But I don't understand...I'm not doing—"

He leaned forward, squeezing her arm, and she knew part of the truth had unfolded itself. He whispered into her ear. "Open your eyes."

An icy shock filled her. If she had seen it from the beginning then she would have known better. She blinked several times. The figures around her had begun to blacken and char. They had ceased their struggle and were falling into crumpled piles of ash. Smoke rose high over the flames. She stared up and saw that her father's smile was still visible through the growing inferno. Then she felt it and her eyes widened.

Tom spun her around and roughly grabbed her by her left wrist.

"OPEN YOUR EYES!"

She shook her head, looking down at her numb hands. The fire that was flooding the city was originating from her open palms. "No!"

She closed her fists over the fire, but it leaked from between her fingers as she fought to extinguish it with force. In desperation, she slammed her *fists into the cement, destroying her hands beyond the repair of normal medical means. She struck the ground over and over, creating molten craters. Her knuckles bled to the bone as she crushed the flow of flame within her broken hands. Tom watched her with an examiner's concentration and inscrutability as she continued on. A tormented shriek was soon wrenched from her lips as she fell to her knees. The last flames rippled into nothingness with whispering hisses. The lavish building in their backdrop was again pristine and whole. Tom moved to kneel in front of her.*

*"It's not over yet," he said. "Stand up."*

*She met his eye then reached for his hand and stood.*

*"Remember this, Cam," he continued. "This is your chance. Now, come on. It's time to go."*

*He pointed up the street to a heavy door, its base still glowing red hot. She cried softly as the burnt bodies blew away with the last embers. She followed him toward the door where he paused. He turned to her, moving to the side to allow her to ready for their departure. She nodded and stepped up. She placed her hand on the handle, her eyes fixed resolutely.*

*"This is my chance..." she said.*

*Tom placed his hand over hers as she felt an added power. Together, they pushed on the handle.*

*"This is my chance to see."*

●

The next morning was difficult, but Cam managed to arrive on the field before six o'clock in the morning where she found herself alone with Krytos.

"Where's Tom?" she asked.

"On his way," Krytos said. He wore all white and held a sword at his side. "I want to see you use your power first. If you could, please show me what you can do."

"What?" Cam asked. "Wait, I don't even know how to...ignite it?"

"Just picture what you want to happen and *will* it to occur," Krytos said.

Cam threw her hands up.

"Your instructions are, well, ambiguous," she said.

"Are you saying you can't do it?"

"Of course, I can."

"Then do it," Krytos insisted.

Cam sighed, reassuring herself that this was just an introduction to training. She extended her hand, palm up, concentrating on an image of fire but nothing happened. Krytos eyed her, his gaze piercing, as she stood on the field with her hand goofily held up in front of her. Frustrated, she closed her eyes.

She could still feel Krytos watching her attentively which gave way to embarrassment then to anger. Then she felt the spark. A tingle rushed from her head down to her fingertips. The palm of her hand began to itch. Somewhere in her core, she could visualize a bundle of energy. It glowed softly in canary yellow as her body tensed with the new power. Her skin grew hotter and hotter with the impending rush of fire until her right arm burst into flame.

"Not bad, though a bit weak," Krytos said.

Cam lowered her hand and frowned.

"Weak?" she asked incredulously. "I just *made fire*!"

"Don't be so easily offended," he continued with a grin. "Besides, it won't be that way for long."

They continued to practice. By the close of two hours, she was able to produce flame instantly.

"Getting better," Krytos remarked as she held a large flame in her open palm.

"That's it," she said, extinguishing the flame. "Getting better? I think the phrase you're searching for is 'getting awesome.'"

"You have a lot to learn, Camilla," Krytos said with a short laugh. She opened her mouth to protest when they felt the wind stir.

"Morning, Krytos," Tom said cheerfully as he walked onto the field. His mother and Gun followed closely behind.

"Good morning," Krytos said. "Thomas, please stand with Camilla. I began training you as a child and, for years, we trained you as the principal fighter. Now, you must learn the essentials of teamwork. You two need to work together."

Tom nodded.

"Good," Krytos said. "Shun and Gun, please stand back for this."

They obliged.

"Now, I want you to use your power, Camilla," Krytos said. "Hit me with your fire. That is your only goal at the moment. Thomas, yours is to assist her."

Cam glanced at Tom and he gave her an almost imperceptible nod to advance.

She raged forward with fire burning in her fist as she made to fling the fiery projectile at Krytos. The wind stirred as Tom moved with her. Her legs were propelling her faster than she had ever moved before, her speed amplified by Tom's power. Her feet barely touched the ground as she ran with astoundingly light steps. She threw her fiery fist at Krytos and it hit with a deadening force that reverberated through her bones.

Triumphant, she looked up only to realize that he had not even attempted to evade her. His hand was on his chest, a great shield of ice protecting him. Cam stared with amazement as Krytos lifted his hand to retaliate the strike. Tom moved forward, his movements barely stirring the air, as he distracted Krytos from his attack.

"Now, Cam!" he shouted. She lifted her hand, poised to strike. Flames soared from her hands. She pushed it forward, inch by inch, only to have it die before it could strike her intended target.

Krytos sighed and threw Tom forcibly across with field with one powerful arm. He landed with a thud that knocked the wind clear from his lungs. Cam turned to face Krytos. He advanced on her with remarkable agility despite his size. She turned to Tom who was on the ground, several feet from her. Then she turned back and saw that Krytos was standing directly before her.

He had moved with more power and skill than she had ever imagined possible. She had no defense left but her fire. With nothing else to guide her but her most primitive instincts, she struck her hand out at him. Flames rushed forth like hell's gates bursting open as he countered swiftly with ice.

A booming crash echoed through the mountains as flame touched ice. It was the most power Cam had ever felt and she was growing manic with the rush of it.

She wanted to win.

Ice prickled her forearms, a calm before the storm which then struck her hard. She flew backward, flying for what felt like miles. The air around her was cold, and her chest tightened painfully from the strike. Then she struck the ground, bouncing with sickening thumps as she rolled across the wet grass.

Blood bubbled in her throat as her potentially fractured nose throbbed. She tried to move her hands, in order to prop herself up, but her muscles were dead, heavy and cold. Instead, she rolled onto her back. The sky was beautiful and blue, as if from some faraway dream that mattered nothing in the real world. The clouds moved together as they floated peacefully over her, synchronized to their own beat.

"You alright?" Gun asked, extending his hand to hers. She nearly collapsed as he pulled her to her feet. Behind them Tom was being tended to by his mother though he seemed to be in much better shape. "Oh, man, Tom told me you were 'Of No Last Name' but I had no idea what that actually meant! I mean, that was incredible! The power!"

"He got me," Cam said, disappointed.

"No, he just 'got' you better," Gun said. "Take a look."

She leaned over Gun and saw Krytos standing between her and Tom. The white sleeve of his shirt had been burnt clean off. Blisters had formed with anger over his already scarred arm. Shun rushed to him and touched one of the bleeding blisters with care. Cam smiled, a bit satisfied, before hobbling over.

"That was very good for your first time, though it was not the perfection that will be required of you," Krytos said, putting a warm hand on Cam's shoulder. "Let's start with weapons. Shun and Gun will be your enemies."

He tossed Tom dual daggers and Cam a sword. Shun and Gun had already readied themselves with a quarterstaff and a mace respectively.

They spent the next hour sparring relentlessly. The clash of metal on metal reverberated through the mountains. They took a break at noon and sat beneath a nearby oak, discussing the progress of the first training session. Cam battled with Krytos over several points, wanting him to say she had achieved something. Tom, Shun and Gun had left to bring back lunch while Cam was still fiercely debating her position.

"I did a good job, you have to admit that," Cam said. "Plus, I'm fairly certain that I surpassed your expectations."

Krytos looked up at the sky and let out a small laugh.

"My expectations," Krytos said. "You were trying to reach *my* expectations? That's ridiculous."

She frowned as she stared past Krytos to the forest behind him. She had too many responses and no time to say them all.

"What you're not understanding is that what I think ultimately doesn't matter," Krytos said. "What you need to meet are not my expectations, but your own."

Cam said nothing as she shifted the dirt between the blades of grass with her boot.

"You can't hurl a grand fireball at me or take on the legacy of the great Edan without the power of your own will," he said. "And you can't save your brother without it either."

His words cut deep and she felt the heavy tide of failure wash over.

"Well, what if I have no expectations of myself?" Cam whispered.

Krytos scoffed.

"So, you have no expectations of yourself and your great power?" Krytos mused with a smile. "You don't believe in yourself, so why strive to do better?"

The last thing she had expected was for him to mock her and she found it incensing.

"You want me to believe in myself?" Cam asked angrily. "What makes you think I'm capable of believing in myself? My parents are dead. Wes is dead. You tell me that I'm supposed to be some kind of hero. You and everyone else. But what if I can't? What if I can't save..."

Cam trailed off, her mouth still trying to form words. She drew in raspy gasps that reminded her of Ke's sickly wheezes. Her heart was pounding out of her chest as panic began to grip her.

"What if you can't save your little brother?" Krytos finished for her.

His intense eyes met hers, full of sympathy, and she stood. She could not sit still anymore and play out the rest of the conversation as if she were fine. Her chest burned with sudden and desperate fury. Then she screamed as her skin erupted into flames, flames larger than any she had produced during that day's training.

"What the hell is wrong with you? Why would you say that out loud?" Cam screamed. "*I'm going to save him.*"

The fire burned with such power that she was overwhelmed. Tears fell from her eyes, evaporating before they reached the tips of her eyelashes.

"Yes, I'm sure you will," Krytos said with a grin as he stood. He raised his glittering blade from the ground with a flourish. "Feel like proving it?"

She watched his feet leave the ground as he charged. The sunlight reflected brightly over his scimitar as the scene before her snapped sharply into focus. But something was wrong.

The world had gone gray, as if her anger had somehow siphoned away the color. Instead, she saw colorless flames and a faceless, silver figure coming toward her. She saw the outline of the man and knew it was Krytos as the silhouette of his sword came into view again. He ran toward her, but his body was slow as if the movement of time had lengthened just for her. Krytos raised the blade across his chest, and she cocked her head to the side in interest as it fell toward her, leaving an arc of gleaming light in its wake. She stepped backward, watching it gracefully slice the air parallel to her body.

Krytos stood behind her, an impressed look on his face as he repositioned himself to attack again. He swung and she dodged with ease. It was like outrunning a snail.

Growing tired of the game, she thrust her hands out toward the moving weapon. Fire shot from her palms with such force that she almost could not believe it was coming from her. She had not needed to concentrate on creating the flame this time. She had willed it forth as easily as she had taken a breath.

She smiled and pushed the flames against Krytos' blade. Her body was calm and her senses oddly focused while the anger she had released was still roaring with life. She pushed a little harder and felt his blade fall a few inches. The anger continued, though she knew now that it was not directed at Krytos. As the flames arched off his blade and rose above their heads, she realized that the anger she had created was aimed only toward herself.

She hated the Gi Force and what they had done to the people of this world. She missed Ke and despised herself for allowing him to contract the sickness. Her mind was spending most days exhausted and her body was constantly shaken. The world was crumbling, and she was destined to save it, but she did not know if she had the strength.

A renewed wave of wrath burst forth from her. The fire screamed like a thousand murderous beasts as she raised her eyes to look up at Krytos. He was already watching her critically and that was when she realized that he had been holding back, waiting to see her next move so he could analyze her abilities further. As if to answer her revelation, he threw her back with one heavy swing of his arm. She flew backward several feet but managed to counter her fall with a jet of fire.

Cam hurled fireball after fireball, but he deflected them easily with his blade. She needed a new tactic as he was predicting her current ones without effort. She saw his foot shift slightly to his left to mirror the movement of her right shoulder, her tell that she was about to attack. She had been so obvious throughout the fight, too brazen, too angry, but now she was going to manipulate it to her advantage.

Cam opened her hand, creating a fireball. It dazzled for a moment before she feigned, careening toward Krytos from her left instead of her right. He moved preemptively in the wrong direction as she ran at top speed toward his unprotected side. He corrected and turned with her movements but was still too late to counter. The fire streaked over him as his clothes ran alight.

Krytos roared as the flames did the same. A thin layer of ice crept over his skin as he grimaced and the fire began to die.

Tom had returned and was watching with vivid interest. Cam stood, waiting for Krytos to call the match as he had fallen to his knees. She wondered if she should be helping him. She took a step forward, but he stood on steady legs.

Krytos was brilliant in the midday sun, powerful and frightening. The remnants of his white shirt fell away in a soft rain of ashes. His back was facing her as his scimitar fell to his side, the tip brushing the blades of grass.

"Are you okay, Krytos? Are we done?" Cam stopped as he turned toward the sun and closed his eyes.

Cam looked over at Tom, but he ignored her, his eyes trained on Krytos. She turned back and saw Krytos watching her again, but the eyes staring at her were not their normal, glossy, deep brown. His pupils were awash in brilliant, fluid silver. He smiled again as he took firmer hold of his weapon.

"What the hell?" Cam asked, shaken.

Krytos moved toward her with ease, dragging the scimitar along the muddy ground to war. She ignited and shot several fireballs at him. Not one made contact as Krytos moved with phenomenal speed. He was halfway to her in a single step that more closely resembled teleportation.

By now, Shun and Gun had come to watch as well as several other members of the Equintas. Krytos stopped, barely twenty paces from her. She did not know what to think or what to do as Krytos grinned. Then he shifted five more steps toward her in the blink of an eye.

"Oh, she's gonna get it now," Volpi said, grinning wickedly.

Cam took a deep breath and felt her entire body run alight with flame. Several of the people who had joined at the sidelines gasped. Krytos, however, remained impassive as he lifted his hand and ran it over his blade.  It chilled and ice formed, webbing over the metal.  She readied herself as well as she could, but her mind had gone blank.

"Break," he whispered.

The blade glimmered, ice and steel, before bursting into pieces.

Shattered shards of frozen steel came rushing toward her.  She did not know how to protect herself.  All she could do was throw her hands up to shield her face from the sword, now broken into a thousand daggers.

CHAPTER 13
FALLOUT

"You're fine, Camilla," she heard someone say.

She opened her eyes. There was no pain or blood. The blades had stopped and were hanging in the air, inches from her face. She stared. Max was standing beside her as the strange glow of neon orange warped her vision. It was a shield.

"What?" Cam asked, shaking.

Krytos blinked and his eyes returned to the deep brown she had come to recognize.

"Good effort," Krytos said with a jovial smile, "and, if it means anything, that was more than I'd expected."

He turned to walk away, but Cam was furious now.

"No!" she shouted. "This isn't over!"

The crowd broke into hushed whispers, each watching with rapt attention. She ignored them as Krytos turned back to face her. Sweat rolled down her face, making her hair frizz. Her clothes were ripped and she was still out of breath. Krytos sighed.

"This wasn't a fight, Camilla *of No Last Name*," Krytos said. Many in the crowd gasped and began to talk heatedly with each other. Several nodded their heads while others looked on in astonishment. "This was just a necessary dance, the rehearsal before opening day. I hope it served its purpose."

Krytos turned with blazing grace and walked off the field toward the village. Cam stood, sweaty and alone, still encased in the shield.

•

A week passed and the training sessions she had with Krytos thereafter were considerably tamer. She was beginning to master defense with one-handed swords in combination with her flame. Tom tried to reassure her that she was progressing well but, for everything she had learned, no session was as meaningful as the first. Now, when she was in the village, curious people ran up to her to ask:

"Are you truly 'Of No Last Name?'"

To which she would simply nod her head, and they would stumble over themselves in their eagerness to introduce themselves. It was days before Tom explained its full meaning.

"So, what do they mean when they ask me 'Of No Last Name?' I've gathered that it's something really significant, however, I don't get why," Cam said as they sat in one of the unused training fields. She was making small fires in her palm, watching expectantly as Tom raised a soft wind to build them higher.

"Sorry, I thought you knew what it meant," he said.

"Oh, right, I didn't tell you? Aside from the fire thing, I'm also psychic," Cam replied sarcastically as she closed her fist to kill the fire.

"Sarcasm will not help you get your questions answered," Tom lectured jestingly.

"Fine, sorry," Cam said with a smile. "Please tell me what my lack of a last name means?"

"Since you asked so politely, I shall oblige," Tom replied. "Edan was born with a surname, but then the Markstre invaded and he knew his family was at risk. So, he sent them far away with instructions to never use or divulge their family name again. See, that's one of the reasons why you've been so difficult to find. You have no last name, no way to distinguish you from any other Camilla or to prove by paper that you're Edan's descendant. Everyone here knows what the surname, or lack thereof, means and that's why they're so elated."

"Whoa," Cam said. Small flames were dancing across each of her fingers as she looked away from Tom.

"Wait, did I just say something depressing or offensive?" he asked. "You look upset."

She turned to him quickly and smiled, though it was visibly strained.

"It's just that I've—" she stopped and took a deep breath. "I've spent my whole life as a slave. I didn't really matter to anyone except for Ke, Mel and you. Now, I'm supposed to be some kind of superhero who's going to swoop in and save the world from the tyranny of the Gi. Those are some really high expectations and I just, you know, don't want to fail."

The last words were choked as she fought to spit them out. Tom sighed then turned to her and poked her on the nose. She swatted his hand away and looked up.

"I know you don't want to let everyone down but, for one thing, you're absolutely not alone in this," he pointed to himself. "I'm one of the Templum Three, too, remember? The responsibility falls just as heavily on me. We're a team. Success is *ours* to attain, right?"

He held his hand up for a high-five which she reciprocated with a chuckle.

"Okay," she said then added. "Though that also means failure is ours to share as well."

"Come what may," Tom smirked, "and we'll defeat it together."

He stood, stretched, and then helped her up.

"Alright, I told Sam I'd meet him to help move the new equipment into the clinic and I'm pretty sure I was supposed to be there like an hour ago," he said. "I'll see you at dinner."

"See you," Cam said, waving him off.

She stared up at the warm sun, noting that it was still early afternoon. The river had become one of her favorite spots to spend her off hours, and she decided it would be a pleasant place to continue reading the book Tom had lent her. She skipped across the field and onto the now familiar forest path that wound between the timeworn pines.

The peaceful, never-ending rush of the river soon met her ears as the trees parted way to reveal the crystalline water. She found her favorite seat upon the fallen tree that lay across the sandy banks and extracted the book from her jacket pocket. A few minutes of tranquility passed. Her attention was deep within the pages of the story, when she heard someone approach. She looked up and saw Tom.

"Tom?" she asked. "What are doing here? Did Sam not need your help or something?"

"Oh," he said tersely. "Yeah, it was already done."

"Okay," she said as she reopened her book. Over the top of it, she could see him staring at her. "What the hell are you doing? Stop staring like that, weirdo."

He didn't smile or even react, and his eyes were cold.

"Seriously," she said, sitting up and closing the book. "Stop it."

"Cam, I think it's time that I told you the truth," he said.

"You can't possibly have more secrets," Cam scoffed. "In fact, if you had—"

"Shut the hell up," he said, his voice was loud and etched with irritation. Anger rose in her at his unwarranted tone. "You need to just shut up and hear me out."

She closed her mouth and waved for him to continue as she fought to keep her fire from breaking out. She noticed it became difficult to control when her emotions were heightened.

"I'm officially done with your whiny bullshit," he said. "There, I've said it. I can't take it anymore."

Cam found herself at a loss for words. She searched his face for a hint that he was joking but found nothing.

"Okay, I'm sorry if I've been emotional needy," she said, sincerely though slightly unapologetically. "But your sudden inability to deal with it is a bit strange."

"I've been there for you in the past because I had to," Tom said icily. "But, to be honest, you're not on the same level I am and you don't even deserve to be one of the Templum Three."

"What? Not on the same level as you?" Cam exclaimed as an angry tremor rolled down her spine. "Nice ego, assface."

"Here come the insults," Tom said, rolling his eyes. "Sorry that I hurt your precious little feelings, but you need to be stronger than that. Right now, you aren't."

"No shit, I'm not," Cam said, crossing her arms. "I only just got these fiery powers a couple of days ago. Don't I get a bit more time to master them?"

"Please, I mastered mine by the time I was six," Tom sneered. "Don't you see how this has been working? I protect *you* to the best of my abilities but, at the end of the day, you should be saving *me*...saving *us*!"

He gestured toward Rebel's Glade as Cam extinguished the rogue flames bursting in the palm of her hand.

"But you aren't. So, grow up. Thicken your skin. Do whatever you have to do, but don't try to involve me in your emotional crap anymore," he said. "I think we need to just be fellow soldiers, not friends, or we'll probably lose this war."

He turned before she could utter a reply and left with long, purposeful strides. The air was still as Cam took a deep breath to stifle the fury that was building. She screamed in frustration. A circle of fire erupted around her, and everything within a two-foot radius began to burn.

●

It was almost dawn and only a few peeking rays of the sun could be seen over the snow-capped mountains. Krytos had sent Shun to gather together ten people. She had woken Tom and Cam first. She led them to the familiar smoky room of Krytos' kitchen where they sat for several minutes in awkward silence, waiting for the others to arrive.

Tom was avoiding Cam's eye, but that was fine with her. She had tried to sit away from him, but Shun had insisted they sit together. After more than a few discomfited moments in the unnervingly quiet room, someone else arrived. It was Gun, followed by Alex and her husband, Max, who yawned loudly. Several minutes later, Cam heard the door open again. Shun had returned with Kalen, Martin, and Luanna, the leaders of their respective divisions within the Equintas.

Kalen was a masterful psychic. He did not appear to be nearly as old as he was. His hair was still full and a healthy shade of auburn. He wore a pair of thin spectacles and a charcoal vest over a crisp, white shirt. He nodded to Tom and Cam as he sat down.

Martin followed. He was the Equintas' illusionist. He was a colorful man dressed in robes of vibrant yellow. A sweeping mass of blue hair fell to his shoulders, framing his mint green eyes. He waved jovially toward them as he tripped over one of the chairs in his usual clumsiness.

Luanna came in last. She was the Equintas' most experienced healer. Her light blond hair cascaded to her knees like a veil. It was the source of her healing ability and she used it to manufacture bandages that could hasten the healing process. She, too, sat at the table.

"Thank you all for coming today," Krytos said. "Good morning."

Several people nodded while the others stared on in rapt attention.

"Well, I'll get to the point," Krytos said. "We're breaking a new cell."

A murmur spread throughout the room as Alex spoke up.

"We're freeing more? So soon?" she asked.

"Yes," Krytos said. "We'll be freeing cell D24 as shown on the maps before you. Seven people occupy this cell, with one I hold particular interest in. Yes, Camilla?"

Everyone turned to stare, and she felt her face redden.

"Why only one cell? Why don't we just save everyone?" Cam asked. Many people were staring at her in disbelief while Tom looked embarrassed by her question.

"Camilla, the first truth in saving people is that you can't save everyone. You can want to," Krytos said. "But if you're dead, then you can't save anyone."

Cam stared at him.

"We are currently one hundred and fourteen strong. But only forty-three of those are trained and powered as offensive players. We have thirteen more as defensive and the remaining fifty-eight are passively powered," Krytos said. "Do you know how many are currently in the Gi? Shun?"

"As of last census, the Gi boasted over ten thousand," Shun said.

"That's not that bad," Cam said.

"That's just the guard for the Lord General," Shun said. "They have about two hundred thousand more in the city of Tengoku and their entire force recently surpassed the thirty million mark."

"Over thirty million," Krytos hissed under his breath. "Over thirty million people, trained solely as offensive soldiers. So, as you can see, we're slightly outnumbered."

Laughter filled the room.

"They have a department within the Gi that is dedicated to capturing and killing Gi deifiers," Shun added. "The department is made up of Gi soldiers and civilians, alike. Fifty of the eight hundred personnel in that department are looking for the Equintas specifically. Now, imagine that department grows each time we free a cell or do anything against the Gi. Let's say it grows by just two people. If we freed all five hundred cells, then we'd be looking at the entire department hunting us. We can't afford that when that department alone outnumbers us seven to one."

"We can't afford that *yet*," Krytos corrected. "But this is why we're freeing another cell so soon after the last break. If you haven't already been informed, we have two of the Templum Three before us. Thomas and Camilla."

Everyone turned to them.

"We've been waiting for this," Krytos said with a hint of exhilaration. "With just two of the Templum Three, we could soon handle a thousand Gi hunting us. We could save more people. I believe that, with the both of you, we have a real chance at defeating the Lord General."

Silence blanketed the space, attention still focused on Cam and Tom.

"We leave tomorrow at midnight," Krytos continued. "We'll convene again, the evening of at nine o'clock."

The meeting ended. All of them grabbed their briefings and began to leave. Cam left with Gun, ahead of Tom. The moon was brilliant overhead, larger than she had ever seen it.

"Hey, Cam," Tom said. "I'm sorry I didn't explain it all to you earlier. That probably made it confusing."

"Why the hell do you care?" she asked with the same indignation he had shown her.

"Whoa, calm down," Tom asked, turning to her. He put his hand on her shoulder. "What's wrong with you?"

Cam felt heat rise in her core with an uncontrollable velocity. She quickly turned and punched him in the face. He fell backward with the sound of rushing air then landed painfully on his back. His nose began bleeding profusely, and he touched the blood with trepidation.

"Don't pretend like you give a damn how I feel," she said.

She turned away and said. "I'll be staying at Gun, Sam and Volpi's. I'll grab my stuff in the morning."

"You're staying with us?" Gun asked in confusion, but she gave him a forceful look and he recoiled. "Okay, I guess you're staying with us."

Cam nodded and gave one last glance at Tom. He was still on the ground. His clothes were muddy and covered in blood. She gave him the best snide smirk she could muster then left.

●

The new morning was fresh and cloudless. Cam sat with Gun on the front porch of the house he shared with Sam and Volpi. He was having his morning cigarette and decided to take the time to teach her about weapons.

"See this," Gun said, brandishing a large sword. "Krytos stole it from a high-ranking Gi last cell break. It's a katana. It's meant to be held with two hands and, there, see the curved blade? It was designed to slice the enemy through the torso then be dragged back for more evisceration damage. It's one of my favorite close-combat weapons."

"And all that knowledge comes from the ability you got from Vinestra?" Cam asked.

"Yup," he said, running a finger over the blade's edge. "I can hold any weapon and know the most effective way to use it. Heck, it works with some things that aren't even really weapons."

"Like what?"

"Take this tree branch," Gun said, holding the branch up. "I know from touching it that I can use it in the Kendo style like a wooden sword and have nearly the same effectiveness. I could also use it in the old world Chinese style but not as an otta as it not curved. Or I could replicate the Filipino style, which I personally find to be really fun."

"That's pretty awesome," Cam said in awe. Gun grinned as Tom approached them.

"Oh, look, it's the person I'm not talking to," Cam said to Gun.

Tom's eyes narrowed. He opened his mouth to speak then decided against it. Instead, he put his hands in his pockets and walked away. Gun frowned.

"So, you guys had a little spat?" he probed.

"More like a nuclear fallout," she said.

The front door opened behind them. Sam and Volpi emerged. Volpi, irritated at Cam's sudden presence in her home, walked past without greeting.

"Breakfast's ready," Sam said cheerfully. "Come on."

They stood and ventured to the community center, which was loud and warm. Over a hundred people being gathered in one room was still something Cam had yet to grow accustomed to. Tom was sitting alone at one of the corner tables, and the others rushed to join him.

Cam eyed the other open tables and chose to sit at one alone. Tom stood, abandoning his table, as he moved to sit beside her.

"We need to talk," he said.

"I don't really feel like being subjected to whatever it is you have to say," she replied coldly.

He shook his head.

"Fine, continue to be like that. But we have a mission, a mission where real human lives are at stake, and I bet you haven't even read the briefing yet," he said. "You might want to do that if you're in this for real."

Cam pouted. She was using most of her restraint to keep from hitting him again. Seconds passed and then minutes as silence continued. Tom was wisely choosing to say nothing. Reluctantly, she pulled the brief from the large pocket of her jacket.

"Well, I'm reading it now," Cam unrolled the paper onto the table. The paper was thick and knotted at the left-hand corner with a piece of twine.

*Mission Set Time: Midnight, the twenty-fourth of July*
*Objective: To free cell D24 of the Ether's group prison cells. As always, all cell occupants are to be released.*

She scanned it. Krytos would be leading the team that Cam and Tom belonged to. They were the offensive team that would be the principal group involved in the act of breaking the cell. Gun was listed as well as Alex, Max and Martin. The defensive team was led by Shun. It was comprised of a list much larger than their team's. She was overseeing more than twenty people who would either be in Rebel's Glade or in Tengoku. Some were spies networked into the capitol city while others were able to do their jobs from their homes, such as Kalen the psychic.

Her eyes roamed down to their assignments. Each person had a specific task that was assigned to them. Alex, with her power of invisibility, would keep herself and Max safe while Max provided shields for everyone. Martin would use his illusions to alter their appearances into less conspicuous people. Gun and Tom were the guards who would only act if necessary.

Cam's part was small as the "lock picker" in which she was expected to melt the cell bars. She was not sure why she was even going.

"It's important that you go," Tom said as her eyes lingered over the paper.

"Can't someone just pick the locks the old fashioned way?" Cam asked while maintaining her scathing tone. "I mean, I appreciate that Krytos wants me to feel involved but—"

"It'll be much quicker if you do it," Tom interrupted. "Lingering is when we usually find trouble."

"It seems like a risk to add an unnecessary person to the team," Cam said. "I think I'm going to suggest to Krytos that I don't go."

Tom slammed his fist on the table, causing dozens of eyes to turn toward them.

"Why are you being so difficult?" he asked.

"I'm not, I'm being rational," she said, though it was only partially true. She was not particularly excited about spending time in close quarters with Tom, especially when they would be risking their lives.

"You want to be rational?" Tom asked in frustration. "Then go on the mission and stop being such a baby."

Cam glared at him, making forceful eye contact. It was a mistake on her part. His expression was so familiar and so unlike the previous day. The difference was so prominent that she contemplated her mental health for a moment.

"Does your silence mean you'll go?" he asked.

Cam dropped her eyes to her plate.

"Fine," she said quietly. He seemed pleased, but she didn't want to see him smile. She stood quickly then ran into someone and fell backward. "Um, ouch."

From her sudden seat on the ground, she looked up to see Volpi standing over her.

"You know," Cam said crossly. "Generally, when you approach someone from behind, you should say something like 'hi' or 'tomato bisque soup.' Even something that irrelevant would have sufficed to introduce your presence."

"Sorry," Volpi said. Her voice dripped with insincerity. "Thomas, I wanted to talk to you about tomorrow's mission."

*Sure you want to talk about the mission.* Cam pursed her lips.

"What about it?" Tom asked. "I was talking to Cam."

Volpi's eyes narrowed at Cam as she stood, straightening her jacket.

"Just things," Volpi said casually. "I'll be working with your Mom. So, there were some points I thought we should cover."

Tom looked like he was about to hesitate, but Cam snorted an interruption. "No, go ahead. I was just leaving."

CHAPTER 14
THE FALLEN

The week sped by in a blur, and soon it was the evening of Cam's first mission. Dinner was noticeably quiet that night. It was obvious that every mind in town was dwelling on the impending cell break. Cam ate eggs, bacon, and white pudding followed by seconds. She enjoyed the meal but ate quickly and quietly. She glanced up occasionally and noticed Tom hadn't eaten much of anything. He was sitting straight backed against his chair, staring at his napkin. They had not spoken once since the day they were given their mission.

She watched him and found herself still livid at his earlier degradation of her. The candle in the table's centerpiece flared upward with her momentary anger, catching one of Gun's sleeves on fire.

"Are you serious?" Gun asked her as he tried to extinguish the flames.

"I'm so sorry," Cam pleaded. "I'm just, just—"

"Crazy?" Gun pulled off the still smoldering shirt.

"I was going to go with 'nervous about the imminent mission' but I'll get you a new shirt," Cam offered timidly.

"It *was* my lucky shirt," Gun grumbled as he eyed the charred sleeve like a mourner at a funeral. "I'll need a really, really nice one to replace it."

Cam continued to apologize as the meal ended, at which time, she and the others who were involved with the mission were asked to stay. Krytos stood up from his table and walked to the center of the room. He was wearing a casual ecru button up under a tawny leather jacket. She could see a small kukri hidden in the side of his belt. He began recounting the plan from beginning to end to ensure everyone understood their roles.

Cam listened attentively, not wanting to miss a single detail. He went down the list of each person's tasks, and she cringed when he came to hers. She felt like dead weight again. She was only there to unlock a cell door, and she knew she could not be the only one capable of completing this task. It was her suspicion that Krytos only added her miniscule role to include her in Equintas operations. It was a nice gesture, but she felt more useless because of it.

"Now, you've all been wondering why I would risk breaking a new cell so soon," Krytos said. "Why would I want more Gi to be out there looking for us when we're not quite ready? Why not wait?"

He glanced around the room as curious faces met his.

"There is a young girl in cell D24," Krytos said. "This girl is a technopathic infiltrator."

A ripple of interest ran through everyone in the room. Significance gleaned on Gun's face as Tom leaned forward in his chair.

"The best part is they don't know what this little girl can do and what kind of unique power she is," Krytos continued.

Agreement rolled over the group as they understood the urgency in the mission while Cam remained confused.

"In addition to this," Krytos said over the rumble of whispers. "We know with certainty that there is a musician, an etholopath, and a young woman who can breathe underwater."

The room was silent as Krytos eyed them with a hint of pride.

"You know, they thought every last one of us was disposable," Krytos said in a low voice. "But they didn't understand the strength that we possess. Our sheer will to survive and overcome is our greatest asset."

A few whoops echoed in the hall as he grinned.

"They thought we were weak," he continued, "that we were no threat."

Cam felt a collective anticipation fill the room.

"But we proved them wrong," he said as people began rising to their feet.

"We, who were the fallen, now build the resistance," he said, his voice booming louder. "It's time to save some lives, ladies and gentlemen. Let's bring the fallen home."

Cheers erupted, and Cam followed suit. When it was time, she followed Gun and Tom out toward the river. The Equintas had a large truck that they used for mass travel up the mountain. Those who were in Krytos' group crammed into the truck's cab and bed. Cam found herself in the corner with only Tom within speaking distance.

"Now that we're on mission, can we start talking again?" he asked.

"I don't think so," she said shortly.

"Are you experiencing prolonged PMS or something? I mean, come on," he said. "Why can't we, at least—"

"What's a technopathic infiltrator? I want to know what power this girl has that we're working so hard to save," Cam interrupted. If he only wanted to be fellow soldiers then she would only speak to him about the mission. He smiled, satisfied that she was willing to let him speak.

"A technopathic infiltrator is essentially a computer hacker," Tom explained. "From what I've heard, they can break into the system with their mind like a psychic. Honestly though, I don't really know the extent of the power because I've never met one."

Cam thought about this as the truck bumped and bumbled up the steep dirt roads. She looked behind them and saw that her side of the truck was barely hugging the thin path. She could see the valley running far below her as her eyes traveled down the sheer cliff face. The trees appeared to be tiny green darts from their vantage, and it was quickly becoming difficult to discern where the ground was. She gulped at the thought of the driver, Tommy, hitting anything as the shortest swerve of the tires could send the truck sailing off the mountain.

"Don't look so scared," Tom said, nudging her. "Driving is Tommy's ability."

The journey up the mountain was slightly less nerve-racking after she learned of Tommy's power. They stopped, after an hour or so, at an outcropping that overlooked Tengoku. Cam was confused. Other than the spectacular view, there appeared to be nothing special about the spot.

"Krytos is going to create a door," Tom said. "He can't make one outside of the city wall. They have some sort of protection around it."

"But we are still outside of the wall," Cam protested.

"No, technically, we're inside," Tom said, pointing below them. "Look down, we're *above* the city."

Cam peered over and saw that it was true. The ledge was over the city, if barely, but it was enough to be considered within the walls.

Krytos made his way forward. He walked up to the edge until his toes hung halfway over the side. Then, with his eyes closed serenely, he drew his right leg back to form a more stable stance and struck his left hand out in front of him. Silver waves flowed from his palm and a stormy gray portal appeared.

"Whoa," Cam breathed.

The portal was over ten feet tall, glowing in deep blue. Lighting, flashing white and silver, surged within it.

"How can the citizens not notice this?" she asked Tom.

"Martin's using his illusions," he said. "He's probably doing some sort of camouflage that blends us and the door with the rest of the scenery."

The opening swirled in a counter clockwise motion with the menacing appearance of an electric, preternatural tornado.

"See you on the other side," Krytos said with smile. Then he walked off the ledge and into the portal.

Everyone followed suit, going through one at a time. It was obvious to Cam that she was the only one who had never done this before. She watched calm face after calm face disappear through the shadowy threshold with apparent ease. Cam was next and she looked down at the city below with a shudder at how far the fall was. Then, securing her faith and trust in her newfound partners in crime, she took a step into the portal.

There was no sensation of falling like she had expected. There was no rush of tornado-like winds against her skin. In fact, there was no feeling at all. She felt nothing, and in that lack of sensation she found that she was unable to move either. The only parts of her that continued to function correctly were her vision and her brain. Colors and unfamiliar scenes flew from every direction. She squinted at them but could only discern minute bits of the rushing images. At one point, she saw a horse drawn carriage then soldiers in a desert. She saw hordes of machines roaming over a valley then naked, undead men devouring each other. She screamed inaudibly as a mushroom cloud blossomed before her like the culmination of a thousand silent screams.

She tried to open her mouth to scream again, but then, with a sudden force that she had not expected, she saw black. Sensation returned to her and she landed on the ground with a hard thud. Her knees smacked the floor loudly, and her hands skidded against smooth tile.

"Ouch," she said to the floor. The skin on her palms felt raw. Then hands were on either side of her arms, lifting her to her feet.

She glanced around. They were in the stall of a restroom. A whoosh came from behind her and she saw Martin come through, landing softly on his feet. He was the final person to arrive, and the portal closed behind him.

"You okay?" Gun asked from her left. "It's pretty weird the first time."

"That's a wonderfully stated understatement," Cam muttered. Gun released her, but someone was still clinging to her right. She knew who it was immediately from the touch. She pulled away and Tom let go. "By the way, what the hell was that? Where did we go when we were inside the portal?"

"Even Krytos doesn't know," Tom said. "He said his power isn't fully developed yet."

"And why are we in a bathroom?" Cam asked as she noted their surroundings.

"Krytos can't make a door that leads directly into the Ether. It's protected like the city's walls," Tom said. "He can make one to get us *out* but only from a certain room. Like I said, the power isn't at its maximum potential."

Cam was about to inquire further when she heard Martin clear his throat.

"I'll be putting an illusion over us now," Martin said. "Gun and Krytos will appear to be soldiers. The rest of us will be prisoners being led to the labs as discussed in your orders."

Martin took a deep breath then pushed the rogue blue hairs from his face. He closed his eyes, then calmly opened them again.

"Alex and Max will follow us, invisible," Krytos said, turning to them. "Stay no more than three paces behind."

"Got it," Alex said as Max nodded. They smiled at each other as Max took her hand, and they both disappeared.

"Shields, please," Krytos said.

"Done," Max said, his voice coming from the empty spot where he had been standing.

"Does Alex make the shield invisible too?" Cam asked.

"Sure does," Gun said. He took a knife from his belt. It had a blunted end at the hilt and he tapped the end of it in the air an inch from her nose.

She cringed instinctively, but the knife merely bounced off the invisible shield that encased her.

"Stealthy," Cam noted.

"We're ready," Krytos said. "Now remember that we have an illusion over us. Gun and I are guards. Martin, Thomas, and Camilla are prisoners. Act as such."

Cam was a bit disconcerted by the supposed illusion that was over them. Her hands still looked like her hands and Tom still looked like Tom but, as they walked by the bathroom mirrors, she gasped in shock. Her skin was pale and sunken. Her back was hunched over, and she appeared so sickly that it was logical to assume she was near death. Tom's illusionary prisoner form was not any better as starved ribs poked through tattered clothing, and his calloused hands gripped the fake shackles. Krytos and Gun were both young and dressed in starched Gi uniforms. The Gi's blazing black and gold sun cross was affixed to their arms.

They began to move out of the bathroom with Alex and Max leaving first to check if the path was clear. Once it was, they filed out into the hallway that led to the Metraline's lobby. The hallway was small and lacked natural light which only worsened the feeling of claustrophobia. They were forced to form a single file line in order to fit. Cam followed Tom and kept her eyes on the ground as they had been instructed, but when she saw the sunlight flood over the golden floors, she had to look up to take in the splendor.

The lobby they were in was for military personnel only. It was an enormous circular space with hallways and archways stemming in all directions. The smooth ceiling rose several stories above her head and was accented in gold. The only window sat on the west wall. It rose from floor to ceiling, reaching almost one hundred feet in height, and was curved to fit the circular dimensions of the room. The walls were ivory, and beautiful sculptures of golden roses sprawled from the ceiling down to the floor. The lobby was bustling with military personnel. The front desk held two dozen busy receptionists clad in gold and black. It was so loud and so crowded that no one even noticed them.

Krytos led them across the magnificent lobby toward a nondescript doorway in the back corner. He flashed a forged security pass at the armed guard. The guard nodded and pressed the access button, giving them entry. They walked down six flights under harsh fluorescent lighting and the scrutiny of every armed guard they passed. Fifteen quiet, nerve-racking minutes passed as they progressed.

The silence was causing Cam to sweat. Her concentration began to falter as her palms grew clammy, and she felt the beginnings of panic. She was trying to breathe quietly, but in order to do so, she had to take twice as many. Each step downward was giving her the sensation of falling off a mountain. Her ankles twitched with every movement and her heart was beating rabidly in her chest. Something needed to happen to end the stillness overcoming her. It was slowly becoming unendurable as the voices began their terrible whispers, but then she felt Tom's knuckle inconspicuously nudge her arm.

"Are you okay?" he mouthed. She frowned. He would be the one to notice. His hand ran down her forearm quickly and quietly as he discreetly grabbed her shaking hand and squeezed it. She took a very deep, deliberate breath.

"Are you?" he mouthed again. She nodded and he withdrew his hand from hers before she could reject him.

They had finally reached the bottom of the stairs. At the platform, sat two more guards with assault rifles. The door was similar to the one they had gone through in the lobby except for this one had a biometric fingerprint scanner. Cam kept her head down but stared up through her hair at Krytos. She knew the guards could not see what he was holding because, if they could, then they would have shot him on the spot.

A stubby, severed finger was held in Krytos' hand. Cam assumed Martin must be extending his illusion to include the bloodied finger as the guards resumed their positions. The scanner was silent for a moment, then a buzzer rang, and a green light flashed over the door.

Krytos pushed the door open, and they walked into a basement. More fluorescent lights flashed on as they entered. The room was empty except for the wall mounted cameras that followed them as they progressed. Another biometric scanner was at the next door. Krytos discretely pulled an eyeball from his pocket and held it up. The door buzzed and again gave them entry. They walked through, and Cam broke her sickly façade to gain a better view of the new room.

She had become accustomed to the industrial concrete, the sterility of a military base, but this room was different. The room was cavernous in height and the floor was covered in dry sand. There were no light fixtures but, somehow, it was still quite bright as if the room had its own little sun.

The ground was so warm that she could feel it tickling her toes through the soles of her shoes. Every inch of the walls were the color of the sand and engraved with foreign words she could not read.

A large pillar, wider than a city bus, stood in the center of the circular room. It also had carvings in the same ancient language as those scattered across the walls. Her eyes ran from the pillar's base up to shocking brightness. She was unable to tell how far the structure traveled up as the ceiling was hidden by the blinding light.

*Could it be?*

Cam stopped, her feet kicking up a cloud of dust like the rising of a small tide.

*It's coming together now. The heart has returned to see me after so many years. I thought I was lost to being an immovable decoration. It's finally going according to plan.*

The voice was soft, a genderless echo, that moved the walls and shook her. She was accustomed to hearing voices others could not, but something in the way this voice spoke convinced her that it was not a figment of her imagination. Tom turned to her and saw her staring up at the endless pillar.

"Come on," he hissed.

"So, you didn't hear that?" she asked.

*Oh, now I see. My ears spent so many years to the ground that I have become deafened. They took my eyes, but they couldn't take away the heart. I can feel everything, and I felt you when you came in.*

"Cam?" Tom asked as the other Equintas turned to watch her as well.

"Quiet," Cam said.

*You are not him, but you will do, if you can prove yourself to me. Are you the hero he created?*

"Um, I'm not sure," Cam said, lost in the conversation with the voice inside her head.

*Restore the Templum.*

"Right, thank you for clearing that one up, it all makes sense now," Cam said, growing irritated. She was aware of everyone watching her in bewilderment. "What the hell does that mean?"

There was a pause.

*There are soldiers coming up to your level from the gardens. They don't know who you are, but they will suspect something if you continue to stand there. They'll be coming through the door in forty seconds. We can speak no further. Take them and leave now.*

"Cam?" Tom asked cautiously.

"Not now, Tom," Cam said, turning to him. "There are soldiers on their way. They'll be here any second. We need to keep moving."

They must have believed her as they all reformed their line and camouflage quickly. They had not taken two steps toward the door before it opened and three Gi soldiers entered. The one that stood in front of the others was unmistakable. He was portly with a long mustache that curled at the ends and a cat o' nine tails on his belt. It was Colonel Holkstoin.

Tom gave her a knowing sideways glance. Cam felt rage roll over. She had not realized how much she abhorred him. It took everything she had to keep herself from torching him where he stood. She swallowed, closed her eyes, and concentrated on the steps she was taking. Her scars were burning, and she could feel Holkstoin's piggy eyes watching her every movement.

She pictured Martin's illusion and imagined what Holkstoin was seeing. He would see her as a prisoner, again, her clothes barely clinging to her sagging skin. He would see the heavy manacles leaving crescent bruises on the tops of her feet. He would see her weak stature and know she was not a threat. Then he would not have a second to react before she lunged at him, breaking the illusion. He would see her as she was, as Camilla, and that would be the last thing he would ever see.

She blinked and looked around nervously. They were almost at the door. Her feet were about to cross the threshold when she glanced back. Holkstoin was walking away with the two soldiers. He had not looked at them once.

●

Mud spattered the floor of the next room. The smell of crops and fertilizer smothered them in a thick blanket. The walls rose upward, laden with rows upon rows of shelves.

Oversized tomatoes grew before her eyes aided by artificial enhancements. They were abnormally large, their skins thick and their color dull. The harvesting machines were barely able to keep up with their growth rate. A group of scientists with measuring instruments and clipboards were observing the plants. The scientists purposefully paid them no attention as they plodded through the chamber.

Cam thought back to the mission briefing, and her mind brought up the map of the Ether. This room was the Gi's laboratory for agriculture where they cloned, bred, and bio-altered crops. They created crops in the manner that was needed for the region of Gi territory requiring it. Once they were created, and the method to recreate them was found then the information was beamed to the outlying crop camps. Slaves, like Cam had been, worked these as well.

The next room they entered reeked of fresh manure and unwashed animals. Livestock of all kinds were crammed into the pens that lined the walls. Most of the animals were crying. They were forced so closely together that they were unable to move. They were defecating on each other from the lack of space.

On the other side of the room, more scientists were working. Two of them were attaching a piglet to a meat hook. Cam had thought it was dead due to the copious amounts of blood running down its body, but then it cried out and she started. The scientists began to dismember it, unraveling its tendons and skinning it down to the muscle.

A goat lay in an unnatural position on another examining table. The contents of its abdomen were spilling over its ribs and dripping off the table. Its intestines rose from its body cavity to drape over three hooked poles that loomed over the carcass. Scientists stood at the other end of the entrails, stroking the spongy noodle-like innards. This was unmistakably the Breeding Room.

Cam shut her eyes as they passed through a set of automatic doors and emerged into a sterile, white hallway. Another hallway branched to their left, but they proceeded straight. Numerous sets of heavy red doors ran down both sides of the hallway. The floor was made of large tiles, shiny and spotless. Her shoes squeaked against the polished top. She concentrated on the rhythmic shuffles until a loud squeaking broke in her ears.

The squeaking built around them as they marched on. Then it was followed by a rumble as the doors on the other side of the hallway opened.

The noise was coming from a large cart that was being pushed by a woman in a nurse's outfit. As they walked toward her, Cam could see something dripping down the sides. Whatever the substance was, it was dirtying the pristine floor in a manner that she found disturbing. Soon, they were level with each other, and Cam could see exactly what the cart was carrying.

Human body parts were scattered in the bowl. The smell was putrid. The lifeless skin on the limbs was sloughing down to the ivory bones. Arms with chemical burns poked out of the gruesome collage, their fingers twisted in odd directions. There were legs with no feet, feet with no toes. All manner of innards were piled in among the sludge. Human hearts, spleens and intestines were tangled together in a sick mess of meaningless gore. Decapitated heads, lacking eyeballs, stared up at her through chipped eye sockets. Cam's hands trembled as she remembered what wing they were in now, the Trial Rooms. It was where the Gi experimented on humans.

They moved quickly through the next doors and entered the prison cells. The rows of cells ran on and on. Weak and terrorized faces surrounded them. Cam stared up at the five levels of cells, stunned by the enormity of the secret prison. Moaning, crying, and screaming could be heard from every angle. The cells were fifteen feet wide and ten feet deep but each held at least six people. They smelled even worse than the Breeding Rooms.

"D Block is this way," Krytos whispered.

They had timed their arrival with the changing of the guards' shifts. The one guard that they did pass on their way to D Block merely nodded as he continued his patrol. Cam looked out at the sea of weakened faces and bodies. She could see their frailty on the number of ribs she could count. The guards, guns, and security cameras seemed like overkill for these helpless people.

"We're here," Krytos said, halting the group. "Martin, remove the concealment."

Cam felt a chill run down her spine and an immediate sense of vulnerability. She had not noticed the weight that the illusion had placed over her until it was gone. Then she heard a gasp behind her and she jumped.

"Hey!"

She turned to face cell D21 and saw an old man, his brittle hands clinging to the rusted bars of his cell. His eyes were wide and full of happiness as he looked at Cam.

"Yes, you," the man said. "Remember me? It's Vern."

"I'm sorry, I don't know you," she said. The Equintas were huddled together, enacting the last parts of the plan.

"No, you have to remember me," Vern said with urgent desperation. "You told me someone would save me someday."

"I'm sorry," Cam said. The man's eyes began to well with tears as he pressed his wrinkled forehead into the bars.

"You promised!" he shouted. "You swore to me and to the rest of us before you were moved to solitary. Don't tell me those were lies."

Cam stammered. She was unsure of what to say. Maybe he had gone mad from his years in captivity, but his eyes held unmistakable truth as they poured lost promises onto the rusted, decaying bars.

"Cam," Tom said as he grabbed her by the elbow. "Come on."

Cam let him pull her to cell D24. The old man continued to sob and she felt something horrible break within her. Tom quickly pushed her in with the rest of the Equintas who were now surrounding the cell. Most of its occupants had awoken and were staring at them with fearful interest.

"Hello. We are the Equintas, a group very opposed to the Gi and to the unjustified imprisonment you are suffering. We're going to get you out," Krytos said. "Please stand back."

The prisoners backed away automatically as they were used to taking orders. Krytos signaled to Cam, and she placed a hand on the bars.

She visualized the fire, focusing on its concentration rather than its size, until she felt it burst forth. Yellow-orange flames spun from her palms. She ran her hands over the bars until they began to weaken, melting with the symphony of crumbling metal. Within a minute, she had created a rough door.

"Good job," Krytos said as the remnants of the bars continued to burn.

The prisoners stared on with confusion and fear.

"Don't be scared," Alex said, rushing forward in a motherly fashion. Her invisibility fell away, allowing her and Max to be seen. "You're free now."

Several of the prisoners held their heads up at this. They were so many and so little. Cam could only stare at their starved bodies and deprived eyes. Some were losing chunks of their hair while others were mutilated with scars and burns. Nausea crept upon Cam as she imagined the horrors they had been subjected to. Alex kneeled beside one of the prisoners, a little girl with clumps of black curls. Cam guessed that she was their primary target as she was the only female child.

"Hi," Alex said in a soothing voice. "I'm Alex."

"I'm Amelia," the girl said timidly. Her voice rang through the cell like a chorus of high bell chimes. "They say they're going to hurt us more. They'll find us, if we run."

"No, they won't. See all of these people with me?" Alex asked with a gentle smile. "It's their job to protect you."

Cam remained outside of the cell. Its walls were dark, and they loomed in on her. She could not bring herself to enter with the others as they coaxed the remaining prisoners out. Something in the desolate confines of the battered cell had dissolved her courage. Tom remained by her side, noticing her discomfort. Angry as she was with him, she was still grateful for the gesture. She caught his eye and was in the process of opening her mouth to speak when an alarm sounded.

"Quick! Follow us," Krytos said to the prisoners.

The Equintas shuffled the people down the hallway toward the solitary cells. Krytos stood by and watched them file out. The freed prisoners, realizing that it was not some trick of the Gi, ran down the hall with more urgency.

"Please, help!" a feeble voice cried from behind Cam. "I beg you, don't leave us!"

Cam's breath stuck in her chest. Time slowed as she turned toward the voice. Down the hall, a few cells away, Vern's thin hand was prying between the bars. Sound fell away as her legs began to move of their own will. Somewhere behind her, Tom's voice was issuing a cry of return, but her feet continued to propel her until she stood before Vern's cell.

"Please, help us," Vern said from behind the bars. "Cal!"

"Cal?" Cam repeated in confusion as she grabbed the bars. Then her eyes widened. The reason why he thought he recognized her was because he was confusing her with her mother, Calliope. "Do you mean *Calliope*?"

"Yes, yes!" Vern shouted in earnest. "Please!"

Cam saw the rest of the Equintas running away from her, toward the departure point. They were whispering and pushing the new members through the exit route, too busy to notice Cam was not with them. She looked up at Tom. He was staring at her, imploring her to follow. She shook her head, apologetic for what she was about to do, as she turned back to Vern.

"Cam, no!" Tom cried, running with his phenomenal speed though he knew he was too late.

She raised her hand to the bars and let the fire burn freely. Melted steel fell quickly into puddles as she applied more pressure to ensure the hurry. Within seconds, she had created a hole large enough for them to exit.

"Come on," Cam shouted. "Run!"

Not needing further instruction, the prisoners ran toward the Equintas. Two children, three adults, and two elders rushed by in the direction she was indicating. Their faces held no expressions, merely the wide-eyed look of a long time prisoner not yet believing freedom had come. From up ahead, Krytos was staring at her with icy eyes.

"Cam!" Tom said, grasping her shoulders forcefully. "What the hell do you think you're doing?"

"Don't pretend like you don't secretly approve," she said.

Tom stared.

"Well, what the hell do you think *you're* doing?" she asked, after a moment. "Come on!"

They ran forward with the rest until they were standing in one of the solitary cells. Krytos had created another door in the back of the empty cube. He stood solemnly, watching Cam as she past. The sirens whirred, and they could hear a multitude of footsteps coming toward them. She entered then Krytos followed her through as the portal closed swiftly behind them, returning to its original state as a cement wall.

•

Cam's second trip through the portal was just as jarring as the first. Images flew by her eyes at breakneck speed. The result of the tumultuous journey left her so disoriented that, upon landing, she walked straight into the passenger side mirror of the truck. Her nose started bleeding in a fashion that was excessively dramatic to the small but embarrassing injury.

"You're bleeding!" Alex exclaimed. She rushed over and touched Cam's cheek.

"I'm fine," Cam said as she pinched the bridge of her nose. Alex tilted her head back.

"Well, it looks like it's already stopping," Alex said as she examined Cam. "Yes, it's just about done. Here. Use this to clean yourself up."

Alex handed her a plaid handkerchief.

"Thanks," Cam said, wiping the blood from across her upper lip.

"Listen up everyone. Since we only have one truck, we'll have to do this in two or three trips," Krytos said. His eyes settled on Cam who refused to meet his gaze. "We'll take the women and children first. Tom and Gun, could you please assist them?"

Cam watched as they helped them into the truck bed. Their bodies were so frail that they could barely walk, but their mood was a dramatic statement to the new hope they were experiencing. After they had been seated, Krytos quickly took his place next to them. Tommy shifted the truck into gear, and they took off with a dramatic peal of the tires.

Cam glanced over the handkerchief as she sat on the outskirts of the clearing, alone. Alex and Max were speaking to the rest of newcomers, regaling tales of the food they would enjoy once they reached the town. Martin was sitting cross-legged in his plum-colored robes. Cam noticed that the bold, outlandish hues of his clothes actually played well with his coloring as they offset the shock of his steel blue hair and large mint green eyes. He was holding a wildflower, casting it in different colors using his illusions.

Cam looked around again and numbly realized that two people were watching her. The first was Tom, who was glancing over at her in regular intervals. He was attempting to appear impassive, but the glint of irritation in his eyes gave away his true feelings. She tried to ignore him, but was only marginally successful.

The other person watching her was Vern. He didn't even bother trying to be discrete in his state of confusion and shock. He had thought she was her mother. He appeared to be working out how to differentiate the two of them. Cam had questions for him, and she knew he must have some for her as well, but her guilt over what she had done was weighing down on her. She didn't have the strength to maintain, let alone initiate, any type of difficult conversation.

After a couple of hours of uncomfortable silence, Cam heard the truck rumbling up the steep mountainside. They again loaded as many people as possible into the bed.

"Do you all mind waiting again?" Krytos asked, eyeing the full truck. "One of you may have my seat, but the other two will still have to wait for Tommy to come back up."

Gun, Tom, and Cam were the only ones not in the truck.

"No, Krytos," Gun said. "We don't mind waiting."

"Are you sure?" Krytos asked.

They all nodded.

"Okay," Krytos said as his eyes fixed on Cam. "See you at the bottom of the mountain."

Then he jumped into the back of the truck, and the familiar noise of tires skidding against the wet ground echoed around them. The sound soon faded, and the clearing became painfully quiet once more.

Tom continued to give Cam sideways glances with the same look on his face. Gun was standing far away from both of them at the mouth of the clearing. He was staring out over the valley of Rebel's Glade and was effectively ignoring them both. Cam retreated to the rock she had been sitting on earlier as she tried to ease her tired mind.

The silence slowly became more and more weighted. Tom's fingers began to twitch between the stares that had slowly evolved to glares. The frustration grew in his eyes as his jaw began to clench. Cam stared at the ground in an attempt to ignore him, but it was increasingly difficult as the hours crept by and her anxiety worsened. Soon, he had added knuckle cracking and sighs of exasperation to his angry routine. To make matters worse, his irritation was beginning to irritate her. The anger that had been originated by his actions suddenly erupted as he added variable foot tapping to his angry twitches.

"You know you could stop that any day now," Cam said to Tom with scathing force. "I will cut off your toes, one by one, if you crack your knuckles or grind your jaw one more time. Also, for the love of all that is as good and wonderful as cotton candy, please stop staring at me with that stupid look on your face. If you have something to say to me, then say it. If not, just stand still and be quiet like you normally would because I cannot take any more of your annoying crap. Remember that I am not unwilling to hit you to make you stop."

"Go ahead then, hit me. It wouldn't be the first absurd and ridiculous thing you've done," Tom retorted. "Actually, it wouldn't be the second or the third or—"

"Seriously?" Gun interjected. "Are you guys really going to do this now?"

"I would tell you to stay out of it, but I think you already know that that's the best course of action," Cam said as she turned back to Tom. "And you! Just say whatever it is you're trying to say!"

"Fine," Tom said, walking up to her. "What the hell did I ever do to you?"

"What?"

"Haven't I been your friend?" Tom asked. "Haven't I taken care of you? Supported you and tried to help you save Ke's life when every ounce of rationality in my body told me to do otherwise?"

"Again, what?"

"What you did in the cells was so unbelievably stupid that I've now lost my frame of reference for what stupidity really means," Tom said. "How could you endanger the Equintas like that?"

"You wouldn't understand," Cam said. "No, I rescind that. You wouldn't even try to understand."

"You're being so unreasonable. You can't even apologize for being stupid," Tom said exasperated. "I mean, don't you realize that the Equintas is my family?"

"Don't you realize that I don't have one?" Cam shouted at him as she thought of Vern mistaking her for her mother.

"So, you'd take mine away? Maybe I should tell Krytos that saving Ke is foolish and that his safety is irrelevant," Tom said. "See how you like it."

Cam screamed at the mention of Ke and her hands ran alight with flame as any semblance of willpower she had had vanished hours ago. Tom took a step back.

"Well, maybe I should burn you to ashes," she said with zealous wink. "See how you like it."

A furious gale whipped downward, swirling the air in dangerous spirals that rapidly became tornadoes.

"Now, come on guys. Is it necessary to involve powers?" Gun asked. They glared at him icily. "Never mind, I'll just stay out of it."

"He has a point, Cam. It's not necessary to use powers," he said. She frowned and flung a fireball toward him. He dodged it with ease and scoffed. "Now, that was just needless violence."

"Needless?" Cam asked. "Like you think I've been this whole time?"

She shot another jet of fire that flew toward him like an arrow. He sent it ricocheting back with a gust-fueled strike. Not expecting such a riposte, she barely evaded the attack. She threw her body to one side, rolled sideways through the dirt and shot another stream of flames toward him. This time he let it come within arm's reach before deflecting it. In an elegant flash, he brought both hands together and pushed a blast outward, effectively extinguishing the fire.

"You know, I really wish that I knew what you were talking about so I could properly retort," Tom said. "What do you mean 'like I think you've been this whole time?'"

"Stop playing games just because someone else is here to hear you," Cam said, looking sideways at Gun. Gun, having decided with resolution to not get involved, backed up even further. "You know exactly what I'm talking about, Tom."

"No, I don't," he said. "But I do know that you're psychotic. Between all of your damn mood swings, I've lost track of what you imagined I did in order to deserve your wrath."

Cam laughed dryly. Dancing flames of orange burst from her fingertips and ran up each arm. The fire glowed and cast threatening shadows against the earth. The impending sunset lengthened her shadow into distortion as it wove together with Tom's retreating ones to form the likeness of a demon.

"You seriously don't remember what you said to me at the river?" Cam asked annoyed. "Did you get a lobotomy in the last week?"

Tom's eyes flitted over her face. Then he eyed the menacing flames on her arms that had grown high enough to resemble wings. His mouth twitched wordlessly.

"I really don't think he knows what you're talking about," Gun said, chiming in. They both turned to face him. Together their power was not only palpable but frightening. Air and fire swayed together in a song of threatening supremacy. "Actually, I should just shut up and stay out of it as I readily recognize the fact that you both could kill me with ease right now."

Cam rolled her eyes and turned back to Tom.

"You know what I'm talking about, Tom."

"No, I really don't and I'm getting so tired of your crap!"

The words rang in her ears, familiar and painful. She looked up at him as resolve chased away her other thoughts.

"Then leave me alone and you won't have to deal with it anymore! That's what you said you were going to do anyway!"

Tom shook his head, throwing his arms in the air.

"Cam, you've officially lost your shit," he said. "What the hell are you talking about?"

It was the wrong thing to say, and he knew it instantly. She had barely been able to contain the true fury that ran under her skin and now it breathed with new life. Her eyes flooded silver and the fire doubled in height. Gun fell backward as Tom angled himself defensively.

"Stop lying, Thomas."

The flames leapt from her arms in one immense explosion, and the fire flew from her outstretched hands toward him. Her eyes were full of rage as the massive, blazing projectile flew. He thrust both of his hands in front of him. The small tornadoes that had been lightly encircling them joined together as he channeled it out toward the fiery blast.

The impact of the two separate energies colliding was cataclysmic.

Both Cam and Tom were pushed backward several feet. Their shoes left long marks in the ground going in opposite directions. Funnels of fire and rushing wind melded together. The result of the combination generated a tornado that burned wildly and swept an unpredictable path around the clearing. Tom and Cam both scrambled, trying to regain control of their powers. Gun watched, mouth slack, as he retreated even further from the clearing.

"Cam, look at what you did!" Tom shouted.

"What *I* did?"

The tornado grew and began to produce the ominous clamors of impending disaster.

"Well, yes, it is what *you* did," Tom said, trying to extinguish the fiery tornado that was gaining speed. "You attacked me first, thus placing the blame pretty squarely on you."

"Maybe I attacked you first, today," Cam said, unconsciously fueling the fire in the tornado. "But I didn't start this."

"Damn it, Cam!" Tom said. "Grow up already and realize that I don't have the faintest hint of a fraction of an idea of what you are talking about. Drop it. You're making yourself angry for no reason."

"No, fuck you, Tom!" Cam screamed. "You said everything I said you said and more."

The fire grew hotter as the orange waves rolled with the wind in a dangerous coil. Tom stared up at the monster they had created then back at her.

"Well, then I'm sorry," he said after a few moments and his tone was unwaveringly sincere. "I want to tell you I'm sorry specifically for whatever it is that I did, but I can't. I have no idea what I did, but ever since that day the mission was announced...you've been different."

"Because of what you said, dumbass," Cam said, thinking of the lecture Tom had given as he told her he was superior to her.

"Again, I don't know what I said to make you this mad. But I miss you," he said, his voice almost pleading. "We're not just two warriors fated to fight this war side by side. We're friends. Just tell me what I did. Please. For the mission's sake, for Ke's."

His words now directly opposed what he had said to her that day, but something in the weight of his statement seemed truthful. The fire relinquished itself from her body, dousing itself in whispers. The now sizable inferno flew up into the sky, exploding over them in a shower of tiny, orange sparks. The velocity of the energy's sudden direction change caused the two of them to fly toward each other. They hit with an echoing thud and fell to the ground.

Cam looked up and saw baby flares of orange sprinkling the air. The wind had died down and the mountaintop was oddly still. She tasted blood then realized her molars had crushed through her tongue. Her nose was bleeding profusely once again and the skin on her forearm was raw. She looked over at Tom who was pushing himself into a sitting position. His lip was cut and a variety of abrasions decorated his skin. Then her attention was snagged by the sound of brakes and halting tires. A car door flew open and a tall figure ran out.

"Thomas? What happened? Are you okay?" came Volpi's voice from the entrance to the clearing.

"Please let that voice be an auditory hallucination," Cam muttered.

"What did she do to you? I saw the fire," Volpi said. She was leaning over him, dabbing his cut lip. Her nails, polished scarlet, matched the color of his blood.

"She didn't do anything," Tom said, standing up. He glanced at Cam then reneged. "Well, it wasn't *all* her fault."

"Don't lie for her, Thomas," Volpi said vehemently while staring daggers at Cam. Then she added in a placating coo. "You're hurt."

"No, I'm fine," he said, pushing her away. "Cam, are you okay?"

"Dandy," Cam said as she tried to stop the flow of blood from her nose. Gun helped her up and they walked over to where the truck was. Volpi ran up to Gun, ignoring Cam completely.

"What happened?" Volpi demanded. "Thomas won't say anything."

"I think it's pretty self-explanatory, Volpi," Gun said plainly. "You saw it...fire tornado."

The blood flow began to slow from Cam's nose as they neared the truck. Tom walked over to them, trying to disguise his new limp.

"You *are* hurt!" Volpi exclaimed. "Gun, help me get him into the truck."

"You're being ridiculously overdramatic," Tom said, trying to fight them off. "I'm fine!"

Cam stopped, trying to stay out of the way as they helped Tom into the bed of the truck. Then Volpi walked over to Cam, her expression vicious. Cam's energy was gone and she was too slow to react as Volpi slid a set of brass knuckles from her back pocket. They were silver with Vinestra carvings over the knuckles in the shape of human skulls. Cam heard them click over Volpi's delicately polished fingers.

She hit Cam once across the left side of her face. Cam's feet lost their hold on the earth, and she felt her body fall backward. Her head struck the ground, and the skin on her already raw arms was shaved down even further.

"Volpi, what the hell?" Tom shouted, rising from the truck.

"You are the stupidest person I have ever met!" Volpi spat at Cam, ignoring Tom. "The Gi could've seen you! You're just lucky Martin decided to come back with me. If he hadn't, then they would've seen that 'fire tornado' you made for sure. As it was, he barely had enough time to cast an illusion—"

Cam looked over and saw Martin, a dozen yellow flowers in his hand. He smiled sheepishly at her.

"—and all this after you broke an *extra* cell!" Volpi continued. "How idiotic are you? I never wanted you here. I had a bad feeling about you from the start. This is not where you belong. You aren't the hero we deserve. You should be saving us, not putting us in more danger!"

Something in the way she said her last statement, sent chills up Cam's spine. She recoiled at the words, remembering Tom saying the same thing to her at the river.

"Volpi, back off!" Tom shouted at her.

"Yeah, calm down," Gun said. "Let's not do this here."

Volpi looked back at them.

"Fine," Volpi conceded. "Let's go."

Gun ran over to Cam. Tom looked like he was about to as well, but Volpi pushed him back down. Cam felt something in her mouth. It was hard, like a small rock. She spit it out and saw that it was one of her teeth, covered in saliva and bright red blood. She felt her face and knew, before she felt it, that the flesh on her cheek had been bitten completely through. Rage began to boil in her veins again, but she didn't have the energy to do anything about it. Gun lifted her into the truck bed and she leaned away from them, holding the injured side of her face. Volpi was still, ineffectually, trying to tend to Tom.

"Cam, you're bleeding a lot," Tom said, finally breaking free of Volpi's grip.

Cam ignored him and hid her broken flesh. The incident had left more than physical marks and she did not feel like sharing those. Volpi's anger returned at the snub Tom had given her. She rounded on Gun.

"You know this is partly your fault, too," Volpi snapped at Gun while shaking a finger in his face.

"Me?" Gun asked incredulously.

"You could've stopped them!" Volpi said. "Or, at least, you could've done something!"

Gun raised his eyebrows and gave her an exasperated sigh.

"Okay, maybe I wasn't clear with the imagery earlier, Volpi," Gun said slowly and deliberately as if he were speaking to a child. "*Fire tornado*."

Having no retort, Volpi resigned herself to silence with a roll of her eyes. The trip back was quiet, and Cam was left to her thoughts of what reprimand waited for her upon their arrival.

# Chapter 15
## Consequences

They pulled up to the outskirts of town after the sky had been thoroughly drowned in darkness. A thin veil of transparent clouds floated over the stars, filtering the moon's glow. The truck squealed to a stop and they departed. The town was quiet as Cam glanced around at the small village with its few buildings and wondered where the new residents would sleeping that night. Kiri, the Equintas' lead architect, would be busy building new homes.

"Cam, let's go to Luanna and get you fixed up," Tom suggested. Volpi rolled her eyes, muttered something that sounded like "whatever" then left.

"I'd rather just go lie down," Cam said.

"You don't look so good," Gun added.

"What a wonderful thing to say! You've just made this the best day ever," she said sarcastically.

"Cam, seriously, just let me see it," Tom said, pulling her hand off her face.

"Whoa," Tom and Gun said together.

Both of them stared at her swollen face as if she were a two-headed, mutant puppy.

"Fine," she said, giving in. "Let's go to Luanna."

Tom and Gun followed her through the town to Luanna's house which also served as the town's clinic. The large patio was lined with benches and chairs, each one different from the rest. Cam managed to glimpse a canary yellow rocking chair, a simple wooden bench and a blue stool with delicate rosemaling before Tom pushed her onward. One of them knocked, but Cam was unaware of who as her wounded face was beginning to throb.

"Come in!"

Gun held the door open while Tom led her through. The living room was white and sterile. Six of the freed prisoners were milling around while Luanna was examining another. Cam stood awkwardly by little Amelia who sat on the ground, playing with an old telephone.

Amelia was only eight or nine. Her midnight black hair was frizzed and naturally set in tiny ringlets. She had olive-green eyes framed by a plane of porcelain white skin. She was sitting cross-legged and was staring intently at the phone.

Cam heard a small crackle as the phone was suddenly dismantled. Each piece of its structure was floating before Amelia, everything from the cord to the microphone to the hook switch. She smiled gleefully and leaned forward to examine them.

"So, she's the technopath," Gun remarked.

"She's not just a technopath, remember?" Tom said. "She's an infiltrator, too. Who knows what the extent of her gift is."

Amelia returned to her sitting position. Cam heard the crackle again and saw some of the parts reassemble. The remaining pieces fell discarded to the floor. Cam leaned forward, intrigued, as a voice began to speak through the headset.

"...and so the warmth of the Lord General's mercy could be seen in all. It can be seen in the faces of every man and woman, of every smiling child..."

Cam looked around the room. She saw six gaunt faces under stretched and graying skin. She saw Amelia sitting on the floor, her bones protruding from malnutrition.

"Is that a radio?" Tom asked Amelia. She looked over at him and nodded proudly.

"Uh-huh," Amelia said with a little smile. "It's not very good. I could make it better if I had more parts."

"Amelia, dear, it's your turn," Luanna said.

"Bye," Amelia said. She turned back to the phone, blinked once and the phone retook its normal configuration.

"So, why do you guys need a technopath so much?" Cam asked.

There was silence.

"Do you know why we don't break the cells more often?" Tom asked, finally.

"Krytos said it's because of the Gi," Cam said, thinking back. "He said the Equintas weren't prepared for more of them hunting us yet."

"Well, that's part of the reason," Gun muttered.

"What do you mean?" Cam asked.

"There are only two ways to get into the Ether," Tom continued. "You either have to be someone with access or you have to be able to hack their security system."

"So?"

"Since we didn't have a technopathic infiltrator..." Gun began. His voice trailed off, and he stumbled to find it again.

"We had to get someone with access," Tom finished. "That means we had to *kill* someone and steal their access."

Cam looked down at the ground, remembering the gouged eyeball and the bloody finger. She did not have a response so she made no attempt. They sat in silence for the next twenty minutes as Amelia and the others were examined. Cam was exhausted and she knew it was late. She had her head between her hands, her mind in the limbo between waking and sleeping, when she heard the front door open.

A nightly chill blew as Krytos walked in. He stood by the threshold until the last of the new residents had been examined and given vitamin supplements. Cam, meanwhile, slowly sank lower and lower into her seat as each minute passed. Soon, she was so low against the couch that she was slipping off the edge. Her trepidation increased to a freezing point as she watched the last patient leave.

"Now, Camilla, let me see you," Luanna said, gesturing for her to come have a seat.

"Hold on a minute, Luanna," Krytos said, holding up a halting hand. "Tom? Gun?"

Tom and Gun stood so quickly that Cam fell off the couch with a thud.

"While it's awfully nice of you two to stay," Krytos began, "I think that's it's about time you went home. I'd like to speak with Camilla, privately."

Gun didn't have to think twice.

"Okay, bye," he said while nearly sprinting for the door.

"You want me to leave, too?" Tom asked.

"Yes, Thomas," Krytos said.

Tom gave Cam a nod and a poorly attempted sympathetic glance then left. Cam sat awkwardly in front of the sofa as Krytos approached.

"Did you come here to sit on the floor?" Krytos asked her. "It would appear that you have some pressing injuries that need tending to?"

Cam stood and walked over to the chair Luanna used for examinations with her eyes fixed on her shoelaces.

"Okay, Camilla, part of my power is the ability to see beneath your skin like an x-ray. I'm just going to touch your face," she said. "It may be a bit jostling."

"Um, okay," Cam said.

She felt Luanna place a hand on her. Luanna closed her eyes and a chill ran under Cam's skin. The coolness intensified around her swollen and injured tongue.

"That's a pretty deep cut on your tongue," Luanna noted. "Wow, you nearly bit a chunk clean off."

Cam nodded mutely in agreement.

"Funny how you weren't injured when I left you guys at the top of the mountain," Krytos said. "How did you sustain that injury?"

"Well, it was sustained at the same time as the bloody nose and the raw palms."

"Yes, Martin conveyed it to me as a 'fire tornado' or something like that," Krytos said with a small grin. "You can explain that at your convenience."

"There was a little misunderstanding with Tom. You know, my fire, his tornado..." Cam began. "But it was really my fault."

"Oh," Luanna said suddenly. "There's a fracture on your left maxilla."

"Was that also obtained in the 'fire tornado' incident?" Krytos asked.

Cam thought about it. What good would it be to tell him about Volpi? Hadn't Cam deserved it? She glanced up at Krytos from the corner of her eye. He was expressionless and immovable.

"Yes," she lied.

"The two of you generate quite a force," Krytos said. "Is there anything you can do to heal it, Luanna?"

"Not without using a scalpel," she said, opening her eyes which had become silver. "It isn't really necessary though and it may increase her recuperation time. I recommend we let it heal naturally."

"Sounds good. Thank you, Luanna," Krytos nodded before returning his attention to Cam. "Had you two ever combined powers like that before?"

"No," Cam said.

Luanna withdrew from Cam, blinking to regain her normal state.

"It's something you two should work on," Krytos said.

"Sure thing," Cam said, trying to avoid his gaze.

"Here are some painkillers and a special bandage," Luanna said, handing her a white pouch. "Take one of the painkillers every four to six hours but no more, okay?"

Cam nodded.

"I gave you only one bandage," Luanna continued. "Put it on your face tonight. The skin should be almost fully healed by tomorrow morning with just the one but, if you need more, let me know."

"Thanks," Cam said as she took the pouch.

Krytos moved in front of her and stared at her broken face.

"Why'd you lie about your facial fracture?" Krytos asked.

"What?" Cam's eyes snapped up to his.

"It's rather obvious you were lying about how you got it," Krytos said.

"I may have omitted the truth," Cam conceded.

"You mean you lied through omission," Krytos said.

"I got punched," Cam said flatly. "Not a big deal."

"By who?"

"The tall, self-centered one."

"Volpi?"

"Yup."

Krytos nodded.

"Why did she do that?" he asked.

Cam opened her mouth but no response came. She looked around the room, searching for the best way to answer. Krytos waited patiently while he toyed with the spiraling scars on his arms.

"I guess because I deserved it," Cam said.

"Deserved it how?"

"Because I broke the extra cell and because I used my powers in an argument with Tom," she said. "He says I'm impulsive and I guess he's right."

"Do you understand the ramifications of your actions in the Ether?" Krytos asked. "They'll be looking for us even more now. Members of the Equintas could die because of you."

"I understand," Cam said, her breaths coming quickly. What else could she say? "And I'm sorry."

"Good," Krytos said as he began to walk away.

"Wait," Cam said, turning toward him. "That's it?"

He turned back.

"Yes, that's it. I think you understand the consequences well enough. I can't do more than hope that you learn from your mistakes because, if you don't, then I'm going to have to restrict you from any future missions," Krytos said. "By the way, I don't accept *any* kind of corporal punishment from *any* member of the Equintas. She had no right."

Cam nodded solemnly.

"Go get some rest," he said.

He left, striding swiftly from the room and out of the house. Cam followed, walking out into the cold night with her heart still racing. She went back to Gun, Sam and Volpi's house. Her heart continued to pound as nausea from the creeping anxiety began to build. She went to the restroom, shakily put the bandage on her cheek and took one of the painkillers. Then she crawled onto the sofa and pulled up the quilt. Only after an hour of sweeping anxiety, after the painkiller had begun to wash its numbing ease over her, was she able to fall asleep.

●

*Cam stood in a hallway, decorated like a birthday cake in yellows and creams. A door at the end stood slightly ajar. She walked to it. The hallway lengthened itself for over an hour before abruptly ceasing to allow her entry. A karate movie blared from the television and a man was sitting on the sofa.*

*"Gun?"*

*He turned to her.*

*"Why are you here...so far into this place?"*

*"I'm not sure, actually," she replied.*

*"Well, then why are you running?"*

*Cam frowned.*

*"But I'm not running."*

*"Oh, that's right," he said. "You're not running yet."*

*"Running from what?"*

*"From the thing that's been chasing you," he said. "Though, I can help with the fighting. I'm supposed to be fairly decent with weapons."*

*"Thanks for the offer," Cam said. "But nothing's following me."*

*"It's steering you in the wrong direction."*

*"No, it's not. I'm fine."*

*"Whatever. I tried," Gun sighed. "Personally, I always thought this was a fight not a race, but if you insist on running, then wheel your little self around and run that way."*

*Gun pointed toward the sliding door opposite her. Cam felt a small pull lurch her body forward. Her ghostly reflection shone back at her off of the glass. The urge to move suddenly became overwhelming as she found herself pushing the door open.*

*A cold breeze struck. She was in a warehouse, poorly lit by the fluorescent lamps encircling her head.*

*"You can stop running," came a deep voice.*

*She spun and saw Krytos. The door she had just used was gone, replaced by endless rows of storage racks and the occasional lift car.*

*"You need help," he said.*

*"I'm okay."*

*"No, you're not," he said. "You need to become stronger. I can help you."*

*"I'm already strong," she said. "I don't think I need your help."*

*Her confusion continued as Krytos scoffed.*

*"You need a friend, Camilla," Krytos said. "Someone who can stop you from running away, stop you from being alone."*

*Cam stared at him, anger boiling, as her muscles tensed. Then she turned and ran. The other side of the storage room morphed, and a blue door began to materialize. She kicked it open and tore inside.*

*"Cam? Are you okay?"*

*She reacted quickly to the sound, jumping back. The room she had entered was a hospital examination room. She heard water dripping from the faucet as she saw Sam sitting in an office chair. She automatically backed away.*

*"Do you need help with something?" he asked.*

*"Why does everyone keep asking me that?"*

*Sam rose from his chair.*

"Maybe they can see what you cannot," he said. She stopped and, cautiously, searched for an exit.

"I don't understand," she replied.

"You know, I can help you if you're hurt," Sam said.

"Thanks," she said slowly. "Pretty sure I'm okay though."

"But you are without your greatest asset," he mused, his tone almost mocking.

He smiled as he patted her on the head. She shoved his hand away, taking a step back. A metal door appeared like a warning, and she scampered through it.

The sound of crushing club music pressed down on her with devastating barbarity. Strobe lights flashed and flickered, but something was terribly wrong. The air was dense as she breathed in a sickening, metal smell. The lights flared again, and she saw that the club was filled with mutilated bodies. A figure stood ahead of her.

"Who's there?"

"I have very often found that bloodshed is necessary, you know?"

"Volpi? Is that you?"

"Who else could do this much damage?" Volpi asked. "Actually, you could. Couldn't you? You've got that same kind of rage."

Cam stopped herself from responding.

"You killed them all?"

"Singlehandedly," Volpi said smugly.

Volpi grinned, raising her eyebrows in a look of self-satisfaction.

"That's horrible," Cam said.

"Please. It's only vengeance. Or is that too far outside your realm of understanding?" Volpi asked. "You know, I can help with that when the time comes."

"Oh, right," Cam said, rolling her eyes. "Everyone keeps telling me that. What do they know of what I need?"

"They're just willing to help you get revenge."

"I don't think I want that kind of help," Cam said.

"Oh, wait, I understand it now," Volpi said. "If you had his help, it wouldn't be as sweet. I get that."

"I meant that I don't want to kill anyone," Cam said.

"But you might have to," Volpi said. "You might have to destroy a childhood or two because, if you can't, then others will die."

Cam looked up and met Volpi's eye.

*"You mean Ke," Cam said.*

*"Yes."*

*Cam ran, pushing Volpi aside as she found a new room behind the DJ stage and entered it. She flew into a narrow alleyway where darkened windows loomed high around her. She turned down multiple, isolated alleyways before coming upon a lonely vendor stall with a sign reading "Keys and Other Illegal Things" over its many display cases. The stall sat in the middle of the alley beside an overflowing dumpster and a fire escape.*

*Cam looked behind her and saw the void, signaling her journey's only possible direction. She turned back and approached cautiously. She peered behind it and saw that it was unmanned save for a little crab. Its black eyes blinked rapidly as it gestured toward the various wares it had on display. Cam stepped closer and saw that each case was lined with assorted keys. The crab motioned eagerly to the key fixed directly in front of it.*

*"You want me to open this?"*

*The crab began jumping enthusiastically in place. Cam shrugged and undid the clasp. She lifted the glass lid and ran her hand on the velvety inside before removing the small, silver key.*

*"What's this for?"*

*The crab held up a sign that read: It's the key.*

*"Sort of gathered that on my own," she said, turning the key over. "Let's try for a bit more precision. What does this key go to?"*

*A thunderous flash of light burst from the sky as a cacophonous explosion resounded in the city. Cam shut her eyes as dark clouds mushroomed upward, blanketing the sun in a crimson filter. The same stone door from her previous dreams had crashed into the city. Cam stopped and turned to the door.*

*The crab crawled up her shirt sleeve, coming to rest on her shoulder. It motioned for her to go to the new door. She listened to the screams rising from the crash site. Her body shuddered before she ran toward the alley's exit.*

*The screams were louder in the street. There had been no pain for those whose corpses now covered the sidewalk. Their blood trickled slowly, first into the sewers and then into the tree-lined avenue. The sickening stench worsened as the heat intensified and the streets ran scarlet. She plodded into the red and gold city with apprehension, her instinct to run. The door creaked open at her sudden presence, and a torrent of bright red blood rushed forth.*

*The mangled bodies of the Equintas tumbled out, broken and dismembered. Gun's drifting body was the nearest. His intestines drooped over the thick, bloated mass of his tongue as Volpi's and Sam's bodies followed. The street was red with the display of horror. A tear of regret fell to the hot pavement as the consequences of every bad decision she had ever made rolled down the gutter.*

## CHAPTER 16
## CRASH

After breakfast, the Equintas mingled with its expanded population. They had added fourteen members to their ranks. Cam met Deanna, the etholopath, and Ronen, the musician. She met Paula, the sculptor, and Nate, the biologist, but the person she wanted to speak to the most had slipped out earlier. She left and walked around the town until she came to the edge of the camp. A huddled figure was before her, sitting on a log bench.

"Vern?"

"Camilla," he said enthusiastically. "Come! Sit."

Cam took the rock opposite him and smiled. Her nerves were on edge as she stared at him with questions swimming in her mind.

"How are you doing, dear?" Vern asked with a wrinkled smile.

"I wanted to ask you something," Cam said, "about Calliope."

"Ah, yes," Vern said with a look of forlorn. "I'm sorry about that. You just look so much like her. She was in the cell with me, you know. I just wanted to see her again so badly that I did."

"Well, it was an easy mistake to make," Cam said, "because I'm her daughter."

Vern looked up at her. His eyes were wide as he sputtered.

"Your mother? Of course! After all, you have her smile."

"Wow, really? Thank you," Cam said, grinning. "How long did you know her for?"

"For five years or so," Vern said. "She always told us stories. She was fantastic at the art of storytelling. She told me that someday the world would turn and that we would be saved. She told us that we only had to stay alive long enough to be there."

Cam frowned and thought of something Alex had said earlier.

*Milo mentioned someone who told him stories. Told him that he would be saved and that all he had to do was live to see that day.*

Cam sighed as she stared at Vern. The notion that her mother had been alive for so many years after she had thought she were dead was unbearable. Those were years lost for her and Ke. Years that had been taken from them. Her heart began to quicken its pace but not from her usual anxiety. It came from resolution. Her body was preparing for battle.

"Thank you, Vern," Cam said.

"For what? You saved me," Vern replied.

"No, I think *you* saved *me*," Cam said.

She smiled at him as she headed off toward the house, her footprints leaving soggy imprints in the soil. The sky rumbled, and she looked up. Rain began to fall, and she let it cleanse her in preparation for what would come.

•

The rain began to fall that afternoon as Cam sat on the front porch of the house, listening to the water splash on the ground.

It was almost unfathomable that her mother had died, not of the false sickness, but at the hands of the Ether's scientists. Her mind involuntarily flashed images of the terrible ways in which her life may have been stolen. The thought served as a reminder of her desperation to save Ke from either fate.

Memories of the Slums, of Ke and Mel, swirled endlessly over her. She tried to imagine them both whole and with her among the beauty of Rebel's Glade. Mel would love the scenery, and Ke would love the people.

"Cam," Gun said.

She glanced at him in acknowledgement as he sat beside her.

"I just wanted to tell you that, well," he stopped and lit a cigarette, "that I think you did alright yesterday."

Her eyes snapped to his as her brow furrowed.

"Really?"

"I know you broke protocol but, to me, it doesn't really matter now," Gun said. "We successfully saved more people from the evil crap that the Gi do in there."

"You mean I was lucky that we were successful," Cam said as she thought of her new friends who could have easily lost their lives as a result of her foolishness.

"Maybe but I'm still glad," Gun said. "Did you know I spent my whole childhood in the labs?"

Cam shook her head.

"I was five when they threw me in there," Gun said. "I used to live in a Second Tier neighborhood in Tengoku. My best friend was Golden Tier and her family had a rare slice of pure Vinestra they kept on display. One day, we were playing around. We broke the case and both accidently touched it. Her grandfather found us right after."

"Was her grandfather powerful with the Gi?"

"Yes and, as it was, our friendship was frowned upon," Gun said. "You know how the Gi feels about non-whites. I'm a mix of a lot of races and I look it. They tolerated me for her sake but touching Vinestra drew the line."

"That's awful."

"Next thing I know, my parents had been killed and I was sent to an orphanage," Gun continued. "They wanted to cover up what had happened. In the schoolyard, I started picking fights and that's when I discovered my power with weapons. Then the Gi found out and carted me off to the labs. They did some really bad things to me in there. By the time I was twelve, I had lost hope and was thinking of ways to kill myself. That's when Krytos broke my cell. He wasn't looking for anyone in there, but he had done it anyway in addition to the cell they'd already freed."

"Wait, so Krytos did what I did? Why?"

"Don't know, never asked," Gun said. "I'm just grateful he did."

He exhaled. Cam watched the smoke rise into the rafters.

"So, what happened to the girl? Your friend?" Cam asked.

"Nothing, I suspect," Gun said. "I never saw her again. She was my only real friend in that stupid city. She taught me how to string bow. I still think about her sometimes, Rhea Murphy."

Cam froze at the name. Gun quietly stamped out his cigarette, not noticing her astonishment.

"Anyway, I have to get going. Got to help with the latest shipment from Birmings," he said, standing. "I just, you know, wanted to let you know that I think I get why you did it."

He placed a friendly hand on her shoulder before he left. The rain began to fall more and more heavily, until all she could hear were tiny water bombs detonating against the town of Rebel's Glade. Water pooled around the fire pit and the trees swayed in the stormy breeze, moving with the will of the wind.

The quiet was eroding the calm she had tethered herself to. She had not spoken to Tom since the previous day when she was at Luanna's. She had seen him at breakfast where they had made awkward eye contact. Neither one of them really knew what to say to mend the friendship. In the distance, the trees began to sway more and more violently. Then a tumultuous pain came crashing down upon her.

Her heart was beating so fast that she was unable to hear anything else but its constant, quickening beat. She took sharp breaths whenever the pain would loosen its hold long enough for her to manage it. She moved to stand and another thunderous stab struck her and she fell sideways off the porch.

*Maybe it's time for you to wake up.*

She barely noticed the physical fall as she was concentrating on the mental one. The anchor that had helped control her, keep her fixed in reality was not there to break her fall. Where she normally would have crash landed into the arms of her best friend, she was just falling beyond the boundaries of sanity.

*FALL OR JUMP, CAMILLA?*

She wasn't sure how long she had been laying sideways in the mud and rain when she came to. Due to the weather and time of evening however, nobody saw her episode.

Her head throbbed as she pushed herself up on her elbow. The rain was still crashing down with tumultuous force. She looked down at where she had been laying and saw a Camilla-sized crater in the mud, two inches deep. She rolled her tongue over her bottom lip, tasting blood. Her arms were raw from the nail marks that she could not remember inflicting on herself.

She was weak and her head was aching as she stood up. She dragged herself up the porch stairs and into the house. Gun and Sam were in the living room. They were playing cards. Cam ducked her head and walked straight to the restroom. She was relieved that they had not noticed her extremely disheveled state.

"Watch it," Volpi said as Cam ran into her.

Cam ignored her and kept walking.

"Hey, I was talking to you," Volpi said. "What? Now you don't have common sense *or* manners? Apologize."

Cam did not have the strength to deal with her. She was soaking wet, covered in mud and bloody. She turned and faced Volpi, who did a double-take at Cam's appearance.

"I am really not unwilling to hit you," Cam said, feeling a smile pull at the corner of her mouth. "Actually, I'm really not unwilling to do a bit more than just hit you."

A warm tingle emanated from her palms, but she kept the fire at bay. Volpi stared at Cam with her mouth parted in shock.

"Whatever," Volpi said. Much of the cockiness had dissipated from her voice. "You're freaking psycho."

"Maybe I am," Cam replied as the temperature in the little hallway began to rise. "Maybe today is the day you should test me on that."

She took a step forward, and Volpi backed away quickly, clearing her path. Cam took a quick shower then changed into something with long sleeves. She stared at the small star on her left cheek, the scar that Volpi had left behind. Then her eyes traveled down to the little bottle of painkillers sitting on the white countertop. She popped the cap off and threw four of them into her mouth.

She went into the living room where she watched Gun and Sam's game. Volpi had left swiftly after their confrontation according to Sam. Cam could feel the painkillers numbing her body and mind. It was nice to not have to think for a bit, to not hear the whispers. Up until the drugs had taken effect, she had been unable to concentrate on much else.

"Wonder why Tom's not here?" Gun pondered. Cam jumped at the sound of his name. The drugs had allowed her forget about their fight as well.

"Was he supposed to be here?" Cam asked.

"Yup," Gun said, taking a swig of his beer. "Bet he's with Volpi."

Sam looked up.

"Is that where she went?" Sam asked.

"Probably," Gun shrugged. "That's where she tends to go when she leaves like that."

"How do you know?" Sam asked.

"Tom complained about it," Gun said. "She's there all the time to 'ask Shun a training question.' Funny how she always goes there when everyone knows Shun's gone."

They fell silent for a few minutes until Cam said something in her inebriation that made everyone laugh. Then they decided to turn in for the night, leaving Cam to drift into dreamless sleep.

•

Two weeks passed in dull agony as her mental state deteriorated. In her boredom and need to avoid any prolonged silence, she had begun to write letters to Ke. It had become a daily ritual for her to sit at the river's edge and write whatever thought popped into her head.

*Dear Ke,*

*As always, I hope that you are still alive and that you'll read this someday.*

*Something tells me that you have to be.*

*But, at the same time, I don't want to get my hopes up or set myself up for disappointment. I think a smarter person would be accepting the inevitable, preparing for loss...but I'm not smart and I can't stop imagining the day when I'll come back to you with Aeraden, the day that I'll save you.*

*But what if I'm too late.*

*I can't stand this anymore! Too much time is passing. We're straddling the line of whether or not I'll make it to you in time. We need to do something. I'm tired of basic training. I know there are things I still have to learn, but there is too much dead time during the day where I could be doing something else.*

*It's during these times that I've been experiencing the "episodes." They were slowly getting worse but, now, they are almost impossible to manage. I never told you about them before because I didn't want to scare you and it seemed so unimportant at the time. But I'll never keep secrets from you again.*

*I haven't spoken to Tom in two days and, even then, it was only during a training session where I was apologizing for burning half of his hair off. Oops.*

*Shun's still gone. I think it's going on three weeks now. I have no idea where she's been but she's on mission, I suppose.*
   *I guess that's all I have to say for now.*
   *Well, here's to hoping that you're still breathing.*
   *Love, ~~Cam~~ Camilla of No Last Name*

Cam signed the letter, folded it into a triangle and set it in her pocket before putting her feet into the water. The river was cold but the shock was rejuvenating. She leaned forward and let the water rush numbly against her fingertips.

She contemplated going to the training field where she knew Tom would be. When his mother was gone, he assumed her position as instructor for hand-to-hand combat. Then she thought of all the things she wanted to say, the things she was able to articulate well in her head but that she would not be able to say aloud. Instead, she knew she would end up saying something that would be misinterpreted. She debated returning to the house when the horribly familiar feeling of panic hit her.

She had had worse attacks before but, still, it was never pleasant and never wanted. She desperately shoved her hand into the river sand, trying to find something to grab. Her other hand reached across her torso, clawing violently at the trees as she tried to find a hold. Breathing became difficult as she leaned back against a log.

"Cam?"

Her shaking intensified to hysterical tremors as she heard footsteps rushing to her side. Her eyes were shut, and she refused to open them because she knew who would be there when she did, knew that he would see her like this.

"Cam!" Tom shouted as she willed her eyelids to open.

She felt his hands on her shoulders, shaking her, as she trembled in agony. Her body began igniting violently as fire flared off her skin, extinguishing and relighting itself in rhythm to the spasms of her heartbeat. The air reeked of burning flesh. She looked down and saw Tom's blistered hands shaking her.

"No," she said, reality snapping back. She grabbed Tom's wrists and threw him back with surprising force. He flew backward several feet, falling partway into the river. She stood on shaky feet, her instincts screaming for escape. Her eyes were finally able to see and interpret reality again, but she was still falling.

*You're already drowning in it.*

Her eyes met Tom's, his widening until the blue irises were surrounded by a sea of white. She was unable to see what he was seeing, but she knew it was something terrible as the pain doubled, dull blades against exposed nerves.

ALL OF THIS IS YOUR FAULT. YOU CHOSE TO FALL.

She felt her heart beating in her throat and the strong urge to vomit.

STOP RUNNING AND FACE THIS!

Then she threw her head back and enormous flames jetted from her mouth.

She could only see the fire, could only feel the rising panic as flames burst from her fingertips. Her veins bulged from under her skin as she felt her feet lift off the ground. The torment grew devastating, and she found herself desperately wishing for death. She could not bear it anymore. She hovered above the river, flames flying freely from her.

"Cam!"

Then she felt a hard jolt as Tom's body collided with hers, knocking her to the ground. She landed with a thump as the fire died away and she found her body still. The pain remained but it had been reduced to a soft ache. She leaned back against a tree and slipped into a sitting position.

"Are you okay?" Tom asked.

She tried to nod as nausea rocked her.

"Uh huh," she mumbled, leaning forward to drink some of the river water.

"That's good," he said uneasily. "So, how often are you having the attacks now?"

Her eyes snapped to his.

"I'm not answering that as it's none of your business," she said, but then her expression grew suspicious. "Wait, how did you know this wasn't the first time?"

"You had them before," he said simply.

"Not to the extent that you would've noticed," she said, calling his bluff.

"Fine," Tom admitted. "Volpi told me."

Cam remembered the night of the first severe attack and the consequential confrontation in the hallway with Volpi.

"Oh, was she worried about me?" Cam asked sarcastically.

"Actually, you scared her," Tom said amused. "She came over right after, screaming about how you were going to kill her."

"Oh, right," Cam scoffed. "*I* was going to kill *her*."

They both laughed at the pure absurdity of it. It felt good to laugh with him again, but then a serious look washed over his face.

"Cam, what happened to us?" he asked. "To our friendship?"

"It fell apart," she replied stonily. "You know, things break."

"I suppose, but it's odd. We were really good friends," Tom said. "Our friendship was one of a kind, plus we're sort of tied together by destiny and all."

"Yeah," Cam said. "How many people can say their by chance friendship turned out to be a predetermined link that was established generations before their births?"

"Seriously, Cam, no games," he said. "What happened? What was it you think I did to you?"

"No games, huh? Please, like you really don't know."

"I *don't* know," Tom said. "But I don't want another argument that's going to lead to any fire and/or wind-fueled disasters. Could you please just say what I did wrong? I'm stupid, apparently, so I need it spelled out plainly."

She bit her lip.

"Fine," she said resolutely. "You were standing right there. You told me I was not being the hero you all deserved. You said I was weak and that I didn't deserve to be Edan's descendant. While tact has never been either one of our strong suits, I still thought it was rather ruthless."

She knew her tone was not as casual as she had intended it to be. She looked over at him, waiting for him to either deny it again or to apologize. Instead, a look of confusion flashed as his eyes darted back and forth in time with his thoughts. Then his eyes grew big and he laughed hollowly.

"Wow," he said. "That's downright cold...maybe a bit brilliant? No, no, it's just mean."

"Please say something comprehensible before I set you on fire," Cam said.

He laughed again as he faced her.

"You know how Volpi's kind of, well..." Tom said, struggling for the word.

"A bitch," Cam suggested. "If that's her power then I won't be shocked even a little bit."

"I was going to go with temperamental," Tom said. "But her power is similar in that fashion. She's a shape shifter."

Cam saw the pieces come together and groaned.

"So, she can make herself look like *anybody*?"

"Yes."

"Then that was her who told me all those very rude things?"

"Yes, apparently so."

"Wow," Cam said. "Bitchiness is definitely her power."

"I would agree," Tom nodded.

Cam stopped.

"Wait, so why did she do all of that?" Cam asked, pausing as she contemplated.

"I wouldn't know what's going on in that crazy lady's head," Tom said.

"Did she think you and I were together *together*?" Cam wondered aloud. "Was she trying to break up our nonexistent romantic relationship?"

"Again, I don't want to delve into the horror house that is Volpi's jacked up brain," Tom said. "Drop it."

"When I first met her, she mentioned something about this spot at the river being yours and hers only," Cam continued, ignoring him. "Then she does all of this irrationally jealous evil scheming..."

"The mystery was solved when we figured out it was her," Tom said. "Let's talk about something else."

"And that's the second time in the last minute that you asked me to change the subject," Cam said, pointing a finger at him. "Is there something you're not telling me? A failed romance with the one with the blue mohawk, perhaps?"

"Actually, she just had brown hair back then," Tom admitted.

"Uh huh," Cam said, satisfied that she had deduced the truth. "Go on."

"Okay, we casually dated once upon a time. Emphasis on the word 'casual' as we were not a good match," Tom said uncomfortably. "Suffice it to say, I stopped the relationship from escalating rather quickly and she did not take to that well."

Cam frowned.

"Wait a minute, that sounds like a roundabout way of saying you slept with her once and then proceeded to not date her," Cam said as Tom became preoccupied with the foliage. "Are you that kind of jerk? Do I need to punch you for Volpi?"

She turned quickly to face him as he braced for an assault.

"Oh, wait, that's right," she said, theatrically thumping her head. "I dislike her a lot and I don't want to do anything on her behalf because she's a mean person."

Tom relaxed.

"Though, you should note that you've lost moral standing in my book," she lectured. "You could have at least let her down easy."

She felt Tom cringe beside her.

"Come on, I was semi-joking there," she said as she turned to see his blistered hands shaking. "Oh, that's right, I brutally burned your hands a few minutes ago. We should get you to Luanna."

"No, I'm fine," he said, brushing her off.

"Come on," she said, pulling him up. "I think the weeping blisters are a clear cry for medical attention."

●

After they left Luanna's clinic, they stood in the middle of town. Normally on a Sunday, Cam would be sitting on the sofa she slept on or reading by the river. She assumed Tom would have been at his home doing whatever he did on his days off. She shifted uncomfortably on the spot then turned to leave.

"Where are you going?" Tom asked.

"I don't know," Cam said honestly. "I don't really like these days off. There's very little to do that's productive."

"Well, I usually read or train," Tom said. "Those are productive."

"That's not what I meant by productive," Cam said. She looked down at her feet. "I guess what I meant was that nothing feels industrious anymore unless it's directed at saving Ke. It's always in the back of my mind, hanging on every action I take."

He looked at her with an impassive face. She could tell he was overthinking his next words.

"Did anyone tell you where my mom is?"

"No," Cam said, thrown by the new topic.

"Krytos sent her to the Slums again," Tom said. "Well, actually he sent her to Tengoku for whatever her mission is, but he also asked her to go to the Slums to check on Ke."

Cam was speechless. Krytos had asked Shun to go far out of her way to check on her little brother's status.

"Don't tell anyone though," Tom said. "She said Krytos said not to tell you and that would have been easy enough, you know, with us being nonverbal to each other and all. But, now that we're talking again, I feel irrationally obligated to."

"Uh, thanks," Cam said. Her fears of being too late to save Ke were returning.

"Wow, calm down," he said sarcastically. "Your exclamations of gratitude are really quite overwhelming."

"Sorry."

Her mind had wandered to Ke and his status now preoccupied her.

"Well, come on," Tom said. She looked up and saw that he was a few feet away. "Let's go get your things."

"Go get my things for what?"

"We did make up, didn't we?" Tom asked. "I, maybe presumptuously, assumed that meant you were moving back in?"

"Oh," Cam said, considering it. "Yeah, I'd like that."

They arrived at Gun, Sam, and Volpi's a few minutes later. Gun and Sam both expressed that they would miss having her as a roommate, though she was fairly certain those were just pleasantries as they seemed very grateful to have their sofa back. They would see her almost daily whether she lived there or not.

To her surprise, it took her time to pack this time. Her possessions now filled one bag and one backpack. She had inherited some clothes and other small items during the course of her stay.

One of her favorite new possessions was the old derringer pistol Gun had given her. He had two working versions that were newer thus he saw no need to keep it. The pistol was stainless steel with accents made of Vinestra. The barrel was a rounded pentagon that wrapped around five short barrels. She found it to be one of the most beautiful weapons she had ever seen and was exceedingly grateful to own it. After she was relocated, Tom suggested they practice with it. They spent the next few hours at the town's range where Cam learned that she was an awful shot.

After dinner, she stayed at the house while Tom left to speak with Krytos regarding Shun's imminent arrival. Tom had several old records that had once belonged to a Gi officer. She was listening to a saxophone solo on one of the jazz albums when she heard the front door close. It was Volpi, and she appeared agitated at the sight of Cam.

"So, you're back here again," she said.

"Yes, which means we'll probably be seeing less of you," Cam said, not bothering to turn around. "I think it's a win/win situation myself."

She could feel Volpi staring venomously at her.

"Where's Tom?"

"Hiding," Cam said. "Logically."

"Whatever," Volpi said. Cam heard footsteps followed by the sofa cushion deflating.

The saxophone drifted off. Cam removed the record and replaced it with a new one. An up-tempo guitar began to build as the song progressed. The notes were warm and quick, plucking the air with their vibrations.

"Turn that off," Volpi said.

"No. As you correctly deduced earlier, *I* live here," Cam said. "But if you really dislike it, *you* could always leave."

Volpi scoffed.

"Or, maybe, I shouldn't be merely suggesting that you leave," Cam said. "Maybe I should be demanding it with one of my fists breaking *your* face."

"Oh, please. Go ahead and try," Volpi said with a coy smile.

"Is it exhausting to constantly be so unpleasant?" Cam asked. "Try being nice. You know, cheerful instead of jeer-ful?"

Volpi laughed haughtily.

"Good, you do have a sense of humor after all," Cam said as she heard the distinct clink of brass knuckles. "Oh."

The guitar strummed higher and louder, over more pronounced notes, as the air pulsed from behind Cam to indicate Volpi's position. Cam spun from her place on the floor and swept her foot up, striking Volpi in the stomach. Volpi stumbled.

Cam came up behind her, grasped her forearm and pulled it taut. Volpi cried out as Cam seized her wrist, forcing Volpi's fingers to spring out rigidly. The brass knuckles clattered to the floor.

"See, while you were doing all of your evil plotting and such, I've been training," Cam said, kicking the brass knuckles out of Volpi's reach. "I think I'm becoming rather proficient."

Volpi grunted and brought the heel of her foot down on Cam's. Cam felt her grip on Volpi's wrist loosen then break as Volpi slammed her elbow into Cam's ribcage. Cam caught herself on the bookcase by the sofa just in time to see Volpi aiming a fist at her. Cam ducked and tackled Volpi by the knees. They rolled, swinging fists that sometimes made contact. Small splatters of blood webbed over the white area rug. Cam rolled on top of her and began to throw heavy, violent punches.

"What are you two doing?"

They both stopped in a tangle of bloody knuckles and raw kneecaps. Tom, Gun and Sam were standing in the entry way. It had been Tom who had spoken.

"Whatever it is, keeping doing it," Gun said excitedly. Volpi rolled her eyes as Tom smacked him in the back of the head.

"I think that was meant to be a rhetorical question," Sam said.

"Ouch!" Gun exclaimed. "Come on, man."

Volpi pushed Cam off. Neither of them had any injuries that required medical attention and that thought left Cam worried their fight was incomplete. Cam had a nose bleed and a few growing bruises, while Volpi's injuries were similarly mirrored. Tom eyed the blood stains on the rug, the scattered records, and broken bookshelf. Cam saw his jaw clench as he took in the extent of the blood stains.

"New rule," he said, taking a calming breath. "Brawling is now strictly an outdoor only activity."

Cam and Volpi apologized then helped repair the damage to the room. Together, they repositioned the furniture and scrubbed away the blood. They swept away the broken vinyl and returned the remaining ones to their box. It was just as they had finished mending the bookshelf that the front door opened and Shun arrived.

CHAPTER 17
IMPACT

Everyone left shortly thereafter. To Cam's surprise, Volpi whispered an apology to her for the fight on the way out. Shun then asked to speak with Tom alone to Cam's great disappointment as she was eager to hear about Ke. Regardless, she excused herself to her bedroom where she fell into a heavy sleep.

•

*The world had grown black and white. Oak trees speckled the landscape as the nearby river rushed foaming births of white. Cam stood in a valley between rolling hills. She felt her hand knock away the fly buzzing around as she examined her white dress. The gauzy fabric reflected the spotty sunlight filtering in through the sparse foliage.*

*"Well, I guess it always has to be something though I was hoping it would be something that makes more sense," Cam mused.*

*"Actually, I think black and white is far less ambiguous," came a voice. Cam spun to face the river as she searched for the voice's source. "At least in this instance, there's a stark metaphorical choice."*

*A pair of eyes were watching her with interest. Heavy, glossy lids lined the familiar, clear eyes. She knew that, despite the noir filter, they were the same color as hers.*

*"This is also nonsensical," Cam remarked. "Hello, me."*

*She was Cam's mirror image but clad in a black dress.*

"We require no pleasantries," the other Cam said. "Let's just get down to business."

The other Cam's appearance was uncanny, and yet her smirk was alien. Still smiling, she nodded up the river. They turned as one lonely raft bobbed toward them. Cam approached the riverbank, her shoes sticking to the sand. A shadowy figure was suspended above it, strung up by an invisible rope. She peered upward, wondering who would be infiltrating her dreams at such a time. The blurry shape progressed until the face became focused, and she fell back in horror. It was finally near enough for her to see the answer. It was the soldier Tom had killed in Tengoku.

"I need to help him," Cam said.

"No, you failed before and you'll just fail now," the other Cam winked. "You should know better. He was already lost anyway."

Cam felt her hand jerk upward then freeze rigidly in place. Without any internal push from her, fire filled her palm then flashed outward in a scorching line. It was slowly connecting itself with the other flame, forming a fiery bridge. She wanted to scream a warning, but she could barely breathe.

"Now, raise our hand," the other Cam said.

The wind was gone, and the soldier's body was floating closer over the rapids. It was apparent that he was still alive though his breathing was abnormally shallow. Her eyes traveled from him up to the bridge, and she felt her heart stop. The bridge was too low. If she did nothing, he would soon be beheaded. She tried to move her hand but found it to still be frozen as she pulled with more desperation.

"Raise the bridge!" Cam shouted. "Please! Raise it! Raise the bridge!"

A terrifying gleam flashed in the other Cam's eyes as she smiled and shook her head. The soldier was nearing them. His eyes flew open as he turned to face Cam.

"Please—" he began.

There was a scream. It tore through him as the fire struck, cutting and simultaneously cauterizing the skin on his damaged neck. Cam cried out, flailing against her invisible restraints as the soldier's head floated by. Fear rose in her as the current began to shift and she felt the increasing cold, the ominous chill. She turned as another raft began to drift down the river. The other Cam followed her gaze and sighed.

*"We better lower it," the other Cam said as she tapped the floor, her expression bored. "Ke's already ten, but he is a bit short for his age. Malnutrition, I suppose."*

*Cam's eyes snapped up to meet Ke's small, unconscious form. She fought with more intensity, hitting the air around her imprisoned arm despite how ineffectual she was. Her muscles twisted painfully with her wrenching movements, threatening to break her bones under the pressure. Her body kneeled in sync with the other Cam's, her legs and right hand out of her control. The soldier's death had been her fault but, this time, she wouldn't fail. She would break free, break away from the invisible wall around her arm that was becoming a panic trigger. She searched the riverbank for anything she could use. Then the fabric of her dress rippled, stroking her empty hand, and she looked down with curiosity. Something was gleaming between the layers of moss and flattened reeds.*

*It was the shining blade of a silver knife.*

*Ferocious resolve erupted in her. She turned eagerly toward it and threw her body forward. Spots of color flashed before her eyes as a sharp, overwhelming pain seared her senses. Her wrist and leg bones struggled in their sockets, trembling hard. She clenched both of her fists and gritted her teeth before lunging downward.*

*A nauseating pop detonated in her ears as her wrist bone snapped. The new break gave the fixed position of her mutilated arm just enough elasticity and give to reach the knife.*

*"We'll be safe if we stay together! Don't be so stupid!" the other Cam shouted. "Don't break what has already been broken!"*

*Cam stared at the darkly-mirrored person screaming on the bank across the river. She gripped the blade with a feeling of renewed motivation and euphoric need. She grasped the hilt, preparing for the pain of self-destruction. Her eyes locked with the other Cam's before she brought it down with the sacrificial determination of a failed hero. Sound disappeared as she struck herself over and over. Ke was still too close. She exhaled, breathing Ke's name as her shut eyes twitched in anguish.*

*Eventually, the knife fell through and met no resistance. The barrier of her flesh and bone had been obliterated. A bloody stub was all that remained of her hand. It plummeted to the ground, forming a shoal depression in the sand that quickly filled with blood. The fingers twitched then fell limp. She watched blearily as the bridge dissipated, and the silhouette of Ke's unconscious form floated safely by. An almost reposeful warmth tingled along her spine, displacing some of the unrelenting pain. She concentrated heavily on the new feeling, welcoming it.*

*"You are one dumb bitch!" the other Cam shouted. "You don't understand what you have done. You have ruined everything!"*

*The air pillowed her descent as she fell upon the grass, knowing she had finally become who she was meant to be. Her body sank into the moist ground as a shadow paralleled her movements on the opposite bank. Cam turned to face the mirror of herself, sighing. They still had one final dance to complete.*

*"You can never truly cut me out," the other Cam whispered. "I'm always here."*

*"You know what?" Cam asked. "I've grown really tired of hearing you talk. I murdered my dreams just to save you. It's time to rectify that."*

*Cam gripped the hilt of the knife, taking in the tarnished craftsmanship, before shoving it deep into her neck. Together, she and her shadow began to fade as their life ebbed in pulses. She watched the tendrils of sticky, mortal webbing pour from her like deadly ribbons against the backdrop of white fabric. They spiraled, creating little patterns along the pleating before blurring together. Her dress soon grew gray with her own blood, but she was content. For this time, she had not failed. She had saved Ke, her baby brother. A smile crossed her face once more before her body melded with her blood and melted into the gray.*

●

Cam woke up, shaky and unstable from the dream. Her body tingled from her spine down to her toes. Normally, this would have preceded an attack but, instead, she felt quite rejuvenated. It was a clear morning and the sun was already dancing brightly against the window. She kicked off the boots she had fallen asleep in, changed into a fresh shirt, and threw on her necklace. When she was done, she walked into the hallway and saw a figure sitting on the sofa.

"Morning, Tom," Cam said automatically, but the figure didn't turn to face her. "Tom?"

She began to move toward the living room. As she looked closer, she realized the man was not Tom. This man's wavy brown hair was longer and his shoulders were broader. Cam's feet left the soft, beige runner in the hallway and fell onto the cold hardwood of the living room. The floor creaked. The man turned at the noise and their eyes locked. They both gasped.

"It's you!" they said simultaneously.

Cam stared in shock. It was Eric Von Clousen, the soldier whose identity they had stolen in Tengoku. He had dark bags under his eyes and his skin was ashen, but it was undoubtedly him.

"Why are you here?" Cam asked.

He tilted his head in curiosity. His large form made him appear rather formidable but something in his lost expression also emanated helplessness.

"Wuh-wuh-weh-we s-s-saw you," he said, pointing shakily at her. His stutter was prominent like vocal speed bumps.

"What are you talking about?" Cam asked. A stream of memories ran through her mind like a film. She saw Tom strike him over the head, saw the alarming quantity of blood on the bed sheets.

"D-d-dream," he said.

"How did you get here?"

His tongue flicked over his bottom teeth as he tried to form the words. Cam couldn't understand what was wrong with him as he sputtered and spewed consonants over drawled vowels.

"You don't know?" Cam suggested.

He nodded once.

"You said you saw me in a dream," she said as he nodded once again. "I saw you in mine, too."

"I-I know."

The familiar feeling of panic came rushing back to her like a blow to the chest. The line keeping reality true was becoming blurred again.

"That's impossible," Cam said. "This would only make sense if I'm still sleeping. Am I?"

He stared at her with blank blue eyes.

"Am I hallucinating? Dreaming?"

He struggled with the words.

"Is any of this real?" she asked desperately.

Her body trembled as she silently urged him to answer.

"Wah-wuh-we duh-d-don't know," he whispered.

He looked so sad.

"That wasn't the reassuring answer I was looking for," she said with a small smile.

"Camilla?"

It was Shun's voice. It rang through the air in the room and pulsed firm support to Cam that she was awake.

"Hi, Shun," Cam said.

"Hi, Shun," Eric echoed behind Cam. She noticed how smoothly that particular sentence came from him.

"How are you?" she asked Cam.

"Good," Cam said. "And you? You were gone for a while."

"It was an arduous trip but I'll recover," Shun said. Something in the sudden tightness of her face and the storminess behind her caramel eyes made Cam falter. "Thomas is in the kitchen. Why don't you two go have breakfast?"

"Okay," Cam said, her eyes lingering past Shun to Eric's feeble figure.

Cam walked out of the living room. She turned her head and noticed Shun watching, waiting for her to leave. Cam made her way into the kitchen and saw Tom sitting at the table. He was staring at an open book as he robotically drank coffee.

"Interesting book?"

"Depends on the contextual intent of the word 'interesting,'" he said, not looking up. "I've read this sentence at the top of the page, well, some ridiculously high number of times. I guess that could be construed as having my interest."

"Are you okay?"

He did a double-take, looking up at her as if he had just noticed her presence.

"I didn't sleep last night," he said, trying to surreptitiously adjust the tenor of his voice to its normal tone.

"I'm sorry," Cam said. "Though, I probably wouldn't have been able to either if I had just seen a *ghost*."

She hissed the word "ghost" at him in a harsh whisper.

"Oh," Tom said. "So, you're probably wondering about *him* then."

"Maybe just a little bit," Cam said sarcastically. "I do generally become concerned when people rise from the dead."

"Let's talk about it somewhere else," Tom said.

They walked out of the house and followed the well-worn path that encircled the town. The sunlight was augmented by the contrasting reflections of the glossy landscape. Cam shoved her hands into her coat pocket as the icy morning breeze swooped over them.

"So, are you going to tell me why I'm seeing dead people?" Cam asked.

"I guess *he* was the mission Krytos sent my Mom on," Tom said.

"Why? Is he part of the Equintas?"

"No," Tom said. "He's just a Gi soldier like we thought."

"You mean a dead soldier of the Gi," Cam corrected. "He better not be a zombie."

Tom scowled at her.

"Sorry. I tend to joke when I'm disconcerted," Cam said.

"Oh, I'm with you very much on the disconcertion," Tom said. "My Mom said the news story on his death was fake and that the Gi took him instead of just fixing his wound and redeploying him. Krytos couldn't figure out why they would do that, and it made him curious. Eric was being held in a mental ward for evaluation on which experimentation group they were going to put him in. He was actually on his way to the Ether when my Mom intercepted him."

"Wait, why was he in a mental ward and not the Ether?"

"Oh," Tom said. The tired look in his eyes doubled as he took a breath. "He's had some undetermined brain damage and it's possible that I'm responsible for it."

His voice quieted.

"It could have been the Gi," Cam said. "He was taken to their ward. Who knows what they did there?"

"According to the records my Mom stole, they hadn't had a chance to really do anything yet," Tom said.

"I wouldn't trust the Gi's records."

"It doesn't matter, Cam," he said, defeated. "It's already done, so it doesn't matter whose fault it is."

They walked with synchronized footfalls across the damp soil. Birds flew overhead, casting misshapen shadows over the town. Tom was silent, staring out at the trees that fenced them in.

"On the positive side," Cam said. "This is a good place for him to rehabilitate. Safe."

"Right," Tom replied sullenly.

"Have you talked to him yet?" Cam asked.

"No," Tom said. "We gave him the couch and he fell right asleep. Why?"

"I did," Cam said.

"When?"

Cam told him about the odd conversation she had had with Eric that morning.

"—and, twice, he said the same words I said," Cam said. "It was strange. He spoke those two sentences normally."

"That is strange and he said he dreamt about you?" Tom asked. "I wonder what his power is. Maybe there's a correlation."

"Like what?"

"A mind connection or something," Tom said. "Maybe he's telepathic."

"Maybe," Cam said.

They continued to discuss the possibilities. Cam was attempting to keep him distracted. He did not display any prominent signs of distress, but she could tell his mood was darker than normal in the way the wind would pick up in rolling bursts of remorse. They broke off the main path and followed the thinner one down to the river. The path disappeared at the bank. They followed the river up to a collection of large flat rocks that sat at the smallest waterfall.

"You want to sit?" Tom asked rather formally.

"No, I'm fine," she said as she looked for pebbles to skip.

"I think you should," he said.

She stopped.

"What's wrong?"

"I brought you out to the river for a specific reason," he said, staring at the sandy ground. "I thought it would be best, I mean, I think it's kind of soothing. You know?"

"Yeah, sure," she said bewildered, sitting down. "It's a good river."

"See, I didn't just want to talk about Eric," he said. "I actually had something else entirely to tell you. You remember the side mission Krytos asked my Mom to go on?"

Cam's face stiffened and her mouth went slack. She remembered.

`It's not going to be good news.`

If it had been good news, Tom would have already told her. He wouldn't be watching her with wary eyes, waiting for the moment when he would have to stop her from falling apart. Her mind went blank. She suppressed everything else in preparation.

*This dance is over.*

"Yes," she replied, forcing herself to sound calm.

*MAYBE YOU SHOULD RUN WHILE YOU HAVE THE CHANCE.*

"Well, it took her some time to find Ke."

*JUMP OR FALL? IT'S TOO LATE TO CHOOSE.*

"There were...complications."

**HE'S DEAD.**

"But he's alive."

Cam had been steeling herself for the answer that would crumble her world.

"He's still alive!" she squealed, grabbing Tom in a bear hug. "Thank god, so I still have time. We can still save him!"

"Yeah, we can," he said quietly.

"What were you playing at there? You sat me down with the super—serious expression and everything," Cam rambled merrily as she skipped around. "But it's okay, I forgive you because this is great news! I'm sure Krytos is formulating some kind of plan to retrieve Aeraden as we speak. I'm so happy!"

"Good," he said, his face growing pale.

"I mean, this is the best news ever," she said, looking up at him. She stopped at his expression. "What?"

"That wasn't all," he said, voice low.

"What? What else could there be?"

He took a deep, pained breath before speaking.

"Cam, they took Ke away," Tom said. "The Gi took him to Tengoku...to the Ether."

"No," Cam said, panicked. "We've got to get him out of there. What are we doing just sitting here and talking? We need to put a team together. Let's go talk to Krytos right now. Maybe we could leave tonight and—"

"Cam," Tom interrupted.

He grabbed her by the shoulders. He was staring at her with sympathy coupled with pity and she understood.

"There's more," she whispered. "Isn't there?"

"Cam, the Gi went into the Slums to take Ke away," Tom said. "They went into your house and Mel was there when they broke in—"

*Here it comes.*

"—he tried to fight them off, but it wasn't a fair fight by any means..."

*Here it comes. The tidal wave that will finish you off.*

"Cam, I am so sorry," Tom said in a whisper. "Mel's dead."

The world stopped. Time and sound broke away. The river ceased its flow. The wind halted its pace. The birds fell silent.

`You were too late, after all.`

Her veins flooded cold as the flood finally broke the dam. Something vital within her core burst. It was too much to have both fury and pain bottled up so tightly in her small, futile body of flesh. In its release, her mind began to implode. The voices detonated, all of them together at once.

OVER AND UNDER. FALL OR JUMP?

*Ocean's rising and you're drowning.*

SHOULD HAVE FUCKING RAN.

Strips of screaming code, filled with the unforgiving rage of fresh agony, ran across her vision. She wanted to cry and scream but her brain was not capable of completing those tasks. The voices, the words, wrapped more and more tightly around her.

**REVENGE. REVENGE. REVENGE.**

`Died alone.`

Burn.

The sane bits of her mind were screaming as the madness swept through. Her heart was pumping with the tumult of invisible, bleeding fists. In her mind, imaginary rooms were being filled with imaginary Gi soldiers. They were being drenched in their own blood and a rain of broken glass. Their mangled bits of flesh were being ripped, torn to shreds as crimson further stained the room. Then she felt something in her mind tear as the culmination of the pain she could not endure and the weakness she could not fight broke free. Everything was silent as she heard one voice whisper softly to her.

**KILL THEM ALL.**

# CHAPTER 18
## WRECKAGE

Cam swept numbly through the remainder of the day. The scar of wanton revenge was seared in her psyche, overpowering all else. At breakfast the following morning, she surprised herself by how well she was able to maintain a cheerful demeanor. She drank fresh orange juice and ate an omelet. She even managed to keep it all down. None of them knew that something hateful had surfaced in her mind.

Her act seemed to be fooling everyone except for Tom. He confronted her later that afternoon.

"Cam," he said.

"What?" she asked as she continued to walk.

"You don't have to do this," he said. "There's no repercussions here for grieving because every single person in this town has had someone stolen from them, too."

"I'm fine."

"No, you're not."

She spun to face him.

"Okay, I'm not," she admitted. "But I'm not in the place to play the damsel in distress for you right now, so back off."

"What? I'm not asking you to play anything," he said, taken aback.

"Yes, you are," she said. "You want me to break down and cry on your shoulder. Then you get to try and make me feel better, but that won't help *me*. All that does it make *you* feel like *you're* doing something. That's sort of selfish. If you're really a friend and willing to sacrifice to make me feel better then don't ask me to do this."

Tom took a step back.

"I'm sorry, I wasn't trying to do that," he said. "I just don't want you to hurt yourself by bottling it all up like you did when Ke got sick."

Cam felt hot tears form behind her eyes at Ke's name. She looked down at her feet as she caught her breath to stop them from falling. Tom noticed, but he did not remark on it.

"Camilla."

They turned as Krytos approached them.

"How are you?" he asked.

"Fine," she replied.

Krytos exchanged a swift look with Tom.

"You would normally have training with me today. Do you want to skip it?" he asked.

"No," she said quickly. "No, I would just like to stay on my normal routine."

Tom opened his mouth to speak, but Krytos raised a hand.

"Thomas, you are needed up the mountain today for the monthly exports," he said. "The truck is leaving in twenty minutes."

"Of course," Tom said. He gave Cam a sympathetic smile before departing.

"Now, Camilla," Krytos continued. "If you're sure you would like to train then let us head to the field."

Cam nodded, following him out to the vast training fields. They stopped on the large, southern plot. It was heavily shaded and the grass was still wet. Krytos walked to the opposite end, pulled a book from his pocket and began reading. Cam narrowed her eyes.

"Are we going to start?" she asked.

"We're waiting for someone else," Krytos said as he continued to scan the pages.

"For who?"

Krytos ignored her as he chuckled under his breath at something funny in his book. Cam threw her arms up in the air and shut her eyes in frustration. She was on the verge of setting his book on fire when she heard footsteps clinging to the grass. It was Sam.

"I'm here," Sam said, panting. He was out of breath and had a hand clinging to his side. "Sorry I'm late, Krytos. I overslept."

"It's okay," Krytos said with a smile. "I actually planned on it."

"Oh," Sam said, reddening.

"Go ahead and have a seat," Krytos said. "You know what to do."

Sam nodded then waved at Cam. She waved back with curiosity at his presence. He sat down, leaning against a massive oak. All three were silent as Cam grew uneasy.

"Where do we start?" she asked.

"You mean when," Krytos said.

"What?"

"Where seems rather obvious as we are on the training field already."

"Okay, *when* do we start?" she asked, irritated.

"When you wish."

"So, I should just attack?"

Krytos nodded. Cam glanced over at Sam, trying to decipher the situation, but he had also brought his own book and had begun reading voraciously. Cam's fingertips tingled as heat spread across her palms, growing hotter every moment. The fire sparked and fell over her open hands, creating an impressive, molten mass.

"You want me to attack? Then fine, I will!"

The fire roared with such sudden intensity that Cam felt her body lift off the ground for a moment. It flew toward Krytos in a river of brilliant death. The power she had conjured was much more than she had anticipated and it left her lightheaded. Gold and orange flames continued to rush from her hands as she regained her balance. Her vision snapped back into focus and she saw that Krytos had not defended himself.

Terrified, she tried to stop the barrage of rushing flames that were engulfing Krytos. Smoke began to billow, and the putrid smell of burning flesh rose into the air. Krytos roared a shattering cry from within his prison of flame.

"Krytos—" she stopped as she saw Sam taking off toward Krytos with a dagger in his hand. "Sam, what are you doing?"

She began running toward Krytos, too. Her heart beat wildly as Sam raised the dagger over his unshaven chin. The screams of agony continued to bellow from Krytos as Sam's dagger came striking down.

Cam stopped as silence fell.

She watched with bated breath as the flames unfurled themselves and the smoldering embers died. Krytos was barely recognizable. His face and torso were burned so badly that she could see the charred edges of exposed innards. Together, she and Sam laid him down gently on the grass. Fresh blood was pooling over Krytos' chest. Cam tried to find its origins, to treat the source. A few minutes of fruitless searching passed before she realized the blood was not coming from Krytos. It was coming from Sam.

The dagger he had run at Krytos with was lying on the ground, covered in bright red rivulets. Blood was running from Sam's forearms in streams. He flexed his arm and poured the fresh blood over Krytos' wounds. Cam stared as it flowed across the horrible burns.

"Sam," she started.

"Cam, not now," he said, wincing.

Sam continued to drip his blood over Krytos until all of the burns were covered. A soft, silver light radiated from Krytos' body as Sam's blood seeped into his flesh like a sponge. His tissue rapidly began to meld and reform. The healing began within Krytos' body then moved outward. Within moments, his skin had woven itself back together. Cam was speechless as she stared at Krytos, whole and uninjured.

"What the hell was that?" Cam exclaimed, turning to Sam.

"I'm a healer," he said, quietly.

"I'm getting that," she said, staring at his forearms. Without the white bands around his wrist, she could see thick layers of knife scars marring his youthful skin.

"When I bleed I heal others," he added at her confused expression.

Cam was about to reply when Krytos suddenly coughed and sat up.

"Krytos! Are you okay?" she asked. "I am so sorry. I thought you were ready—"

"Good job, Sam," Krytos said to Sam. "Thank you for coming."

Sam nodded.

"Wait," Cam said. "You *let* me hurt you?"

"Yes," Krytos said as Sam helped him up.

"I don't understand," Cam said as her body shook, "and, to be frank, I'm rather pissed off about it."

"I wanted you to understand what it would feel like," Krytos said. He winced as he held up his hand which was still burnt and oozing. "Damn."

"What *what* felt like?" Cam asked as Sam bent over Krytos and swiftly cut his palm with the dagger.

"Sam, don't worry about it. It's not life-threatening," Krytos said, ignoring Cam again.

"You'll have a scar if I don't," Sam said as he squeezed his palm over Krytos'.

"You worry too much," Krytos said, patting him on the shoulder. "Besides, new scars tend to heal old ones."

"Krytos!" Cam shouted, trying to snap his attention back to her. "What *what* feels like?"

"Hurting someone."

"Hurting someone?" Cam repeated. "I know what that feels like."

"Not really," Krytos said. "I needed you to know the details."

Cam thought about the details: the smell, the touch, and the lingering adrenaline of panic. Her heart pulsed.

"Was this a new feeling, Camilla?"

"I suppose," Cam said then added with a sigh. "Okay, yes, violently so."

"What did it feel like?"

"It was bad," Cam said. "Disgusting, actually..."

"And?"

"Distressing."

"Why?"

"Well, I felt bad doing what I did to you," Cam said exasperatedly, "which is a logical reaction, by the way, being as you didn't attack and all."

Krytos looked down as Sam retreated to his spot by the tree.

"Was it because you felt bad attacking a stationary target or because you were attacking a voluntary one?" Krytos asked.

"Voluntary?"

"You realize that every single Gi soldier became who they are freely. Of the many things the Gi mandates, their enlistment is not one of them. It would be unnecessary anyway. The military has so many applicants that they have to turn down half of them," Krytos said. "I needed you to understand this first and foremost. Every time you singe a hair on one of their heads, you will feel this tenfold."

"But I won't," Cam said, confused. "They're the enemy."

"To you," Krytos said. "But who are they to their parents? Their children? Their friends?"

Cam looked at the ground, trying to discern how she could see a Gi soldier or member as anything else. It was difficult simply to categorize them as humans.

"They are family to someone," Krytos said. "As I like to think I am to you or will be someday. It will hurt you to hurt someone at some point during this war. It's just a matter of time. I wanted you to know beforehand, to prepare you."

"Well, that's courteous of you," Cam said scathingly.

"It's okay that you're angry with me," Krytos said. "It's just a defensive mechanism to camouflage the guilt. You think it feels bad now but imagine how you would have felt if I had died."

"No, that's okay. I'd prefer not to imagine that," she said.

"That's fine. I'm not going to force you to," Krytos said. "But not doing so now will just make it worse later. It's even harder when you watch them die, harder when they're lying at your feet, dying at your hand, and praying that their children will never forget them. Nothing can ever make that feel right. In fact, it can make you doubt your purpose. So, it will make it easier if you can accept that guilt now."

Cam stared up into his eyes and tried to appear brave.

"In other words, you're conditioning me to be a killer," she said.

"Not to be a killer, Camilla, and I'm not 'conditioning' you for anything," he said. "I'm just giving you the truth of what it means to be a warrior, not because I want you to be one, but because you'll have to be."

Cam looked away.

"I wish we didn't need to fight at all, Camilla," Krytos said. "But there is no other way. There won't be any peace talks with the Gi or negotiations. If we tried, they'd kill us. If I don't help you become a warrior now, then they'll win. Unfortunately for us, this fight, this rebellion, is the only chance we have for freedom."

Cam nodded, accepting the truth while despising that she had to.

"We're at a disadvantage. Freedom has historically been too easy to take away and too difficult to restore. So, if we must fight this losing battle," Krytos said, a steadfast gleam in his eye. "I'm going to ensure that we leave a mark."

•

Cam was now training every day with Krytos from sunrise to sunset. It was a necessary distraction to keep her from plummeting into despair over the loss of Mel and the kidnapping of Ke. She had become proficient with many weapons, and her hand-to-hand combat skills were improving exponentially under his guidance. On the seventh day, she sat down at the dinner table and threw her head into her arms. The relentless training was beginning to exhaust her mentally and physically.

"Day seven," Gun said as he poked her head with his fork. "How're you holding up?"

"Not well," Cam mumbled over her newly bruised lips. "I think I'm approaching that stage where I'm in so much pain that I'm going numb. Or is that just wishful thinking?"

She spent the rest of the meal concentrating on her food. Her right hand was fractured, forcing her to use her left to eat her salmon. She held the utensil between her thumb, middle, and ring finger as she tried to keep the fork level with the plate. Her hand shook each time from the effort. Meals had become very tedious. Sam jokingly offered to give her an intravenous drip while Tom, who was ambidextrous, showed off by switching which hand he used to eat with. She kicked both of them under the table and was quite happy that she had been going through strength training.

After the meal, she made her way to the field. She had not been in so much pain since her whipping. Her hands, elbows, legs, and face were covered in scabs. Her muscles punished her each time she took a step. It was a relief when she met Krytos and he invited to her to take a seat.

In the middle of the field, a bar stool stood. She sat on the stool, noticing that the legs were slightly off balance. Krytos stood before her, taking quiet drags from his pipe. His eyes were shut and his expression was thoughtful. Several minutes passed as Cam twirled her thumbs, waiting.

"Why have I been sitting on a stool in the middle of the forest for the last ten minutes?" Cam asked. "Aren't we going to train?"

She waited for his response. He opened his eyes as he secured the pipe between his teeth.

"What do you fear?" Krytos asked.

Cam was silent, taken aback by the question.

"Nothing," she replied quickly.

Krytos raised a knowing eyebrow and laughed.

"Nothing?"

"Nothing," Cam said, but the hesitation covered her words like a lacquer, shining with falsity.

"Sure," he said mockingly.

"What do you want me to say? Something that'll seem really profound, I'll bet. Like that I'm scared of death or love or vampire puppies," she said. "My death is most likely going to be due to someone else's theft of it. Something like that just doesn't scare me anymore."

Krytos laughed.

"You're so young," he said. "At your age, you think everything is so extreme, so black and white. Now, come on, what *really* scares you?"

She pondered his words for a moment.

"I guess the Gi do," she said.

"The Gi scares you," Krytos said with a small nod. "They do have that effect on a lot of people. What scares you about them?"

"Their efficiency at stealing freedom and using it to hurt others," Cam said. "The innocent are their first casualties and that doesn't seem to leave a mark on their consciences."

Krytos nodded.

"Actually, now that I think about it, it's not the Gi Force in its entirety that scares me," she said.

"It's not?"

"Well, the Lord General scares me the most," she clarified. "Without him, none of the other Gi Force soldiers would do what they do. I can't even imagine what my life would be like if he had never existed."

Krytos cast his eyes up to the warm sun as he took a slow drag from his pipe.

"He is a scary man," he said as the smoke billowed in wispy tendrils. "Though, Camilla, there is nothing more to a scary man than the fear you let him take."

Cam thought about his statement for a moment.

"So," she said. "Live without fear or something equally impossible?"

"No," he said. "Live *with* fear. Let your enemy take it. Let your enemy be the scariest thing in the whole wide world and then—"

He broke off as he stared into the forest behind her, deep in thought.

"And then what?"

Krytos turned to her and grinned.

"Then you show him what fear truly means."

•

After dinner later that night, Cam went with Tom and Gun to the town's fire pit. Most nights, someone lit the bonfire and there would be a small gathering of people. They would drink and share stories until late into the night. Cam had never attended before, but she found it to be a nice experience. Kiri the architect was sharing a glass of wine with Ronen, the musician they had just freed from the Ether. Alex was cuddled against Max under a red flannel blanket. Cam and Tom drank stouts brought in with the last imports while Gun flicked the ashes of his cigarette into the fire.

Despite the size of the bonfire, the darkness of the forest at night was overwhelming. Outside of the warm, orange halo that ringed the fire pit was nothing but black. The dense shield of warmth emanating over them was their only protection against the darkness. Cam let her thoughts roam further than usual as the shadows flickered, preventing her face from betraying her emotions. She said very little for the next couple of hours, allowing herself the simple luxury of listening.

"So, you and Sam were born here?" Ronen asked. Alex had been sharing old stories of when Tom and Sam had been toddlers.

"Yeah, we were the first generation of children born as Equintas," Tom said. "Technically speaking though, *I* was the first ever."

"Oh, please. The first by one day," Alex said.

"I was still first," Tom said smugly.

"Whatever, you just always have to be first," Alex said, waving her hand in the air. "When we gave him Vinestra for the first time he used his ability to beat Sam in a foot race. Tom bet his favorite toy for Sam's. Sam accepted because he didn't know Tom had the power to run faster than the wind. He was so upset when he lost!"

"Harsh, man," Gun noted.

"I was five," Tom said, defensively. "I didn't know any better."

"So you don't give the children Vinestra until they're five?" Vesna asked. Vesna was a young woman who had been in the cell Cam had freed. She had an aptitude for linguistics.

"We worry about giving it to them before they're emotionally capable," Max said.

"But is a child really that capable at five?" Vesna asked.

"So far," Max said. "The child grows up learning their power at the same time they are learning everything else."

"See, children don't get their power the same way an adult would," Alex added. "Adults receive a blast of Vinestra and their power can become known in a matter of minutes, but children seem to absorb the Vinestra differently. They don't show the signs of their power for a week or two and, even after that, it takes months to develop to a noticeable point in most cases."

"But you said Tom used his right away in the race with Sam?" Ronen pointed out.

"Well, I'm just special," Tom said, smirking.

"Krytos thinks it's because he's one of the Templum Three," Alex said. "There were other developmental markers as well that were indicative of his unique power."

"Yeah, I didn't have to train my power for it to strengthen when I was little," Tom said. "It just adapted and grew on its own."

"Camilla's one of the Three as well," Kiri said, speaking for the first time. "What are your powers like?"

Cam looked up at her, startled by being directly addressed. Kiri's bright green eyes were like beacons of curiosity, prodding her for an answer.

"Um," Cam stammered. "I make fire."

"I don't think that was the detailed answer the group was looking for," Gun said, nudging her.

"Well, it hasn't been as easy for me to develop them as I guess it was for Tom," Cam said. "I wasn't exposed until really recently, so it's been pretty overwhelming."

"But what about all this demon stuff Kiri's been telling me about?" Ronen asked. "Can't you talk to demons or something like that?"

"It's more like I can decipher their language," Cam said. "The one time it happened, I was telepathically sent this huge code. All of my other senses were gone until I decoded it. It was odd, to say the least, and I don't really know how to describe it correctly."

"But you *can* talk to demons?" Vesna asked.

Cam nodded.

"Wow," Vesna said, running a hand through her layers of auburn ringlets.

"Hey, Alex," Ronen said, changing the subject. "You said you were going to tell us the story about how Krytos got the, you know, crazy scars."

"Oh, that's right," Alex said. "It was about twelve years ago. Krytos learned that Aeraden was kept in the vault in the Ether. We had broken a few cells at that point so he knew he could make a door that was relatively close. He and a few others broke into the vault but they were stopped immediately by this enormous ghost monster with talons."

"What?" Ronen asked, disbelieving. "You're making that up."

"No, Krytos said it was the size of a house and transparent with two huge, scarred eyes," Alex said. "We had expected armed guards and weren't prepared. Only a few of our team escaped and that was only because of Krytos' ice shield. When he took it down to run himself, the beast mercilessly attacked. Shun and the others had to carry him back half-conscious to the portal."

The discussion of the beast and Aeraden's vault drifted away as a realization dawned on Cam. The *Book of Trappings* had mentioned a demon called Oni-Orochi. It had been captured and blinded by the Markstre who later became the Gi. Cam felt a genuine smile cross her face as she considered the possibility.

Could the invisible beast be Oni-Orochi, one of the Seven Demons of Ortus Canitia?

If her revelation proved true then she could communicate to it. She could ask it to allow them into the vault just as she had done with Leviathan. She needed to talk to Krytos. This was her chance to save Ke.

Cam began to fantasize about Aeraden and saving Ke from the Ether. The group slowly began to thin as time passed. Cam lingered until the only ones who remained were Tom and Gun. They were discussing weapons when Cam stood and walked resolutely toward Krytos' house.

"Cam? Where are you going?" Tom asked.

"Krytos' house," she replied as she continued to walk. She heard Tom and Gun shuffle to their feet.

"Right, Cam, I don't think this is the best idea," Gun said. "I like my thumbs sans screws, thank you very much."

"I really do agree with Gun," Tom added. "I think that waking up Krytos would be very stupid. He's rather partial to his sleep."

She did not reply as the silhouette of Krytos' house came into view.

"Tom, she seems serious," Gun said.

"Should we go with her?" Tom asked.

"Do we have to?"

"Well, I want to know what she's so fired up about."

"Ha, 'fired' up about," Gun laughed. "That's silly."

"Plus, I think it would be ungentlemanly if we didn't," Tom continued. "That way, when her frozen body turns up in the morning, we can at least pretend like we tried to save her from Krytos' grumpy wrath."

"When, of course, we're going to just be hiding behind the furniture while he ices her?"

"Correct."

They followed her reluctantly onto the gravel pathway leading to Krytos' door. They arrived at the small porch, stopping as the wind chime began to sing. Cam took the first step, and the porch creaked loudly under her weight. Tom and Gun jumped. She approached the door and lifted her curled hand, poised to knock.

"I really wouldn't do that if I were you, Cam," Tom warned.

"Why not?" Cam asked. "I want to wake him."

"I meant that it's already open," Tom said, pushing the unlocked door with his index finger. She gave him an annoyed look before pushing her way inside.

The living room was darker than the night they had departed from. She wove her way through the dining room, navigating around towers of books and piles of scrolls. She stopped at a glimmer of light coming from the farthest corner of the kitchen. There was a small figure stooped over on the sofa.

"Milo?" she whispered. He was sitting with his back turned to them, sketching quickly in his notebook. Cam cautiously leaned forward to see what he was drawing. It was a demon, half dragon and half crustacean, blowing fire from its jaws. A figure was riding its back with a body-length sword drawn to attack. The figure was so realistic that Cam thought she was looking into a mirror.

"You guys are stupid. He's gonna be mad," Milo replied, his voice at its normal volume. They all started.

"You are the third person to tell me that," Cam said once she had recovered. "You would think that, as the leader of the Equintas, he would be accustomed to being woken up at all hours."

"Duh, that's why he likes his sleep," Milo said, rolling his eyes.

"Oh, I guess that does make sense," Cam admitted as they heard several loud footsteps.

Tom and Gun both stiffened as Cam stared. Milo gave them an "I told you so" look as Krytos emerged from the nearest door.

"What the hell is going on?" he demanded. When no one answered, he added with more force. "I said, *what is going on in my house*?"

Tom and Gun straightened as Milo returned to his drawing.

"Well, is anyone going to answer me?"

Cam stood.

"I need to talk to you," Cam said, her once coherent thoughts breaking. "We need Aeraden—"

"You woke me," he interrupted, "to tell me we need Aeraden. I think that is a little bit obvious and a subject that could've waited until morning!"

"We need it as soon as possible," she said. "I have a plan that I need you to hear."

"Right now at 2:43 in the morning?"

"Yes," she said.

Krytos sat at the dining table and sighed.

"Sit," he said, motioning to the table before them. "Now, Camilla, go ahead and tell me about the plan that was so exceptionally urgent."

Cam looked out the window at the silver sliver of moon as she formulated her words.

"I think the thing that guards Aeraden is one of the Seven Demons of Ortus Canitia," she said. "I think I should go there and try to communicate with it. If I succeed then we could lead a group into the Vault. We could finally get Aeraden."

She took a deep breath. Gun was staring at her with his mouth open while Tom shook his head. Krytos crossed his arms, eyeing her sternly.

"That sounds like a well-thought-out plan," Krytos finally said.

Cam looked at Tom then at Krytos.

"I'm sorry," she said. "Was that sarcasm? Your tone stayed pretty much the same there."

"Camilla, here's my problem with your 'plan.' What happens if you fail?" Krytos asked her. "I'll tell you what will happen. Many of us will die and the blood will be on your hands."

"But what if I don't fail? What if we're successful?" she asked. "My little brother is in the Ether, too. Isn't it worth the risk to at least try? We could save a life as well as retrieve the healing stone."

"It's potentially a suicide mission. Defeating the Gi is important, but the victory is lost if we're also mourning unnecessary, preventable deaths," Krytos said. "I took people in there before and I got them killed. It's a mistake that I won't be repeating."

Anger brewed in her. Mel was already lost. She would not allow Ke to die a tortured death alone in the Ether.

"Maybe I won't let it be your mistake to make," she said.

The room was silent. Even the crickets stopped their evening song to listen.

"Was that a threat, Camilla?"

"My little brother is on the verge of death. Consider it more of an ultimatum."

Her gray eyes were glimmering with the ferocity of determination. Krytos let out a small chuckle.

"I can see there is no placating you on this," he reneged. "So, instead, let's make a deal."

She raised an eyebrow.

"What sort of deal?"

"Present your plan to the council," he said. "If the majority approves of it then I will gladly help you."

"The council?"

"The leaders of each division within the Equintas," he explained. "I'll set the meeting for tomorrow after dinner. Now, go home and go to bed. You have preparations to make."

# CHAPTER 19
## END OF THE LINE

The following evening, Cam arrived at Krytos' house after dinner as he had instructed her to. She knocked on the door and heard shuffling footsteps. Milo peeked through the window and, upon seeing who it was, waved. A moment later she heard the doorknob turn, and the door swung open.

"Hi," Milo said. "They're in the kitchen."

Cam smiled then walked into the kitchen to the rich aroma of freshly brewed coffee. The oak dining table had been cleared of the books and knick knacks that were usually scattered atop it. Krytos sat at the head of the table with a full mug and his pipe. Shun was on his right, sipping tea. Martin, Luanna, Kalen, and Alex were there.

"Camilla," Krytos said. "Go ahead and sit."

She sat down at the empty dining chair that stood opposite Krytos. Everyone at the table was watching her and, coupled with the heat of so many bodies in the small kitchen, she flushed with embarrassment. The silence mounted as she resolutely stared at the taupe table runner and the melted candles in the center. Then she heard a knock at the front door, followed by Milo's voice. Forceful foot falls echoed into the kitchen.

"Milo says I'm late. It's exactly seven-thirty. How am I late?" came Gun's protesting voice.

"You're not late," Krytos said. "You're just the last one here."

"Oh," Gun shrugged. Then he saw Cam and smacked her on the shoulder in a painful but friendly gesture of greeting. "Hey, Cam."

Gun sat and poured himself a large mug of coffee.

"Now that everyone's arrived, I can explain why you're here," said Krytos. "Camilla has made a proposition in which to acquire Aeraden. Each of you overlooks a different branch of our operations which, in turn, makes each of you responsible for lives other than your own. We will collectively determine whether or not to proceed with her plan. Remember, while you may supervise others, you have no control over their choice to serve in accomplishing the mission. Consider carefully the opinions of your people."

Everyone nodded.

"Now, Camilla," Krytos continued. "Let me explain how this deliberation generally works. Each person here represents a group in the Equintas. Shun represents the infiltrators and those who are undercover within Gi cities. Kalen represents the psychics and Luanna the healers. Martin represents the manipulators and shifters that can change objects. Alex represents those who can change themselves. Gun now represents the fighters, and I represent everyone else who does not fall into one of the aforementioned categories. A majority vote here means that we'll proceed unless the true majority disapproves. Camilla, if you would please, explain the details of your plan to us."

All eyes turned to her again. She had never been in such a situation in her life. Her brain scrambled to reorganize her plan's logical virtues and organize them into a sensible presentation.

"Um, well, I was thinking about the beast that guards the Gi's vault in the Ether," Cam said, her voice shaking under the pressure of their gazes.

She stopped and took a deep breath. Alex smiled at her encouragingly, though it only served to escalate the pressure.

"You all know what my powers are," Cam said. "I can control fire and talk to demons. Although I wouldn't quite call it 'talking' so much as blasts of scrambled bits of information that I have the ability to decode."

She laughed nervously as they continued to stare.

"Anyway, I'll get right to the point," she continued quickly. "I think the beast guarding Aeraden is one of the Seven Demons of Ortus Canitia."

Furtive glances were exchanged along with a few whispered words.

"Do you have any evidence, Camilla?" Shun asked. "How can you be certain?"

"It could be anything," Kalen said. "There were no physical characteristics that could help us truly discern its species."

"Well, there is one thing," Cam said. "Other than the talons of doom, what was the only other characteristic of the creature? Krytos?"

"The eyes," he said.

"Or lack thereof," Cam said. "The beast had visible scars where its eyes should have been. This characteristic is shared with a demon in our history, Oni-Orochi."

She pulled the *Book of Trappings* from her bag and set it on the table. Shun gasped. Gun gave Cam a quizzical look.

"The *Book of Trappings*!" Shun exclaimed. Her usually cool demeanor melted with her excitement. "You told us about it before, but to see it in person..."

"What's the big deal?" Gun asked. "It's just a book."

"No," Shun said. "It's the only book left in existence that recounts the Trappings Era, the time when the Gi assimilated the world."

Gun's mouth fell open. Everyone else at the table, except for Krytos, seemed to be equally in awe.

"There's a chapter in this book that's from the journal of a Markstre officer," Cam said. "That chapter talks about some excursion where they encounter a demon."

"A demon?" Kalen asked. "They specifically called it a demon?"

"Yes, this demon, Oni-Orochi, was protecting something," Cam said. "As it fought the invading Markstre, killing most of them by the way, it was wounded. The Captain of the Markstre pierced its eyes, blinding it. After the Markstre became the Gi Force, I'm guessing they had its eyes completely removed before they used it as the guardian for their vault."

"So, you're postulating that the shapeless creature guarding the vault is *this* same demon?" Shun asked.

"Yes," Cam said. "I believe that the beast is Oni-Orochi, one of the Seven Demons. I think we need to break into the Ether and get to the vault entrance where it is kept. I need to see it and try to communicate with it. If I'm right, then I can command it to give us entrance to the vault. We can get Aeraden and save my brother. We can save everyone."

It was quiet for a long time. Rogue drops of coffee boiled between the pot and the hotplate. Cam, relieved to have made it through the presentation under their scrutiny, kept her vision confidently squared on Krytos.

"Who would like to begin this deliberation?" Krytos asked, looking at each of them in turn.

"I will," Kalen said. He stared down his nose with stern, spectacled eyes. "Your plan is naïve. Tell me, what happens if you can't communicate with it?"

Cam sputtered.

"Then we run?"

She realized afterward that she had phrased her answer like a question. Kalen raised an appraising eyebrow.

"We wouldn't be able to outrun it," Krytos said, tapping a finger to the scar on his face.

"So, there is no exit strategy?" Luanna asked. "The other healers and I can't heal anyone if they're being digested in the beast's stomach."

"But what if she's right?" Alex asked.

"Are you saying that the lives of our family are worth the gamble?" Kalen asked in outrage.

"No, but look at everything she's shown us," Alex said. "Look at the book she's brought. I think the odds of her being correct are pretty good."

"Pretty good is not good enough," Kalen said. "If she fails and we can't get our people out, then I cannot agree to this."

"I concur," Luanna said.

Silence followed as the division among the group became apparent. Shun's eyes narrowed in thought as she looked at Cam. Cam was reminded of Tom.

"I think this matter is ready to be put to a vote," Krytos said. "If you choose to, you may disclose your reasoning for reaching your decision. Kalen?"

"I don't think this a good idea," Kalen said. "I will not risk the lives of the Equintas for a gamble where we have no way to escape. Camilla, I think you are a lovely girl with bounds of talent, but your plan is flawed. Your idealism is touching but, ultimately, foolish."

"Luanna?"

"I vote 'no' for the same reasons Kalen gave," Luanna said, tossing a long strand of pale blond hair over her shoulder. "As a healer, I see the wounds, and I see the death. I don't want to see any that could have been prevented. I'm sorry, Camilla."

She turned to Cam for the apology at the end.

"Alex?"

"Yes, I think we need to do this," Alex said. "I was a slave and I watched too many people die from the sickness. The amount of people we could save is practically endless. I think it's worth the risk."

"Martin?"

"Yes," Martin said. "I think that, with new members such as little Amelia, we stand a chance of escape. I want to believe that Camilla has deduced the origin of the beast correctly and that she will be able to communicate with it."

"Shun?"

Shun crossed her fingers as she pursed her thin, pale lips. She stared at Cam for several long moments.

"Shun?" Krytos asked again. Shun turned to him as a gentle smile spread on her face.

"Yes," she replied. Krytos waited for her reasons and moved on when they did not come.

"Gun?"

Cam held her breath. The vote was three to two in her favor and his vote would give her the majority. He stared into his coffee. His large fingers drummed a quick beat on the table.

"Cam," Gun said. "I'm really, really sorry, but I vote 'no.'"

"What?" she exclaimed. "What about my brother? You were trapped in the Ether for years. How can you vote to abandon my brother there?"

He squared his shoulders as he forced eye contact with her.

"Cam, do you even know why I'm here?" he asked. His voice was weighted in such an unfamiliar way.

"Because you're head weapons guy," Cam said. "Krytos just said that."

"That means I got promoted," Gun said. "Do you know why I got promoted? It's because Paula, who used to hold this position, is dead."

Cam looked down as she gripped the tablecloth.

"She's dead because the Gi caught her," Gun continued. "They tortured her, killed her, and hung her severed hands from a tree by the Whipping Post."

"Gun," Shun said, putting a hand on his arm. He took a deep breath.

"So, that's why I can't vote for your plan, Cam. If you had asked me yesterday, my answer would have been different," Gun said, clenching his fists. "I will not put our family in the line of fire on a chance. I'm sorry, but I just can't. We bury too many people as it is."

Cam was unable to respond properly, so she merely nodded. Krytos cleared his throat and the attention returned to him.

"Thank you for your input," Krytos said. "My vote is 'no' as well."

Cam felt the familiar rise of anger in the pit of her stomach. It was causing her limbs to tremble.

"The proposition has not won a majority vote," Krytos said. "I'm sorry, Camilla. We will find another way to help your brother, I promise."

Under the table, Cam felt her fingernails bite into the calloused skin on her palms. The skin curled and crimped as it rolled up underneath her nails. She clenched her teeth as Kalen continued to look down his pointed nose at her. The room suddenly felt too small. Her chest tightened as she took a deep breath and tried to keep the image of Ke dying on the floor of a Gi cell out of her mind.

"Fine," she said with a smile as a drop of crimson slid from between the wrinkled, broken skin on her palm. "Thank you for your time."

She stood, walking swiftly from the room. The Equintas talked of family, of its importance and sanctity. She now knew they were right. Ke was her only family now. The relationship between her and the Equintas was over.

•

When Cam awoke the next morning, she packed her bags. It was time to leave. She knew how to get to the tunnels that would lead her to the city. The sun had just begun to rise over the majestic horizon when she finished. She left the luggage on the bed and crept out of the house. There was only one item left needed for her plan, and she knew she could not acquire it herself.

Amelia had been living with some of the other kids at Alex and Max's house. Their house was one of the largest as they had adopted six children over the years. She could hear Alex and Max bustling around the house, followed by the noises of their children. Cam took a deep breath and knocked on the front door. Bobby, the boy who could create earthquakes, answered.

"Hi, Cam," he said, yawning.

"Hi," Cam said. "Is Alex here?"

"Yeah," he said. "You can come in. She's making pancakes."

Cam smiled and entered. She watched Bobby shuffle into the living room to her left where a sizable tower of blocks stood. He sat down beside them then placed his hand on the carpet. Cam felt a slight rumble under her feet as the blocks fell to the ground, forming a large smiley face. Bobby grinned up at her.

"Bobby," came Alex's voice from the kitchen. "I told you, no earthquakes *in* the house!"

"Sorry!" he shouted back.

Cam began to make her way to the kitchen. She saw James, the oldest child in the house at fifteen. Before she could blink, he was gone. Then she heard a whoosh ahead of her and saw him reappear in the hallway.

He squeezed by the second eldest and newest addition, Annabel. She was thirteen and could breathe underwater. Cam walked into the kitchen and saw Alex running after the twins, Kenshin and Miyu, while Max was at the stove.

"Hi," Cam said.

"Hello," Max said with a wave of the spatula.

"Hi, Camilla," Alex said from the table where she was seating the twins. "What's up?"

"Oh, nothing much," Cam said, trying to decide what someone who was not being deceitful would do. "I just wanted to thank you, you know, for voting for me yesterday."

Alex grinned and walked over to give Cam a sympathetic hug. Cam reciprocated, though it only made her feel worse about her dishonest intentions.

"Have you had breakfast yet?" Alex asked. Cam shook her head. "Well, why don't you eat with us?"

"Sounds great," Cam said, plastering on a smile that felt very fake.

"Max, where's Amelia?" Alex asked. "I seem to be missing a child."

"She should be in the playroom. I gave her an old calculator to dismantle," Max said as he continued to flip the pancakes.

"James, would you please go get Amelia?" Alex asked as little Kenshin made a run for the back door. James rolled his eyes but stood anyway. Breakfast was ready but it took the better part of half an hour to get all the children seated.

"Bobby, wait your turn. Don't just reach over your sister like that," Alex said. "Camilla, would you please help Amelia with the pancakes?"

"Sure," Cam said, taking the enormous platter of pancakes from Max. She lifted one up with her fork and put it on Amelia's plate. Amelia immediately ripped a small piece off and, using her fingers, dipped it in the puddle of syrup she had poured earlier.

Breakfast was very loud, but Cam preferred the noise. There was no pressure for her to make conversation which meant fewer opportunities for her to give away her plan. At the meal's conclusion, Cam assisted Max with the cleanup. He was quiet but, again, Cam did not mind as she was quite busy drying the plates. The kids dispersed the minute Alex announced breakfast was over. The first chance Cam had she went to look for Amelia. She found her hovering over a scientific calculator. It was in pieces across the floor.

"Hey, Amelia," Cam said.

"Hi, Cam," Amelia said, looking up.

"What are you doing?"

"Breaking this," Amelia said, holding up a mangled motherboard. "But I'm not breaking it forever. I can make it better later."

"Oh," Cam said, sitting down. Amelia had the pieces hovering before her face, reassembling them. Her little olive green eyes were stark in comparison to her pale face, which was made starker by the dark curls. She was so young and, yet, Cam was going to ask her to be a conspirator. Cam sighed. "Amelia? Can I ask you for a favor?"

"I guess," Amelia said with an indifferent shrug.

"This is our secret though, okay?"

Amelia nodded, her interest piqued with Cam at the mention of its secretive nature.

"Well, you're a tech-infiltrator," Cam said. "But what can you really do? See, I need a security system hacked, but it's in Tengoku."

"That's too far," Amelia said. "I can't see Tengoku from here."

"So, you have to *see* the machine to hack it?" Cam asked.

"Yep," Amelia said. "I had to touch it before, but I'm stronger now. I can just look at it now and it goes poof!"

"That's impressive," Cam said encouragingly, though she knew her plan was lost without a way around the Gi's high security.

"Why do you look so sad?" Amelia asked.

"Well, I'm trying to help someone," Cam said. "I need to get to Tengoku and through their security."

"That sounds scary," Amelia said, staring at the ground. "I think you should just stay here."

"I would, but I have a little brother," Cam said. "He's in Tengoku and I need to save him."

Amelia's little face scrunched up. Her nose wrinkled as the forgotten bits of the calculator fell to the floor.

"Is he in the bad place? Where I was?" Amelia asked, looking panic-stricken.

"I think so."

Amelia stood and wrapped her thin arms around Cam's neck.

"You gotta get him out," Amelia said, her already high voice elevating. "They hurt us really bad in there."

"I know," Cam said, patting Amelia on the back.

"They poke and pinch until you bleed. They put lightning through me. I told them it hurt, but they didn't stop! They just kept hurting me!" Amelia cried. "I never want to go back!"

"No, you won't! You're safe here," Cam said, struggling to say something comforting. Amelia's little body shuddered with sobs as Cam hugged her more tightly. "I promise, you're safe here."

Amelia cried, her little hands clinging to Cam. After a few minutes, her body finally relaxed. Cam wiped the tears away with her shirtsleeve.

"Do you feel better?" Cam asked.

"No," Amelia said with a loud sniffle.

"I'm sorry," Cam said. "I'm sorry I made you so upset."

"It wasn't you."

"Still, I'm sorry."

It was quiet for a few minutes as Amelia sat in Cam's lap. Then Amelia looked up and tugged on Cam's shirt.

"What?" Cam asked.

"I think I *can* help," Amelia said with a big smile.

Amelia took Cam outside to the back of the house where a swing set stood. They walked around the side to the Equintas' main garage. Amelia grabbed the metal handle of the door and, with Cam's help, swung it open. Small dust plumes burst from around the door frame. Cam coughed.

"Come on," Amelia said, grabbing Cam's hand. "It's in the back, but you can't tell anyone. I'm not supposed to know about it. It's Max's."

"Know about what?"

Amelia jumped up and grabbed the chain for the light. A soft yellow light flooded the dark corners of the space. Amelia pulled an old drop cloth away, scattering more dust. Cam looked over at her with confusion. Propped between an over packed shelf and a stack of boxes was a dull, gray motorcycle.

"I don't get it," Cam said.

"If I can't help you get *into* Tengoku," Amelia said, patting the bike's seat. "Then I'll at least help you *get* there."

"But I don't even know how to ride a bicycle," Cam said. "Let alone a motorcycle."

"That's okay!" Amelia said, enthusiastically. "I can make it so it drives for you."

•

Cam slung her backpack over her shoulders and snapped the front clasps for extra security. A black helmet was tied to her pack as she pushed the refurbished motorcycle out from its hiding spot by the river. The sun was peeking over the waterfall, one of the many landmarks for her journey. She pushed the motorcycle out toward the dirt road on the outskirts of town. The forest was quiet with the stillness that only early morning brings. She flipped the kickstand down with her foot as she slid the customized helmet on. Amelia had assured her that all she needed to do was press the green button by the clutch and the bike would do everything else. Cam gulped as she remembered that Amelia was only eight years old.

The lightweight dual sport had been reassembled and refurbished to perfection. It shone with a glory that it probably had not seen since its manufacture. Its previously lackluster gray exterior was now a stunning silver. Cam swung one leg over the bike and grasped the handles. She plugged the wire that ran from the bike into the port at the back of her helmet. She took a deep breath and pressed the green button.

The kickstand sprang up into place as the back tire spun against the dry earth. A dust cloud erupted around her as the bike thrust itself into a wheelie before speeding up the mountain. Amelia had programmed the bike to understand terrains, inclines, declines, and weather. Cam's helmet utilized a non-invasive, brain-computer interface to navigate. The camera in the helmet sent the images to the bike's computer where it processed the images she saw and calculated them into optimum driving performance.

Cam fearfully held onto the bike as it swung around the sharply curved road. She had little knowledge of the tunnels, but the computer assessed her memories of her initial trip to Rebel's Glade and projected a small map onto the helmet's inner screen. With her destination in mind, the bike navigated itself knowledgeably. It did not stop to take in the view as it continued at breakneck speed, following the road toward the tunnels.

The tunnel entrance seemed much smaller to Cam as she flew in at turbulent speeds. She felt compelled to close her eyes, but she knew that the bike would most likely stop abruptly and launch her off. As she careened from brilliant daylight to the darkness of the tunnel, she felt the bike shift. The darkness prompted her to wish for some kind of light to which the bike responded by turning on its headlight. The one hundred mile journey was completed in thirty minutes.

The bike warned her when the tunnel was ending five miles ahead, which gave her just enough time to figure out how to ease to a stop. Her legs were numb, and her skin was trembling from the vibrations as she dismounted and unplugged the helmet, leaving the bike propped against the cavern wall.

She quickly changed into her city clothes then went up the steep set of stairs. The climb left her winded as she slid the door's peephole open to check for any activity. It was pitch dark in the Equintas' secret entrance.

She opened the door and entered the dark refrigerator. She strode casually through the kitchen and into the Garden of Sin club. Confident at her progress thus far, she straightened her posture and walked out onto the dazzling floor of the Golden Fire Casino.

The casino was well air-conditioned, and it was a nice change from the cramped, muggy tunnel. Not knowing where to start, she hitched her bag higher on her shoulder and followed the masses. High-end restaurants and loud bars congested the space. Glass windows framed mannequins, gold and figureless. Scarves and gaudy jewels were draped around their necks. The classic ringing of the casino floor eventually met her as she stepped onto the burgundy carpet.

The scent of smoke thickened the air and added potency to the smell of so many bodies pressed together. She maneuvered between drunken gamblers and waitresses in golden leotards before hearing the click of her heels on the tile, indicating she had reached the front lobby. The ceiling rose, doming high above her, as natural light flooded the space. She felt a soft breeze emanating from the doors as she drew closer then, as her hand met the golden door handle, she heard a voice.

"Camilla?"

Cam turned. She did not recognize the man who had spoken. He came up to her and placed a cold hand on her shoulder. She flinched away, inching toward the door.

"I'm sorry, I don't know you," Cam said.

The man leaned in closer. She saw a glint of something flash in his hand before feeling the barrel of a gun press against her back.

"Do yourself a favor and don't cause a scene," he whispered.

She looked behind him and saw two suited men. They all wore small badges on their belts that declared them to be from the military's investigatory branch.

"No," Cam said, her voice rising in volume. "I've done nothing wrong."

"You will come with us. The only choice you have," the man said pressing the barrel harder into her side, hard enough to leave a bruise, "is whether you'll come with us in one piece."

Cam shook her head and laughed.

"Sorry, but that's not my only choice."

She spun, grabbed the man's wrist and broke his arm. He screamed, his gun flying into the air. She caught it then struck him swiftly across the face. A pair of strong hands collided with her as they wrapped around her torso. She dug her heel into his toes then flung her elbow back. His blood sprayed across her forearm, but he still did not release her. The third man joined his now copiously bleeding colleague, tackling her. She fell on the tile and felt her cheekbone thud against the hard surface. Her fingers scrambled against the tile as both men wrenched her arms back. She screamed, arms firmly pinned, as flames burst forth.

Both men flew backward. They landed on the lobby desk over thirty feet back. The fire ran in an arch from her left hand to her right as the large crowd retreated, their eyes fearful. Smoke billowed as the fire extinguished itself, and she stood, knocking the cuffs to the ground.

"You're not going anywhere."

Cam turned just in time to see a gun fly toward her. She heard the deafening blow echo against her skull before she felt the pain. Her body spun. She looked over and met the eyes of the soldier who had spoken to her initially then she fell to the floor, unconscious.

CHAPTER 20
## DRAWING BLOOD

The lights above were swimming like frosted orbs rolling over blurry waves. She tried to lift her head, but her vision distorted further and she felt sick. Her hands automatically moved to rub her eyes, but they were stuck. She tugged and felt her wrists catching on something. She blinked then fixated downward and saw fuzzy halos of gold securing her down. Several minutes passed before the room swam slowly into view.

She was tied to a large metal chair that was bolted to the floor. Gold rope strapped her hands tightly to the chair's arms. Her feet were growing numb. She struggled to move her frozen toes as she felt something odd beneath her. She looked down and saw plastic sheeting. Her toes curled over the plastic with an ominous crinkle as she raised her head and forced her eyes to focus.

The chair stood in the middle of a long, vast room. The walls and floors were made of rectangular stones taller than a full-grown man. Panels of fluorescent lights ran down the center of the room, illuminating two wide marble steps leading up to a platform. Atop the platform, sat a rich mahogany desk. A gold and green lamp doused the desk's expansive top in a muted, orange glow. A high-back leather chair sat behind the desk, turned away from her.

"So, you're finally awake," came a voice from the chair. The voice boomed across the walls, ricocheting down to her. Her eyes grew wide as she immediately recognized the man speaking.

"Holkstoin," she spat in disgust.

He rose from the chair and snapped his fingers. A door opened and two soldiers wheeled in trays. Holkstoin curled his ridiculous mustache as he began to walk toward her. The soldiers set the two carts beside her chair. The shorter soldier appeared pained as she caught Cam's eye. Cam saw the lumps sitting under the white cloths and understood that she was looking at the outlines of torture implements.

"Now I remember you," Holkstoin said, waddling over.

"Took you that long?" she taunted.

"They told me you were an intruder," Holkstoin said, ignoring her. "Do you know what I do to intruders?"

"No, but, judging by your sizable pants, I can guess at what you'd do to a thirty pound turkey," Cam said. She tried to ignite her flame in her hands but nothing happened. She tried again with more desperation. Nothing.

"You made quite a mess for us," Holkstoin said, approaching her. "You shouldn't have used you powers like that."

"Somehow I'm not apologetic," Cam said as she tried frantically to produce a spark.

"Not yet," Holkstoin said, throwing the cloth off the nearest tray. "Oh, and your powers are useless here, by the way."

Cam stopped. Holkstoin chuckled as his gloved hands hovered over the various tools.

"See, that's *my* power," he said. "I can stop yours as I wish."

She stared into his porky eyes as his finger brushed the pliers. She tried to wipe all expression from her face, but her heart was beating so rapidly that it rattled her ribcage.

"I need to know what you're doing here. Why did you break into the city?" Holkstoin asked.

Cam weighed her options then spat in his face. His rolls of blubber quivered as his skin mottled red with anger. He grabbed the pliers and squeezed her left hand. She could feel the slime of his palm sweat through his gloves as he shoved the pliers under her fingernail and pulled.

Cam screamed as Holkstoin grunted with the exertion. She felt her ankles twinge sharply as they struck out against their bonds, nearly breaking from the force. Her breath was ragged and halting as he tossed the fingernail to the floor. She watched the bloody bit roll to a halt atop the plastic, leaving a thin trail of red behind.

"Disrespect will only make this worse for you," he said, his breathing just as strained as hers. "You should just answer my questions."

"Well, you should learn how to use a treadmill," she said, breathing heavily as her vision swam with tears.

Holkstoin didn't acknowledge her answer. He snapped his fingers and the door opened again. A skinny, adolescent boy walked in. His sweater hung off his bones, and his hair was abnormally thin. His eyes bulged from the sockets in a sick, unnatural way. Cam noticed how Holkstoin refused to make direct eye contact with him.

"This is Hugo," Holkstoin said. "You don't want to become acquainted with his boy. He is much more *creative* than I am. Now, tell me why you're here? Who are you working for?"

Cam felt the corner of her mouth pull upward.

"Screw you, you fat fuck."

Holkstoin frowned.

"Hugo, please assist her in answering my questions," Holkstoin said as he turned his massive back to her.

He returned to his desk as Cam turned her attention to Hugo. His face was so gaunt that it resembled a skull painted flesh tones. He stared at her with red-brown eyes, and she felt her body pressing itself into the seat out of instinct. His middle finger bounced on the handle of a small pair of shears.

"Take," he said absently as he handed her the shears. His finger pointed to her upper arm. "Snip, snip."

The gold ropes binding her wrists uncoiled though she was still unable to move. Then she felt her hand reach for the shears, her fingers wrapping around the handle against her will. The spring's tension fought her grip as she held the handles shut. Then she brought the shears down to where Hugo had pointed.

She tried to stop, but her hand was being guided by Hugo's mind alone as her body mimicked the movements he made. She watched as he lowered invisible shears to his own arm. Sweat coated her frame. She knew it was coming, and that she could not prevent it from occurring. Then a scream bubbled shrilly from her as the shears cut a "v" into her skin.

Hugo smiled.

She screamed again as he forced her to cut another "v" an inch lower. He repeated the process over and over until her arm was splintered with cuts like a row of gills. Her skin burned as Hugo smiled serenely at her.

"I'm having fun," he said. He grabbed her hand and shook it with genuine glee. "I hope you are, too."

"Yeah, the torture's great," she muttered.

He turned her hand over in his. His clammy fingers ran along the inside of her palm as his smile crept wider and wider. She shuddered.

"You're exactly the kind of friend I like," he whispered as he bit his white lips. "I like girls."

Cam felt her body tremble. Her bravery melted as he stared at her. She could see the depravity in his eyes, and she knew that he would relish in her agony as much as possible. It would probably go on for a couple of days before her body failed. She stared up at Holkstoin's desk. He was sitting at the chair with his back turned to her. For one reason or another, she found his cowardice to be empowering. This was her mistake, and she was not going to divulge anything about the Equintas. Even if they managed to torture her for months, she would not let them win.

"YOU'RE NOT PAYING ATTENTION!"

A loud crack resounded. Spots danced before her eyes as she clutched her broken finger. She felt Hugo's bony hand under her chin, lifting her face to stare into his demented eyes.

"Yes, I like you a lot. Such pretty, gray eyes," he said, his smile large and playful again. "We'll cut them out last."

Soon, a thick coat of her blood was splattered across the plastic sheeting around her feet. Bits of her skin and ragged fragments of her fingernails dotted the floor along with a couple of teeth. For the most fear-inducing hours of her entire life, she sat helpless as Hugo forced her to torture herself. It was only after her face was covered in blood and vomit, crusted with chunks of orange-green and congealing black, that she fell unconsciousness, and the branding iron fell from her hand.

•

"Cam?"

Cam knew she was either dead or hallucinating. Either sounded quite appealing.

"Cam?"

She could smell the Slums. Something familiar was touching the periphery of her memory. It was parental. She slowly opened her eyes.

"Mel?" she asked at the sight of her Godfather's face.

"Are you okay?" Mel asked, putting a warm hand on her face.

Cam smiled and, realizing her hands were now free, grabbed Mel's arm. A sharp jolt rocked her as she grunted loudly.

"Wow, being dead hurts," Cam said, tensing from the pain that washed over her. It came in waves sometimes burning, sometimes cutting.

"You're going to be fine," Mel said. His face seemed more youthful. She smiled. Sam had told her that if you are granted entrance into heaven, you are happy and young for the rest of eternity. Was that where she was? "Look at what they did to you. My poor Camilla."

Cam saw the darkness behind Mel sharpen. She saw stone floors and plastic sheeting. Her head hung low, swaying as her vision tried to refocus. She saw a metal chair. Her weak, almost numb, fingertips brushed the chair's arm. They came up sticky and black.

"I thought we told you to *capture* her," Mel said to someone behind Cam. "Was that a difficult order?"

"No, sir."

Cam lifted her head, grunting with the exertion, and saw the rotund figure of Colonel Holkstoin.

"Then why did you do *this* to her?" Mel asked, straightening up to his full height.

Cam had not been hallucinating. Mel was younger. His figure was athletic and trim. The crook in his posture was gone. His face was smooth and thick brown hair covered his head as he glared down at Holkstoin.

"I'm sorry, sir," Holkstoin said. "Usually when you have me detain someone, you always have me...interrogate them. I just assumed..."

Cam felt bile rise in her throat as nausea nearly overcame her. She could barely understand what they were saying. Why was Mel here?

"She is very special," Cam heard Mel say. "There will be punishment for your ineptness today. You could have killed her. Now, leave us."

To keep herself from vomiting, she tried to keep her mind focused on something else. She saw a thick band on Mel's finger and stared at it. A sizable circle lay across the top of the band with a pattern etched into it. Cam blinked and tried to focus again on the ring, to focus on something other than the overwhelming pain. Then her breath caught in her chest as the world became sharply focused. In the center of the ring were two, gold concentric circles against a black background.

It was the insignia of the Gi Force.

## Chapter 21
## Family Bonds

Cold panic iced her core. She was still alive and still in Holkstoin's office. Mel was present, and he was wearing the ring of the Lord General's Advisory Council.

"So sorry about all the unnecessary pain you're in," Mel said, patting her roughly on the shoulder. Cam winced as his fingernails scraped her broken skin. "Unfortunately, some of my subordinates fall into the lower spectrum of human intelligence."

"Mel, what's going on?"

"Bring him in," Mel said into his intercom, ignoring her.

Cam heard the door open. She raised her head and saw two nurses enter. They were carrying a stretcher on which a sleeping form was lain. She saw a starved outline and brown, curly hair. She blinked to readjust her aching eyes, and her heart dropped.

"Ke!" she shouted, reaching forward. She fell out of the chair, her legs too weak to support her. Her face struck the ground, sticking to the congealing blood.

"Now, now," Mel said, grasping her shirt collar. He lifted her to her feet as though she weighed nothing. "None of that. You're already hurt."

He dropped her into the chair.

"It's nice to have the family back, isn't it?" Mel smiled as he ruffled Ke's hair. "It's just like old times."

"But you're one of them!" Cam shrieked, finding her voice.

Mel looked down at her. His now youthful, handsome face was like something from a nightmare.

"Oh, come on, Cam. Give me some credit," Mel said smugly. "I'm not just 'one of them.' I'm the Lord General's third in command. The only higher ranking officers are Bacchus Murphy and the Lord General himself."

"No," Cam said in disbelief. "You're my Godfather. You've been raising me since I was ten!"

"Right, well, living in the Slums was a sacrifice I was willing to make," Mel said, leaning toward her. "Do you know why?"

Cam stared at him, at his formerly comforting face, unwilling to answer. This was the man who had helped her take care of Ke, who had brought her Kaibe when she was mourning her parents and was unable to eat. This was the man who had introduced her to some of her favorite stories and who had given her hope for a better future.

"It's because you're special," Mel said with a frightening smile. "You're Edan's active descendent. You're the fated leader of the Templum Three."

Her heart dropped as she strained to preserve her previous solemnity.

"How did you know?" she finally asked.

He pointed to the wall where a panel was shifting aside to reveal a large bank of security monitors. Footage of the Golden Fire Casino began to play. Cam watched as she appeared on the screen. Her fight with the undercover GFIF soldiers ensued, concluding with her potent display of fire. She smiled to herself as she watched their broken bodies fly aflame through the air.

"Through decades of hard work," Mel said. "Fifteen years ago, we had narrowed the pool of possibilities to a few hundred thousand spread across the globe. The Lord General decided to send in operatives to the most concentrated locations. The issue with you people, Cam, is that none of you have proper documentation of your lineage. We had to go in and befriend you pitiful wastes so you would disclose what little you knew of your heritage. It was tedious work, but I volunteered. I asked if I could be one of those operatives because I had a gut feeling that the descendant was a Raquineste slave."

Mel eyed Cam with pride before continuing.

"I was stationed undercover in the unit next to your parents," he said. "They were trusting, naïve fools and they let me into their lives with no questions asked. The other slaves, however, were not so easy. Over one third of the Raquineste slaves were possible descendants and none of them wanted to talk to me."

He turned to Ke, watching his shallow intake of breath.

"I worked tirelessly for a decade. Progress was so slow," Mel said. "That was until your sweet mother had her tragic misfortune. I'm sure you remember that day, you were ten or so I believe."

Cam shuddered. Some of her most vivid and horrific memories were of the day when her mother had accidently been exposed to Vinestra formed.

"I was with her when the poison was to be administered," Mel continued. "She displayed the most amazing prophetic ability I had ever seen. I knew she was special so I had her sent to the Ether. I believe she lasted for several years before the trials became too much for her body to bear. The data we gained has proven to be invaluable."

Cam was too weak to display the fiery turbulence she was amassing.

"Your father contracted the sickness shortly thereafter," Mel said. "He died rather quickly after that, and you two were left all alone."

He walked to Cam and kneeled beside her, taking her numb hand in his.

"It was so tragic," Mel cooed mockingly. "But then I saw an opportunity. I took you both in and my display of charity won over the hearts of those mindless drones in the Slums. They began disclosing their secrets to me at such a pace that I almost couldn't keep up with the reports. I was eliminating candidate after candidate in record time."

He released her hand and moved behind her.

"Then Ke fell ill and you disappeared. I didn't think much of it. I had work to do," Mel said. "Then the old crone in the unit below us died. She never trusted me even after I took you brats in, but her grandson was another story. He had just turned eight and was all alone. He wanted me to care for him like I did with you and Ke. I told him we could be a family but only if he shared the secrets his grandmother had refused to. He all but ran home to bring me their heirlooms, one of which was a very rare document."

His fingers rapped quickly against the chair.

"His family was old like yours," Mel began. "They had been the Armistdan Order's historians. The document was a chronicle of their coming-of-age rites. The ceremony for Edan's eldest daughter was described in great detail as he was their leader. Apparently, Edan had had a special item crafted for her, one whose description was very familiar."

His hand moved to her necklace. He raised the gem, angling it toward him as he scrutinized it. She protested, but her body was still too weak.

"It was a silver necklace with a small circular pendant of Vinestra," he said. "It was *this* necklace."

He laid the pendant back against her skin and sighed. Cam laughed.

"So, exactly how much did it blow for you to find out that it was me all along? I mean, by the time you realized it, I was already gone," Cam said, forcing a grin despite the pain.

"It didn't matter as you practically told me where you were going," Mel said viciously. "You were coming to us."

Mel began pacing back and forth. Cam kept her eyes trained on him as a small amount of energy had recouped itself. Holkstoin's power had been keeping hers suppressed, but now he was gone. She tried to ignite a small flame in her cupped hand.

"Then I faked my death and came home with Ke. It was logical that you would eventually try to save him," Mel said, "but weeks passed, and I began to think you had died or given up. Then I heard about the break-in in the Ether, and I reviewed the security tapes. Your illusionist is quite gifted. Krytos really knows how to pick talent."

Cam's eyes widened at Krytos' name then at the flame that had briefly ignited in her palm.

"Your fearless leader, huh?" Mel mocked. "The Equintas had been a bit of a pest in the past, but they were never of any importance to us. They're too weak. But the fact that you had joined them meant you were preparing for something and, given your predictability, I knew that something would be saving Ke. He really has been the best kind of bait."

Cam laughed as it was her only outlet for the rage that was building. She felt another flame spark in her closed fist. It held for several seconds longer than the last.

"Well, retribution's a bitch, Mel," she said. "I'm stronger than you know."

"Really?" Mel asked, amused. "From my perspective it appears that you only have two options. You can join us and help us to create the perfect world the Lord General has envisioned for us. Your power is the key to the manifestation of a real Utopia. We'll heal Ke, and you both can live for hundreds of years in the new world. I mean, look at me. You'd never guess that I was one hundred and twenty-four, would you?"

He ran a wrinkleless hand over his youthful face and winked.

"Or, of course, you can resist," he continued. "But I don't see a lot of logic in that choice. You'll still wind up helping us reach our goals. You'll have no choice. Plus, Ke will wither and die in a prison cell. He'll die alone, and you'll have to live with the knowledge that you could have prevented it."

He took a step toward her.

"Now, be a good girl and say that you'll join the holy ranks of the Gi Force and that you'll serve the benevolent Lord General to the best of your ability," Mel said. "Will you join us?"

Cam forced herself to stand. Mel approached, his hand outstretched. She took it and smiled, showing the blood that was stuck between her teeth and the mangled remnants of her sliced gums. Mel eyed the collage of burns that ran up and down her arms. They were oozing clear liquid, collecting the pieces of dried blood in its path. She took a breath and her slit nostrils flared inward, flapping the damaged cartilage.

"Yeah, thanks for the offer," Cam said. "But I'm going to have to hotly decline."

Cam wrenched Mel's hand, shoving her mutilated thumb between his metacarpals. She evoked her remaining energy and willed the fire to soar from her palm. The flames encased Mel's hand, scorching with the resolve attained by her wrath. Mel yelled as she stiffened her grip.

"Oh, and sorry about all the unnecessary pain that you're in," Cam said.

She pulled Mel's hand down and slammed her other fist into his nose. He reeled and fell back. The skin of his burning hand melted, sloughing away completely at the point of tension. Gravity weighed his arm downward as she doubled her own force. Then she heard a loud, painful pop. Mel screamed and fell to the ground as Cam looked down.

His scorched and severed hand was clutched in hers.

Cam knew this was her only chance to escape. She ran for Ke and swept him off the cot. Her bare feet slapped against the stone floor as her heartbeats echoed deafeningly. She was at the door, and she slammed her shoulder into it, banging the doors open with a crashing thud.

There was only one guard outside, and he could not have been older than Cam. He pulled his gun from his holster with shaky hands and pointed it at her. She was about to knock the gun away when she felt a strange tug around her abdomen. Suddenly, she and Ke were flying backward, back into the room.

"No!" Cam shouted.

She saw the door shrink rapidly as she was flung to the other side. It was as though a vice were gripping her torso. She hit the wall and gasped as the wind was knocked from her. Ke fell from her arms, his unconscious body rolling several feet before stopping. Her arms and legs were then forced down, pinned against the wall.

"Ke!" she coughed, taking in painful breaths as the invisible force held her. Her throat burned from the lack of oxygen.

"Did you really think it would be that easy to escape?" Mel asked, snarling.

"What is this?"

She struggled against her new bonds.

"I'm a telekinetic, Cam," Mel said. Cam felt the same force expand to grip her throat. It pushed inward, severing the flow of air, "a very powerful one at that."

Her fingers grew cold and numb. She tried to move her head to open her airway but could not.

"Despite your little display, I still think you can be reasoned with," Mel said. "Maybe a few days of watching your brother deteriorate will be an incentive."

Hot tears pooled in the corner of her eyes as she recognized the direness of her situation. Ke's frail frame still lay crumpled on the ground where he had fallen.

*Joining the Gi will save Ke. Maybe we should just say "yes."*

Cam could hear Ke's pained breathing. Saving him had been her goal, the impetus for self-preservation.

*We can try to get him out. We can send him to Tom. We know they'll take care of him there.*

Cam agreed with the logical side of her mind.

*If we can't escape, we have to die.*

Remaining in Gi capture was not an option. She was too valuable to the Gi's plan, to their continued domination. This was the only way to rectify her mistakes.

She clenched her jaw as she sought the resolution needed. She looked at Mel, seeing nothing of the man who had raised her. This Mel was a stranger. He was Mellech now. Cam knew it would be easy to lie to this man, to give a false pledge of loyalty. She took a deep breath and opened her mouth to speak.

Then a booming crash resonated, followed by the door flying off its frame in pieces. The lone guard flew into the room with exceptional force. The air in the room eddied, sending ribbons of plastic sheeting and brown chunks of Cam's skin upward. Gun rushed into the room behind the tornado with his sights on Mellech. Holkstoin was on Gun's heels.

Mellech turned with a look of annoyance on his face. He lifted an eyebrow as Gun armed himself with two bowie knives. Mellech waved a casual hand in his direction, and he flew into the opposite wall. Holkstoin lumbered up with an apologetic expression.

"Are you really this incompetent?" Mellech shouted. "How did they get in here?"

There was silence as Holkstoin slowly raised his head to make eye contact.

"Like this."

A sinister smile stretched across Holkstoin's face before it melted and smoothed into a bright red pout. Then his porky body melted into the curves of a woman. Volpi, tall and leather-clad, threw a brass-knuckled fist into Mellech's face. Mellech fell, unconscious.

Cam felt the force that had been keeping her pinned to the wall, slide away. Gravity peeled her from the wall. She began to sink until she felt the tornado hurtle toward her, moving up the wall. Then arms, warm and familiar, wrapped under her knees and back.

She smiled, she couldn't help it.

"Not fibbing, Tom," Cam said as he set her down. "I'm kind of glad to see you."

"You look like crap," he said.

"Torture tends to do that," she replied.

Sam ran over, blood already drenching his arm as he let it fall over her. He let so much that Cam worried he would lose consciousness. Instantly, the smaller wounds healed. Some of the larger ones, like the circular gouges surrounding her exposed bone, were slower to heal. However, she felt enough strength return within a couple of minutes for her to stand on her own.

"Thanks," she said. Sam smiled.

"Come on," Volpi said, tapping her foot. "We didn't come all the way down here to get caught, too. We should go now."

"Okay," Cam said as she picked up Ke. "Is there another way out of here?"

"There's only the one way out," Gun said. "Volpi's going to transform into Holkstoin again."

"Can't wait," Volpi sneered, slipping the brass knuckles into her pocket.

"We're going to act like prisoners," Tom said.

"Again?" Cam asked.

"Then we'll follow her out and, um, hope for the best," Gun finished.

"Okay," Cam said, not particularly comforted by Gun's tone.

They took turns binding their hands and locking their chains. Without Martin to camouflage them, they were reliant on props. Volpi transformed into Holkstoin again. Her skin bloated and bubbled as her clothes flapped, stretching until they resembled his uniform. The newly-formed Holkstoin looked up and smiled.

"Let's get the hell out of here," came Volpi's voice.

They lined up behind her and followed her out of the room. They filed out into the Breeding Room from the hallway connected to Holkstoin's office. The scientists looked up from their clipboards and saluted Volpi. She nodded in return as they walked toward the lobby. Cam felt the discomfort in her mouth increase as she realized her sliced gums had not been healed. To distract herself, she concentrated on holding Ke's stretcher with Sam. Ke was facing her, eyes closed and hands over his chest. Giddiness rose in her as she absorbed his presence. They opened the doors to the lobby and Cam saw the looming stone pillar standing before her.

*Are you leaving?*

Cam cursed under her breath. She had almost hoped the voice she had heard before was a hallucination. She glanced around the room to ensure only their party was present before answering.

"Why do you care?" Cam asked quietly.

*Please, you mustn't leave yet.*

"Give me a reason not to," she demanded. She stopped and felt Sam tug on the stretcher then falter. He stared at her as she regarded the pillar in concentration.

*You have to go back.*

"I'm kind of in the middle of an impending escape here," Cam said. Tom, Gun, Volpi, and Sam were now collectively staring at her.

*You left your other half behind.*

"Please, nothing cryptic," Cam pleaded. "There is really no time for it."

*In order to find victory, you must go back down into the Ether. You must find your other half!*

"Who are you talking about?"

*Your oni.*

Oni-Orochi. Cam had forgotten about the demon, and her original idea to communicate with it.

"You want me to go to it *now*?"

"Cam!" Tom shouted, interrupting her silent conversation. She looked at him, realizing that he was shaking her shoulders. Gun was holding the stretcher now. "What the hell are you doing?"

"We have to go back," Cam said. "Actually, *I* have to go back."

Tom inclined his head. "Okay, this might be a stupid question on some level, but why?"

"Oni-Orochi," she said. "I was right. The voice just confirmed it. I've got to free it."

"Yeah, we're not going to do that, Cam," Tom said. "We're practically free. Once we leave the Ether, it'll be easy to get home."

"I know," Cam said. "But, long story excruciatingly short, I was told by an 'entity' of the old Ether that we must free Oni-Orochi. More specifically, we must free Oni to gain victory."

"Am I the only one who thinks the Gi must've gotten her very, very high?" Gun exclaimed. "We can't go back."

"What are you guys even talking about?" Sam asked.

"Okay, I've had suspicions that Oni-Orochi is one of the Seven Demons of Ortus Canitia," Cam explained. "If it is, I can communicate with it. I can ask it to help us or, at least, ask it to not kill us while we steal Aeraden. Krytos didn't want to take the risk, and that's why I came here myself."

"Right, and *we* came here to rescue you," Gun said. "For that reason alone, we're not going back."

"I agree," Sam said. "Even now that I know the story, it still seems foolish to go back in."

They broke into simultaneous arguments. Cam attempted to debate her side but was overrun by three firm declinations. Then the most unexpected voice broke over them.

"I agree with Cam!"

Silence fell as they turned to Volpi. The Holkstoin illusion was gone and her expression was resolute. She appeared to be unhappy agreeing with Cam as her jaw was set tight.

"What?" Cam asked, worried that her ears had suffered permanent damage.

"I think you're right and I think you should go get Oni," Volpi said, "and, if you guys won't help her, then I will."

There was silence. Sam looked conflicted as he wanted to agree with Volpi, despite his better judgment, in order to gain her affection. Gun, having not yet recovered from Cam's desire to return, was still in shock. Tom turned to Volpi.

"Why?" Tom asked her. "Why do you of all people think she's right?"

Volpi's lip trembled.

"Because she has to be," Volpi said. "You know all the stories about the Templum Three and the demon's power. That demon is the key to defeating the Gi. It may be foolish, but I'm willing to die protecting Cam long enough so that she can try."

Tom's face was impassive as he contemplated Volpi. Then he smiled.

"Okay then," Tom said, clapping his hands together. "Well, you heard Volpi. I, for one, am not going to let the ladies go back by themselves."

"I'll go, too," Sam said, looking a bit uneasy.

They all turned to Gun. He rolled his eyes.

"Whatever, I guess I'll go, too," he said. "But what are you going to do about your brother?"

"We'll take him with us," Cam said. "It may actually help us blend in by having Ke on the stretcher."

"Sounds good except, Volpi, you can't be Holkstoin," Tom said. "The scientists in the labs will suspect something if they see you again."

"I know," Volpi said. "But I was more worried about camouflaging you guys since they've seen all of your faces already."

"We don't have any disguises other than what we're wearing already," Sam said, tugging at his prisoner's clothing.

*Camilla?*

"Oh my god, what?" Cam asked, addressing the room. No one said anything as they watched her seemingly one-sided conversation.

*I may be able to help. Do you see where the sand dimples by the base of this pillar?*

Cam walked closer to the pillar, staring at the base until she saw a place where the sand was funneling slowly through a hole in the stone.

"Um, yes," Cam said.

*Tell everyone to stand as close as possible to it. Take Kevin off the stretcher and hold him up. You'll need to compress yourselves together as much as you can.*

"Okay," Cam said, unsure as to why she was so readily agreeing. "Help me get Ke. Gun, you're the strongest, you hold Ke upright and as close to you as possible."

Gun nodded and lifted Ke from the stretcher with Sam's aid.

"Sam, hold the stretcher upright," Cam continued. "Everyone stand as close to me as possible."

They huddled together in a suffocating group hug.

"What now?" Cam asked the ceiling. "This isn't exactly comfortable."

*Tell Thomas to prepare for a hard landing.*

"Right," Cam said, rolling her eyes at this point. "Tom, the voice in my head wants you to 'prepare for a hard landing?'"

*Now hold on.*

"To what—"

Cam's voice rose into a scream of surprise. The ground fell away from beneath their feet, and they plummeted. The air rushed around them as their speed increased. She clung to the nearest person as she felt someone do the same to her. The air was deafening in her ears, and she could not tell who was still screaming until her mouth grew dry.

They were in a tunnel that was lengthening itself as they plunged. They could hear the loud, rolling grind of the rocks and earth as they moved aside. A light broke, and they all looked down. A green floor met their eyes as they fell through the ceiling of the prison cells.

Cam felt the wind change and squinted up at Tom. His eyes were closed in concentration. The air puckered, mushrooming around them with a small blast as their speed slowed. They floated down at a soft but somewhat unsettling speed. Tom, eyes closed and teeth gritted, swayed slightly with the exertion of controlling the force. Cam grabbed his arm and steadied him. As they landed, he leaned into her for support.

"Hands up!"

Disoriented, Cam turned and saw what the others had already seen. They were surrounded by seven Gi soldiers and seven well-aimed pistols. Cam raised her hands, following the others' leads. Volpi smiled as Tom slid Cam a sideways glance. She understood and reciprocated with the slightest nod.

"Would any of you be willing to put your guns down and let us go?" Sam asked, knowing their plan as well. "I'm rather anti-violence, and yet I'm pretty sure I'm about to witness all of you being beaten to within an inch of your lives."

The soldiers sniggered, but their laughter was cut short. Tom sent a cutting blast toward them, sending two into the wall as Cam helped Sam pull Ke away from the fight. Volpi slammed her fist into the face of the nearest soldier. A piece of his tongue soared from his mouth as she struck him again and he fell unconscious. Gun pulled two batons from his belt and leaped over Volpi, swinging them in front of his chest to gain momentum. As he sailed between another pair of soldiers he let the batons fly out, striking each soldier's skull with perfect precision. They fell like dominoes until only one lone soldier stood before them, his pistol shaking like madness in his hands.

Gun walked up to him, tossing the baton casually. The soldier took a step back as if he had forgotten about the pistol in his hands.

"Boo!" Gun said with a grin, taking a sudden step forward.

The soldier gasped and dropped his pistol, taking off for the door. Gun turned back and laughed as the pistol hit the floor and discharged. They heard a thunderous bang as Gun collapsed to the ground.

# CHAPTER 22
## OPENING THE DOOR

"Gun!" Cam shouted, running forward. Gun lay on the ground with a blank look on his face. Blood seeped from his chest in a rapidly growing puddle. Cam grabbed Gun's hand while Tom held him down by his shoulders. Volpi grabbed his feet as Sam kneeled.

"Wow, being shot really hurts!" Gun grunted.

"Sorry, this is going to hurt worse," Sam apologized as he delved his fingers into the wound. Gun cried out and gripped Cam's hand so tightly that she nearly cried out, too. Sam worked quickly as he deftly removed the bullet.

Gun's body relaxed, but he was rapidly growing pale. Sam tore the bandages off his forearms where the wounds that he had used to heal Cam were still oozing. He pulled his knife from his pocket and slid it across his skin. His peachy flesh parted like butter as drops of blood oozed.

Gun's wound healed slower than Cam's, but the reconstruction was still conspicuous. After almost a full minute, Gun's skin began to meld together again. He sat up cautiously, drained from the ordeal. He clapped Sam on the shoulder as Tom pulled him to his feet.

"You okay?" Cam asked.

"I'll live," Gun said as he examined his repaired stomach.

"Let's go," Tom urged. "Reinforcements will be coming."

They hurried down the rows of cell blocks, each containing shrunken figures huddled in the background. At this point, it was faster for Cam to throw Ke on her back and run. She stared straight ahead as they cut through the maze of cells. The moans and cries of the prisoners crept into her ears, but she fiercely concentrated on her footfalls. She hitched Ke higher around her shoulders as they reached the double doors leading toward the labs. Gun, weapons ready in unclasped holsters, pushed open the door.

The white hallway was quiet. Cam saw the doors on the other side but knew they were not their destination.

"We need to go down that hallway over there," she said.

They moved quickly with great caution when a door opened somewhere ahead of them. The door clanked loudly against the wall as squeaky footsteps followed. Tom signaled for them to stay back as he proceeded silently down the hallway. The footsteps began to move in the same direction they needed to go. Tom peered around the corner then waved them forward.

Two guards were facing away from them two doors down. Tom gently extended his hand, and the draft billowing from the air conditioner roared down the hallway. The guards turned in time to receive the blast as their bodies were propelled backward. They crashed into the door and fell into a crumpled heap.

"Go," Tom said as they ran down the hallway, pausing before the doors that led to the Refining Room. Tom picked up a security badge from one of the guards.

"Gun, Sam," Tom said. "Guard the door while we clear the room."

They nodded. Cam handed Ke to Gun as Tom swiped the security badge. The door clicked open and they stepped through with trepidation.

The sounds of expansive machinery overwhelmed their ears as they entered. The room was large by most standards but miniscule in comparison to its counterparts in the Ether. Bulky machines sat in rows as pieces of Vinestra were filtered down the assembly line of mechanical pincers and chemical solutions, refined down to the form distributed to the citizens.

"Hello?" came a woman's voice.

The clink of brass knuckles and the flick of a switchblade rang together as Tom and Volpi fortified. Cam turned in the direction of the voice as dainty footsteps echoed against the cement floor. She had no weapon so she lamely put her small, semi-battered fists up.

"Who's there? Identify yourself."

Cam saw tiny feet in a pair of black kitten heels come around the machine. They were attached to a short, thin woman in a rich woolen skirt and silk blouse. Her hay-blond hair fell straight to her chin, and her green eyes widened at the sight of them. It was Rhea Murphy.

"Who the hell are you guys?" she asked. "Show me your authorization to be here."

Silence followed her demand as she stepped forward, angrily.

"You will show me your authorization, or I'll remove you myself," she demanded.

Volpi laughed then ran confidently forward as she was almost a foot taller than Rhea. Cam tried to stop her, but she was too slow. Volpi's fist was clenched tight around the brass knuckles as she aimed with precision. Rhea smiled, sidestepping the attack effortlessly. Volpi's overshot caused her to fly forward as Rhea raised her hand and pressed a single finger against Volpi's back. The air rippled with sudden force as Volpi's body slammed to the ground, cracking the cement floor. Volpi grunted as she tried to sit up only to realize her arm had snapped upon impact. The corners of Rhea's mouth twitched upward again as she stared with satisfaction at Volpi's incapacitated form.

"Now, why are you here?" Rhea asked, turning back to Cam and Tom.

Cam contemplated several lies, but all of them seemed ridiculous.

"We're here to steal Aeraden," Cam said honestly. "My little brother's dying. I need to save him."

Rhea, not expecting such an answer, sputtered for words.

"You are?" she finally asked, taking a step toward Cam.

Tom shoved Cam behind him.

"Stay away from her," he warned. It would have been a funny threat to make against such a diminutive woman had they not seen a recent demonstration of her abnormal strength.

"I just asked a question," Rhea said, amused. "Don't get so defensive, tough guy."

Cam skirted around Tom, trying to get to Volpi who was in visible agony. Rhea grabbed a sledgehammer that sat beside one of the machines. She lifted it with one hand and swung it easily in front of Cam, blocking her path.

"Your friend will be fine," Rhea said. "Stay where you were."

Cam backed up as Rhea flipped the hammer casually in her hands. Tom, who had been calculating Rhea's ability, took a step forward. Rhea swung the hammer out so that it settled just before the tip of his nose. He smirked at her then threw an enormous blast of energy outward.

Wind cascaded in a spiral toward Rhea with enough power to send a grown man flying, but Rhea barely budged. She put her free hand up to block the biting wind as she took a steadier stance. The gusts soared toward her slender palm but could not move her. She snickered as she pushed the cyclone aside, deflecting it with ease.

Tom frowned and pushed a more powerful whirlwind toward her. The machinery shook, ringing in highs and lows like a song. Rhea quickly slammed the sledgehammer into the concrete, burying the head securely in the ground. She held on as the augmented winds threatened to lift her off her feet. Tom decided to strike while he had some advantage. He ran toward Rhea with such fleeting speed that Cam could barely see him. He struck Rhea on the side of her head in an attempt to swiftly render her unconscious. The blow knocked her to the ground as the wind slid her to the other side of the room.

Tom followed in a flash. Rhea was still conscious, and it appeared that the hit had shocked her more than it had injured her. Tom kneeled and struck her again across the face. Cam felt tempted to pull him away as he hit her over and over amid the dissipating wind. When he stopped, Rhea was laughing with only a cut lip to show for the tremendous beating.

"That was really, really interesting. I've never seen anything like that," Rhea remarked. She jumped to her feet and wiped her face delicately. "That'll just make this all the more fun."

She charged, aiming her tiny fist. Cam heard the crush of bone on bone as the collision sent Tom flying. As he fell, he maneuvered his feet to meet the ground and catch his fall. The moment his toes touched the floor he was moving again, speeding around Rhea like a whirlwind.

She was unable to reach him when he moved so quickly, but the one strike she managed to execute sent him sailing into the side of a refinement machine. Tom pulled himself out of the depression his body had created and stood, facing Rhea. Cam was debating how best to intervene when the doors abruptly swung open. Sam and Gun, carrying Ke, burst in.

"What's going on?" Cam asked.

"Guards," Sam said. "At least thirty."

Gun heaved Ke onto his back as Sam threw the door's security bar down. They both stopped when they saw Tom's rapidly swelling eye and Volpi leaning against the wall.

"What the hell is going on?" Gun asked.

Sam leaned over Volpi, examining her broken wrist.

"Sorry," Sam said preemptively as he cut his arm.

"Just be fast," Volpi said. Then she squealed in pain as he cut the flesh around her wrist, deep enough to expose the broken bone. He quickly filled the wound with his blood as her skin healed over, creating a sac around the injury. Sam's powers were limited in the fact that his blood could only heal what it could touch. The bone was broken, but it had not punctured the skin, eliminating a direct path to the wound. Volpi touched her wrist gingerly as Sam helped her to her feet.

"Thanks," she said.

"You guys have to go," Rhea said abruptly. She ran to a door on the other side of the room and typed into the security pad. "This door leads to the Vault."

The security system beeped as a puff of air burst, releasing the air lock. Sam, half carrying Volpi, ran through the door. Tom followed, giving Rhea a peculiar look that she did not acknowledge as Cam stopped in front of her.

"Thanks," Cam said. "But why—"

Rhea put a hand up to cut her off.

"You don't have any time. They won't be able to follow you in. Only an officer ranked as a Colonel or higher can even set foot in there, so it'll take some time for them to follow. Lucky for you, I happen to know my grandpa's code," Rhea said. "I just hope you know what's on the other side of this door."

Rhea turned to leave and bumped into Gun's massive chest. She looked up at him and jumped back as if she had seen a ghost. Gun's mouth fell open and he blinked several times, nearly dropping Ke in his shock.

"Rhea?"

He reached out to touch her shoulder, to make sure she was real, but she pulled away. Her eyes grew so wide that the green irises were framed in white.

"Is that really you?" Gun asked, again.

Rhea took a step back as her tears fell fast and free. Then she turned and ran from the room. Gun started to follow, but Cam grabbed his arm and pulled him into the hall as guards began to fill the room. They fell into the hall together, and the door closed behind them. Gun propped himself up on his elbows, his eyes transfixed on the sealed door.

"Gun?" Cam asked quietly. She was unsure if he wanted everyone else to know.

He turned to her as if he had suddenly realized where he was and what was happening.

"Come on," she urged. He blinked deliberately then nodded. They stood and turned to face the others.

Tom, Volpi, and Sam were gaping at the largest door Cam had ever seen. The full enormity of the double doors was lost to them as the top was indiscernible in shadow. The door was tarnished in slate hues with twin handles made of black stone. A thick border framed the door, filled with alien symbols.

Cam walked forward and ran her fingers over the cold engravings. Her breath rattled in her chest as she stared, transfixed. She had seen the door before. She had seen it in her dreams.

"Yeah, this isn't foreboding at all," Cam said. Her hands wrapped around the cold, stone handles as she noticed her reflection in their glossy finish.

"I'm going in," she said, turning to them. "You guys stay here. If I don't come back in ten minutes, take Ke and leave."

"I can go with you," Tom suggested.

"No, you can't actually," Cam said, "and don't do anything stupid like coming in after me, okay? If you do, I'll kick you where it really hurts."

"Well, no one wants that," he said, stepping back.

Cam took a breath, knowing potential suicide lay on the other side. She was apprehensive though self-assured as she pushed on the handles. The doors gave way to her, opening just enough to allow her access. She stepped into the darkness and heard a deafening thud as they closed behind her.

# CHAPTER 23
# ONI

The room was indistinct and gray. There was a faint light source somewhere, but Cam was unable to see where it originated from. The room appeared to be filled with some type of smoke. Her vision was smothered by the haze, though she had no difficulty breathing as the air smelled and tasted clean. She waved a hand in front of her face to disperse the haze but found it to be immovable. The smoke hung serenely in the space, its wispy tendrils probing the air like a whisper.

Cam took a small step forward. She was almost blinded completely by the haziness of the room. Her feet slid over the floor, searching for anything that would trip her. Her arms were stretched out to her sides as she slowly progressed. The light was soft and yellow-orange, but it was growing brighter with each step she took. Then she heard a loud screech like fingernails on a chalkboard multiplied in volume and intolerability.

The haze rippled like water. Cam felt goose bumps rise swiftly over her skin as the air in the room rushed toward the undulation. The temperature plummeted with the movement as silence fell. Immobilizing numbness encased her for nearly a minute before she was hurled backward.

The air, heat, and sound returned plangently as she warily peered upward. The smoke dissipated, revealing the source of the light. Her mouth dropped and her eyes widened as they traveled upward to take in the beast that was standing before her.

It was shapeless save for ten appendages, each with a set of whetted talons. It was indeed transparent as the Equintas had stated, but its vastness was overwhelming. The light Cam had seen was emanating from a glowing orb within the beast's body. The powerful movement of the air had simply been the creature inhaling. She took a step forward as the beast lunged.

Cam stopped as it swooped around the room in a large arch, settling directly above her. Two red, mutilated eyes appeared. She wanted to scream, but her body was frozen. Talons came down on either side of her as the beast inched closer and closer. Her breath was coming in quick bursts as one thought played over and over again.

*I was wrong.*

She scrambled backward. Her body was acting of its own accord, but for every inch she moved, the beast moved two. Soon, she was up against one of the walls, cornered. Her sense of direction was hindered greatly as the smoky haze settled in a great circle around her, making the beast the only thing she could see. Adrenaline struck her, awakening her stunned senses. She thought of Ke as the blinded eyes, each bigger than her skull, charged toward her.

There was no pain. Her mind was oddly blank, and all emotion had fallen away. Her body was tranquil for the first time in a long time as she took a deep, relaxing breath. She looked up and saw the horrifically blinded eyes surrounded by swirling smoke. She should have been afraid as she was before, but she found her normal senses had somehow become secondary. She could still hear the talons scratching against the stone floor and smell her fear-induced sweat drying on her skin. Her brain continued to interpret all sensory inputs, but they were ancillary to the new part of her mind that had awoken as she detected a tendril of intrusion.

The tendril began to spin, replicating itself into thousands of pieces. They trembled together, fusing into various shapes of various dimensions. Silver dots represented the first dimension and were interspersed between two-dimensional and three-dimensional geometric shapes. The fourth dimension was characterized by two distinct tesseracts. One rotated across a single plane while the other rotated across two. To add to the complexity, the shapes were concentrated into the form of another, larger shape that resembled a crescent. The crescent itself also rotated in a manner similar to the tesseracts.

It was a code, and somehow Cam already knew how to decipher it.

The first key was in the crescent shape of the overall code. The crescent undulated inward until it reversed itself. During this movement, it was folded into itself halfway. The number of overlapping dots represented the number of words. Cam saw two.

Both varieties of tesseracts were partnered with a two or three-dimensional shape. Cam located the clusters containing correlating two and three-dimensional shapes, such as circles and spheres. These groupings represented the second key which allowed her to decode the individual letters in each word. Once she had located the correct groups, she substituted them into the equation that she somehow knew would produce the correct letters:

$$(2\text{-}D)(\text{Simple Rotation}) - (3\text{-}D)(\text{Double Rotation}) = X$$

"X" equaled the numeric representation of a letter in the English alphabet. Each letter was assigned a number starting with "1" for "A." The pattern continued in rising numeric order against descending alphabetic order until "26" for "Z" was reached. Cam repeated the process for each shape cluster until she had nine letters. The order of the letters was determined by the rate of each groupings movement. Each letter was arranged from the slowest to the quickest. Cam arranged the letters in the new space of her mind and a smile spread across her face.

"Oni-Orochi."

With her newfound elucidation, her normal senses returned and her brain was once again concentrated on reality. Oni-Orochi roared as its transparent body launched upward and burst into flames with a blinding show of light. Cam threw her hands up and shut her eyes as a great boom echoed from where Oni-Orochi had been.

The walls trembled as the smoke swirling inside the demon transformed into white feathers. They erupted into the air and floated downward like a gentle snow. Cam reached for one which evanesced at her touch. Then the room was flooded with crimson light as Cam found herself looking up into the blind eyes of a fully corporeal demon.

Red and orange scales coated its body. Its torso, head, and tail resembled a dragon while its legs were more akin to a crustacean. Eight shelled legs ran down the sides of its stomach and a pair of claws jutted from the upper half of its torso. Shadowy, bat-like wings rested firmly against its colossal body.

Cam stood and tentatively stepped closer. It made no move to attack her. Instead, it bowed lower into a less aggressive stance.

"Okay, so you are very much one of the Seven Demons. Um, hi," Cam said with an awkward wave. "I'm Cam."

Again, she felt Oni's thoughts seep into her mind. The word was "vision," but it was not the only message conveyed. She saw quick and abrupt flashbacks from the dreams that had begun after Ke had fallen ill. The images flashed with intensity, each scene striking her mind like a bullet.

A flash of silver light flared, and she suddenly saw herself running toward a door down a golden street. Ke was standing by the roadside, calling her "Camilla of No Last Name" and begging her to remember what was given to her. Then there was another flash, and she was in a blood-soaked street. The door still stood before her, and a crab sat on her shoulder. Over and over, the images cascaded into her mind with unbearable weight. She gasped as the image shuddered and reformed again. She was facing her father with his mutilated eyes as he told her she had the chance to see. Then the vision evolved, and she watched the crab grow into the demon before her.

Cam collapsed to the ground, heaving from the nausea caused by the sudden vertigo. As the spinning of her vision slowed, she began to realize the commonalities shown in the vision.

"So, you were behind those dreams. You were trying to lead me here, weren't you?" Cam asked. "By the way, not the best way to accomplish that. Maybe a dream with less random imagery and more clear instruction like a sign that says 'Hi, I'm Oni, and you need to come to the Ether to get me, please.'"

The demon stood motionless with its head turned toward her. One of the ragged, empty eye sockets twitched as if it were trying to blink. Cam waited for a response but none came either verbally or mentally.

"We're supposed to be able to communicate, right?"

Oni-Orochi shifted its head curiously as it sniffed the air around her.

"You know, conversations?" Cam asked with more firmness. "Here's an example, and you can take notes on how *I* give concise directions unlike some demons who shall remain nameless. I say something such as 'I want to get a cheeseburger without pickles and extra dressing.' You could then respond with something like 'I don't know, burgers give me the runs maybe we could go for tacos.' See that give and take of verbal output? That's called a conversation."

Oni remained silent. Cam was growing frustrated. It had sent her a random set of code and a violent flash of visions that had made her sick. She had been expecting a much easier form of communication.

"So, the only way we can talk is through codes then?" Cam asked exasperated. "No more visions, please. The last ones you sent made me sick, and I can't be sick every time you want to have a heart-to-heart."

Oni made no movement aside from the slow rise and fall of its chest as it breathed. The gentle and rhythmic breaths drew Cam's eye to the door behind it. It was a smaller version of the doors she had passed through earlier, and it led to the Vault. Cam remembered the reason why she was there in the first place and turned back to Oni. The events with the demon had left her confused and tired.

"Okay, I don't know if you can understand me or not. But here it goes," she said. "The reason I'm here is to steal something out of the Vault behind you. My little brother is sick and that's the only way to save him."

She paused to see if Oni would respond but nothing happened.

"Well, I'm going to just go in that door now," Cam said with a sigh. She stood and gave Oni a wary glance. "Please don't eat me. I'm sure I'll just give you indigestion."

She walked toward Oni with her shoulders back and her chest puffed out in a poor attempt at feigning confidence. Oni's eyes were nothing more than ragged scars thicker than her leg, but it shifted its head regardless. She continued to tread around the demon until the mutilated eyes were no longer visible. Then Oni moved, shifting its body around with swift grace and Cam let out a shrill yelp of shock. Oni cocked its head to the side with a perplexed expression.

"Sorry I screamed. You just scared me," Cam said, taking a deep breath. Oni sat down and was still as stone. Cam let out a sigh. "This is ridiculous. I have no idea whether you can even understand me. I should just—"

Cam and Oni turned as the double doors flew open. Tom, Gun, Volpi, and Sam rushed in with Ke in tow.

"Cam!" Tom said. "Cam, are you...oh."

They stopped and stared up at the flame-colored demon. Oni stood and widened its stance defensively.

"Is that what I think it is?" Sam asked, pointing.

"Oh, my god," Gun muttered.

"Apparently you all are either deaf or unable to follow simple directions," Cam said, annoyed. "What happened to 'don't come in after me?'"

"Well, you, um, screamed," Tom said, eyes unblinking as he stared at Oni. "That's generally an indicator that someone's in trouble."

"Oh, my god," Gun repeated louder.

Cam looked over at Ke, hanging from Gun's back.

"Well, we can discuss all this later," Cam said. "I think we should find Aeraden and get out of here, quickly."

Cam pointed toward the other set of doors. Oni stretched its legs out and sat down, having understood they were no threat. Gun took several steps back at Oni's movement.

"Is that your way of saying that it's okay for us to go in there?" Cam asked Oni. "I'll take your pointed and continued silence as a 'sure, go right ahead.'"

They followed her as she skirted around Oni's massive body. Gun was particularly cautious as he kept himself as close to the wall as possible. When they reached the smaller door, Cam put her hand on one of the handles and pushed.

The two doors swung open to reveal a long stone room. Large sconces lined the walls on either side, spreading warm light over the space. Sturdy mahogany cabinets ran the length of the walls, spread intermittently between the stone pillars. Cam's eyes traveled to the end of the room where a glass cabinet stood. Inside the cabinet, sat a milky, white stone.

"Aeraden," Cam said.

She walked down the hallway with the others trailing behind her. With each step that fell upon the well-worn pavers came a shock of exhilaration. Her vision narrowed, tunneling to the bottom shelf where the little orb waited. The culmination of everything that had happened since Ke became sick crashed down upon her.

They had done it. They had saved Ke against all the odds and determents. She let her joy, so raw and so sincere, go. It was a cataclysmic explosion of emotion so exhilarating that it hurt. She smiled as she stepped up to the glass cabinet and put her hand on the door. Her reflection smiled back, jovial for the first time in a long time. Then she felt a soft vibration run along her forearm.

Her skin tingled, and the hairs stood on end. A force gripped her arm tightly as her vocal cords constricted. She sputtered, managing only to let out a tiny gasp.

"Wow, you are just so damn predictable, Cam," Mellech said amusedly. "You should have left when you had the chance, though you were never the shiniest tool in the box, were you?"

Cam felt her body lift into the air as Tom and the others turned to face Mellech. Her invisible bonds rotated her. As Mellech came into full view, so did Holkstoin backed by thirty armed soldiers. Cam struggled to breathe.

"Let her go!" Tom demanded as the air stirred.

Mellech smiled as Cam felt the force pull her back.

"Let her go?" Mellech asked with a grin. "Gladly."

Then, with swift strength, the force released her and threw her toward the stone wall. She cried out. The stirring air quickly turned into a fierce gale as Tom threw himself between her and the wall. He maneuvered the wind to act as a buffer for them while he tried to slow their speed. Even so, Cam felt the air kick out of her lungs as they collided with the barrier.

Mellech turned and nodded to Holkstoin.

"Arrest them," Holkstoin ordered.

A group of eight soldiers, assault rifles poised, broke from the group and advanced. Cam and Tom lay in a painful heap against the wall, trying to regain their bearings after the impact. Cam gasped sharply as her lungs fought for air. Through teary eyes, she saw Ke being quietly transferred from Gun to Sam who carefully laid him on the ground and out of harm's way. The soldiers advanced until there was only a few feet between them.

"Put your hands on your head," one of the soldiers ordered. "Now!"

Each of them did as they were told. The soldiers broke out of their formation again. Four of the soldiers moved toward Cam and Tom while the other four divvied up to arrest the others. As one of the soldiers advanced on Volpi, she grabbed him by the neck and flipped him onto his back. The soldier hit the ground just in time to receive a sharp jab to the nose.

Gun drew two daggers from his belt. The first was thrown in a graceful, spiraling arch at the soldier in front of him. It hit its target squarely in the center of the pupil. The second dagger was thrust backward and lodged into the stomach of the soldier behind him. Together, Volpi and Gun rendered another unconscious.

Cam saw two of the soldiers that had been by Tom fly across the room into the wall. Her arms ran alight with flame and the soldier holding her screamed. She broke out of his grip and sent out a fiery blast that scorched the remaining soldiers. She turned as nearly two dozen more advanced.

"While I found that little show quite amusing, I should remind you how outnumbered you are," Mellech said as he turned to his subordinates. "Go."

The remaining soldiers took up their weapons and charged. The heat within her rose until it boiled over as rage. She was too close. It was unthinkable to allow them to stop her now. The fire that had been smoldering over her arms burst out toward the oncoming onslaught. The spiraling mass of flames exploded as a tornado melded with the fire. She glanced sideways at Tom who was responsible for the added cyclone tearing her emboldened flames down the hall.

The soldiers' eyes widened as their bodies flew back with force, the blast picking up Mellech and Holkstoin along the way. The soldiers spun through the fiery mass and collided with the double doors. Cam and Tom ran forward. Most of the soldiers appeared to be unconscious and those who weren't were fleeing with speed. Cam spotted Mellech lying face down on the floor, and she moved to him. She turned him over while keeping a hand clenched around his throat. He looked up at Cam, weakly, as a cackling laugh rose from his chest. Cam cautiously tightened her grip, poised to strike as Mellech continued to laugh.

"I'm not seeing the funny here," Cam said. "Seems to me that you should be doing something more productive, such as begging for your life."

Mellech laughed harder. Cam dug her thumb and middle finger into his throat. He choked, gasping until Cam loosened her grip.

"You're missing the big irony here for me, Cam. Here I was, so frustrated to know that I had once had you, Edan's descendant, in my grasp," Mellech said hoarsely. Burns coated his skin and a thick chunk of his forehead was missing. "Only now, I learn that *he's* been a descendant, too."

Tom came up and stood over Mellech.

"Right under your nose it would seem," Tom said. "You Gi folk are awfully dim."

"I never liked you much, kid," Mellech said, lip curled in a snarl. "I always thought you were a bad influence on my little Cam."

"Good thing I never listened to you on that one," Cam said with a grin.

"Oh, but you should have," Mellech said. "You're just like your father, so arrogant. You think you'll always win. You know, after your mom was taken, your dear old dad just couldn't take it. He wanted to form a rebellion with the other slaves and leave the Slums. He wanted an uprising, but he was stupid. I wasn't about to let him ruin the decades of my life that I had spent on research. So I stabbed him three times in the back and had his body sent to Curro where they ground it into chum for the fishing boats."

Mellech laughed as he watched Cam's face fall. The saliva ran dry in her mouth as she looked down at the man who had been her second father, the man who had only gained such standing by killing her real father. She could not help the sorrowful tremors that ran down her body.

"Oh, there, there," Mellech said mockingly. "At least your dad didn't suffer like your mom did. Your mom endured some of the worst torture imaginable. It was so bad that even *I* cringed reading the reports."

Cam's fingers twitched as her vision swam red.

Mellech's eyes bored into her as a sick smile crept across his face. "Would you like to know the details?"

Cam could not move. She was paralyzed with rage. Her vision was fixed on Mellech's murderous face.

"The day she finally died was pretty gruesome," Mellech said. "We were working on power enhancements and had to drill into her spine. Oh, the screaming was horrible. You have no idea. I had to wear earplugs—"

"Shut up!" Cam screamed.

"But I'm having so much fun," Mel protested, still smiling.

The fires began to die as smoke filled the room. Disgust and fury overwhelmed Cam at the sight of the slimy smile still tickling the edges of Mellech's mouth. Her ire was resolute as the fire in her palm burned into the shape of an arrow. She allowed it to hover over him before she bore it slowly into the center of his chest.

"Stop right there, you two!"

Cam turned her head and saw Holkstoin. Holkstoin had his pudgy arms wrapped around Ke's limp, unconscious form. A fixed blade was in Holkstoin's hand, and he had it pressed against Ke's throat. Cam glanced around and saw Gun lying unconscious on the ground. Volpi and Sam were at the Vault's entrance, too far away to assist. Cam turned back to Holkstoin.

"Put your hands on your head or else the boy—"

But the sentence was never finished. In the confusion of the gray smoke, a disoriented soldier had stumbled into Holkstoin as he attempted to run from the room. Holkstoin lurched forward, and Cam watched as the dagger delved into the soft, buttery skin that lay over Ke's jugular.

CHAPTER 24
REVENGE

In hindsight, Cam could remember the look of shock that had swept over Holkstoin's red, blotchy face. Her vision flooded redder than the blood that gushed from Ke. Holkstoin dropped Ke clumsily to the ground and retreated. The bloody dagger shook in his porky hand and fell with a clatter. A messy, asymmetrical pool of blood spilled from Ke, highlighting him in a crimson aura.

Cam's mind focused on Holkstoin as a target formed around him. She did not remember letting Mellech go or walking toward Holkstoin. All sound melted away and she could only hear the quickening thumps of her prey's heartbeat. Her movements were trained, slow and precise, as she knocked Holkstoin to the ground and wrapped her burning hands around his neck.

She cried out in a murderous rage that was deaf to her own ears. The flame growing across her body began to swell. The enormous room was suddenly too small to contain her power. The flames danced high, growing steadily with each jarringly calm breath. Then something snapped.

Something that had been tethering her power, keeping it earthbound, broke under the strain. A rush of adrenaline unlike anything she had ever felt sprang forth and her body erupted in emerald green flames.

*Break.*

The heat of the fire amplified as Cam watched Holkstoin burn. The power was unlike anything she had ever felt. His skin bubbled under her palms as his eyes widened in terror. He screamed, fighting vainly against her. His fat boiled and burned, sticking to her clothing. White and yellow lumps of fat pooled around him like bits of raw egg as his flesh turned red and soft. She squeezed her fingers and felt them slip as his burning skin sloughed into steaming piles on the ground. Bile filed his mouth and nose as the fire ate away his face. His lips were shiny wet as they burned and swelled.

Cam felt wave upon wave of pure hatred and unending anger compound her senses. Most of the rage was directed at Holkstoin but a little was reserved for herself. She had let herself feel like they had won, like she had won. She had allowed herself to feel the painful rush of glory and happiness that accompanied success. For months, she had kept any sense of accomplishment or true joy at bay. She had been too quick in relishing success, and she hated herself for being so weak, so impatient.

*Is this how you run?*

The voices had joined her, but she was unafraid as she watched the fat clusters turn to black, charred disfigurements. Holkstoin's cheekbones jutted upward as the flesh fell away. His missing skin and exposed innards were a retribution for the mutilation of her life and the destruction of her dreams. As the fire raged she felt herself slowly sink as the heaping mass that was once Holkstoin's torso fell away.

`Grand justice for a shattered euphoria.`

As Cam held onto Holkstoin, she watched him burn. She hoped that he was dying and that he would die after she was done. She knew he would suffer more if he lived and that was not her intention. If he survived the burn treatment, and if Aeraden was applied quickly enough, he may only be scarred, but then there would be no escape from the monstrous existence that would follow. He would be scarred so horrifically that his skin would be smooth like doll plastic. His wife would leave him, and his children would never call. At work, he would receive sympathetic nods, and no one would be able to finish a meal with him at the same table. The pain of years and years of believing he was a monster as the logical response to the way he was treated was more punishment than she intended. The fire raged with more fury as, in her eyes, he only deserved to die.

*Is this how you drown?*

Her knees hit the stone floor as her hands throttled his naked spinal cord. His partially disintegrated body jerked and convulsed. The charred bits of himself formed a perimeter around him, a ghastly snow angel.

His eyes had rolled back in his head and had begun to shrink in the heat. Cam found herself straddling his boiling intestines and the smoking remnants of his uniform. The smell of burning fecal matter thickened the air. His jaw was set into a permanent scream as Cam held on past the point where she knew he was dead.

*...THE LAST THING HE'LL EVER SEE.*

Movement by her hand caught her eye as she saw a dark square. It was Holkstoin's wallet, and she pocketed it. She felt a gust twist against her fire as Tom's hands pulled her back. She quickly let go as time sped up and her senses returned to normal. Her rigid fingers came away sticky with partially liquefied skin. Tom pulled her into a standing position and she flexed her fist, noting the sickening squish. Volpi and Gun were staring at her while Tom did the opposite. A few feet away, Sam was cradling Ke's body. The bandages were again discarded as his reopened scars repaired Ke's wound.

A sudden spark came over her as she realized Ke was not dead. She should have remembered that Sam was able to save him. She killed Holkstoin as revenge for a murder that never happened, as an outlet for allowing Mellech to go unpunished.

"Is he okay?" Cam asked, finding her voice.

Her body was weak and her hands refused to stop shaking. She was not just a killer but a murderer.

Sam eyed her warily.

"He'll survive, but not for long," Sam said. "We need to get him out of here. My blood isn't healing the wound entirely and I think it has something to do with the poison."

"Where's Aeraden?" Cam asked. Regaining control was the only substitute to dwelling on Holkstoin's remains.

"We got it," Gun said, pulling the orb from his pocket.

A cacophony of footfalls echoed from the Refining Room, and they turned in the direction of the sound.

"Soldiers," Tom said.

"We almost didn't survive last time, even with the fire tornado thing," Volpi said.

"Now do you see what I meant about the fire tornado?" Gun asked her.

"That sounds like more soldiers than before," Tom said. "But we're going to have to fight. There's only one way out."

A sharp screech stung their ears as Oni approached them. His disfigured eyes turned toward Cam. She thought of the last story Ke had told her back in the Slums as the gray smoke billowed around them.

"Oni can help us fight," Cam suggested desperately. "Let's all hop on then we'll have the advantage of height, too."

"Are you sure?" Gun asked, eyeing Oni with trepidation.

"Guys, we don't really have time to debate this," Sam warned, still on the floor with Ke. "They're here."

Blurred shadows clambered into the room as they quickly took turns pulling themselves onto Oni's back. Volpi went first followed by Gun, who appeared rather nervous. Sam was next then Ke and Tom. Oni stayed perfectly still as Tom extended a hand to Cam. She jumped up just as dozens of soldiers approached their location. The first line stopped at the sight of Oni, looking up in shock.

"Are you going to attack them or should we—" Cam gasped as she gripped the silky red scales.

Wings extended from Oni in one swift movement that almost made Cam's heart stop. The shadowy, translucent wings spanned the length of the entire room. The air rocketed forward and knocked the soldiers over. The smoke cleared from their side of the room with Oni's single movement. Cam gulped, holding on firmly as they rose into the air.

"What the hell is going on?" Volpi shrieked as they continued upward. "Can't it see there's a ceiling up there?"

"No," Gun said. "Actually, it looks pretty blind to me."

"It's blind?" Volpi asked incredulously. "Yeah, I wouldn't have gotten on this thing if I had known that."

Cam clung to Oni as the ceiling loomed closer and closer. She heard Volpi scream and felt Tom's grip tighten around her torso. Cam shut her eyes as Oni drove them into the ceiling.

Cam waited, but there was no impact or change of speed. She peeked out, reluctant with fear.

They were in a tunnel that seemed to be creating itself just like the path the pillar had produced. It was more than wide enough for Oni. Cam looked down. Smoke and dust billowed with them as the debris from the suddenly generated tunnel crashed down. The air surrounding them was building force as Oni reached higher speeds. Then the air reversed its pull and Cam saw daylight flood the tunnel. Smoke filled the air around them and exploded outward as they broke out into the light of the Metraline's lobby.

Screams filled the air as Oni dug its claws into the marble floor, breaking the slabs like butter. Soldiers, secretaries, and scientists scattered across the room in panic. The gray smoke drifted upward and pressed against the domed glass wall that overlooked the city, filling the lobby like water in a fishbowl.

Cam felt Oni's body expand as it inhaled deeply. It was quiet as the Gi onlookers dared to peek out from behind the safety of desks and pillars. Then Oni exhaled and the gale shattered the wall of glass.

Razor-edged pieces of the highest quality glass rained down in sedan-sized chunks. Oni reared and they were flung into the air again. The charcoal smoke burst from the front of the Metraline as they broke through the gray smoke and flew out into the bright blue sky.

CHAPTER 25
FINDING HOME

Oni flew them well into the stratosphere before adjusting direction. Cam had had no communication with the demon since the visions it had shown her, and yet Oni knew exactly where to go. He flew them south, following the mountains and the river toward Rebel's Glade. Cam held on to Ke who was lying in front of her against the back of Oni's neck.

Cam grinned as they flew through a low bank of clouds. She was thoroughly enjoying the experience. Flight seemed natural to her as she found she was more comfortable in the sky than on the ground. She had almost forgotten that she had the melted body fat of a Gi colonel stuck to her palms.

Tom and Sam seemed to share her exhilaration of flight, whereas Volpi had not opened her eyes since they had left the Metraline. Gun was staring straight ahead with a greenish tint to his skin.

"I wouldn't advise throwing up on the demon," Sam said to Gun. "It might get mad and buck us all off."

"Thanks, man. The mental image of us being thrown from a demon's back midflight is so helpful," Gun said as he clutched his stomach.

"I'm just kidding," Sam laughed. "Besides, this is the coolest thing I've ever done and it seems perfectly safe—"

Then they felt Oni lurch. They looked at each other as Oni regained level balance for a brief moment before plummeting into a dive. They soared into the valley between the mountains. The air was cold and biting as Oni drew level with the treetops. Cam observed the lush green forest that thrived between the mountain pass below them. A flock of birds soared alongside them as the river reflected glossy silver. The air was again crisp and exceptionally clean. The sun was directly above them, casting their shadows small as they landed in a forest clearing north of Rebel's Glade. They dismounted with the sudden landing prompting Gun to vomit in a bush while Sam laughed about it. Tom pulled Ke down and hitched him high on his back.

The moment after they had all dismounted, Oni began to change. Its body grew paler and paler until it was once again the transparent, formless version of itself. Cam felt everyone else back up. The surface of Oni's body glinted bits of silver as its skin began to ripple. The movements became faster and more pronounced until the ground beneath their feet began to vibrate. She took a step closer but was blinded by a brilliant flash. When she opened her eyes, she saw a small white crab no bigger than the palm of her hand.

"Oni?" Cam asked uncertainly.

The crab turned and winked with its tiny black eyes. Instinctively, Cam kneeled down as the newly miniaturized Oni-Orochi crawled to rest on her shoulder.

"Weird," Cam said, petting Oni who nestled cheerfully into her neck.

"Maybe he knows he's about to meet more people," Sam suggested. "I mean, he's probably gathered by now that his other form is a bit off-putting to some."

"Sure, makes sense," Tom said, shrugging as he examined Oni with curiosity.

"It's sort of cute like this," Volpi commented.

"I still don't like it," Gun said. He was the only one remaining at a distance. "It may fool all of you, but I still remember the scary that lurks under that innocent, crustacean exterior."

Cam rolled her eyes.

"Come on, let's get going," Cam said as her mind drifted back to Ke. "We're pretty far from Rebel's Glade and Ke still needs help."

•

Cam was exhausted. They took turns carrying Ke but, even with their assistance, her body was worn. Her calves burned and her back was sore.

She looked around and noticed how remarkably alert everyone else was. Granted, they had not been tortured for the better part of the previous night but it made her realize how often the others had been on perilous missions where death was an inch away. This was her life now, too. She had been pre-destined to fight and to survive.

"Can you believe we did it?" Gun asked through a veil of cigarette smoke.

"Did what?" Volpi asked.

"Stole Aeraden," Gun said with a grin. "Has that realization sunk in with any of you yet? We did the impossible. We are going to change the world."

The river roaring beside them began to fork, marking the one hour mark. Cam felt a small pinch on her shoulder as Oni shifted in its sleep.

"Think of all of the people we're going to save," Sam said in awe.

"Where will we even start?" Volpi asked. "There's so much we can do now that we have Aeraden."

"Krytos will probably want to get it to the sick in the Slums somehow," Gun said.

Cam looked at Ke's little face. His big eyes were closed and his mouth was half open. His tiny body was even smaller than she remembered and his skin was gray.

"The best part for me is how angry the Lord General must be right now," Tom said, grinning. "I mean, this time, *we* won."

The path wove between the trees and the light grew dimmer as they traversed. The river widened as the forest gave way to the mountain range. Chimney smoke rose from the houses as the town came into view. Cam felt a tingling flash in the pit of her stomach. She was excited to be back in Rebel's Glade, which could only mean that she had missed it and had gained an emotional stake there. It was almost like coming home.

It was Alex who saw them first. She smiled and ran out to meet them. She was soon followed by Max, their brood, and then half of the town. The welcoming crowd pressed around them in unanimous relief of their return. Hands clapped their backs and hearty greetings were echoed around them. Cam hitched Ke higher on her back as she noticed Tom soaking up the attention with a cool, almost nonchalant, demeanor.

Cam, on the other hand, could barely breathe. She returned their smiles as she did feel gracious toward them for they genuinely cared for her safety but her tongue was heavy in her mouth. Her mind ran over hundreds of responses to the inquiries, but each one was imperfect. She remained silent with a smile still plastered to her face, feeling dumb for not wanting to say anything. The voices whispered incomprehensively as her mind raced. The crowd followed them to their house where Shun was standing at the threshold, arms folded. Cam, with Oni on her shoulder, nearly ran up the stairs and into the house.

Tom followed her in, waving casually to everyone as he shut the door. They carried Ke into the bedroom and laid him gently on the bed. Cam pulled the soft blanket over him as Oni crawled to lay beside Ke's left ear. She carefully brushed Ke's hair from his eyes as Shun's silhouette appeared in the doorway.

"Well," Shun said softly. "Did you get it?"

"Yeah," Cam said as she removed the milky stone from her pocket. Shun's eyes widened, and she took in the most subtle gasp. "We got it."

"Tell me what happened," Shun said eagerly.

Cam let Tom recant the arduous journey. He began the story with Cam being tortured in Holkstoin's office. For over an hour, he detailed what had occurred. Shun nodded appropriately and asked the occasional question, but she could not contain her curiosity or enthusiasm when Tom introduced Oni.

"So, this little guy is Oni-Orochi?" Shun asked, indicating the sleeping crab. "You were right after all, Cam."

Cam nodded weakly.

"Yes," Tom said. "He's some kind of shape-shifting demon. Cam saw him in a non-corporeal form, and we all saw him as this enormous flying beast. Sam thinks he changed into this form to be less intimidating to us while he's not needed for combat."

"Amazing," Shun remarked as she gently stroked Oni's shell.

"Cam was amazing, too," Tom said as Cam kept her eyes locked on the pattern of the quilt. "She had a power evolution already."

"Really?" Shun asked, eyebrows raised.

"What's a power evolution?" Cam asked, looking up.

"It's what Krytos calls it," Tom said. "Your power with fire reached a new level when—"

He dropped the sentence awkwardly. Shun noticed and narrowed her eyes. Cam knew he had almost said "when she killed Holkstoin."

"—when your fire became green," Tom finished lamely. "When that happened, the temperature in the room rose exponentially. It was really spectacular."

Tom pressed on. Cam could not help but notice how he continued to omit what she had done to Holkstoin. Cam tugged on a loose thread of the blanket, absentmindedly. She had barely thought of Holkstoin after Oni flew them away. She tried to concentrate on the crosshatch stitching as thoughts of him flooded her mind. Her eyes traveled over and under with the threads of the blanket. Her heart was beating loudly in her ears again as her thoughts followed her eyes, over and under. Then the familiar stabbing in her chest returned with her quickening breaths, synchronized with her heart and eyes as they continued to travel, over and under.

OVER AND UNDER. JUMP OR FALL?

"Cam."

Cam looked up. It was quiet again. Tom and Shun were staring at her. She took a breath. A cool rush filled her lungs as she looked down and saw a sizable pile of loose threads next to her. Her fingers were still clenched around the string, knuckles white.

"Cam," Tom said again. "What are you doing?"

"Sorry," Cam said. "I guess I was, um, in my own little world."

•

Later that evening, Cam sat on a grassy patch behind the house alone. Oni appeared to have grown quite protective of Ke and had refused to leave his side. The evening chill had crept over the town as it did most nights. Luanna and Sam arrived to begin work on Ke's remedy. The library in the town hall had several ancient texts stolen from various Gi offices. One of them, *Pharmacopoeia*, held the old techniques for Aeraden extraction. In order to alter the essence of Aeraden, several alchemical reactions had to be completed. The resulting product created the base for the elixir known as Aeranekutide, the preserver of life.

Cam was told she could not personally do more to help aside from allowing them to work unimpeded. She had mingled in the kitchen for a while before the tense and silent atmosphere forced her to leave. She tugged at her sweater as she sat, listening to the wind weaving its patterns among the trees.

Tom had reminded her to change her clothes as she was leaving. Thick slabs of Holkstoin's skin had melted into her dark pants. The distorted flesh had accumulated a thick layer of ash when it had still been sticky from the burn. It almost blended in with the dark color of the fabric though the stink of his boiled innards was permanently branded within the threads.

"Hey."

Cam turned to see Gun leaning against the building with a quizzical look on his face.

"What are you doing back here?" he asked.

"They're working," Cam said. "I got antsy waiting."

"Oh," he replied, sitting down. He pulled a partially smoked cigarette from behind his ear. "Can I get a light?"

Cam snapped her fingers and held up the flame. He took a deep drag and sighed.

"So, how are you doing?" he asked. "After everything..."

"Okay," Cam said. "Tired, I guess."

She knew what Gun was trying to ask, and she was not prepared to answer. She was still peeling bits of Holkstoin from her palms. This was not a conversational topic. Mutual silence dusted the air between them as well as wispy spirals of smoke. Gun seemed to interpret her silence correctly as he pulled a bottle from his brown leather jacket.

"Want some?" Gun asked.

Cam took the bottle and drank a mouthful. She felt a toxic burn scurry down to her stomach. She leaned back against the house as night began to creep over them. Gun was looking down at his fingers as he flicked the ash in a freefalling arch away from them. He was being so quiet.

"Are *you* okay?" Cam asked as she took another drink.

"Yeah," Gun said with a forced smile. "I'm fine."

"Okay," Cam said. "I just know it must have been hard to see her again. You know? Rhea?"

"Oh," Gun said, turning to look at her as he allowed his melancholy to show. "I forgot I told you about that. It's not a big deal though."

Gun let the smoke billow around him as he smashed the cigarette into the mud, eyes averted.

"There's something you should know about her," Cam said. "She sort of saved us in there."

He looked up.

"Sounds out of character," he muttered, trying to camouflage his curiosity. "Not that it matters."

"She opened the security door that led to the Vault. I don't think we would've gotten through that door without her help," Cam said.

"Why are you telling me this, Cam?" Gun asked, suddenly irritated. "I told you it doesn't matter."

"Sorry," Cam said. She took a swig and held the bottle out to Gun.

He took the bottle from her and leaned back against the building. They sat in silence, letting the waves of inebriation form. Both of them trying to forget and cut their losses. Like rolling out the carpet to cover the stains, they pretended that the holes in their hearts didn't exist.

Three hours later, Gun was passed out on the soft grass mumbling "gnomes...back off...shoestring potatoes...ice cream sandwiches." Cam was tossing crumpled leaves into the air and shooting them to ashes with miniature fireballs. The nearly empty bottle lay clumsily between them.

"That's a fire hazard," Sam said as he came around the building.

"Hi, Sam," Cam said. His black hair was tousled messily, and he wore a tired expression.

"What are you two doing back here?" Sam asked. Then he spotted the bottle. "Never mind."

"What are *you* doing back here?" Cam asked as she tried to ignore the dryness of her tongue.

"Trying to find you," Sam said. "Luanna said it should be done in an hour or so. I've got to run over to her place and get some more things."

"Oh, that's good," Cam said with a great sigh. "The sacrifices were worth it then."

"Sacrifices?" Sam asked.

"Nothing," Cam stammered quickly. "I mean, 'sacrifices' is the wrong word. He was an obstacle. I didn't mean to say that either. Damn you and your booze, Gun."

Cam trailed off. Sam put a firm hand on her shoulder as he kneeled next to her.

"So, what does the Christian bible say about revenge anyway?" she wondered aloud.

"Quite a bit," he said, his tone warm. "Lots of damnation for the vengeful and such."

"Great. Good to know."

She resumed burning the fallen leaves as Sam let out a long sigh.

"But I'm not sure how much of that applies here," Sam began. "You know how they say an eye for an eye—"

"—will make the whole world blind? Heard it before and, yes, I get it," Cam interrupted. "I'm a wretched person who's going to get what's coming to me."

Sam smiled. It was a soft, gentle smile that brought her comfort.

"I was going to say that what you did probably felt vengeful. It probably *was* vengeful," Sam said, "but, to me, it was simply justice."

She looked up.

"What?"

"That man killed a lot of my friends," Sam said. "I'm not condoning the taking of *anyone's* life but, at the same time, I know I won't be crying over his death. You cry when you feel loss. The world didn't lose anything when he left, in my opinion."

Cam stared at him. She did not know what to say in response to his statement. He had the most congenial face that practically screamed honesty. It was odd that this was their first real conversation.

"Come on," Sam said. "Let's get Gun home."

They lifted Gun together and carried him to their shared house. Volpi was lying on the sofa and listening to a thumb-sized music player when they came in. She opened one eye and raised an eyebrow at Gun.

"So, that's where the liquor went," Volpi said. "Did he take the big bottle or the little one?"

"What do you think?" Sam asked.

Volpi chuckled as they dragged Gun to his room. They laid him on the bed and closed the door.

"I've got to go," Sam said. "I need to get the old alchem set out of Luanna's workshop."

"Right," Cam said haltingly as she decided what to say. "Hey, thanks for what you said. You can't take back the past so it's nice to have some comfort with you while you resolve the present."

"You're welcome," he said with a smile.

He turned to leave. Volpi gave him a playful kick to the leg, and he retaliated by throwing a pillow at her that she deflected with ease. Then he waved and was out the door.

Volpi, now sitting up and leaning against the back of the sofa, was staring at Cam. Cam looked down, uncomfortable under Volpi's crushing gaze.

"I didn't think you had it in you," Volpi said with a devilish raise of her eyebrows.

"Had what?"

"You know *what*," Volpi said. "You're a killer."

Cam looked down as her face grew hot, and her skin turned ice cold.

"That's one way of putting it," Cam said, moving toward the door. Volpi stood and began matching her pace.

"It's the *only* way of putting it."

"Leave me alone, Volpi," Cam said.

Volpi grasped her arm and spun her. Cam's back hit the door, causing it to shudder. She fiddled for the handle but Volpi was upon her, blocking her way.

"No," Volpi said, slamming her fist next to Cam's head. Cam felt the door vibrate behind her. "It was revenge, and you know it."

"Why the hell do you care?"

Volpi's expression became manic. Her eyes narrowed and her muscles twitched. Cam shrank back further against the door.

"Because I wish I'd done it," Volpi whispered.

She backed away, leaving Cam pressed nervously against the door.

"You just don't get it, Cam!" Volpi exclaimed, her body shaking. "You don't know how much I wanted to kill him, to kill them all. You don't know how I lay awake at night picturing the ways I'd cut them if I had the chance. You're not the only one who wanted that porky son of a bitch dead."

Cam was speechless. She was not accustomed to this emotionally honest version of Volpi.

"Why?" Cam asked, breaking the silence.

"Why what?"

"Why did you want Holkstoin dead?"

Volpi took a deep breath and turned to face Cam with anger in her watery eyes.

"Did you know I was a slave, too?" Volpi asked. "Over half of the Equintas were born into it. I worked the mines, just like you."

Cam nodded, a bit confused as to why Volpi was telling her this.

"It was just me and my dad," Volpi said. "My mom died in childbirth. My life was typical of the misery that most slaves endure, relentless work for no pay and barely enough food to live. In this weird sort of way though, I miss it..."

Volpi stopped to blink away her tears.

"I was fourteen," Volpi continued. "It was the end of shift. I went for a walk down Hangyaku, like I normally did. Then I felt a blinding pain at the back of my head, and everything went black. I woke up in one of the guard towers. There was this man there. He had a Gi uniform on and these ridiculously fancy dress shoes that were tasseled in gold. I remember being so confused. He didn't say anything to me, not once. He just stared."

Cam's breath caught in her throat.

"Then, in a flash, he threw me down on the table," she said. "He held my hands back so hard that my wrist fractured. Then he took his pants off. I just remember the pressure of his weight. I couldn't move, couldn't breathe. But I screamed. I screamed so loud that I couldn't speak for days after. Not like it mattered anyway. Who was going to save me there?"

Cam's vocal cords had disappeared. She barely managed to nod.

"He left me bleeding in the middle of Hangyaku," Volpi said, her voice growing harder. "It had started to rain by the time I was finally able to stand up. I was so broken, ripped to shreds. Everything hurt. The rain cleaned away all the evidence on the long walk home. I didn't tell anyone. I just went to work the next day like I would normally."

"Volpi..."

"Funny thing is, I'd just gotten my period," Volpi said with the saddest laugh Cam had ever heard. "Had it four times then, well, I didn't get it anymore."

Cam gasped.

"You know you can't hide something like that," Volpi said. "Not in the Slums. He saw it and he wanted it, wanted *my* baby. The bastard thought I had good genes. So they stole me away to Tengoku but not after I made the mistake of telling my father what happened. I told him everything, confessed it like I had done something wrong. I told him about the guard tower and about the baby. Then the next morning I was gone.

"My dad tried to murder him, tried to get me back. The Gi stopped him, of course. They publicly tortured him on the west hill by the Whipping Post. *He* made sure that I knew every detail. You probably heard about it. Slaves never attempt to murder a Gi. It's pointless. So my dad's execution was a big deal."

"I heard," Cam said, cringing at her literalness of her statement. She remembered the night when she had heard him screaming. No one slept in the Slums that night.

"I got the news in the delivery room right after that son of a bitch took my son," Volpi said, biting her lip. "They threw me in the labs and, well, you can gather the rest."

"Volpi, I'm so sorry," Cam said.

"That's why I helped you back in the Ether and why I followed your crazy plan all the way to a demon," Volpi said. "I need to believe in you and in the Templum Three. If I don't, then I can't believe we have a chance at winning this. It's kind of all I have left to hold onto."

Volpi looked over at Cam. Her expression quickly hardened back to its normal state.

"You tell anyone that story, and I'll slit Ke's throat in his sleep," Volpi said as she walked toward her bedroom.

"Wait, one question?" Cam asked. Volpi turned. "Does Tom know?"

"No," Volpi said firmly. "Now, you keep good on your word, or I'll keep good on mine."

●

Cam wandered aimlessly around town until she found herself at the river. She sat down and stared blankly at the water rushing by. She had realized over the course of the last few months what being Edan's descendent truly meant. She knew many were depending on her to save them, to serve their justice or to exact their revenge. The weight of responsibility had been slowly crushing down on her but, now, it was suffocating. She barely noticed when Tom sat next to her.

"You should get back to the house," Tom said. "They're almost ready."

"Good," Cam said distractedly.

Her thoughts ran in time with the river. She could barely mull over one before it slipped away to be replaced by another. She glanced out of the corner of her eye and noticed Tom watching her intently.

"What are you doing?" Cam asked. "It's creepy. Stop it."

"Are you okay?"

"People really need to stop asking me that," Cam said.

"Do you want to talk about it?" he asked. Cam knew instantly what he was referring too.

"Not particularly," Cam said. "It's barely sunk in, the fact that I...killed him."

Cam felt her voice crack and stumble over the word "killed." A slimy rush of bile hit her throat and she swallowed hard as she tried to think of something else.

"So, are you going to talk to me about Holkstoin, too?" Cam asked Tom angrily. "Are you going to tell me it was good thing, what I did? Because your opinion would be unanimous with everyone else's."

"No," Tom said. "I'm not going to tell you anything. I just came over in case you needed someone to listen."

Cam let out a long sigh of frustration.

"I'm trying to be strong here, you know. I'm trying to be your hero," Cam said. "But, here *you* are, making me feel like *I'm* the one who needs to be saved.'

Tom shook his head.

"But doesn't a hero need someone to save them once in a while?" he asked. "Maybe that's what I'm supposed to do."

He reached into his jacket pocket and pulled out a charred wallet. He handed it to Cam.

"I found this when I was cleaning, or rather throwing out those clothes you were wearing," he said.

Cam shuddered as she took the wallet from his hand. She had nearly forgotten that she had taken it in her foggy, rage-fueled attack. The wallet fell open in her lap. A few thousand GV spilled out followed by a clear tri-fold. Cam stared at it. The first slot held a picture of a teenage boy and the second a little girl with blond pigtails. She recognized the eyes as they matched the ones she had watched burn at her own hands. The third picture was of Holkstoin with his arms around a round-faced, blonde woman who was smiling sweetly toward the camera. The two children from the other pictures were sitting on the ground in front of them. A cornflower blue backdrop filled the empty space.

Cam tried to remember what Krytos had told her about hurting someone, about knowing that they are connected to others in the world. She concentrated on the atrocities the Gi had committed as guilt tried to force its way into her thoughts, tried to break down her barriers. She thought of Holkstoin's face, full of self-satisfaction as he whipped the skin off of her back. She thought of him kicking Ke as he lay unconscious on the floor of the mine. She thought of Volpi and her tragedy at the hands of the Gi. She saw her parents, alive and happy. The memory of their youthful and exuberant smiles reminded her of how young they had been when they were murdered. She tried to remember that Holkstoin had been the enemy as raw memories flooded her consciousness. Then, for the second time that day, she felt something break, and she screamed.

Emerald green flames covered her body. She could feel her eyes changing as they flooded silver. Her body was stuck in its blistering cage as the nearest foliage caught fire. Images of old and terrible memories raced across her vision at an alarmingly intense speed. Her heartbeat matched the speed of the images and each beat felt like a hammer was being slammed against the inside of her ribs.

*It's survival of the fittest. His death means you can stay afloat a little bit longer.*

"Shut up!" Cam screamed as she shut her eyes.

"It's worrisome how often I have to ask, but who are you talking to?" Tom asked. The green flames leapt from Cam's body as Tom suffocated the smaller patches of fire.

`This is your world.`

"No," Cam whimpered as the voices grew in volume. Whispers filled the background, speaking unintelligibly.

**KILL THEM. KILL THEM ALL.**

A sudden gust blew over. She opened her eyes and watched as the emerald flames that danced from her skin were pulled away. Then Tom was there, arms wrapped around her firmly as he pulled her up from the ground, his face panic-stricken. White puffs of smoke rose, encircling them. It took her a moment to realize that she had been crying and that the white wisps were the steam produced from her drying tears.

They were standing inside of a tornado. Green flames rotated, containing them in a tunnel of sparking flashes. Her hair whipped her face as her body continued to shudder.

"Cam," Tom said firmly. "Stop this."

The fire churned and flared with a power that nearly overwhelmed her. Anger and sadness bit at her in waves. She could not stop until the pain was gone, until she burned to ash.

"Cam, stop!" Tom shouted, holding her more and more tightly.

The wreck of pain she had been enduring for so long, almost felt right now. It was unbearable but inexorable, and she was unsure what would happen if she felt something else. The mere thought constricted her breathing to near hyperventilation.

"Cam!"

She looked up into the steely blue eyes of her best friend. They were so full of concern, so full of honesty, that it was overwhelming. In that moment, Cam felt safe and she did not mind being dependent on someone else. In that moment, it did not matter whether or not she had to be a hero for everyone else as long as he could be there with her. His embrace tightened as she forced calm into her body and the fire began to fade.

They parted and the wall of emerald fire fell away. The river continued its trip down the valley with no interruption as charred bits of leaves, some still edged with green embers, rained down.

"Um, we should probably go back to the house," Tom said, after a moment. "They should be ready by now."

"Right," Cam said, her voice straining to be audible.

He squeezed her shoulder and forced a smile. He was so warm, so good, and familiar. It was like finally finding home.

# CHAPTER 26
## SILVER LINING

When they returned to the house, the sun had set, and the town was blanketed in darkness. The lights were on at their house, and Cam could see movement inside as well as on the patio.

"Look, there's Cam and Tom!" Cam heard Amelia shout from the patio. Amelia waved to them from her perch on Max's shoulders.

"Hey, Amelia," Tom said as he nodded to Max before going inside.

"Hi, Tom! Hi, Cam!" Amelia said excitedly as Max set her down. "Daddy said my bike worked!"

"It sure did," Cam said. "Sorry about that, Max. I just had to borrow it. You got it back, right?"

Max smiled.

"I understand, Cam, and I did get it back," Max said. "It worked out for the best. We have Aeraden and your little brother—"

"—and you have a *way* cooler bike now," Amelia said to Max. "I was just thinking of ways I could make it even better."

Cam leaned down and gave Amelia a hug which was reciprocated with enthusiasm.

"Thanks," Cam whispered. "I really couldn't have done it without your help."

"You're welcome," Amelia chirped happily. "I'm just happy that your brother will be okay."

Cam nodded as she went inside the house. Shun and Alex sat at the kitchen table drinking tea. They both waved as Cam continued to the bedroom. Luanna was sitting beside Ke and was cleaning his arm with antiseptic. Sam and Tom were at the dresser which had been converted into a makeshift alchemy station. Krytos stood at the back of the room with a tense expression.

"They say it's ready," Tom said, coming to her side.

"We'll be administering the serum intravenously," Luanna said as she inserted a needle and catheter into Ke's arm. Oni had awoken and was watching with rapt interest. "If we've done this correctly, then we should see some improvement within a few hours. Even so, it could be a few weeks before he wakes up."

"Wait, what?" Cam asked. "What the hell do you mean 'if?'"

"Cam," Sam said, turning to her. "No one, other than the Gi, has made this serum in over three hundred years."

"We've followed the old book of pharmaceuticals," Luanna said. "If the directions in that book are accurate then it will work but, as Sam said, that text is very old. I'm allowing for a degree of uncertainty."

Tom reached an arm around Cam as Luanna connected the bag to the syringe. The serum was milky like Aeraden itself and a soft glow radiated from within the core. Cam watched as the medicine made its short journey from the bag to Ke's blood stream.

"Now, all we can do is wait," Luanna said with a heavy sigh.

Cam sat down on the bed, waiting for a change in Ke's condition. Hours passed deep into the night. Krytos retired to the living room where Milo and Amelia were. Luanna joined Shun, Max, and Alex in the kitchen. Sam was slumped against the dresser, asleep, and Tom was in a similar state by the nightstand. Oni had curled its body into Cam's lap as she tried desperately to stay awake, though the task was becoming increasingly difficult. She had not slept in over two days.

Cam transitioned into a state that was half awake and half asleep. Her eyes were open, but her mind had become unfocused. The room had slowly filled with a soft, repetitive melody that was swiftly becoming a lullaby. The first sound was the soft, delicate drip of the IV. Then came Sam's slow inhalation followed by Tom's as they slept in their respective corners. After which, came Ke's raspy intake of breath. It rattled the air with its hoarseness. Cam listened to the melody as it droned on: drip, breath, breath, gasp.

Drip. Breath. Breath. Gasp.

Drip.

Breath.

Breath.

Then there was a second of silence. Cam woke herself and listened more intently.

Drip.

Breath.

Breath.

...breath.

Her heart fluttered with excitement as she leaned over Ke. He was breathing in the same rhythm as before, but the harshness had begun to subside.

Cam was numb with gleeful shock. She leaned down and kissed Ke on the forehead. Then she leapt from the bed, throwing Oni onto the pillow in her excitement as she ran over to Tom.

"Tom!" Cam exclaimed, shaking him. "Wake up! It's working!"

"What? Ouch, stop it," he said groggily as he swatted her hands away.

"I said 'it's working,' the serum is working," Cam said before turning to Sam. "Sam, wake up!"

"Wow, he sounds so much better," Tom said, now fully alert.

"What?" Sam said, rushing up with a stethoscope. He listened for several moments. "I'm getting Luanna."

Sam dashed from the room and, in a matter seconds, the room was filled with people. Luanna cut to the front of the group and began to examine Ke. Cam felt Amelia latch onto her arm as she peered cautiously at Ke.

"Is that your brother?" Amelia asked quietly.

"Yes."

"Is he better now?"

"I think so," Cam said.

Luanna quickly finished the exam and stood with a smile on her face.

"It's definitely working," she said.

A collective sigh of relief filled the room. Krytos was grinning from ear to ear. Hugs were being exchanged and there were tears in many eyes. Possessing Aeraden and the recipe to utilize it were previously thought to be impossible. The world was changing.

●

The next morning, Krytos asked everyone to attend breakfast at eight o'clock. Cam took her shoes off at the door and felt the warmth of the Vinestra floor travel up her legs. She sat at the back of the room with Tom and Gun. The room was filled to its capacity as everyone in the town filed in. After a few minutes, Krytos stood and moved to the center of the room. Silence followed as he cleared his throat.

"We've been very busy lately," Krytos said. "A number of events have taken place, some planned and others not. Our general infiltration operations within Tengoku have now spread to Birmings. We have grown enough to accomplish this while still maintaining coverage. With these new posts, we have gained an immense wealth of knowledge that would have otherwise been lost to us.

"We have also gained Camilla who is, as you all already know, of No Last Name. We now have two of the Templum Three, and both have chosen to fight alongside us.

"Recently, an unexpected mission was conducted deep inside the Ether. The purpose of this mission was to steal Aeraden from the Gi."

Murmurs stirred throughout the group as Krytos summarized the events in the Ether.

"This unexpected mission was successful," Krytos said. "They managed to penetrate the security that led to the Vault and steal Aeraden. It is now in our possession, and we have successfully utilized it to produce the healing serum, Aeranekutide."

The murmurs rose quickly in volume until they culminated in a cheer. Krytos allowed it to continue for a moment before raising a kind but interruptive hand.

"Yes," Krytos said. "This new development is immense. It is the next step in this fight. With this, we can save the sick slaves in the mines, the fields and the sea. We finally have an advantage that the Gi does not."

Krytos stopped to take a breath. His expression was somber as he readied himself to continue.

"Last night, when we discovered that we had successfully created Aeranekutide," Krytos said, "I felt something I had not felt in a long time.

"I felt hope.

"I was suddenly hopeful that we could win this war and, as you all know, I'm not an optimist. I spent the rest of the night picturing a better future, dreaming of it. Then I woke up and I thought of what I would say to you today. I wanted to share this feeling with you. I wanted to tell you about hope against uncertainty and hope against the oppression of the Gi. I wanted to make you all hopeful for a better tomorrow, hopeful for change.

"Then I thought of those who wouldn't be here, those who were lost. That was when I realized hope will not save us. Hope cannot carry this torch, but that's okay because we have something far stronger. We have the will and an ever-growing ability to change this world for the better.

"So, today, I don't just hope for change, for a better future. Why? Because, today, I *know* it will be better. What I mistook for hope last night was simply a realization of the inevitable, and the inevitable is that we are going to change this world, and we are going to win."

•

Over one hundred miles from the forest of Rebel's Glade, a visibly-stressed Mellech was standing anxiously before a golden elevator at the top of the Metraline. His gloved, prosthetic hand held a thick, black binder. The elevator came to a halt and the doors opened, revealing an elegant hallway. He walked forward as the tapping of his fine shoes echoed against the marble. He approached a pair of mahogany doors and rapped the back of his knuckles sharply against the surface.

"Come in," came a deep voice.

Mellech turned the handle and entered. Bacchus Murphy, Rhea's grandfather and the Lieutenant General, sat behind the massive desk that encompassed most of the room. His uniform was decorated with medals and badges. His salt and pepper hair was the only indicator that he was older than forty.

"Mellech," Bacchus said indifferently. "Sit."

"Bacchus, sir," Mellech said, making no move to sit. "Here are the protocol and security reports from...the incident. I'm sure the Lord General will be calling a meeting with you soon to discuss—"

"It's already scheduled," Bacchus interrupted. He chuckled as he flipped through the binder. "So, have you been demoted yet?"

Mellech's expression grew cold.

"No, for your information, sir," Mellech said. "I will, in fact, be tasked with several new projects. One of which I wanted to discuss with you now."

"Oh," Bacchus said, his tone becoming serious.

"Yes, sir," Mellech said. "We need to enhance security in certain sectors, especially one in particular. I believe you are already aware."

"Yes," Bacchus said. "I am fully aware. Will you be overseeing this from now on?"

"No, I'll be coordinating additional security," Mellech said. "The Lord General does not want to take any chances."

"I should think not," Bacchus agreed, leaning back in his high back leather chair. "Is there suspicion that the Equintas knows?"

"No, sir, not yet," Mellech said. "But we weren't aware that they had such knowledge of the Ether or the Templum Three either."

"Shameful that this tiny, pathetic group of rebels seems to always be a step ahead of us," Bacchus said. "Don't you agree?"

"I'm sure they feel somewhat victorious now," Mellech said. "But they won't feel that way for long."

"No, I should think not. Those naïve little fools," Bacchus chuckled. "If only they knew that we already have the final piece to the puzzle."

He tapped the black binder with a satisfied grin, his fingers brushing over the label.

*Enhanced Security Protocols*
*Cardenash's Descendant*
*A. Murphy*

END

| 16 | 3 | 2 | 13 |
|----|----|----|----|
| 5 | 10 | 11 | 8 |
| 9 | 6 | 7 | 12 |
| 4 | 15 | 14 | 1 |

# ABOUT THE AUTHOR

C.A. Zitzelberger is a dedicated writer, avid reader, and enthusiastic gamer. She is a devoted fan of fantasy, science fiction, and anime. She currently lives in Sacramento California with her husband, her cat, and her two dogs.